AVA McC

Aiveen McCarthy was born in Dublin and attained degrees in Physics and Nuclear Medicine before going onto work for the London Stock Exchange for six years as an analyst programmer. She currently works in software in County Dublin, where she lives with husband Tom and two children.

AVA McCARTHY

The Courier

HARPER

Harper
HarperCollins*Publishers*
77–85 Fulham Palace Road
Hammersmith, London W6 8JB

www.harpercollins.co.uk

Published by *Harper*, a division of HarperCollins*Publishers* 2010

1

A catalogue record for this book
is available from the British Library

ISBN-13 978-0-00-728592-1

Set in Sabon by Palimpsest Book Production Limited,
Grangemouth, Stirlingshire

Printed in Great Britain by Clays Ltd, St Ives plc

Mixed Sources
Product group from well-managed
forests and other controlled sources
www.fsc.org Cert no. SW-COC-1806
© 1996 Forest Stewardship Council

FSC is a non-profit international organisation established to promote the
responsible management of the world's forests. Products carrying the FSC
label are independently certified to assure consumers that they come
from forests that are managed to meet the social, economic and
ecological needs of present and future generations.

Find out more about HarperCollins and the environment at
www.harpercollins.co.uk/green

To my husband, Tom, for rowing in through thick and thin and taking on whatever needs doing. My love and appreciation always.

Acknowledgements

Grateful thanks to my agent, Laura Longrigg, for her encouragement and support throughout the writing of this book, and to my editor, Julia Wisdom, at HarperCollins for helping me to make it a better one. Thank you also to Anne O'Brien, sharp-eyed copy editor extraordinaire. A special thanks goes to Jerome O'Flaherty, techno über-wizard, for allowing me to bend his ear. And thank you also to Grant Watson and his mother for the Afrikaans translations; to Pilar Molina for the Spanish translations; and to Caroline de Moraes for translating into Portuguese.

1

Harry had a rule about breaking into safes: never do it for a client you couldn't trust. She studied the woman sitting behind the desk and wondered how on earth she could tell.

'We don't have long,' the woman said, picking at Harry's business card with her nail. 'He'll be back in an hour.'

Harry tried to read her eyes but couldn't see them behind the oversized sunglasses. 'Perhaps we should do it another time.'

The woman's mouth tightened. She dragged a hand through her hair, spiking up her short pixie cut.

Her name was Beth Oliver, or so she'd said. She'd called Harry an hour ago, asking to meet at her home on the seafront to discuss a specialized job. So far, they'd skirted around the details, but Harry could tell there was more.

Beth jerked to her feet and began pacing the room. Her figure was boyish, flat front and back, making it hard to pin down her age. She came to a halt by the large sash window that overlooked Dublin Bay.

'I can't wait any longer.' Her fists were clenched. 'It has to be today.'

Harry glanced over at the tall, stainless steel construction that occupied one end of the room. 'You're sure the laptop's inside the vault?'

Beth nodded, shoving her hands deep into her pockets. Her outfit was casual, trainers and jeans, the kind Harry favoured when her own scams needed a quick getaway.

Inwardly, she sighed. Six months ago, her internal wiring would've sorted through all the signals, but lately her judgement had been off. Maybe it wasn't surprising after all she'd been through, but surely she should've snapped out of it by now?

She snatched up her case and got to her feet. Playing it safe was not in her nature, but her instincts were too unreliable to take a chance right now.

'Your best option is to call the vault manufacturers,' she said. 'They could probably open it for you.'

Beth spun round. 'But they know my husband, they'll ring him to check it's okay.'

'Any reason they shouldn't?'

'I told you, he can't know about this.' The pitch of Beth's voice was ramping up. 'Besides, I need you to examine the laptop. That's what you do, isn't it?' She pushed Harry's business card across the desk, the Blackjack Security logo

2

visible in one corner. 'Recover information from hard drives?'

Harry shrugged. 'Among other things.'

'Well, that's why I'm hiring you.'

'Look, Beth, I'll be straight with you here. For all I know, you could be a stranger off the street who's just broken into this house.' Harry held up her hand at Beth's outraged look. 'And even if you are who you say you are, I have no legal authority to break into your husband's safe and examine his laptop without his permission. I just can't do it.'

Beth's knuckles were white. 'What if I could prove the safe belongs to me?'

Harry frowned. 'Does it?'

She snorted. 'Everything in this bloody house belongs to me. Cars, bills, mortgages, I pay for it all. Garvin's been bleeding me dry for years.' She resumed her patrol of the room. 'He's always on the point of making it big, but everything he does is a disaster.'

She stopped in front of the steel vault, arms folded, shoulders hunched. Harry moved up beside her, the polished metal reflecting her own approaching image: navy suit, tangled black curls, dark smudges for eyes. Beside Beth's pipe-cleaner frame, her own modest curves looked buxom.

For the first time, Harry studied the vault up close. It was the size and shape of a triple wardrobe, with a heavy-duty door along its centre panel. Mounted on the handle was a brick-sized entry device complete with small keypad and screen. A red light blinked on and off in one corner.

The back of Harry's neck tingled. She was close enough to the vault to reach out and touch it, and the challenge to crack it open made her fingertips buzz. She dragged her attention back to Beth.

'So you can prove you own this?'

She tried to keep the hopeful tone out of her voice. There was a lot here that needed clearing up before she could accept Beth as a client.

Beth marched back to the desk and snatched an envelope from one of the drawers. 'I'm well used to people not believing what I say.' She handed the envelope over. 'Especially where Garvin's concerned.'

Harry opened the flap. Inside, she found a passport and a bank statement, both in Beth's name. The passport showed a woman with high cheekbones and a slight upward tilt to her eyes. Harry glanced over at Beth. It could've been her, but the bug-eyed shades made it hard to tell.

The bank statement showed a payment to Bull Safehouses Limited and another to a local computer store. Stapled to the back were a receipt for a Dell laptop and an invoice for the vault, both dated some six months previously.

Harry raised her eyebrows at the woman's efficiency. Either her personal accounts were in better shape than Harry's, or she'd been planning this for some time. She ran her eye over the rest of the statement, noting the substantial payments made to men's clothing outlets, utilities, supermarkets and petrol stations. It was clear Beth paid for a significant chunk of the household outgoings, whether her husband contributed or not.

Harry handed the paperwork back to Beth. 'So what's on the laptop that's so important?'

'Proof that he has money of his own.'

Harry threw her a sharp look, and Beth nodded.

'He's had money for some time, I'm convinced of it,' she said. 'Six months, maybe more. His suits are flashier, he's upgraded his car. And I haven't been getting the bills.'

'Surely that's good?'

Beth stared at Harry from behind her dark shades.

'I'm about to divorce him. I need to show he has money of his own, otherwise he'll come after mine.' A tiny muscle flexed in her jaw. 'And he's had all he's getting from me.'

Harry flashed on the scam she'd pulled in the Bahamas that year. She'd soft-soaped a banker with tales of a cheating spouse and the need to hide her assets before her divorce. Sympathy and plausibility. Vital ingredients for any fraud. Was Beth's story really any different?

Harry stared at the woman's pinched profile reflected in the vault door.

'Has the black eye anything to do with it?' she said.

Beth shot her a look, and Harry pointed at the shining steel.

'The glasses hide a lot, but you can still see it from the side.'

Beth checked her reflection, then dropped her gaze.

She slipped off the glasses and fiddled with the stems, not meeting Harry's eyes.

She looked older without the shades, her weathered skin at odds with her youthful frame. She was probably in her mid-thirties, just a few years older than Harry, and she had the slanted eyes and fine bone structure of the woman in the passport photo. The only difference was her left eye. The skin around it was plum-purple, the cornea shot through with blood.

'How'd that happen?' Harry asked.

Beth didn't answer. Instead, she tugged her shirt collar tighter round her neck, but not before Harry had spotted the bruises. For a moment, neither of them spoke.

Finally Harry said, 'Are you planning on cleaning him out?'

Beth hugged her chest. 'I don't want anything from him, I just want to get away.' She glanced at her watch and rubbed her arms, as though trying to keep warm. 'Look, are you going to help me or not? Because we're running out of time, and believe me, you don't want to be here when he gets back.'

Harry studied her for a moment, tossing around the possibilities. The bank statement, the passport, the black eye. Her eyes flicked towards the gleaming vault, its winking light daring her to crack it open. She made up her mind.

'How long do we have?' she said.

Beth's good eye lit up. 'Forty minutes, maybe less.'

Harry whipped a standard contract out of her bag

and filled in the blanks. As she watched Beth sign, her mind ran through a checklist of the tools she'd brought along: torch, pliers, plastic bags, screwdriver, bottled water and a packet of wine gums. She'd left her laptop on the back seat of her car. She could go back out if she needed it.

She tucked the signed contract into her bag, then turned her attention to the vault. Below the small screen on the security panel was an ATM-like slit. Below that was a recessed opening with a flat metal pad about the size of a large coin. And engraved in gold at the bottom of it all was a tiny padlock logo.

Beth shifted her feet. 'Like I said on the phone, it's got biometric access. Have you bypassed that kind of thing before?'

'A few times.'

In truth, Harry had only done it twice. Hacking biometric security was an unpredictable science, and mostly it took time. She peered at the slit and the small metal pad. On the face of it, she'd need two things, neither of which she had: a digital keycard and one of Garvin's fingers.

'He always keeps the card on him,' Beth said, as if reading her mind. 'Even at night. There's no way I can get hold of it.'

Harry nodded. In her experience, people kept a backup for something that important. She moved over to the desk, scrutinizing the items on its surface: phone, pens, notepad, some disconnected cables and a silver-framed photo.

She rummaged in her case and found her torch. Then she crouched down low, training the beam on the underside of the desk. She'd once known a target who'd taped an envelope to the bottom of his desk, a secret stash for all his bank accounts and passwords. Ever since then, she'd paid attention to nooks and crannies.

She craned her neck, squinting between the cross-planks and into all the corners. Nothing.

Harry straightened up and sank into the office chair, scooting in close to the desk. Most people kept notes to jog their memories, but this guy kept things clean. No doodles, no scraps of paper, no printed reports. Her own desk was a lot more topsy-turvy.

She opened the drawers. Paperclips, spare pens, boxes of staples. She hitched the drawers out of the desk, hoisting them around and checking every surface. Still nothing.

Beth prowled around the room, checking her watch at ten-second intervals.

'Relax,' Harry said. 'You're making me nervous.'

'You don't know what he's like. The last time he came home and found someone unexpected in the house, he just threw her out.' Beth waved a hand in the air. 'Oh, he was very civil about it, but she must have known something was wrong. She still left, though.' Her voice grew quieter. 'She was family, she should've known.'

Harry shot her a look. Beth was slumped against the vault, picking at her nails.

'Known what?' Harry said.

8

Beth shoved her hands into her pockets. 'That he'd turn on me. The minute she'd gone, he smashed up a chair and used it to break my ribs.'

'Jesus.' Harry stared at her. 'Why?'

'No reason. There never has to be a reason.'

Harry blinked. She tried to imagine being tied to a man who made you feel afraid. Without warning, she flashed on a familiar face: someone she'd trusted, who'd later tried to kill her. Her heartbeat picked up, and she shook the thought away.

She drummed her fingers on the desk, trying to re-focus. Her gaze flicked over the silver-framed photo, and she reached out for a closer look. A young girl in a school uniform smiled up at her with Beth's tilted eyes.

'My little girl, Evie,' Beth said. 'She's in boarding school. Safer there.'

Harry nodded, and turned the photo round in her hand. The glass seemed loose, the backing board not quite flush with the frame. She prised up the clips and tipped the photo out on to the desk. Tucked in against the backing board was a blue plastic swipe card, with a gold padlock logo in one corner.

Hairs rippled at the back of her neck. Beth strode towards her.

'Don't get too excited.' Harry headed over to the vault. 'We still need your husband's fingerprint.'

She fed the card into the slot. The red light flipped to amber, and the screen prompted for her next move:

Beth fidgeted behind her. 'What now?'

'If we had more time, we could lift Garvin's prints from around the house.' Harry wrinkled her nose. 'Maybe make some kind of mould. Problem is, with ten fingers to choose from, it's a bit hit and miss. We only get three shots before the vault locks us out for good.'

Beth groaned. 'We've only twenty minutes left.'

Harry peered at the recessed opening. 'When did your husband last open the vault?'

'This morning. Why?'

'Has anyone touched the finger sensor since?'

'Not that I know of.'

Harry fetched her torch and shone it into the recess. The beam picked out a faint smudge of grease on the metal pad. She snapped off the light and ran through her options. She could hack the sensor in a few different ways, but the priority here was speed.

'What are you going to do?' Beth said.

Harry shrugged. 'Use the only fingerprint we have. The one on the sensor.' She saw Beth's blank look and explained. 'I'm going to try and reactivate it.'

Harry bent down low so that her mouth was on a level with the metal pad. It was a capacitive sensor that measured electrical changes across its surface when a human finger touched it. A high measurement meant a ridge in a fingerprint, and a low measurement meant a valley. The sensor put it all together to reconstruct a fingerprint pattern.

The trick now was to make it think that Garvin's finger was still there.

Harry swallowed, and licked her lips. She needed to breathe on the surface of the sensor, letting the moisture from her breath gather between the lines in the grease stain. With luck, it'd be enough for the sensor to measure the capacitance and mistake it for an actual finger.

Gently, she breathed on to the surface of the pad, exhaling for three or four seconds. The screen beeped, and she glanced up at the message:

Access Denied: Finger Detection Failed.

Damn. Probably too much moisture. She must have exhaled for too long. She could try it again, but in her experience, tricking around with her breathing technique wasn't going to help.

'Now what?' Beth's voice was shrill.

Harry aimed for a confident tone. 'Plan B.'

She reached for her case, but before she could open it the desk phone rang. Harry jumped. Beth's hand flew to her throat and they both stared at the phone.

'Aren't you going to answer it?' Harry said.

Beth shook her head. After four rings, the answering machine kicked in.

'If you're there, pick up the bloody phone.' The man's voice was gravelly, his accent clipped. New Zealand?

He waited a beat before continuing. 'Forget it. I'm nearly there, I'll see you in two minutes.'

The call ended with a click. Beth stepped backwards, wide-eyed. Her fear was infectious, and Harry found herself checking over her shoulder.

'Can you do it?' Beth's voice was a whisper.

'In two minutes?' Harry swallowed. 'Maybe. Or you could bail out now?'

Beth's headshake was almost imperceptible. A voice in Harry's head shrieked at her to run, but she blocked it out. Fumbling through her case, she found a clear plastic bag and a bottle of water. Trying to hold the bag steady, she half-filled it with water, then tied a knot in the top. She kneaded it, testing its pliability. It wobbled like jelly in her hands. She squeezed a corner of the water-filled plastic into a marble-sized balloon. Then she turned back to the vault.

She felt Beth's eyes on her like a pair of hot skewers. Holding her breath, she lowered the balloon on to the sensor and counted to three.

Beep. Beth cursed. Harry's gaze shot to the screen:

Access Denied: Finger Detection Failed.

Hot sweat flashed down her back. She'd only one shot left. She grabbed her torch and shone it on to the sensor. The smudge was still there, faint but visible.

'One minute left,' whispered Beth.

Harry ripped out the packet of wine gums from her

case, the contents exploding on to the floor. She snatched up an orange jelly. Its surface was soft and dry. She pushed her index finger into it, coaxing the smooth jelly round her fingertip with her thumb and middle finger.

The jelly had the same capacitance as the skin on a human finger. Hackers called it the Gummi bear attack, and there was a small chance it could fool the sensor.

Harry moved her fingers into the recess. Wheels crunched on gravel in the driveway outside, and Beth gasped. Harry froze, a pulse hammering in her throat.

A car door *thunked*.

Harry swallowed and lowered the wine gum towards the pad, her fingers trembling. Footsteps scraped against stone outside. She touched the jelly against the metal, keeping the pressure even.

One, two, three.

The light flashed green. Bolts clinked inside the vault. A split second later, the door to the house crashed open.

2

Finding a diamond could mark a man out for death. Mani knew this, but still he had no choice.

Black dust swirled in the beam from his helmet, thicker than smoke. There was always dust. It burned his throat and crusted against his skin. Most of the time, he could barely see his own hands.

He adjusted the mask over his mouth. It was a poor fit, inadequate for wide, African noses. Most of the men pulled them down under their chins after the first twenty minutes.

'They don't fit,' Takata explained. 'Besides, Van Wycks, they say the dust is safe.'

But Mani knew better.

He tightened his grip on the drill, holding it like a machine gun, one hand in front of the other. Pickaxes clinked in a nearby tunnel, and in the distance someone buzzed up a chainsaw. Mani lodged the bit into a crevice on the blue kimberlite rock and leaned into it, the pressure burning through the knife wound in his arm. His heart pounded against the butt of the drill.

'Mani? Are you all right?'

Mani could hardly see Takata's face, but he felt the old man's bony fingers on his arm and heard his wheezing chest. Mani nodded, blanking out the cramped tunnel and the ceiling that seemed ready to crush him.

He pictured the layers of rock pressing down from above. Three or four feet of loose black soil up near the surface. After that, the soft yellow ground, for another fifty feet. Then the blue ground, where the kimberlite was hard and dense, to a depth of six hundred feet. All of it right above Mani's skull. And all of it packed with diamonds.

'Mani?'

The bony fingers squeezed his good arm. Mani shook the sweat out of his eyes and fired up the pneumatic motor. Vibrations hammered through his body. The drill chewed into the tunnel wall, spitting out chunks of blue-grey rock. The noise blasted his eardrums till they felt like they might bleed.

He released the trigger and squinted at the blast hole. The drilling had ground up more black dust and Mani could feel it coating his skin. The heat was suffocating, the reek of chemical explosives filling his sinuses.

Up until a month ago, his days had been spent in air-conditioned libraries and classrooms. He'd been studying engineering at the University of Cape Town. The student

15

hostel was small but clean, and he'd had his own room. Here at the Van Wycks mine, he shared a locked-down compound with thirty other men. The toilets were filthy and had no doors, and the single shower doubled up as a refuse dump.

'*Roer jou gat!*' Move your arse!

The guard punched Mani hard on the shoulder. Hot pain sliced through the wound in his arm, and he winced. He half-turned, being careful not to meet the guard's eyes. His name was Okker. He stood with his legs wide apart, anchoring his twenty-stone bulk in place. His face was a white moon, slick with sweat.

'*Daardie gat is te klein.*' That hole is too small.

Okker slapped a wooden club into the palm of one hand. Mani knew, as did all the men, that the large business end was weighted with a sheath of lead. The guard stepped towards him.

'*Doen dit oor.*' Do it over.

'Yes, sir.'

Mani knew the switch to English would annoy him. Mani's Afrikaans was fluent, but he rarely gave voice to its guttural sounds. He turned back to the wall, fumbling for the blast hole with the drill bit. He felt Takata's hand under his elbow, guiding him.

A sickening crack split the air. Takata cried out and slumped to the floor. Mani spun round in time to see Okker raise his club again.

'Stupid old man,' Okker yelled in English. 'Didn't you understand what I said? I told him to do it!'

16

He swung the club down with both hands. In the same instant, Mani hurled himself in front of Takata. The club smashed into Mani's shoulder. He yelled, sank to his knees. The old man's chest heaved with his wet bubbling cough.

Behind Mani, wood slapped against skin in a slow, menacing rhythm. He snapped his gaze round. Okker lashed out with his foot, crunching it into Mani's ribs. Stabbing pain shot through him. He doubled over, clutching his side. Dear God. Was he going to die here in this rat hole?

He thought of his brother and gritted his teeth. If it wasn't for Ezra, he wouldn't be here. He flashed on his brother's face leering up at him from the bed, one tooth missing. *The diamonds, they belong to the African people.* And beside him, Asha, beseeching him with her calm, almond-shaped eyes.

Asha.

He tensed his muscles, heaved himself to his feet, and turned to face Okker. The guard was flexing his fingers around the wooden club, his hands small for such a large man. There was no one else around.

A hooter shrieked in the distance, and Okker froze. He narrowed his eyes. Then he rammed the club into Mani's chest, forcing him backwards and pinning him against the wall. Jagged rock bit into Mani's back.

'I've been watching you.' Okker's voice was low. 'And I know what you're up to.'

Mani stopped breathing, every muscle suspended.

17

'I don't know how you're doing it,' Okker went on. 'But I'm going to find out.' He jabbed the club up under Mani's chin, and leaned in close. His breath was hot and sour. 'And when I do, you and the old man are dead.'

Mani dug his nails into the rock behind him, his muscles rigid. Okker's eyes slid down to Takata's motion-less body. Then he jerked the club away and stepped back.

'Get him out of here.'

Mani rubbed his jaw with a trembling hand, then bent down and lifted Takata to his feet. The old man was light, his flesh parchment-thin on birdlike bones. Takata was fifty-three, but his body was older, too old to be down here. His sons and grandsons all worked in the mine. So had his daughter, for a time.

Looping one arm around Takata's waist, Mani half-carried him along the uneven path, ignoring the fiery pain in his own ribs. The tunnel widened. Cones of light criss-crossed through the blackness as other miners spilled from their own tunnels into the belly of the mine.

'You should not have done that.' Takata's voice was low.

'I should have let him kill you?'

Mani felt Takata shrug. He guided the old man towards the lift shaft.

'Your daughter would not thank me for letting you die,' Mani said.

Another shrug. 'Asha, she knows I will not live for ever.'

Mani didn't answer. Together they trudged alongside the metal conveyor that carried the ore to the crushers. It creaked and rattled, hauling thousands of tonnes through the tunnels. The dust here seemed paler but just as dense, whipped up by dry ore on the move. Dry drilling was the rule in the Van Wycks mine. Dust-suppressing water sprays would have cleaned the air, but were forbidden in case they harmed the kimberlite.

Mani pushed into the lift along with Takata and a dozen other men. Daylight bled down through the shaft, and all around him the miners hacked out their damp, rattling coughs.

The ancient crate groaned upwards. Inch by inch, the darkness thinned, the air grew warmer, until finally they broke through the surface. Mani squinted against the sunlight and the blizzard of dust. The lift clattered to a halt, and Takata hobbled out, following the other men. Mani trailed after them, his mask still in place.

The throb of diesel engines filled the air. Tractors and dumper trucks lumbered around the open pit. The men on the ground, mostly black, guided the heavy machinery with yells and hand signals. None of them wore a mask.

Mani flicked a glance at the tonnes of ore piled in the waste pits a few hundred yards away. There were diamonds in those discarded mounds, if you knew where to look.

'I'm watching you, *kaffir*.'

Okker was so close that Mani could feel the heat radiating from his white flesh. He slid his gaze away and

19

shuffled behind the other men, keeping his eyes on the ground until Okker had moved away. Then he turned to stare again at the stockpiles of kimberlite ore. Dust caught in his throat, and he coughed like the other men, pain slicing his lungs like slivers of glass. His eyes watered, blurring his focus. His gaze drifted beyond the waste pits to the shadowy Kuruman mountains in the north. The mountains they called the Asbestos Hills.

Diamonds and dust.

He wondered which would kill him first.

3

Harry yanked open the vault door and scrambled inside, Beth pushing in behind her. Outside in the hall, the front door slammed.

Harry's eyes raked along metal shelves, her heart pumping. Together, they groped through them. Stacks of small coloured envelopes covered every surface. No sign of a laptop.

'What the fuck?' Garvin's gravelly voice echoed in the hall.

Harry whipped around, but they were still alone. She turned back to the vault, craning to get a view of the top shelf. Blood drummed in her ears.

A second voice spoke, lighter than Garvin's. 'Move inside. Now.'

Harry frowned. Garvin hadn't sounded like a man to

take orders. Then her brow cleared. In the corner of the top shelf was a slender black shape.

'Got it!' she whispered. She stretched up, grabbed the laptop and shoved it into her case. 'Come on, let's go. He can't take on both of us.'

She checked on Beth, one hand on the vault door. Beth was on her knees, stuffing blue and white envelopes into a black duffel bag. Why wasn't she moving?

Ratchet-snap. Harry spun round. The spring-loaded action had come from the hall. When Garvin spoke, his voice was shaking.

'You can't shoot me,' he said.

Harry's eyes widened. Behind her, Beth had stopped moving.

'Someone will hear.' Garvin sounded close to tears. 'There'll be witnesses.'

'I never leave witnesses.'

Harry's hand flew to her mouth. She ducked back into the vault and swung the door to, leaving it open a slit.

'The light!' Beth pointed at a button on the door jamb.

Harry pressed it, keeping her finger down, and like a fridge light the bulb went out. She peered through the crack.

A heavy-set man was backing into the room, hands in the air. Crescents of sweat stained his shirt under the arms.

'I've got money,' Garvin said. 'Take whatever you want.'

22

He stumbled against a chair and whimpered, his shoulders sagging. A middle-aged man in a baseball cap followed him in. His hands were clamped around a blocky pistol trained on Garvin's face.

Harry swallowed. Her fingers felt slippery with sweat. Beside her, Beth had frozen.

The man gestured with the gun. 'Face the window.'

Garvin swivelled obediently to his right, like a child anxious to please. Harry could see his profile: the trembling lip, the puffy face. The other man scanned the room, his gaze sliding towards the vault. Harry shrank back, pressing up against the shelves, her finger still on the light switch. Beth had flattened herself against one wall.

Metal snapped and clicked. Harry flinched, waiting for the shot. When none came, she inched forward and peeped out through the slit.

Garvin's hands were handcuffed behind his back. The man jabbed the gun into his shoulder blade.

'Kneel.'

Garvin dropped to his knees, making small mewling sounds. The man with the gun touched the elongated barrel to the back of Garvin's head.

'Any last requests? Sorry, too late.' *Phut-phut*. The muffled shots spat into Garvin's skull. He jerked once, then crumpled to the floor.

Harry gasped. Her finger slipped, and light flooded back into the vault. The man in the baseball cap whirled round and for an instant they locked eyes. Then he raised his gun to her face. Harry screamed, slammed the vault door shut. Bullets zinged against metal, and the door's automatic bolts clanked home.

Harry backed away, her heart pounding. She could hear Beth moaning in the dark.

'Who is he?' Harry whispered, but Beth didn't answer.

The door handle rattled, and Harry held her breath. She cocked her head, straining for more sounds. Nothing.

Slowly, her eyes adjusted to the dark. Beth had slid to the floor, knees up, hands over her ears. Harry had a sudden image of Garvin's bulk, towering over Beth with a broken chair. She hugged her arms across her chest, and tried to be glad he was dead.

She squinted into the gloom. The only source of light was a small red dot blinking on the door, the twin of the light on the security panel outside.

Harry stiffened. The keycard! Had she left it in the slot? She couldn't remember. But she'd dropped the wine gum to the floor, hadn't she? Even if he found it, he couldn't possibly guess its purpose.

Unless she'd left it on the sensor.

Dammit, why couldn't she remember?

The light blinked amber, and Harry froze. He must have found the keycard and fed it back into the slot. She backed up against the wall in line with the door and lifted her case, ready to strike. It was the only weapon she had. Her eyes fastened on the amber dot, waiting for it to turn green.

Nothing happened.

'What's he doing?' Beth whispered, clambering to her feet.

Harry shook her head. She pressed her ear up against the door. The steel was like ice on her cheek. She could make out a faint, scuffing sound, like something heavy being dragged.

Nausea slithered inside her. Dear God. He was going to use Garvin's fingers on the sensor. Harry closed her eyes, blocking out the image of him roughing up a corpse to press dead flesh against the pad.

The numbers. Concentrate on the numbers. Ten fingers, three shots. Maybe they'd get lucky and he'd strike out.

The scuffling grew closer.

Who was she kidding? Those odds weren't real. After all, who used their pinkie on a biometric scanner? Chances were, Garvin had used his thumb or index finger, something the man in the baseball cap had probably worked out for himself.

Four fingers, three shots. Those odds were on the killer's side.

The scuffling stopped. Harry waved Beth to the other side of the door, and raised her case back over her head. She stared at the amber light.

Handcuffs clicked, then clattered to the floor. A trickle of sweat ran down Harry's back. There was a grunt, a final heave. Harry counted to three. Then a soft beep sounded from the other side of the door.

Strike one.

Harry took a deep breath and flexed her fingers on

25

the case. Beth had found a metal cashbox on one of the shelves and was holding it high over her head. She traded looks with Harry and nodded, her eyes wide with fright.

They waited. One, two, three.

Another beep, faint but unmistakable. Harry let out a long breath. He had one shot left. If he failed, he'd need a code to reset the device before he could try again. And the only person who knew that code was dead.

Sweat ran into Harry's eyes and the amber light blurred. Beth's breathing came fast and shallow.

Beep-beep-beep. Amber flashed to red. The man outside roared, and gunshots pumped into the lock. Harry screamed, spinning away from the door. Metal screeched as the vault's anti-attack bolts slammed into place, dead-locking it against assault. Bullets blasted the door, round after round, until finally the shooting stopped.

Harry glanced over at Beth. She was cowering on the floor, arms over her head. Had that become her only means of defence, curling into a submissive ball? Harry rubbed at her ears. They still pounded with echoes, or maybe it was her own blood exploding through her veins.

For a long time, neither of them moved. Hot metal ticked into the vault. The air grew muggy, heavy with exhaled moisture, and for the first time Harry worried about being able to breathe. The walls seemed to crush in on her, and she fought an urge to hyperventilate. How long could they last in here without fresh air?

'Maybe he's gone,' Beth whispered eventually.

'Maybe.' Harry slid to the floor and tried to regulate her breathing. 'Or maybe he's just waiting us out.'

Beth's face crumpled, making Harry feel like a brute for pointing out the truth. She studied her for a moment: the cropped hair, the bruised eye, the fingers that plucked at the black duffel bag.

'Are you glad Garvin's dead?' Harry asked.

Beth shrugged, and didn't look up. She twisted the bag's cord around her fingers.

Harry had another question, though she didn't expect an answer to this one either.

'Why did you stay with him?'

This time, Beth looked up. 'You think that, just by leaving, the violence would've stopped?' She shook her head, jerking at the drawstring on her bag. 'Leaving is more dangerous than staying, sometimes. Unless you plan it right.'

She slid Harry a glance, then dug an envelope out of the bag.

'Know what this is?' She hooked her fingers under the flap and extracted something small. 'Here, catch.'

Harry caught the tiny pellet Beth had flung into the air. She rolled it between her fingers, then held it near the red light in the door. It looked like a piece of clouded crystal, about the size of a garden pea. Even in the tiny glow of light, its metallic lustre gleamed.

'That's over a carat,' Beth said. 'Maybe a hundred and twenty-five points.'

Harry stared at her. 'This is a diamond?'

'A rough diamond, uncut. Africa's finest.'

Harry turned the stone over in her hand. It felt smooth, as though coated in an oily film, and looked more like a chip of polished lead than a diamond. She shook her head.

'So I broke into Garvin's safe to let you steal his diamonds?'

Beth pointed to her bloodied eye. 'Call it compensation.'

Harry stared at the frail woman in front of her. Battered wife or burglar, who could tell? At this point, Harry's internal barometer was swinging wildly.

She held the stone out to Beth, who waved it away.

'Keep it,' she said. 'You've earned it.'

Harry shook her head and tossed the stone into Beth's lap. Then she sprang to her feet, her limbs suddenly twitchy with the need to get away. She switched her attention to the vault door, running her hands along the cold steel. The man with the gun must have gone by now. Surely he couldn't risk hanging around a dead body, live witnesses or not?

'How do we get out of here?' Beth's voice was tight.

But Harry wasn't worried about how to get out. Security was paramount for this kind of vault, but its focus was to keep intruders out, not lock hapless prisoners in.

The question was not how to open the door, but what was waiting for them on the other side of it.

Harry's fingers groped in the dark till she found what

she was looking for: a long metal lever. It was the vault's internal escape mechanism, required by safety regulations in case someone got trapped inside. The regulators probably hadn't had her exact situation in mind, but Harry was grateful for their foresight.

She pressed her ear to the door. Nothing. Then she wiped her palms against her thighs, and gripped the lever. She glanced back at Beth.

'Ready?'

Beth jumped to her feet and nodded, hitching the duffel bag over her shoulder.

Harry pushed the lever down with both hands. Bolts shunted back through metal, one after the other. The light flicked green. Holding her breath, Harry pressed her shoulder to the door. It didn't budge.

Shit. Had the killer's bullets damaged the mechanism?

She slapped her palms flat against the door, arms fully extended. 'Come on, push.'

Beth joined her at the door, and together they heaved. A chink of light sliced into the vault.

'Keep pushing!' Harry said.

'Something's jammed up against it!'

Grunting, they leaned their weight into the door until finally it gave way, breaking open a small gap. Beth's rail-thin figure disappeared through it.

'Beth, wait!' Harry froze, waiting for the spray of bullets. When it didn't come, she peeped out into the room. It was empty.

She grabbed her case and squeezed through the gap,

stumbling over the reason why the door had jammed. Garvin's body lay wedged against it, face down on the floor.

His hair was wet with blood, and Harry caught a whiff of dried urine in the air. She backed away, clutching the case to her chest, then raced out into the hall.

'Beth?'

The front door was wide open. Harry sprinted outside, checking the street. People were out strolling, taking in the sea view over the wall. There was no sign of Beth.

A siren whined in the distance. Harry whirled round, taking in her choices. Behind her, the open front door. To her left, her red Mini parked by the kerb. In spite of the chill blowing in from the sea, Harry's brain was over-heating.

She edged towards her car, raking over the highlights of her morning so far. A safe that she'd broken into illegally. A client who'd disappeared. A duffel bag full of stolen diamonds. Not to mention a dead body. The list wasn't encouraging.

The siren grew louder and she fumbled for her keys. Did she really want to stick around for the police? The last time she'd got close to an investigation, she'd ended up a suspect. Still was, for all she knew. That wouldn't help her credibility this time round.

With trembling fingers, she opened the boot of her car and dumped her case inside. She thought of the man in the baseball cap who didn't leave witnesses, and her throat closed over. She knew she should talk to the police, but for the second time that day, a voice in her head screamed '*run*'.

The siren grew more strident. It wasn't too late. After all, no one knew who she was. The killer didn't know her name, and the police didn't need to know it either.

Harry gasped. Her business card. It was still on the desk inside. She spun round and scrambled back up the steps, taking them two at a time. The siren was close now, in the same street. She raced back into the house and made straight for the office. Averting her eyes from Garvin's body, she scoured the surface of the desk. She hauled out drawers, checked on the floor.

Tyres squealed outside, car doors slammed. A cold shiver rippled down Harry's spine.

Her business card was gone.

4

'Beth Oliver died four months ago.'

Harry turned away from the window and gaped at the plain-clothes detective by the door. 'What?'

'That's right.' He closed the door behind him and leaned against it, arms folded across his chest. 'So now as well as all the other holes in your story, you're saying you were hired by a dead lady.'

Harry squinted at him, as if sharpening her focus could change what he said. He was lean and wiry, his sandy hair cut short like a schoolboy's. His name was Hunter, and he'd been questioning her in Beth's kitchen for two hours.

She thought of Beth: the battered face, the passport, the bank statement. She shook her head, but her insides were sinking.

'She was here, I talked to her.'

Hunter shrugged. 'I don't know who you talked to, but it wasn't Beth Oliver. She died in a car accident last July.'

Harry groaned, and sank into a kitchen chair. She'd known something was off from the start. Why the hell hadn't she just walked away?

She shook her head. She knew why. That damn vault. Even as a kid she'd been the same, hacking into computers just to prove she could. By the time she was eleven she could crack open almost anything, and mostly it just brought her trouble. Maybe at the age of twenty-nine it was time to consider grown-up things like consequences.

She looked up at Hunter and had a hard time meeting his eyes. 'Seems like I misread my client.'

'If there ever was a client.'

'Look—'

'The woman next door saw you charge out of the house, ready to take off.'

Harry glared at him. 'I told you, I wasn't taking off. I was looking for Beth.'

'So why'd you go back into the house?'

She hesitated. She could hardly tell him she'd been looking for her business card, trying to cover her tracks. 'I don't know. To stay with the body, call the police. I don't really remember.'

'But you didn't call us, the woman next door did.' Hunter pushed himself away from the door and sauntered towards her, his thumbs hooked into the pockets of his chinos. 'Imagine that. You're standing here with a dead body and you don't call the police.'

Harry met his gaze and tried not to blink. 'I must have heard the sirens. Why would I call you if you were right outside?'

He stared at her for a long moment, and she made herself stare back. Faint cracks fanned out around his tired hazel eyes, but otherwise his skin was smooth. She guessed he was probably somewhere in his thirties.

'So tell me more about this man with the gun,' he said eventually.

'I've told you all I can remember. He was wearing a baseball cap, and a light blue jacket and jeans, I think.'

'Height?'

'Five feet ten or eleven, maybe.'

'Face? Age?'

Harry shrugged. 'He was tanned, quite lined. Compact build. In his fifties, I'd say.'

'Anything else?'

'I only saw him for a minute through a narrow slit. Ask the woman next door. If she saw me, she might have seen him.'

'We already did. She didn't see anyone. No man in a baseball cap. No Beth-lookalike.' He stepped closer towards her. 'Just you, dumping a case into your car.'

'That was the laptop, I told you. Here.' She stood up, fished in her bag and held out her car keys. 'Red Mini parked outside. Take the laptop, I don't want it.'

Beth probably hadn't wanted it either. She'd only been interested in the diamonds.

Hunter took the keys and tossed them to a uniformed

officer, who caught them and left the room. Then Hunter turned back to Harry, moving in closer. He smelled of coffee and herbal deodorant.

'Harry Martinez.' He peered at her face. 'Any reason I should know that name?'

Her stomach dipped. She shook her head and aimed for a casual shrug. After all, what could she say? That her father was Salvador Martinez, the high-profile banker who'd gone to prison for insider trading? That the fraud squad had been watching her now for six months, convinced she'd helped him stash some of his money?

Hunter's eyes never left her face. 'What's Harry short for? Harriet?'

'Henrietta.' Her father had been the one to start calling her Harry. Harry the Burglar, to be precise, but now was not the time to share that particular detail.

Hunter's eyes dropped to the business card she'd given him. 'Blackjack Security. You own this company?'

Harry nodded. 'I started it up a few months ago.'

'What kind of work do you do?'

She shrugged. 'It varies. Penetration tests to check system security, computer intrusion investigations, computer forensics for litigation.'

Hunter was nodding slowly. 'You make a habit of breaking into people's safes?'

Harry felt her cheeks burn. 'Not without the owner's permission. Look, you don't really think I killed Garvin Oliver, do you?'

Hunter cocked his head, like a terrier processing signals.

Then he waggled his hand, showing how much her credibility hung in the balance. Before she could press him further, the uniformed officer returned to the room and handed back her keys. Hunter threw him an inquiring look, and the officer nodded. Harry looked from one to the other, wondering what damning evidence they'd turned up against her in her own car.

Hunter's phone rang. He checked the caller ID, and his mouth tensed. She could see him debating whether to take the call, then he answered it in terse tones. While he listened tight-lipped to the voice on the other end, Harry thought of her missing business card.

She longed to believe that Beth had taken it, but she knew the chances were slim. More likely the man in the baseball cap had seen it and slipped it into his pocket. The notion made Harry's brain jangle. The killer already knew her face; now he knew where to find her, too.

'She what?'

Harry snapped her eyes back to Hunter. He was glaring at her, deep lines carving up his forehead. Her heartbeat geared up a notch. He listened some more to the voice on the phone. Then he ended the call, his eyes still drilling through hers.

'That was Detective Inspector Lynne,' he said. 'Ring a bell?'

Harry's fingers tightened around her keys. For an instant, she was back in the Bahamas, a suitcase full of banknotes by her side; and waiting for her in Dublin was a detective with watchful grey eyes. She swallowed.

'I think so,' she managed. 'Isn't he with Fraud?'

'I put in a call to check you out. Seems Lynne has dibs on the name Martinez. Gets alerted any time it turns up.' His eyes probed hers. 'He reminded me about the case against your father.'

'So? My father went to prison for six years. Case closed.'

'Apparently not.' Hunter shook his head. 'Sal Martinez. I should've made the connection. Earned millions in insider trading, didn't he?'

'Which he forfeited to the courts as part of his sentencing. He paid out over forty million euros.'

'But according to Lynne, there was more. And it's missing.'

Harry thrust out her chin. 'What's all that got to do with me?'

'Lynne's a tenacious man.' He paused. 'He asked me to give you a message.'

'Oh?'

'He advises you not to plan another trip to the Bahamas.'

Harry flashed on another image: jade green sea, baking sand and the *slick-slick* of cards being dealt. She shook her head.

'Am I being accused of something here?' she said.

'Like I said, Lynne is tenacious.' Hunter glared at her. 'He doesn't give up.'

Harry sighed. Suddenly her whole body ached, as if reminders of the past had sapped her energy.

'Look, if I'm not under arrest for anything, I'd like to go.'

Hunter shrugged. 'You can go. For now.'

She made her way past him towards the door, then hesitated and looked back.

'The man with the gun.' She bit her lip. 'He saw me.'

'So you said.'

'He might find me. He said—'

'—that he never leaves witnesses. You said that too.'

Harry stared at him. 'Aren't you going to do anything about that? Offer some kind of protection?'

Hunter shrugged. 'We'll get a patrol car to cruise by your house once in a while.'

'What good will that do? He's not going to wait in the street with a rifle, is he?'

'I don't know, you tell me.' Hunter narrowed his eyes. 'You're the only one who saw him.'

He turned away, dismissing her. Harry's insides plummeted. She thought of the man in the baseball cap and how he'd locked eyes with her just before he pulled the trigger. She thought of her business card, in plain view on the desk. Her head reeled. She stumbled through the hall and out on to the street. The air was fresh and salty, and she gulped it down. Then slowly, she moved towards her car.

Instinctively, she checked over her shoulder, her eyes sweeping across the array of windows fronting the Georgian terrace. So many places for a man with a gun to hide. She shuddered.

If she could just find the woman she still thought of as Beth, then maybe the police would believe her. But how? Somehow, she was connected to Garvin Oliver, but what did Harry know about him? According to Beth he was a sponging wife-beater, but her version of events was hardly reliable now.

Harry began to regret handing over the laptop. It might have revealed information about Garvin Oliver that could have helped to track Beth down. On the other hand, maybe she should just let the police handle it. Right now, they didn't believe a word she said, but they were bound to discover the truth eventually.

Raindrops spat against her face. She unlocked her car and ducked inside, and immediately her nose wrinkled at an alien smell. The uniformed officer must have been a smoker; he'd left his tell-tale sootiness behind. She opened a couple of windows to generate a cross-breeze, and did a quick visual survey of her car.

Everywhere showed signs of a cursory search. The pile of computer books on the passenger seat had been rearranged and her notepads had fallen to the floor. She flipped open the glove compartment. Her maps and screw-drivers had been disturbed too. She felt a creeping sense of violation at the thought of someone rifling through her things. Then she checked the back seat, and frowned. Her laptop was missing.

Harry's spine buzzed. She leapt out of the car, hauled open the boot and stared inside. The raindrops were heavier now, raucous seagulls free-wheeling inland in packs. Harry reached for the case that lay where she'd left it. Inside it, her torch, pliers and the rest of her toolkit were all undisturbed.

And alongside them was Garvin Oliver's laptop.

5

Callan clanked through the turnstiles, hitching his bag higher on his shoulder. The only thing inside it was a Browning pistol that he'd already fired once that day. He checked his watch. In another twenty minutes, he planned on firing it again.

He scanned his surroundings. In front of him was an oval of immaculate grass, bounded by low hedges. Adverts for Hennessy and Paddy Power bookmakers lined the railings on the inside. The parade ring was empty.

He tipped up his baseball cap, backhanding the sweat from his forehead. He was cutting things bloody fine. The last job had been a screw-up, throwing him off schedule. He pictured the puffy-faced man kneeling on the floor, pissing himself as he waited to be shot. It should've been quick. In, out. No mess, no witnesses.

He fingered the business card in his pocket. Now he had the Spanish-looking girl to add to his list.

People swarmed in front of him, beating a path between the grandstand, the bookies and Madigan's Bar. Leopardstown racecourse always drew the crowds.

Leopardstown. *Baile on Lobhair*. Town of the lepers.

Pain pulsed through Callan's skull, and with it an image: baked red dirt, buzzing insects, the stench of rotting flesh. A village in Sierra Leone, bodies butchered for the ritual cannibalism of the RUF. But in all of the rebels' murderous binges, they never ate the lepers.

Callan blinked, shoved the memory away. He swallowed and edged closer to the ring. Soon the punters would be five deep around it, inspecting the horses for the next race. That was fine with him. He needed the crowd cover.

He opened his programme and checked through the runners for the one o'clock race. There were seven in total, and number four was underlined: Honest Bill. The small print confirmed what he needed to know: Jockey, R. Devlin; Trainer, D. Kruger; Owner, T. Jordan.

Frantic commentary echoed over the tannoy, winding up the 12.40 race. Punters began staking out their space by the parade ring. Callan adjusted the bag on his shoulder. It was light. In the jungles of Angola and Sierra Leone, every man in his unit had carried an AK-47, ten magazines, an extra ammunition belt, an M79 grenade launcher and a supply of white phosphorus grenades. Here, things were different. Here, you only carried what you could conceal.

Hooves clopped behind him, buckles clinked. He turned to see a frisky black horse being led into the ring. His coat was glossy, his chest muscles bulging. Callan consulted his racecard. Number one, Rottweiler's Lad.

'Bit of a sprinter, that fella.' A middle-aged man had appeared next to him at the railings, chewing on a pipe. 'Good deep chest.'

Callan grunted, raking his gaze over the other horses filing into the ring. Numbers three, six and five, all dark brown. They jig-jogged past, stirring up an aroma of hay and manure. Where the hell was number four?

The public address system crackled, the announcer giving the all-clear on the previous race. 'Winner all right, winner all right.'

The signal for the bookies to start paying out. The man with the pipe ripped up his ticket and snorted. Then he turned to Callan, sweet tobacco mingling with stable smells.

'Who d'ya fancy for this one, then?'

Callan's jaw tightened. He didn't have time for ring-side tipsters, but rudeness would attract attention. His urban camouflage was anonymity: jeans and casual jacket, cap over the buzz-cut, everything loose-fitting to hide the muscles so at odds with his middle-aged face. After one o'clock, he needed to be forgettable.

He feigned a smile. 'Honest Bill.'

'Ah, Billy-boy. Great horse. Brave as they come.'

Rottweiler's Lad pranced by, tossing his head and snorting. Jockeys began drifting into the ring, and Callan

43

checked the racecard for Honest Bill's colours: black-and-white cubes. None of the jockeys matched.

'There's your fella.'

Callan turned. A honey-brown horse bounced into the ring. His coat looked sweaty, and his hind legs were sheathed in red bandages. The saddle cloth bore the number four.

The muscles in Callan's neck tensed. His eyes travelled beyond the horse to the jockey who'd stalked in behind him. He was taller than most, wiry like all of them, and his silks were patterned like a chessboard. Rob Devlin. Callan studied him, making sure he'd recognize him again.

Devlin made his way into the centre of the ring, shaking his head at a red-faced man who was waiting for him there.

'Is that the trainer?' Callan said.

The man with the pipe followed his gaze, then shook his head. 'That's the owner, Tom Jordan. TJ, they call him.'

Callan watched the red-faced man. He was standing eye-to-eye with the jockey, trying to stare him down, but Devlin seemed to be doing all the talking. A bell sounded, and the pair broke apart. Jockeys scattered to mount their rides, and a tall, scowling man broke away from another group to give Devlin a leg up.

'That's the trainer,' the man with the pipe said. 'Dan Kruger. One of the best.'

Callan narrowed his eyes. So that was Kruger. He edged around the ring to get a better view. The trainer looked to be in his late thirties, with prominent, dark brows and a tanned face. He patted the horse's neck and saluted the jockey. Then Devlin gathered up his reins and headed out of the ring.

Callan glared at the jockey's swaying back. For now, he was out of reach. But that still left the other two. He fixed his sights on Jordan and Kruger and followed them as they left the ring. They mingled with the crowd now flowing back towards the stands, and Callan melted into their slipstream.

He unzipped his bag a fraction and slotted a hand inside, grasping the butt of his gun. Keeping the weapon in the bag meant he could place the barrel right up against the target. Two silenced shots and the target would go down. The crowd would think he'd fainted, Callan would disappear, and his ejected cartridges would be caught inside the bag. Neat and tidy.

He followed the two men across the concourse. Kruger disappeared inside one of the bars, and Jordan was about to follow when a small boy of nine or ten raced up and grabbed him by the hand. Jordan turned and laughed, allowing himself to be dragged away.

Callan clenched his fingers around the gun. He tracked the pair along the side of the stands as they hurried towards the bookies' enclosure.

He checked his watch. It was almost one o'clock. He lengthened his stride, closing the gap between them. The boy scampered off to the nearest bookie and Jordan stood alone, like a springbok separated from the herd.

Callan hesitated, checking his cover. The crowds here had thinned, the punters deserting the bookies for a place on the stands. He hung back. Too exposed.

The tannoy system crackled. 'They're under starter's orders.'

The boy reappeared. Jordan took him by the hand and together they hiked up into the stands.

'And they're off.'

Callan strode after Jordan, circling, weaving, slipping through the crowds, using whatever cover his combat zone offered him. The commentator droned out his inventory of horses.

'And racing now away from the stands, it's Forest Moon the leader, from Holy Joe and Dutch Courage. Then comes Rottweiler's Lad, with Honest Bill the back marker.'

Jordan and the boy stopped halfway up the grandstand. Callan was already four steps higher, and he stared at the back of Jordan's head.

'Rounding the turn now, it's Forest Moon and Holy Joe. Then Rottweiler's Lad improved into third place.'

Callan sidestepped into a gap, lining himself up behind Jordan. Suddenly, the man ducked, squatting low. Callan froze, then relaxed again as he saw the boy climbing up on to Jordan's shoulders. By the time Jordan was upright, Callan had moved one step down. Two more, and he'd be right behind him.

The commentator's voice shifted up a key. 'And into the back straight, it's Holy Joe, Forest Moon weakening into second, challenged by Rottweiler's Lad, Honest Bill, then Dutch Courage.'

A murmur rippled through the crowds. 'Come on, Honest Bill.'

Jordan handed the boy a pair of binoculars. People craned their necks to get a clearer view and Callan took another step down.

'As they round the final bend, it's Holy Joe the leader from Rottweiler's Lad, then Forest Moon, Honest Bill making ground on the outside but Devlin has left him a lot to do.'

The crowd buzzed, shifting restlessly. 'Come on, Billy-boy!'

Callan inched forwards. Suddenly, the boy swivelled and stared at him through the binoculars. Callan's scalp prickled. He flashed on another ten-year-old boy. Matted black hair, wild eyes. The child soldier with binoculars around his neck and a machete in his raised arms. Chills swept through Callan's frame.

A roar went up from the crowd, and the commentator's pitch shot up an octave. 'And they're into the home straight, it's Rottweiler's Lad, Holy Joe, Honest Bill accelerating on the outside!'

Callan's vision blurred. He could smell the child soldier's unwashed body. He recalled how the boy's shirt had fallen open, exposing red welts where the initials 'RUF' had been carved into his chest with a razor. Callan hadn't hesitated. He'd fired his sniper rifle, spitting two bullets into the boy's forehead.

'And they're inside the final two furlongs!' The commentator was in a frenzy, the yells from the crowd filling the stands. 'It's Rottweiler's Lad, but here comes Honest Bill surging up on the outside!'

Callan remembered standing over the boy's body. He'd stared at the bloody initials where the rebels had rubbed cocaine to induce the boy's savagery. Beside him stood a line of wailing children. The child soldier had been about to hack off their arms.

'It's Rottweiler's Lad from Honest Bill, I've never seen anything like it, Devlin has turned him loose, calling on him for everything he has!'

The boy on Jordan's shoulders turned away. Callan's chest tightened, the memories choking him. He took a deep breath, then descended the final step. He was right behind Jordan, close enough to smell the scent of cigars from his clothes.

The commentator was yelling now. 'It's the final furlong, it's Rottweiler's Lad and Honest Bill, stride for stride, Honest Bill digging deep.'

Callan stretched the canvas of his bag taut around the gun barrel.

'They're neck and neck, what a race between these two!'

The roars had reached a deafening pitch. It was the crescendo he'd been waiting for, the perfect cover. He pressed the gun barrel into Jordan's back.

The commentator hadn't drawn breath. 'It's a desperate finish as they come up to the line, Rottweiler's Lad trying to fight back!'

The stands were a blaring wall of noise. Callan squeezed the trigger twice. The commentator's voice was off the scale.

'And it's Honest Bill the winner! What a horse!'

Callan stepped backwards and sidled through the heaving crowd. From the corner of his eye he saw the boy tumble to the ground, his father crumpling beneath him.

Callan strolled towards the exit.

Winner all right.

6

The most important thing about pilfering confidential data was not to get caught. Harry flicked a glance in her rear-view mirror and wondered how she'd get away with it this time.

A flash of heat washed over her. What the hell was she thinking? She should have taken Garvin's laptop back to Hunter the minute she'd realized the mistake. The longer she held on to it, the worse it would get. Already, she felt as if something radioactive was glowing through the boot of her car.

Harry geared down into third, negotiating the bends on the coast road. Waves slapped against the wall to her left, tossing spray into the air like confetti.

She came to a T-junction and slowed down, considering her options. Turn right, and she could loop back to Garvin Oliver's house and hand the laptop over.

Turn left, and she could be home in fifteen minutes. Harry chewed her bottom lip.

When you got right down to it, the police had been the ones who'd screwed up, not her. After all, it wasn't her fault the officer had snatched the first laptop case he'd seen.

She checked left and right. Naturally, she wouldn't dream of withholding evidence. She gripped the steering wheel and swung left. She'd hand over the laptop just as soon as she could, but not until she'd peeked at it herself first.

Harry wound her way south, her whole body clenched, her eyes darting to her mirror. No one seemed to be following her, but it was hard to tell. On her left the beach curved like a bow, the slate-grey water reflecting the rain clouds above. Her arms ached from gripping the wheel, but relaxing them was beyond her.

She cruised through Killiney Village, cutting left down a rough track tucked in behind a row of new builds. She pulled up in front of the only house on the lot: a small, stone cottage with double-glazed windows and matching white UPVC door. She stared at it and felt herself droop.

Six months ago she'd been renting an apartment close to the city, where she'd basked in Dublin's lively buzz and felt that she belonged. But lately she'd had an urge to buy her own place. She'd rented the cottage as an experiment. Living close to the sea was supposed to be soothing. But instead, there was something unsettling about the greyness of the beach and the isolation of her new home.

Harry sighed and climbed out of the car. Maybe it wasn't just her professional instincts that were becoming unreliable.

She hauled her case out of the boot and trudged inside the cottage, passing through the narrow hall into the cramped kitchen beyond. She dumped the case on the table, then flung open the small windows at the rear of the house. Sharp, salty air perked up the room, but she didn't stop to enjoy the view. Right now, she had other things on her mind.

She eyed up the case. Beth had only been interested in the diamonds, but the laptop must have had some importance if Garvin locked it up in a vault. She wiped her palms along her thighs. It was a long shot to hope it might lead her to Beth, but it was worth a try.

Harry slid the laptop out of the bag. Something small rattled out with it, clattering on to the floor. She peered under the table, and her whole body froze. Almost invisible against the stone tiles was a smooth, pea-sized pebble. Harry bent to retrieve it, then rolled it between her fingers, holding it close to her face. Beth's uncut diamond. It felt cold, as though it had been kept in the fridge. She watched its steely lustre catch the light for a moment. Then she buried the stone in her fist.

Beth must have slipped it deliberately into her bag. Had she been leaving her a gift, or planting evidence? Harry was inclined to believe the worst, but either way, it'd be hard to explain to the police. She shook her head and dropped the pebble into her jacket pocket. She'd work out what to do with it later, but right now, she had a laptop to cross-examine.

She reached out to flip open the lid, then hesitated. Any snooping she did on the laptop could probably be traced. Worse still, her activities might overwrite valuable data on the hard drive. Apart from getting caught, the last thing she wanted was to compromise a murder investigation.

She frowned. Then she marched to the spare bedroom where she kept her field kits and retrieved a stash of hardware: a digital camera, a screwdriver, a sanitized hard drive, a spare laptop and a bunch of cables and switches. Adding a clutch of paperwork to the mix, she set the lot on the kitchen table and went to work.

First, she grabbed the camera and took some shots of the laptop, recording the make, model and serial number and documenting her actions as she went. Next, she unscrewed the laptop chassis, exposing the hard drive and releasing it from its caddy. She photographed the disembowelled hardware, labelled each component, then photographed it all again. It was tedious work, but she needed a record of her activities. If the integrity of the hard drive was ever in doubt, at least she could prove chain of custody. Inwardly, she winced. Her own integrity might be a little trickier to establish.

Snatching at the cables, she hooked up the hard drive to a set of switches, connecting it to the blank drive which in turn was plugged into the spare laptop. She powered everything up, worked the keyboard for a moment and then stood back. It would take a few hours, but soon she'd have a duplicate of Garvin Oliver's hard drive.

Odd to think that somewhere the police were putting her own laptop through the same paces. Acquiring a forensic duplication was the first step in analysing a hard drive for evidence. She'd worked her share of computer forensics cases in her last job with Lúbra Security. Of course, that was before she'd got sidetracked by a crooked trader who'd tried to kill her for her father's money.

Harry shivered. Her eyes swept the room, taking in the slanted ceilings and exposed oak beams. She'd thought it was the need for a slower pace that had taken her out here. She suspected now it was more to do with having somewhere to lick her wounds.

She shook her head. Godammit, enough introspection. The need to pace up and down jerked through her limbs, but the cottage just wasn't built for it. Instead, she flung herself into a chair and thought about Beth. Or whatever her real name was.

She scribbled down everything she knew about her, which didn't amount to much: her physical description; her intimate knowledge of the contents of Garvin's safe. She recalled the woman's likeness to the passport photo belonging to the real Beth, and her story of Garvin's beatings. *She was family, she should've known.*

Harry frowned. Were she and Beth sisters?

She thought of the next-door neighbour who'd seen Harry poised for flight. Neighbours usually had plenty to tell, as long as they were asked the right questions.

Would the woman next door know anything about Beth's family?

Harry tapped a fingernail against her teeth. Talking to the neighbour in person was out of the question. She'd hardly chitchat to someone she'd just witnessed fleeing the scene of a crime. On the other hand, what choice did Harry have? She had no name or phone number. All she had was an address.

The hairs on the back of her neck prickled. She snatched up her car keys and headed for the door.

Sometimes, an address was all it took.

7

The closer Harry got to Garvin Oliver's house, the harder it was to breathe. She cracked open a window and sucked in the sea air. Ahead of her, yellow police tape snapped in the breeze, and an officer stood on guard by the railings. Traffic slowed to a crawl as motorists rubbernecked at the scene. Harry inched her car in behind them.

Her stomach was taut, as though braced for a punch. An image flashed before her: Garvin kneeling, head bent as though in prayer; the gun barrel touching his skull.

I never leave witnesses.

Sweat spilled down her back. The notion that someone out there wanted her dead jammed up her brain.

The officer on sentry duty waved the cars on, bending low to inspect the occupants as they passed. A fair-haired man, lean and athletic, stepped out of the house to join him. Harry caught her breath. Hunter. Shit. How bad would it look to be caught coming back for a voyeuristic eyeful? She yanked at the steering wheel and veered up a side road, her heart banging against her chest.

She'd been stupid to even think of driving past the house. What was the matter with her? She detoured away from the coast road, taking the long way round. Five minutes later, she'd pulled up at the library closest to Garvin's home.

As she pushed through the door, she inhaled the smell of ageing, plastic-bound books. A lot of people thought libraries were dull, but to Harry they were hidey-holes full of free information. And information was artillery for a social-engineering attack. Which was double-talk for executing a scam.

She smiled at the librarian behind the desk. 'Hi there. Do you keep a hard copy of the electoral register?'

The librarian smiled back. He was tall and stooped, with the gentle-giant look that often went with large men.

'You can check it online, you know, to see if you're registered.' He pointed over his shoulder. 'The computers are back there.'

'Yes, I know, but I'd prefer the hard copy if you've got one.'

She'd tried the online system before. For honest citizens just checking they were registered to vote, it certainly made life easy. But for snoopers like Harry it blocked you right at the get-go by demanding both a name and address. No off-course browsing allowed. The printed version, on the other hand, dumped everything right in your lap.

The librarian nodded, and ambled out from behind the counter. That was the other great thing about libraries. No one ever asked you why.

Harry followed her jumbo helper as he wound his way between the rows of shelves. Behind her, scanners bleeped and date stamps thumped. Eventually, the librarian stopped by a filing cabinet and pointed at the stacks of paper perched on top.

'That's most of it for this area, I think,' he said. 'If we don't have the one you need, we can check with the other libraries.'

Harry thanked him and watched him lumber away. Then she hefted the mound of paperwork to a nearby desk and pulled up a chair. She thumbed through the pages. They'd been stapled together in bunches, organized by district and adjoining roads. She traced a finger down the columns of data. The houses were listed by road number, with the occupants' names recorded against them. She smiled, her mouth almost watering. All that juicy information. Then she fished a pen and paper out of her bag and went to work.

It didn't take long to find Garvin Oliver's road. She scanned the house numbers. There it was, last on the list: 91 Seapoint Avenue. Occupants: Oliver, Beth; Oliver, Garvin. The register must have pre-dated her death. No mention of the daughter, which made sense. As a schoolgirl, she wasn't eligible to vote.

Harry's eyes slid back to number 90. There was only one occupant: Cantwell, Margot. Since the Olivers' house was an end-of-terrace, there were no other immediate neighbours. Replacing the stack of paper on the filing cabinet, Harry returned to the front desk where she borrowed a telephone directory and looked up the name Cantwell. None listed for 90 Seapoint Avenue. Damn. Ex-directory. Why did people do that? Did they really think it kept their number private?

She chewed the end of her pen for a moment. Then she swapped the directory for the Golden Pages and looked up video rental stores in the area. There were two, but MaxVision was the closest to Garvin's home, located just around the corner. Harry noted the phone number, along with that of the MaxVision store across town in Malahide.

Then she flipped to the florist section and ran her finger along the page till she found one close to Seapoint. She jotted down the name and number, and was about to return to her car when she spotted the row of computers behind the desk.

Beth Oliver died four months ago.

Harry contemplated the screens. Surely if there was a sister, she'd be mentioned in Beth Oliver's death notice?

Two minutes later, and after a brief chat with the librarian, Harry was logged into the national newspaper archives. For the next hour, she scanned through the death notices. She expanded her search to stretch back more than six months, just to make sure. But Beth Oliver's name wasn't there.

Harry frowned. Then she shrugged it off and headed back out to her car. Settling herself in the driver's seat, she dialled the number for the MaxVision store located in Malahide.

'Hello, MaxVision Rentals.' The voice was male, but just about. A bored teenager, by the sound of him.

'Hi there.' Harry smiled widely. The bigger the beam, the better it transmitted to your voice. 'I was in with you a couple of nights ago and I just wanted to say how helpful the girl behind the counter was. Really, she went to a lot of trouble and recommended a great movie.'

There was a pause while the teenager seemed to grope for a response. Satisfied customers probably weren't covered in the training manual.

'Right,' he said eventually. 'Well, glad we could help.'

Harry kept the smile going. 'I just wondered, could I get her name so I can thank her, maybe write a nice letter to the manager?'

'Uh, well, sure. But we've got two girls working here. What did she look like?'

Harry scrambled for something generic. 'Oh, darkish hair, I think. Medium height. Slim.'

'Slim?' He sounded surprised, and Harry backpedalled fast.

'Well, slim-ish.' She laughed. 'Anyone under fourteen stone looks slim to me.'

'It might have been Lara.' He sounded doubtful. 'Was she sort of, like, pale, dressed all in black in a big tent thing?'

Harry pictured an overweight, teenage Goth. Poor Lara. 'Yes, that sounds like her. Could you tell me your store manager's name so I can drop him a note?'

'Sure, it's Greg Chaney, you can send it here to the store.' He cleared his throat. 'And my name's Steve.'

'Thanks, Steve, you've been a great help. I'll be sure to mention you too.' She hung up and scribbled the names on her pad, awarding herself a mental thumbs-up. Persuading people to part with information always made her day.

Next, she called the MaxVision store near Garvin Oliver's home.

'MaxVision Rentals, Jilly speaking.' Another teenager, but chirpier this time.

'Hi, Jilly, this is Lara from MaxVision in Malahide. Listen, are you guys having trouble with your computers today? Our stupid system has been down for the last two hours.'

'Really? No, ours is fine. Did you try switching it off and on again?'

Harry snorted. 'I suggested that, but who listens to me? Steve here reckons he's some kind of computer genius, says he's on the case. You know what guys are like.'

Jilly sniggered. 'Tell me about it.'

'Anyway, I have a customer of yours here who wants to rent *The Mona Lisa* but she doesn't have her card with her. Could you verify her information for me? Greg Chaney, our store manager, said it'd be okay to ask.'

'Sure, that's no problem. Greg calls us all the time. What's her name?'

'It's Margot Cantwell, 90 Seapoint Avenue.'

'Hang on.'

Harry crossed her fingers, trying to ward off the possibility that Ms Cantwell was a movie-phobe.

Jilly came back on the line. 'Yep, she's here. Do you want the account number?'

Harry let out a long breath. 'Yes, please.'

She jotted down the number as Jilly called it out. She didn't need it, but information was like currency: too valuable to be discarded. Then she closed her eyes, keeping her tone casual.

'Is there a phone number next to that?'

'Yeah, it's 2834477.'

Harry's eyes flared open. Bingo. She scribbled the number down. She had what she needed, but she played things out.

'That's great,' she said. 'No late returns due, I hope?'

'No.'

'Or outstanding fines?'

'No, she's all clear.'

'Great. I'll set her up manually with an account here and enter it into the system when it's back. I'm sure Whiz Kid Steve here will have us up and running in no time.'

They shared another snigger, then Harry thanked her and hung up. She stared at the phone number she'd just acquired. Some people made a living from scoring information they weren't supposed to have. In the trade, they were known as information brokers. The key was to push for just a small piece at a time. Then you traded each nugget for something bigger at every stage of the scam. Harry's biggest trade-up was yet to come. She dialled Margot Cantwell's number.

'Yes?'

The woman's tone was snippy, and Harry pictured her with a 'what-is-it-now' look on her face. She beamed into the phone.

'Hi, this is Catalina from Kay's Florist in Blackrock. Is that Margot Cantwell?'

'Yes.' If she'd added *What's it to you?* Harry wouldn't have been surprised.

'Great,' Harry said. 'I called to your house just now to deliver a bouquet of flowers, but there was no one home. Will you be there if I call again in half an hour?'

'I've been here all day, I didn't hear anyone. Who're they from?'

'Actually, there's no card.'

'I don't want them. Never trust anyone who sends you flowers, that's what I say.'

'They're really beautiful.' Absurd to feel defensive about her imaginary flowers, but who got surly at an unexpected bouquet?

Margot snorted. 'Flowers just give a person something to hide behind, if you ask me. Let the roses say it all so you don't have to commit yourself in words. Saves the trouble of lying.'

Harry blinked. Whatever the world had done to Margot, she was having a hard time letting it go. Still, for all her crankiness, she seemed willing to stay on the line. Harry steered the conversation towards the Olivers.

'I didn't like to leave the bouquet next door,' she said. 'Not with all those policemen around. What happened in there?'

'They won't tell me. I heard some kind of commotion, then this young woman with wild dark hair came rushing out of the house. Looked odd to me, so I called the guards.'

Harry smoothed a hand over her tangled curls. 'Isn't that the Olivers' house? I'm sure I've delivered flowers there.'

Margot sniffed. 'You probably have. That'd be his style all right.'

'Poor Mrs Oliver. We did the flowers for her funeral. It was a car accident, wasn't it?'

'So they said. The police were around a lot that time, too.'

'I never met her husband.' Harry crossed her fingers. 'But I did meet her sister once. She chose the flowers for the funeral. She and Beth were very alike, weren't they?'

Margot paused. 'Beth didn't have a sister. She was an only child.'

Harry frowned. 'Are you sure?'

'Oh yes.' The woman had turned pensive, and Harry strained to read her voice. It was never a good sign when the mark began to think.

'And another thing,' Margot continued in the same tone. 'There wasn't any funeral. Not here, anyway. She was buried in South Africa.'

64

'South Africa?'

'Cape Town. That's where they're from.' Margot paused. 'What did you say your name was?'

Damn. 'Catalina, from Kay's Flowers. Sorry, I must be mixing things up, we do a lot of funerals in here. Listen, it's been nice talking to you. I'll send someone round with the bouquet later today.'

Harry disconnected and flopped back against the seat. That was stupid. She'd reached too far, straying from her nuggets of information. Guesswork didn't always pay off.

She rewound the conversation with Margot. At this point, her efforts seemed like an elaborate scam that had netted her very little. So the Olivers were from Cape Town. She recalled the woman masquerading as Beth. To Harry, her accent had been a plain-vanilla blend of the South Dublin suburbs. No terse South African clip, no foreign inflection. It wasn't conclusive, but together with Margot's information, it seemed to rule out the possibility that the woman was Beth's sister.

Harry drummed her fingers on the wheel. All she had now was Garvin's hard drive.

8

'Diamonds, they come from stardust, did you know that, Mani?'

Mani grunted, his arm throbbing as he helped Takata to his feet. The sun grilled his face as he followed the queue along the barbed-wire corridor.

'Asha, she explained it to me.' Takata sounded surprised that his daughter knew such things. 'Diamonds are older than the sun.'

Mani shook his head at the old man's poetry. Behind him, the last of the hydraulic excavators clanked to a halt. The pit was now a graveyard of dust-covered machinery, abandoned for the day.

Mani's face twisted in pain as a hard lump in his chest ground further into his gut. Takata's voice dropped to a whisper.

'The diamonds, they come from outer space.'

Mani managed a shrug, the lump a jagged fireball inside him. 'It's only a theory.'

He'd explained it to Asha himself the day before he left. He'd sat with her on the ground outside the shack, watching her weave brooms from the grasses she collected. As always, there was a contented stillness about her. He'd wanted to grab her by the shoulders and shake her. Instead, he'd snatched up a stick and drawn a circle in the dirt.

'Do you know where diamonds come from?' he'd said.

She smiled. 'From the ground.'

A pack of shrieking children swooped in front of them, their faces gritty with dust. Asha laughed and waved them away. Mani jabbed at the centre of his circle.

'They come from grains of carbon deep inside the Earth,' he said. 'In the mantle. A hundred miles below the surface.'

He avoided her gaze. He was showing off, and he knew it. Educated student returns to his home village. But he couldn't help it. Keeping his eyes low, he scored a line from the centre of his circle to the edge.

'Volcanoes carried the diamonds upwards, punching lava through the crust.' He pointed, teacher-like, at the line he'd drawn. 'These volcanic pipes, they hardened into kimberlite.'

He glanced at Asha's face. She was watching him with her serene, almond-shaped eyes.

'I know,' she said.

He tightened his grip on the stick. How could she

know? How could she know anything, living in this shantytown of metal huts, with its goat-kraals and chicken coops and rusty hubcaps salvaged from wrecked cars? He glared at her. He could tell her things, things she couldn't learn in this godforsaken place. He stabbed at the centre of his circle.

'Yes, but where did the grains of carbon come from?' he said. 'How did they find their way into the Earth's mantle?'

Her shoulders lifted in a gentle shrug. 'They grew there.'

He shook his head, smiling. She didn't know. 'That's what we used to think. That they came from plants or animals. A bit of plankton, maybe, or an insect, dragged around by the continental plates.' He sneaked a glance at her. 'But now we scientists know better.'

Her eyes were on the swatch of grasses in her hand. She made no comment on his claims to be a scientist. He turned away, his cheeks burning in the sun.

'Go on,' Asha said.

He shook his head, tossing the stick aside. 'I'm talking too much.'

She retrieved the stick, and held it out to him. 'But I want to know.'

Her gaze was steady, the smile gone. He cleared his throat, took the stick, then carved a second circle into the dirt.

'They found a meteor in Antarctica. It broke up a saw-blade when they tried to cut through it.' He filled his circle with dots. 'That's because it was seeded with diamonds.'

Asha plucked at her grasses. Mani roughed out a five-pointed star above his circles.

'Then astronomers discovered diamonds in a super-nova,' he said.

'A *super-nova*?' She stumbled on the English word. He looked at his feet. Suddenly, his urge to impress her seemed unkind.

'It's an explosion of dying stars,' he said gently. 'They viewed it through a powerful telescope and saw diamonds. Now they say the grains of carbon were planted in the Earth by meteorites and stardust.'

Her hands went still, and her eyes drifted away from him. Mani kicked at his crude drawing, obliterating it in the dust.

'It's only a theory,' he said.

Asha was silent. He followed her gaze to the settlement clearing where the children always played, even in the dust storms. Beyond it, the metal huts looked like water tanks with roofs. Van Wycks provided them. In winter they were ice-cold; in summer, sizzling hot. Mostly, families gathered outdoors, unprotected from the kimberlite dust that blew in from the Van Wycks mines.

His eyes came to rest on the grassland beyond the shantytown, where his mother had died the year before. Ezra had got word to him that migrating Congolese rebels, high on cocaine, had stumbled across her and slit her throat open.

He swallowed and looked back at Asha. She had wrapped her arms around her waist, one hand stroking her side. Mani knew she had scars there, and more on her back, from where they'd operated to remove part of her lungs.

'All this because of stardust,' she whispered, shaking her head.

Mani dropped his gaze. Then he leaned closer to her, his fists clenched on the stick.

'You should have come with me when I asked. To Cape Town.' He was whispering now, too. 'You still can. I won't go to the mine, we can leave today. Ezra got himself into this mess, he can get himself out of it.'

Asha shot a hand out and gripped his wrist. Her eyes bored into his.

'You must help your brother – you must.' Her breath was hot on his face. 'If you don't, they will kill us.'

A uniformed guard jabbed the butt of his submachine gun hard into Mani's shoulder. He winced, quickening his pace. Sweat oozed from him as the lump in his gullet tore at his insides, the pain now worse than anything in his arm. He knew he'd feel no relief until the diamond settled deep inside his belly.

The queue wound its way through the barbed-wire corridor. Mani's eyes swept the horizon, taking in the watchtower with its armed guards, and the double electric fence surrounding the compound. The fences were spaced far apart to stop diamonds being thrown out to confederates. Some of the men used catapults to shoot the stones out. Their accomplices were usually savaged by the Alsatians that patrolled the other side.

Takata dug an elbow into his ribs, nodding towards the man in front. It was Alfredo, Mani's bunk-mate. He was Mani's age, twenty-four, but already had five children to feed. He twisted towards them, his shoulders hunched and his face screwed up in pain.

Mani's gut clenched. Instantly, he knew Alfredo was carrying.

He shot a look at the guards. The nearest one was only a few yards away. Mani whispered in Portuguese. Like him, Alfredo was Angolan.

'*Cuidado!*' Be careful!

Alfredo opened his eyes, tried to nod. He cradled his abdomen, shuffled a few steps. Mani's heart raced. Another fifty yards and they'd be inside the x-ray unit.

What was Alfredo doing? No one escaped the x-rays at the end of every shift. Especially if you were black. He glanced at his friend's sweating face, and suddenly understood. Alfredo was gambling the x-rays weren't switched on.

Mani swallowed, the diamond punching through him like a fist. Alfredo was a fool.

Regulations limited the mine to three x-rays per week on any employee; the rest of the time, the machine was meant to shoot blanks. But what did Van Wycks care about regulations? Radiation overdose was like asbestosis or silicosis: just another black disease.

Mani knew from Ezra that there were no blanks. The machines shot full-power x-rays every day.

His gaze slid back over his shoulder. A tank-shaped figure had moved into view: Okker.

Mani spun round, his chest banging. He felt Okker's eyes drilling the back of his neck. Like most of the guards, Okker was a mercenary. The worst kind of soldier. Thugs and criminals, dishonourable discharges shipped in from foreign armies. But even the other mercenaries were afraid of Okker.

Suddenly, Alfredo yelled, clutching his belly. Then he doubled over and thudded to the ground. Weapons snapped, guards sprinted. In seconds, three submachine guns pointed at Alfredo's head. Mani froze.

Okker lumbered over. 'Take him straight to x-ray. Today he can jump the queue.'

The guards hauled Alfredo up by the arms, ignoring his screams. Mani jerked forward, but Takata's bony fingers were like a vice on his arm. He stopped, but not before Okker had seen him.

'Well, well, kaffir boy.' He slapped his club into the palm of his hand. 'Friend of yours?'

Mani's intestines knotted around the stone. He gritted his teeth, trying to keep the pain from his face. Okker jabbed the club into Mani's chest, clicked his fingers at the guards.

'This one, too,' he said. 'Do both of them now.'

Two more guards appeared at Mani's side and dragged him to the head of the queue. They shoved him through the entrance to the x-ray unit, flinging him through a set of double doors into the waiting room. Alfredo's guards were hauling him into the mini-theatre beyond. Mani stumbled after him.

'Wait! Let me go first!'

A fist punched him in the side of the head, slamming him to the ground. Three savage kicks crunched into his lower back. He curled, foetal-like, to protect his abdomen, but the taller guard yanked him up and hurled him against the wall. Mani slid to the ground, panting. The guard raised his weapon, took aim.

'Just stay still, college boy.'

Mani squinted up at his face. It was large and square, like a slab of cement. His name was Janvier, a Belgian mercenary. Rumour had it that he practised his sniper aim from the watchtower by shooting passing miners in the back. Behind him, the other guard looked young and pale.

Mani pressed himself into the wall, his skull pounding. By now, Alfredo was locked inside the x-ray room. Mani checked the warning light over the door. Flashing red would mean the x-rays were on. The light was still green.

He thought of the black specks they'd find in Alfredo's stomach. He closed his eyes. There was nothing he could do.

A buzzer sounded. The light flashed red. Mani began to count. Twenty-five seconds was all it took to scan someone head to toe. Another fifteen to check the results.

Eight, nine, ten.

Van Wycks had every angle covered. Daily x-rays at the end of every shift. More x-rays and searches when your contract ended and you left the compound for good. Sometimes they fed you laxatives the day before just to purge any diamonds out.

Seventeen, eighteen, nineteen.

Nothing was allowed to leave the mine. Any vehicles that came in never went out, in case they carried diamonds through the gate. And if a mine worker died, his family never got his body back. Instead, he was buried inside the compound, so that no one could smuggle diamonds in his corpse.

Mani opened his eyes. Twenty-five seconds. The light turned green.

He listened. All he could hear was his own ragged breathing. He couldn't bring himself to count any more.

Then he heard a yell. Something in the other room crashed to the floor. A door slammed. Mani stiffened, snapping his eyes to the window. Alfredo stumbled into view, crouching. He lurched across the compound, heading for the electric fence. A shot cracked into the air. Alfredo buckled at the knees, sagged to the ground. Blood seeped from his thigh. He clawed at the dirt, trying to drag himself on.

Okker strolled up behind him, swinging a rifle in one hand. Mani swallowed.

Okker laughed. 'Look, he's going for the fence.'

Alfredo stopped crawling and lay trembling in the dust. Okker bent over him.

'What are you going to do, tunnel under it?'

He guffawed again, looking around for an audience. Then he turned back to Alfredo, took casual aim and shot him in the face.

Mani gasped. He shook his head, couldn't breathe. Okker was still laughing. Mani wanted to look away, but he couldn't. Okker snapped open a knife and sliced through Alfredo's shirt, baring his scrawny abdomen. Then he touched his blade to the dusky skin.

'Let's slit him open, see what we've got.'

Mani jerked back against the wall. His limbs twitched, pulsing with shock. He squeezed his eyes shut, trying not to listen to the ripping sounds from outside. The diamond in his own gut scorched through him.

Something clicked near his ear. Mani opened his eyes and stared into the bore of a gun. Janvier smiled. Behind him, the younger guard looked sick.

'You're up next, college boy.'

9

'Someone's been looking for you.'

Harry spun round, backing up against the safe. A pint-sized young woman stood in the doorway, a mug of coffee in her hand. Harry rolled her eyes at her own jumpiness.

'You scared me,' she said.

Imogen Brady stepped into the room. 'He called three times, wouldn't leave his name.'

Imogen's eyes raked Harry's face. Friend and business partner, she occasionally doubled up as Harry's self-appointed keeper.

'He sounded pissed off about something,' she said.

Harry's pulse raced. *Baseball cap, tanned face, the barrel of a gun*. Had he started to track her down already? She turned back to the office safe to hide her panic.

'Probably a recruitment agency.' She swiped her keycard

and punched in her access code with trembling fingers. 'Do me a favour, next time he calls, tell him I've gone away for a while.'

Imogen came to stand beside her, her head barely reaching Harry's shoulder. 'Is that the laptop from the new client?'

Harry bit her lip. She'd told Imogen about the call-out to Monkstown before she'd left, but now she wished she hadn't. Her next move was definitely the wrong side of legal, and the less Imogen knew about it the better. She shoved Garvin's laptop to the back of the safe, then snapped the door shut.

'It's just routine stuff.'

Imogen blocked her path. Her eyes were huge in her pixie face, but she still managed to look stern.

'You look terrible.' Imogen glanced at the safe, then back again. 'What's up?'

'Just tired.' Harry tried to keep her voice light. 'Not sleeping well lately.'

That much was true, at least. For the past few months she'd been plagued by nightmares that slashed like hatchets through her sleep. Recurring flashes of betrayal and death. She suppressed a shudder.

'It's that house of yours, if you ask me.' Imogen plonked a hand on one hip. 'Cooped up in the middle of nowhere, it's enough to depress anyone. Why don't you get a place in town, somewhere closer to the office?'

Harry's gaze drifted around the small, open-plan space where Blackjack did its business. The walls were a mix of exposed brick and pipes, the high domed ceiling a mess of ancient plumbing from the original Guinness Brewery warehouse.

The office was located in the Digital Hub, a cluster of technology companies based in the old Liberties area of inner-city Dublin. Harry had chosen it as the home for her new company a few months before, funding it with money left over from her exploits in the Bahamas. The location had an edginess that had appealed to her: state-of-the-art technology tucked in between the bargain stores of Thomas Street and the chimney stacks of Guinness with its yeasty, Bovril smells.

Harry shivered. Normally, the Blackjack office filled her with pride, but not today. Today it was a place where a man with a gun might find her.

'Here –' Imogen thrust her untouched coffee into Harry's hands. 'You look like you could do with this more than me.'

Before Harry could reply, the phone rang and Imogen bustled off to answer it. Harry took the opportunity to slip away to her own desk, where she'd hooked up her office computer to the copy of Garvin's hard drive. She pulled up a chair and sat hunched over the keyboard.

Given the choice, this was the last place she'd be. But she needed to do some snooping, and this was where she stashed her burglar's tools.

She stared at the screen and wondered where to start.

You could tell a lot about a person just by digging through his computer: what internet sites he browsed, what files he opened, what photographs he downloaded. In fact, you could unearth more information than there was time to analyse, and that was the problem.

Harry drummed her fingers on the desk. Normally, she'd have some context, some obvious starting point. If a client hired her as a computer forensics investigator, her mandate would be clear: find evidence to show an employee was downloading pornography on company time; prove the new sales guy was passing information to a competitor. But what was she looking for on Garvin's laptop? Some clue to 'Beth'? Or to the man in the base-ball cap? Suddenly, the idea seemed far-fetched.

She checked on Imogen. Still on the phone. She'd jammed the receiver into the crook of her neck, her hands free to fiddle with her rings. Harry turned back to her screen and launched her forensic toolkit program.

Small hairs rose on the back of her neck. She was about to cross a line. Garvin's hard drive was evidence in a murder investigation, and she'd no business tres-passing on its data. Whatever way you looked at it, she was probably about to commit a crime.

Her fingers hovered over the keyboard. She thought of the trouble she was already in: of Detective Inspector Lynne, still stalking her past; of Hunter, who'd pegged her as guilty of theft, or maybe even murder; of the killer on her tail, and Hunter's indifference to the danger she was in. She balled her fingers into fists. Was she supposed to clock up brownie points before she qualified for police protection?

To hell with it. Maybe it was time she protected herself. She jabbed at the keys and leapfrogged into Garvin's files.

She took a few moments to scout out the landscape, eyeballing the installed programs, skimming through the logs and noting the most recently used files. It was like nosing around someone's house while they were away, and it took effort not to look furtive. She picked her way around, until gradually she'd built a picture of how Garvin had used his laptop.

It was standard stuff. Mostly he switched between spreadsheets, a word processor and the internet. The everyday tools of the ordinary user. And with them, he'd produced thousands of files.

Harry leaned back in her chair, hands in her pockets. Analysing files was as much instinct as science, but right now she was all out of hunches. Her fingers touched the rounded pebble she'd found inside her bag. It still felt cold. She worried at it for a moment, then let it drop, leaning back into the keyboard. Sometimes the most obvious was worth a try.

She keyed in a search for the word 'diamonds'.

Thousands of filenames rolled up the screen, and Harry groaned. She refined her search, filtering by date stamp, concentrating on files that Garvin had accessed in the week before his death. The list shrank to seventeen. That was more like it.

Harry flipped open the first file and scanned through it. It was an invoice from a company called Safari Diamond Corporation for 'twelve rough 1.5 carat whites'.

The invoice was addressed to Garvin Oliver Trading Limited and amounted to $90,000.

Harry skipped into the next file. Another invoice, this one originating from Garvin Oliver Trading Limited to a Dutch company called Staal Precision Cutters. Garvin was charging them €30,000 for a shipment of eight uncut yellows, ranging from 0.75 to 1 carat.

Harry flicked a glance at Imogen. She was winding up her call, pushing away from her desk. Harry skimmed through the next few files. More invoices and orders, and a handful of spreadsheets that looked like profit-and-loss accounts. Garvin was clearly in the diamond-trading business, and her eyes widened at his bottom-line numbers. 'Beth' was right. Garvin had been making money.

'Want another coffee?'

Harry jumped, and snapped the files shut. Imogen stood behind her, yawning and stretching like a cat.

'Thanks.' Harry scrambled for another errand to keep her friend out of the way. 'I skipped lunch, so maybe a doughnut, too?'

'Good idea. You need the calories.'

Harry waited till Imogen had left the room, then poked through the rest of the files. More invoices, orders and correspondence with suppliers. Garvin had been busy the week before he died.

Finally, she opened the last file, a spreadsheet called 'Stock Inventory October 2009'. It had been accessed earlier that morning.

Rows of data flashed on the screen. Harry blinked,

trying to make sense of them. It looked like a list of stones that Garvin had bought and sold. He'd recorded the quantity and colour of the stones, along with their weight in carats, noting suppliers and customers against each entry. The largest stones weighed up to four carats, and a few of them even had names: Apollo, The African Star, Egyptian Sunrise.

Some of the entries had digital photos embedded in the data. Harry zoomed in. Images of smooth, crystal-like stones filled the screen. Some were foggy white, like the one in her pocket; others a duller yellow or brown. One photo showed a cluster of six misty whites, set beside a matchstick for scale. Each stone was listed as 0.25 carats, no bigger than the match's head.

'Here you go.'

Imogen plonked a mug down on the desk, along with a creamy doughnut. Harry spun round to face her, obscuring her view of the screen.

'That was ChemCal on the phone,' Imogen said. 'They've decided to prosecute.'

Harry raised her eyebrows. Imogen had been working on a forensics investigation for ChemCal Labs. The MD had suspected his chief accountant of embezzlement, and had hired Blackjack to scour his laptop for any tell-tale signs.

'Do they want you to testify?' she said.

'They're talking it over with their lawyers.' Imogen fiddled with her ring. 'I'll pencil in some time, just in case.'

Harry sipped her coffee, willing her screensaver to kick

in behind her. She nodded at Imogen's fidgeting fingers. 'How're you doing with that ring?'

Imogen made a face, then splayed out the fingers of her left hand. 'It's making me grumpy.'

'I'd noticed.'

Imogen had announced her engagement the week before to an architect she'd been dating for six months. From the outset, she'd declared it was only an experiment to see how getting married would feel. Harry had been sceptical. In her view, it was long-term commitment that probably made marriage such a chore. Treating it like a new dress you could take back if it didn't fit seemed to be missing the point.

Not that Harry felt up to long-term commitments, either. She couldn't imagine herself taking that leap, plummeting into a world where wills clashed and two lives were locked together. Just thinking about it made her feel short of air.

Imogen wiggled her fingers, appraising her ring. 'I'll probably give it back today.'

Harry glanced at the twinkling stone, her awareness of diamonds heightened. It was a small solitaire, about the size of a peppercorn. From the little she'd learned, she put it at less than half a carat.

'What about Shane?'

'He'll get over it.' Imogen smiled and put her head to one side, her long ponytail springing out from her crown like an S-hook. 'He's looking a little twitchy himself. The word "hasty" keeps coming up.'

Then she flapped her hand, dismissing the subject. 'I'll send you the ChemCal report.'

'Any surprises?'

'Not really.' Imogen headed back to her desk. 'He'd tried to cover his tracks with some hidden files, but it didn't take long to sniff them out.'

Harry stared after her for a moment, then snapped her eyes back to the screen. Hidden files. She could almost feel her brain shifting.

She'd taken Garvin's files at face value up to now, only considering those in plain view. And why not? After all, he'd been killed during the course of a burglary, hadn't he? Wrong place, wrong time. Just like her.

But what if there was more to it than that? Gooseflesh buzzed along her arms. What if he was killed because he had something to hide?

10

There were plenty of ways to make a file disappear. The question was, which would Garvin have used?

Harry hitched her chair in closer to the desk, her fingertips tingling. There were lots of commercial tools out there that kept your secrets safe, camouflaging your files till they melted out of sight. You couldn't view them, delete them or modify them. As far as the operating system was concerned, the files just didn't exist.

Harry plunged back into her forensic toolkit. The operating system may have been gullible, but her box of tricks wasn't. She rattled her fingers across the keys, setting up a search. Her copy of Garvin's hard drive was more than just a replica of recognizable files. It was a bit-by-bit image, and that included deleted data, unused memory and hidden information. She wouldn't be fooled by a bunch of skulking files claiming to be invisible.

She launched her search for camouflaged files, then sat back in her chair and waited.

Her eyes roamed the room, coming to rest on the office safe. It was smaller than Garvin's, about the size of a filing cabinet, and she used it to store evidence from Blackjack's investigations.

Security and privacy.

Harry shook her head. Technology was supposed to safeguard your secrets, but did it really? She thought of Garvin's vault, protected by his own fingerprint.

Something you know, something you have, something you are.

The security mantra ran through her head. Something you know: a password. Something you have: a keycard. Something you are: your fingerprint.

Harry shuddered, picturing Garvin's killer scrabbling at the dead man's fingers. Biometric security had its uses, but there was nothing she wanted hidden badly enough to put her own body parts on the line.

The computer beeped, and her eyes shot back to the screen. The search had come up empty.

Harry frowned. No covert files. Most likely it meant that Garvin had nothing to hide, but she shoved the thought away. Right now, hidden files were all she had.

'Harry?'

Imogen was holding the phone out to one side, her hand over the mouthpiece. 'It's him again, you sure you don't want to take it?'

Harry's skin prickled. She shook her head, registering

Imogen's frown as she turned to make excuses into the phone. It was probably a legitimate caller, but disclosing her whereabouts to anyone right now seemed like a bad idea. Harry tried to ignore her drumming heartbeat, and dragged her gaze back to the screen.

She chewed on a fingernail. Maybe Garvin had used a less sophisticated approach than commercial privacy products. Her mind drifted back to her first Blackjack case. Her client had been an angry, middle-aged woman who'd wanted evidence that her husband was cheating. It hadn't taken long. His laptop had yielded a slam-dunk photo of himself with his nineteen-year-old secretary. To hide it, he'd simply renamed it from susie.jpg to su.123. Without the .jpg extension, the picture viewer didn't pick it up. And trying to open it with anything else just spewed gibberish on to the screen. Either way, Susie stayed incognito.

Bogus file extensions were quick and easy, and people used them all the time. Harry rummaged through her toolkit and fired off an extension checker search. In less than a minute, two filenames flashed up on the screen:

VW-Stock.got

VW-Cargo.got

Harry stiffened. Two phony extensions. It looked as though Garvin had tried some sleight of hand. She stared at the doctored file types. 'GOT' for Garvin Oliver Trading?

Normally her toolkit could figure out the true file type, but this time it played dumb. She checked the file locations.

They were stored alongside dozens of spreadsheet files, including the stock inventory she'd opened earlier. Chances were, she'd unearthed two more spreadsheets, but it was hard to find an innocent explanation for their disguise.

She opened the first file, VW-Stock. A blizzard of symbols filled the screen: Russian and Greek script, hashes and squiggles, all of it densely packed. The familiar gobbledy-gook of unreadable data.

She opened the second file. More hieroglyphics.

Harry squinted at the screen. Had she got the file extension wrong?

She shook her head. This time she was throwing in with her instincts, and that left her with one explanation: the files had been encrypted.

A shiver scampered down her spine. She felt like she was grappling with one of those nested Russian dolls. Data inside encryption, inside hidden files, inside a vault. What the hell had Garvin needed to hide so badly?

She frowned at the illegible garbage on the screen. To unscramble it, she'd need the encryption key and that could be just about anywhere. Maybe it wasn't even on the hard drive. She was beginning to think Garvin was more technically savvy than she'd given him credit for.

Harry drummed her fingers on the desk, glaring at the filenames on the screen. What the hell were they hiding?

She checked the timestamps on each of the files. They'd been encrypted eight days ago, locked into riddles that no one else could read. And once a file morphed into ciphertext, its plaintext version was deleted.

Or was it?

Harry scooted in closer to the desk and kicked off a search for deleted files. What were the chances that Garvin's plaintext still lurked in the cracks of the hard drive?

A list of recovered files unravelled up the screen. One by one, she sifted through them, looking for a match.

Nothing.

She slumped back in her chair. No plaintext, no deleted data, no encryption keys. Garvin's files were locked down tight, and her chances of cracking them open didn't look good.

Her phone trilled from deep inside her bag. She fished it out and checked the caller ID. Private number. Harry licked her lips, but her mouth was dry. The man with the baseball cap had her number from her card, but that didn't mean it had to be him. She hit the silence key and stuffed the phone deep into her bag.

She hunched back over the keyboard. There had to be something else she could try. She thought for a minute, then straightened up. It was an outside chance, but worth a shot. Her fingers flew across the keys as she set up her final search. This time her target was temporary files.

Hard drives were riddled with them. Conscientious programs created them as backups, saving temporary copies of your files while you worked on the originals. They came in handy if the program crashed before you'd saved your data.

Garvin would have worked on his files in plaintext

before he eventually encrypted them. It was the backup of those plaintext files that Harry needed to find.

She beat a tattoo on the desk with her fingers, her eyes fixed to the screen. Temporary files were usually deleted when the original file was closed, but not always. With luck, the ones she needed were still lying low on Garvin's hard drive.

And if not, she was all out of tricks.

The computer beeped. Her pulse quickened. She stared at the filenames listed on the screen:

VW-Stock.tmp

VW-Cargo.tmp

'Harry?'

Something fluttered in Harry's stomach. She fumbled with her mouse. Supposing they were just backups of the encrypted files?

Imogen appeared at her side. 'You really need to take the call this time.'

Harry bit her lip. Then she pointed her mouse at the first file. Held her breath.

Double-click.

The file opened.

Crystal-clear plaintext filled the screen.

'Harry, it's the police.'

11

'What the hell do you think you're playing at?'

Harry winced at Hunter's tone. She wedged the receiver against her shoulder, her fingers working the keyboard. 'I don't play games, Detective.'

'I could haul you in for this.' His teeth sounded glued together. 'You're being deliberately obstructive.'

'I've told you the truth.' She browsed through the first of Garvin's hidden files, VW-Stock.tmp. It looked like another stock-take of stones.

Hunter snorted. 'From what I've heard, you and the truth don't exactly hit it off.'

Harry breathed through her nose, trying to tune him out. She pecked through the data: numbers, customers, colours, weights. She frowned, backtracking a little. Could that be right?

'You intentionally removed evidence from a murder investigation.'

Harry jerked her gaze away from the screen. She didn't hold the moral high ground on much right now, but he wasn't getting away with that one.

'If you're talking about Garvin Oliver's laptop, then it was your officer who made the mistake, not me.'

'You withheld evidence.'

'I gave you the keys of my car.'

Hunter was silent for a moment. Then he said, 'I want the laptop.'

'Come and get it anytime you want.'

'I want it now. We're right outside.'

Dammit. 'All right, I'll come and buzz you in.'

She slammed down the phone, her eyes straying back to the numbers on the screen. Then she snapped the file shut. That would have to keep for a while.

Imogen hovered behind her. 'Everything okay?'

Harry got to her feet. 'Not exactly. I'll explain in a minute, but right now, I've a pissed-off detective to talk to.' She gave her friend a direct look. 'Promise me you'll stay out of things for the next few minutes? No matter what you hear me say?'

Imogen's eyes lit up for a second, then she frowned. 'What are you getting into, Harry?'

'Just promise me?'

Imogen pursed her lips. 'Okay. But that explanation better be good.'

Harry gave her an attagirl pat on the arm, then headed

92

out to reception where Hunter was waiting behind the glass security doors. His shoulders were hunched, his hands shoved deep into his jacket pockets.

She took a deep breath, wondering how to compose her face for the ten-yard walk to the door. In the end, she settled for a self-righteous glare, which Hunter seemed to have no trouble returning.

She strode across the empty reception and punched the door-release button on the wall. Hunter swung in past her, a gust of cool, yeast-scented air riding in behind him. He wheeled round to face her, his cropped hair spiky from the wind.

'Next time, I'd appreciate it if you would answer your mobile.'

Harry shot him a look. So that was one caller identified. No reason to think the other was a killer with a gun, but then, nothing today had exactly been rational.

He looked past her to the door. 'You remember Detective Inspector Lynne, don't you?'

Harry whipped round. A lean, dark-haired man was standing in the doorway. Forty-ish, neat grey suit, penetrating eyes. He stepped inside. She remembered how silently he'd always moved. Like a cat.

Lynne inclined his head, his eyes never leaving her face. 'Ms Martinez.'

Harry managed a stiff nod. Then she turned on her heel and led them back through reception, her spine tingling with awareness of being watched from behind. Resisting the urge to accelerate like a fugitive, she coached herself to stay calm: *Nice and easy, keep it steady, just give them the laptop and they'll go.* The diamond burned a hole in her side.

The last time she'd tangled with Lynne had been in a hospital corridor four months earlier. Her father had lain dying in the next room, eking out his last days on life-support machines. By then, his helpless body was as thin as a child's, kept alive by tubes hissing air into his lungs. Lynne's questions had been the same as always: *What happened to the money from Sal's insider trading? Did you help him to hide it? Why did you visit a bank in the Bahamas? Where's the money now?*

More persistent than his questions were the silences he waited for her to fill. But she never did. She never told him she still had the money, or some of it, anyway. She'd stolen it to protect herself, but afterwards, she'd kept it for her father. She'd wanted to give him something to wake up to. But then the doctors had told her that her father was going to die.

Harry squared her shoulders, warding the memory off. She snapped her security pass against the card-reader on the wall and marched into the Blackjack office. Maybe a brisk pace would make her look as if she was in control.

She gestured at the safe. 'It's in here.'

Imogen swivelled in her chair, eyes wide, mouth shut. Harry fixed her attention on Hunter as he stepped towards the safe. Up close, she could see that he needed a shave, the bristles glinting like iron filings on his face. He snapped a pair of latex gloves up to his wrists, his eyes trained on hers.

'You've had the laptop for hours, why didn't you say anything?'

Harry shrugged, avoiding Imogen's gaze. 'I didn't notice until now. I've only just got here.'

'How do we know it hasn't been tampered with?'

'I secured it in the safe the minute I realized your mistake.' She drilled him with a look. 'This is a computer forensics lab. Preserving evidence is a priority around here.'

Hunter raised an eyebrow, scanning the room. 'Looks like an ordinary office to me.'

Harry began checking things off on her fingers. 'You can't get in here without a security pass, and there's a CCTV camera pointed at the safe, which, by the way, you can't open without the access code and swipe card. There's no way anyone could have tampered with it.'

Lynne spoke quietly from the doorway. 'Nobody except you.'

Harry locked eyes with him for a moment. She could sense Imogen's open-mouthed stare, and even Hunter seemed unwilling to break the silence. She spun towards the safe, swiped her card and punched in the access code. When the door clicked open, she pointed at the laptop, motioning for Hunter to help himself.

Lynne cleared his throat. 'Make sure you take the right one this time, Hunter.'

Hunter froze, his mouth fixed in a tight line. Then he grasped the laptop with both hands.

'What about my laptop?' Harry said. 'You still have it.'

Hunter's eyes flicked sideways at Lynne. 'We need to hold on to that for a while. You'll get it back eventually.'

A muffled ring tone sounded nearby, and Lynne stepped out of the room to take the call. Harry clicked the safe shut, glancing over at Hunter. She wondered about the friction between the two officers, and whether it might be worth tapping into. She cocked her chin in the direction of the door.

'Isn't it a little unusual for Fraud to tag along on a murder investigation?'

Hunter shrugged. 'Not necessarily. Fraud, Customs, they're all piling in on this one.'

'Really? Lynne doesn't exactly strike me as a team player.'

Hunter snorted, but didn't answer. He busied himself with a chain of custody form, filling out the details. She wondered how far she could push him.

'Is he your boss?'

For a second, his pen froze. 'No.'

'He certainly acts like it.'

Hunter glared at her. 'This is my investigation. I'm in charge, and don't you forget it.'

Sweat glinted on his upper lip in between the stubble, and she took it as a sign that she'd pushed enough. She perched against a desk, arms folded, while he finished off the form. When he finally looked up, his eyes were hard to read.

'We've been watching Garvin Oliver for some time.' He wrestled the laptop into a silver anti-static bag. 'His diamond operation isn't entirely legit, but then you probably know that.'

Harry thought of Garvin's hidden files, then blanked the knowledge out in case it showed on her face.

Hunter drilled her with a look. 'Illicit diamond trading is one thing, but do you really want to get yourself involved in murder?'

Illicit diamonds. Africa's finest, Beth had said. Harry's mouth felt dry.

'Look, you're really wasting your time with me,' she said. 'I'm not involved in all of this.'

Hunter held her gaze. The hazel eyes looked muddy and tired. Then he nodded and sighed, and for the first time seemed to loosen the tight rein that he kept on himself. He held up his hands.

'Okay. It's possible you were just in the wrong place at the wrong time. It happens.' He sneaked a glance at the door, then lowered his voice. 'But if not, I'm warning you, we'll soon find out.'

His eyes locked on to hers, his expression an odd mix of threat and empathy. Then Lynne slipped back into the room and clicked his fingers.

'Let's go.'

Hunter stiffened, and Harry could have sworn she saw his fists clench. Then he snatched up the laptop and

strode to the door. Harry didn't know what kind of polit-
ics Hunter was up against, but it looked as though Lynne
was pulling rank.

She watched them go, her eyes falling on the silver
evidence bag tucked under Hunter's arm. Suddenly her
breathing stalled. The notion of the police getting hold
of Garvin's data started an inexplicable hum in her throat,
and she felt an overwhelming urge to snatch the laptop
back.

'Harry?'

Imogen was staring at her. Harry gave herself a mental
shake. What was the matter with her? There was nothing
on Garvin's laptop that could get her into trouble. She
wheeled round and scampered back to her desk, Imogen
close behind.

'What's going on, Harry?'

'I'll explain in a minute.'

Something in Garvin's hidden inventory file had snagged
her attention and she needed to check it out. First, she pulled
up the original inventory that Garvin had left in plain view:
'Stock Inventory October 2009'. The familiar set of images
flicked across the screen: the cloudy pebbles weighing 0.25
carats, each the size of a match head; metallic specks, 0.03
carats, no bigger than sugar crystals. The largest on the list
was a yellow, 4-carat octahedron the size of a raisin.
According to his records, Garvin had sold it for €10,000.

Then she switched back to the hidden file, VW-
Stock.tmp. Many of the stones were christened, just like
before: Yellow Mist, Helios, Pink Heart. There were

98

almost three hundred stones in all, with dates going back over a year.

She homed in on the images. Most incorporated ordinary objects to lend the diamonds scale, and her eyes widened at the numbers. A gleaming, metallic stone, the size of a gobstopper: 100 carats. Another the colour of weak camomile tea and bigger than a jumbo marble: 175 carats. But most of them were as big as hen's eggs and weighed in at over 200 carats. The last on the list was the largest of them all, a silvery crystal of 270 carats. It had been sold over a year ago to someone called Fischer for almost five million euros.

Harry let out a long breath. Was that what this was about? Was Garvin smuggling large stones, and trying to cover his tracks? She checked the file again. Whoever Fischer was, he'd only bought one stone. The rest had been sold exclusively to a buyer called Gray.

Harry's brain hummed with questions, and she almost forgot about VW-Cargo.tmp, the second hidden file. She clicked it open, her mind preoccupied. Where did Beth fit into all of this? Another array of names flashed up on the screen. At the top was an obscure twelve-digit number: 881677273934. Harry doodled it down on her pad, her eyes travelling over the column of names: Excelsior, Artemis, Dawn Light.

Harry frowned. Dawn Light. The name seemed familiar. Dim memories floated like ghosts. Frosty mornings, bright colours. She shook her head. It wouldn't come.

She checked the name again, and her whole body went still. Her breathing stopped, her fingers froze; the only part of her that moved was the pulse pounding in her jugular. She swallowed, and stared at the screen.

Recorded against the entry for Dawn Light, was the name HARRY MARTINEZ.

12

Mani stumbled into the x-ray room, sweat drenching his body. Outside, he could still hear Okker's yells as he gloated over Alfredo's butchered torso. The image burned into Mani's brain, and he clenched his fists to stop his arms from trembling.

'Over there!'

The guard called Janvier slammed Mani up against the wall. He jammed the butt of his gun against Mani's cheek, forcing his head sideways, while the younger guard shone a torch in Mani's ear. Then between them, they whipped Mani's head around to check the other side. Janvier wrenched Mani's mouth open and poked a spatula inside it until Mani gagged. Then he tore at Mani's eye sockets and crushed his nostrils while the other guard kept him pinned to the wall.

The search wasn't necessary. The x-ray machine

performed a whole-body scan, and stones inside any part of him would be found. But Janvier and some of the other guards still indulged in their own spot checks. They liked the humiliation it caused.

When they were done, they hauled him out from the wall and shoved him to the floor. They patted him down, then turned and left. Mani stayed on his hands and knees, his elbows locked but his arms still trembling. Behind him, the door clunked shut, sucking all sound from the room.

He lifted his head. In front of him, the x-ray cubicle stood open, waiting for him like a giant, Perspex capsule. To his right was the conveyor belt that scanned outgoing luggage and to his left was another guard in a white coat, watching from behind a screened-off booth. His name was Volker, and he'd worked the x-ray unit for the last two years. He rapped on the reinforced glass.

'Stand up!'

Mani struggled to his feet, the diamond slicing through his gut. Volker tapped the keyboard in front of him.

'Name?'

'Mani . . .' His voice cracked. Then he cleared his throat and lifted his chin. 'Mani Eduardo Tavares Villa dos Santos.'

Volker's eyes narrowed at the full Portuguese name. Mani kept his chin raised. He'd spent most of his life trying to live up to that name. His parents had been Angolans, living half their lives under Portuguese rule, the rest under bloody civil war. His surname followed the Portuguese pattern of combining both their names. But his maternal grandmother had been Congolese, a strong, raucous woman who'd lived in the shadow of the Blue Mountains close to the Congo River. She'd asked that her first grandson be given a Congolese name, so he became Mani, meaning 'from the mountain'. He could still hear his father's scornful voice: *The man from the mountain, he should be a warrior with a gun, not a mouse with a book.*

Mani squared his shoulders, trying to ignore the fiery pain in his belly.

Volker stepped out from behind the screen, his red-rimmed eyes fixed on Mani's face. Mani gritted his teeth, then rolled up his left sleeve to show the bandage on his upper arm. Slowly, he unravelled the filthy dressing to expose the knife wound underneath. He sucked in air at the sight of it. Red, raw flesh bulged out through a gaping rent in his skin. The puckered edges were too far apart to knit together, but so far there was no sign of infection. No oozing pus, no bad smell. He knew what to look for because that was what had happened to Ezra.

He took a deep breath. Then he pressed the misshapen folds of flesh. Pain blazed a trail up his arm and he felt himself sway. Fighting the dizziness, he kneaded the wound until two silvery-white stones worked their way out, each the size of a large pea. He picked them up with trembling fingers and dropped them with a clatter into the metal dish that Volker was holding out.

Mani closed his eyes, the hot stabbing in his arm

starting to recede. He could hear the whoosh of running water and the rattle of stones against metal. When he opened his eyes, Volker was back in his booth. Mani fumbled with his bandage, binding up his wound.

Volker flicked a switch on his console. 'Into the cubicle.'

Mani shuffled into the x-ray capsule, positioning himself in the centre of the circular platform. The door slid shut with a *whunk*. A motor hummed as the C-arm of the x-ray machine enclosed the base of the cubicle and began inching its way up along the walls. Mani felt his limbs relax, the pain in his arm now a dull throb. He closed his eyes. Thank God tomorrow was his last day at the mine.

He had only come back because Ezra had begged him to, saying that he was ill. At first, Mani had refused. He had exams to sit, a scholarship to honour. He didn't have time to return to his home village where children coughed in their sleep, and where Asha now lived as Ezra's wife. So he sent money instead. But Ezra pleaded with him, saying that he might die. Blood poisoning from a knife wound, he'd said. He didn't explain till later that the knife wound was self-inflicted.

So Mani had gone to see him, bracing himself for the crushing misery of the shantytown he'd managed to escape. His was a family of diamond diggers. His grandfather had crawled along the Angolan sand dunes, scrabbling for diamonds by hand, carrying them in the tin can that hung around his neck. The mine owners had stuffed a gag in his mouth to stop him from swallowing any stones.

Mani's father had washed gravel by the riverbeds, gripped by a gambler's conviction that the next stone would change his life. When Mani was ten, his father moved them to the Northern Cape in South Africa, where he swapped riverbed mining for the underground pits. He'd been killed in a fight over a diamond the size of a sunflower seed.

'You must take my place in the mine,' Ezra had said when Mani went home. 'Until I am well.'

Mani had looked away. The shack was dark, filled with the oily smell of the Primus stove. He shook his head.

'I will send you more money, I will find another job in Cape Town.' He already worked two jobs between his studies, sending most of his money home, but anything was better than the incarceration of the mines.

Ezra sighed. 'Money, it will not be enough.'

Mani squinted at his brother's face. Ezra's eyes were feverish, his voice weak. What trouble had he got himself into now? Mani knelt beside the bed, the mud floor warm from the heat of the day.

'I don't understand,' he said.

'The Van Wycks mine.' Ezra licked his parched lips. 'There is something about it you need to know.'

And then, in the smoky, stifling hut, Ezra had explained.

He'd been on a toilet break when he found the first stone. He'd wandered up to the waste pit behind the latrine, putting off going back to his shift, and the diamond had glowed at him from underneath the rubble.

Ezra's eyes glazed over. 'It was bigger than a sparrow-hawk's egg.'

He'd hidden it again beneath a deeper pile of stones until he could figure out what to do with it. One thing was certain: if there was one diamond, there were others. But after several furtive visits to the pit, he still hadn't found any more.

Then late one night, he'd thought about the waste rock. Most of it was debris, discarded by the crusher and the separation plant. But piled here and there were larger boulders, the kind Van Wycks had been dumping for years. The geologists had tested them but declared them uneconomical to mine. So they fell uncrushed out of the separation plant and ended up in the waste pits along with the rest of the rubble.

But what if the Van Wycks scientists were wrong?

The next time Ezra had visited the waste pit, he'd taken a lump hammer with him.

Mani stared at his brother in the smoke-filled hut, the crackle of the cooking fires starting up outside. 'You broke up the boulders?'

'Van Wycks, they were wrong.' Ezra's eyes were bright. 'One boulder, it gave me three diamonds, over a hundred and fifty carats each.'

He went on to explain how he'd smuggled the diamonds out. A cousin of theirs supplied cocaine to many of the mercenaries guarding the mine, and according to him, the x-ray operator was in deeper than most. Volker, it turned out, was more than willing to take payment in diamonds in exchange for clearing Ezra's x-rays.

106

Ezra had brought his first stones out of the mine over a year ago and sold them on the local black market.

'For a day, I was rich.' Ezra closed his eyes and smiled, his gums a ghostly grey around his missing tooth.

Mani groaned. Like his father, Ezra never held on to money for long. Drink and gambling usually soaked up most of it. 'What happened?'

Ezra dragged his eyes open, the smile gone. 'Stones that big, it is hard to keep them a secret.'

Avoiding Mani's gaze, he explained how he'd woken up in the dark, after several days of celebrating. His drunken friends were gone, and so was all his money. But he wasn't completely alone. Kneeling over him was a man in dark clothes, his white face smeared with mud. The blade of his knife was pricking Ezra's throat.

Three other men had crept out of the shadows and held Ezra down while the first man wielded his knife. First he carved it along Ezra's chin, then sliced it into his shoulder, then worked his way down into the softer areas of flesh, until finally Ezra gave them what they wanted. From now on, he was to act as their courier, funnelling large stones out of the mine and selling exclusively to them. He'd been following their orders now for almost a year.

Mani stared around the dingy shack. 'But then, where is all the money?'

Ezra swallowed, his throat working hard. 'He pays me next to nothing.' His eyes slid over to the hanging sack that served as a door. On the other side of it, Asha was stoking the fire. 'If I don't do as he says, he will kill us.'

And then Ezra told him what the man with the knife had said, as he'd left him whimpering on the ground. *Go home and see what I have done, just in case you feel like changing your mind.*

And so Mani had learned the truth about how his mother had died.

The x-ray machine clanked to a halt. The cubicle door slid open and Mani stepped outside. Volker was still at his console. Mani didn't know how the guard smuggled out his stones, but white workers weren't subjected to as many searches as blacks.

Mani exhaled a long breath. His body felt warm and sluggish. Today was his last time. The last time he'd open his gullet to swallow a diamond so big it tore up his insides. The last time he'd cram stones into a seeping wound, tears burning his eyes. The last time he'd drink the foul mixture of water and spoiled milk that would purge his body out.

His brief contract with Van Wycks was up. Tomorrow Volker would clear him and the contraband in his luggage as he finally left the compound. And he was never coming back.

Volker raised his head. 'You can go.'

Mani nodded, making his way towards the exit. 'Tomorrow there will be more.'

Volker shrugged. 'I won't be here.'

Mani froze. He stared at the guard. 'But I leave the compound. You must pass me through x-ray, my luggage—'

'You'll have to make other arrangements.' Volker turned back to his console. 'My time here is up, I leave this evening. It's getting too risky, Okker's asking questions. My replacement starts in the morning.'

Mani's head swam. Heat washed over him as he thought of Ezra in his stinking shack, of Asha whom he'd loved since he was ten, of his mother who'd fought to keep him at school, of Alfredo, of Takata. But most of all, he thought of the killers waiting on the next shipment of stones.

What would they do when he couldn't deliver?

13

'Dammit!'

Harry snapped the laptop shut and massaged the corners of her eyes. They felt gritty from staring at the screen.

Wrong place, wrong time. That was supposed to explain her connection with Garvin's death. Even Hunter had conceded it was a possibility. But with her name chiselled into one of his files, who'd believe her now?

She bundled up her laptop, along with the printouts she'd made of Garvin's spreadsheets. She noticed she was making a lot of packing-up sounds, just to create some noise. By now, she was alone in the office. The winter darkness had rolled in like a tide, though it was barely five thirty. She'd intended to leave with Imogen, perhaps give her a lift home. Safety in numbers was a theory Harry subscribed to. But Imogen's fiancé had arrived unannounced and whisked her away before she and Harry had talked.

Now Harry was alone in the dark, which wasn't how she'd planned it.

She killed the lights, set the alarm and scuttled across the deserted reception as though helped along by a tail-wind. Empty buildings had their own ghosts, and Harry's spine was already tingling. She shouldered her laptop bag. She'd review her findings later on, but right now she had someone to see.

She jabbed at the door-release button and trotted out into the street. The building opened on to Sugar House Lane, a narrow, cobbled alleyway that ran alongside the walls of the Guinness brewery. She scanned the shadows ahead. The alley twisted away into the darkness, forking out to the backstreets that skulked behind the brewery. The right fork led past the entrance to the Storehouse tours. The left wound its way into Marrowbone Lane, which was where she'd parked her car.

Harry hesitated, the malty scent of hops filling her nostrils. Then she hitched her bag high on to her shoulder and clopped over the lumpy cobbles. Ancient building walls closed in on both sides. With their bricked-up windows and rusted bars, they looked like abandoned prisons. Harry hunched her shoulders, picking up the pace.

She thought about her name on Garvin's files. Was it a coincidence, or had Beth deliberately set her up? She fingered the cold diamond still in her pocket. At this point, she was inclined to believe the worst.

111

Something rustled in the darkness. She snapped her head around, but all she could see were black, brick walls. Her skin prickled, and she speeded up.

Dawn Light. The name floated into her head. By now, she'd remembered why it seemed so familiar but she needed to be sure, and there was only one person who could help her. She checked her watch. If she hurried, she might catch him before he left.

Feet scuffed on the cobbles behind her. She whirled around and stared into the dark alley. A lone streetlight flickered and buzzed. Her heart thumped against her chest bone. She backed up a few steps. She thought of her car, parked on the backstreet at the end of the lane. She could make it in twenty seconds if she ran.

A shape stirred in the shadows. Harry gasped, her limbs rigid. Then she jerked to life and spun away, breaking into a run. An engine growled up ahead, and feet pounded behind her. A low hum escaped her throat. She bolted down the alley, her shoes smacking the cobbles, her whole body on high alert.

Then she stumbled, pitching forward, and sprawled across the fork in the lane. In the same instant, head-lights blazed into the alleyway: an evening tourist coach, revving towards her from the right. Something spat into the darkness behind her, zinging past her ear. She caught her breath. Then she clambered to her feet, grabbed her bag and lunged for the other side of the road. A horn blared, brakes squealed. Her body slammed into concrete. She curled up and rolled, pain shooting down her arm.

Behind her, glass shattered, people screamed. Harry snapped her eyes back to the alley. The coach was angled across the cobbles, its headlights smashed up against one wall. It was barricading the laneway, blocking her view of whoever was on the other side. Harry staggered to her feet, dimly aware of white-faced tourists gaping from the bus.

She blundered through the twisting backstreet. A block of flats loomed on her left, bleak and dark. Ahead was Marrowbone Lane, her car visible in the distance. It was less than a hundred yards away, but was there time? Her breath tore at her throat. Her instincts said to keep running, but her brain told her to hide. Hide where? In her car? Feet slapped the path behind her. Her muscles clenched. She had seconds to decide.

Harry swung left and vaulted over the low wall surrounding the block of flats. An orange glow on the second floor announced a smoker on the balcony. She sprinted the few feet to the building and swung herself over a set of railings into someone's porch. Running footsteps sounded in the laneway. Harry crouched in the darkness, edging out of sight behind a jumbo satellite dish the size of a tractor tyre.

The footsteps stopped. Something icy squeezed Harry's stomach, and she shrank back against the wall. She strained for sounds from the laneway.

Nothing.

The sweet incense of burning weed drifted down from the balcony above. Harry squinted through the gap between the dish and the wall, but could only make out shadows. Jeering laughter rang out nearby, and somewhere a glass smashed. Harry darted a glance behind her. The flat was in darkness, the window secured with iron bars. Scorch marks flared out over the blistered porch walls, and from the sentiment of the graffiti it looked as though someone had tried to burn the tenants out. Harry shuddered, a tremor starting up in her arms.

A cone of light cut through the darkness. She stiffened. The beam stretched into Marrowbone Lane, sweeping from side to side like a searchlight. Harry ducked down low, peering out. A man stood with his back to her. He was wearing a baseball cap, and his flashlight had zeroed in on the windscreen of her car.

Harry flinched. Her breathing came in short gulps. More glass smashed. She steeled herself to look again. The man in the baseball cap was poking his arm through the shattered window of her car. He unlocked the door, flung it open and searched the interior with his flashlight. Then he popped open the boot and checked inside. His movements were brisk and economical, unhampered by the gun that he aimed straight ahead at all times.

Harry clamped a hand over her mouth to stop herself from screaming. Her stomach churned as she thought of how she'd almost hidden in her car. But how the hell did he know which one was hers? She closed her eyes. Garvin's house. He'd probably waited outside for Garvin and seen her arrive.

The boot slammed shut and Harry jumped. She kept

114

her eyes shut. Footsteps crunched on broken glass, but after a moment there was silence. She huddled closer to the wall, hugging her knees. Like Beth, cowering in the safe.

She stayed like that for some time, until finally a woman's voice called down to her from above.

'He's gone, luv. Done a runner.'

It was a husky, smoker's voice, and for an absurd moment Harry thought of her mother. She had the same hoarse throatiness. Tears pricked Harry's eyes. She opened them and peered out from behind the giant satellite dish. Marrowbone Lane was empty.

Harry hauled herself to her feet. She felt cold and achy, as though she'd spent a night camping outside. Her eyes darted left and right as she clambered over the railings and tottered back out towards the lane. She looked over her shoulder at the ember burning in the dark.

'Thanks.'

But the woman didn't reply. Harry wondered what other things she'd seen from her balcony that made her take all this in her stride.

She scuttled over to her car, eyes raking the shadows. Scrunching over the glass, she swept the driver's seat clear of splinters with her bag. Then she ducked inside, gunned the engine and tore off through the backstreets, zig-zagging left and right until she reached the main road.

The bright lights of Thomas Street felt like a refuge, but the sweat still rolled down her back. Had someone really just tried to kill her? Her head felt scrambled.

She shot a glance in her rear-view mirror, half-expecting the silhouette of a baseball cap to appear in the car behind. She swerved left, switching lanes. Horns blasted her erratic driving, and she took a fitful breath, trying to calm down.

She followed the traffic into the city, a cool breeze whistling in through her punched-out window. What if she told Hunter what had happened? He could check out her car, talk to the coach driver. Surely he'd believe her now? Then she remembered her name on Garvin's files, and felt like she'd hit a wall. Dawn Light. That was going to count as evidence against her, no matter what she said.

Unless she could figure out what it meant first.

Harry checked her watch. Was she too late? She flipped on her indicator and swung right, heading for the brightly lit shopping streets that criss-crossed south of the river. She tacked her way past the restaurants and bars, until she reached the back of the Westbury Hotel. She dumped her car in a metered zone, not bothering to lock it. With a smashed-out window, what was the point?

She trotted towards the hotel entrance, the cool night air fresh against her clammy skin. She smoothed down her skirt and patted her hair. Five-star hotels had a way of turning their noses up at people who looked like fugitives.

She pushed through the doors and strode into the luxurious foyer, with its red velvet armchairs and crystal chandeliers. A grand piano plinked somewhere to her left.

She made her way up to the second floor, where the oak-panelled walls and thick carpet muffled every sound.

At the end of the corridor was an ivory door. Outside it was a tray, bearing the remains of a light snack. Harry's pulse quickened. Had he already left?

She raised her hand and knocked on the door.

Dawn Light. She swallowed, checking over her shoulder. What if she was wrong?

The door opened wide, and she found herself face to face with the only man who could help her. She tried her best to smile.

'Hello, Dad.'

14

'*Cariño, ven acá.*'

Her father beamed at her, sweeping his arm out behind him like a matador. Harry stepped into the room, her shoes sinking into the cushion-soft carpet. Her father had been staying in the Westbury for over a month. Normally the place made her senses purr, but right now her body was preoccupied with not caving in.

She glanced at her father. His snowy beard was freshly trimmed, the sickbay complexion long gone and replaced now by his natural olive tan.

He'd been released from prison earlier that year, but the day he'd got out, one of his trader pals had been waiting for him. A hit-and-run jeep had mowed him down, drop-kicking his brain and pulverizing his insides. For months, the hospital ventilator was all that had kept him alive.

The doctors had tried to wean him off the machines, but his lungs couldn't cope and he'd had to be reconnected. When the weaning trials finally sent him into cardiac arrest, the doctors had wanted to stop. Sal's body had given up, they'd said. Mechanical ventilation was just prolonging the dying process. They gently suggested that, the next time his heart stopped, they shouldn't try to bring him back.

But Harry's mother had refused to sign the resuscitation waiver. She'd requested instead that the trials be resumed, and in the end she'd been proven right. It had taken another month, but finally Sal's lungs had accepted the burden of breathing on their own.

'You're just in time.' Her father was shrugging into a navy blazer with large, brass buttons. With his nautical beard and upright bearing, he could have been a submarine commander. 'Come and help me count cards.'

Harry sank into a gilt-edged chair. It would've been nice to unload and seek advice, but even her father would admit she was probably the only adult in the room. She watched him rub his hands together, a jolly-sailor grin lighting up his eyes.

'Ready?' he said.

'Dad, first I need to ask you something.'

A door clicked open behind her. She turned to see her mother step out of an adjoining room, patting her silver-blonde hair. She stopped when she saw Harry.

'Well.' Her mother seemed to have trouble meeting her gaze. 'I didn't expect to see you here.'

119

Harry raised her eyebrows. The word 'ditto' sprang to mind, but she bit it back. Her mother had called time on her unreliable marriage as soon as her husband had gone to prison. Apart from her determination to bring him back from the dead, she'd kept her distance from him ever since.

Harry glanced at her father. 'I came to see Dad about something.'

Her mother paused. 'Oh. I see.' Then she turned away and snatched a coat from the wardrobe, setting the hangers jangling.

Harry closed her eyes. Dammit. She hadn't intended to give her the brush-off, but confiding in her mother was never easy. And in this case there were added complications. Not only did the safe-cracking make Harry look shady; there was also her unhappy relationship with the police. She couldn't explain it without going into her escapade in the Bahamas. And as far as Harry was concerned, that was between her and her father.

Her mother plucked at the cuffs of her gold silk blouse, then slipped on her cream wool coat. As always, she was dressed with Grace Kelly elegance, and her eyes narrowed as she took in Harry's appearance.

'You look dreadful,' she said. 'What's the matter?'

Harry glanced down at her navy suit. It was crumpled and grubby from rolling in the dirt. She remembered how her thoughts had turned to her mother as she'd crouched in the burned-out porch. Some needy instinct, long forgotten. What would her mother do if she showed the same neediness now?

Harry swatted at the scuffmarks on her jacket. 'I just stumbled outside. I'm fine, Miriam.'

She'd been addressing her mother as Miriam since the day she'd turned eighteen. Somehow, the urge to shed the mother–daughter roles had coincided with the right to vote. Her mother had never objected.

She saw her father sneak a look at his watch.

'We'll see you out, Miriam.' He opened the door with a flourish. 'I'll rustle up a taxi for you downstairs.'

Her mother sniffed, then led the way out of the room. Harry could tell by her stiff-backed frame that her mother didn't believe a word she'd said. Harry sighed. She and Miriam had experienced a brief solidarity when her father had almost died, but it hadn't lasted. Things soon slipped back to their habitual remoteness, both of them too self-contained to know how to stop it. There were reasons for it, Harry knew, but that didn't make it any easier to deal with.

Outside the hotel, her father hailed a taxi and shepherded her mother into it. Harry huddled under the canopied hotel entrance, her back to the door, while her parents made polite goodbye sounds. Streetlights blazed through the darkness, and the thrum of al fresco drinkers filled the air. Dublin's ritzy nightlife was just around the corner, but far from finding comfort in the buzzing crowds, Harry felt her insides shrink.

Her father peeped at his watch again. Then he slammed

the door shut and, with a rap on the roof, sent the taxi on its way. Harry edged out from under the canopy and he turned to her with the giddy air of a schoolboy playing hooky.

'Come on, we're wasting time,' he said.

15

Harry had been an apprentice to her father's gambling career ever since she was six years old.

His idea of babysitting was to bring her to his card games and keep her out till three in the morning. At home, she was his sparring buddy, dealing hand after hand so he could practise his card-counting skills. When he wasn't playing cards, he was betting on horses. Her earliest memory was of minding his binoculars while he handed money to men on wooden crates.

She darted a glance over her shoulder, trotting through the streets to keep up with him. Music thumped through the open pub doors. A glass shattered on the pavement beside her, earning cheers and a round of applause. The drunks weren't rowdy enough yet to be a problem, but she kept her eyes averted just in case.

She scuttled down a side street, catching up with her father as he pushed through a set of glass doors.

'Evening, Mr Martinez.'

The bouncer was dressed in top hat and tails. Harry's father saluted him.

'*Hola*, Juan.'

Harry and the bouncer exchanged a smile. His real name was Bob, but for some reason neither of them ever mentioned it.

She followed her father into the vestibule, where two security officers sat behind a desk and a third stood guard beside a door. Her father gestured for her to go first. She presented her casino membership card, then turned to the small, biometric scanner mounted on the desk.

Dead fingers, waxy flesh.

Harry swallowed, blinking the memory away. She pressed her thumb lightly against the pad. The internal door clicked and, with her father close behind, she made her way upstairs to the gaming room.

The air was filled with the clackety-click of chips being tossed and stacked. The room was bigger than a rugby pitch, and the punters huddled three deep around the tables, like players hunching into a scrum.

Harry weaved her way through the crowds. Steel balls swirled on roulette wheels and rattled into their slots. Conversations were muted, the chitchat kept to a minimum.

She craned her neck, checking out the blackjack games. Her father wouldn't give her his full attention till he was settled at a table, and she knew the kind of table he liked. High stakes, not too busy, a stool at third base would be good. Preferably more than one free spot so he could play a few hands at a time.

She found what she was looking for at the end of the room. Minimum stake five hundred euros, no crowds. There was only one free stool and it stood at first base, but the dealer was shuffling, which meant the start of a new shoe. Where blackjack was concerned, that was a bonus.

Harry signalled to her father, and he nipped into the vacant seat, beaming at the blonde sitting beside him.

'Hola, chica.'

The young woman simpered, and Harry rolled her eyes. Her father had a tendency to ham up his Spanish roots, especially where women were concerned. In truth, he was only half-Spanish. His own father had been a businessman from San Sebastian who'd married an Irish girl and eventually settled with his in-laws in Dublin. Harry's father had only lived in Spain for a few years, though he'd grown up fluent in the language, as had Harry.

The dealer spliced the cards with a snap, and Harry edged closer to get a better view. She watched him riffle the deck, willing him to get on with it. The sooner the game started, the sooner she could talk to her father.

'Forty-five thousand, please.'

A murmur eddied around the table, and Harry gaped at the bundle of notes in her father's hands. Not for the first time, she wondered where on earth he got his cash.

The money she'd acquired in the Bahamas was dwindling. She'd gambled some of it away in the casinos of Nassau, a farewell tribute to a father she'd thought was dying. Then she'd passed off the rest as poker winnings and parcelled it out when she'd come home. Some to her mother; some to her sister, Amaranta. Some set aside for her father, just in case. A chunk had gone to the widow of Jonathan Spencer, a young investment banker who'd died at the hands of people greedier than him. And the rest she'd invested in Blackjack Security. But her father had never accepted a penny from her.

The dealer shoved two stacks of blue and purple chips across the baize. Harry's father picked a blue one off the top and placed it on the betting spot in front of him. Minimum bet, five hundred euros.

Harry flicked him a glance. His eyes were following the cards as the dealer slid them out of the shoe. Harry knew he was counting. She felt her own instincts kicking in, a running score starting up in her head as natural as breathing: minus one, zero, plus one, plus two.

The cards slick-slicked out on to the baize. Minus one for a high card; plus one for a low card; zero for the cards in between. In blackjack, tens and aces were favourable to the player, so it helped to know the relative proportion remaining in the deck.

Harry leaned her elbows on the table. She should probably give her father a chance to settle his rhythm, but she needed to know about Dawn Light.

'Dad, I need to ask you something.'

He tapped the baize in front of him, signalling for another card. Then he sliced a hand through the air, palm down, standing on eighteen. The dealer was showing a nine.

Harry glanced at the other players. Most of them had the pale, clammy look of punters betting money they couldn't afford to lose. Their attention was turned inwards, but she kept her voice low all the same.

'It's about Dawn Light,' she said.

Her father raised his eyebrows. 'Oh, so you already know, then?'

She paused. 'Know what, exactly?'

'That I bought Dawn Light.'

Harry blinked. One side of her brain registered that the count was now plus one, while the other tried to make sense of what he'd said. Memories shifted like shadows. Glossy chestnuts, roaring crowds. She thought she already knew the answer, but she decided to ask the question just the same.

'Dawn Light – it's not a diamond, is it?'

Her father beamed at her. 'He's a diamond all right. Best little racehorse I ever bought.'

Harry closed her eyes and nodded. More memories chased her. Clopping hooves, the smell of hay; her father's horse, Dawn Light, clattering across a yard. She snapped her eyes open.

'But that was years ago. You bought Dawn Light when I was seven or eight.'

He gave her a fond look. 'You remember that? I didn't

think you would. We had some fun with him, didn't we? As a matter of fact, that was Dawning Light, but you're right, same bloodlines.' His smile grew wider. 'Dawn Light is his great-grandson.'

The dealer flipped over his hole card: a ten to go with his nine. A groan went up around the table. Harry's father shrugged as his stake was swept away, then he shoved another blue chip on to the spot.

Harry frowned. Why would Garvin make a note of her father's racehorse in his files? And, more to the point, what was her name doing next to it? She watched her father, his eyes sweeping the baize as the dealer flicked the cards. *Minus three, minus five, minus seven.*

'You're running it in my name, aren't you?' she said.

He gave her a sheepish look. 'Did your mother tell you? I hope you don't mind.'

'But why?'

'Partly for luck.' He lowered his voice. 'But also because my own name attracts a certain notoriety, and I'd prefer to keep my head down for a while.'

Harry nodded and watched him lose another hand, then decided to let him play uninterrupted for a while. There was probably no need. He'd always had a flair for keeping track of the count while holding down a conversation. She had the same knack. Her brain could keep tabs without needing to engage her other senses. But lately she'd noticed failings in her father's memory that hadn't been there before his run-in with the jeep.

She rummaged in her bag, extracting the printouts of

Garvin's hidden files. She'd taken a closer look at them before leaving the office and, despite her first impressions, it was clear that the two files were different. She flicked through the sheets of paper, one eye still on the cards.

She started with the list of large, uncut diamonds, VW-Stock. It was several pages long, jammed with information about weights and prices and the transactions with Gray and Fischer. The second file, VW-Cargo, was just a single page. At the top was the strange twelve-digit number: 881677273934. Below that were two columns of names, her own among them, each marked with a place and a date. At first, she'd thought it was another list of diamonds, but now she knew better. Now she knew it was a roll-call of horses.

She chewed on a nail, staring at the words next to her own name: Kenilworth, 8th November 2009.

Today was 2nd November. Something squeezed at her gut as she wondered what it meant.

She glanced at her father. He was winning and losing in equal measure, his stack of chips much the same height as when he started out. The dealer was playing with a six-deck shoe, and by now had penetrated over half of it. The count was plus two.

'Does Kenilworth mean anything to you?' Harry said.

Her father shrugged. 'I know it's a racetrack in South Africa.'

Harry considered the information, wondering how it helped. She watched her father double down, raising his stake to one thousand euros. Harry tried some other names from the list.

'Ever heard of Excelsior? Or Artemis?'

Her father tapped the baize and caught a ten. Twenty-one.

'Artemis, he's a real stayer. Won by seven lengths in the Lyons Handicap last month. Had five thousand on him at two to one.' He raked in his winnings as the dealer went bust. 'As far as I know, poor old Excelsior is dead.'

'How about Honest Bill?'

'Ah, now there's a horse I'd like to own. Bravest fella you'd meet.' He frowned. 'Stable mate of Dawn Light's, as a matter of fact. It was his owner who was shot today at the races.'

Harry blinked. 'What?'

'It's been all over the news. Shocking thing to happen.' He eased another blue chip out for the next hand. 'He was in the stands and someone shot him in the back. His poor young son was on his shoulders at the time.'

Harry flinched. For an instant, she heard again the *spit-spit* sounds that had chased her in the alleyway. Her vision blurred as she checked the list for the entry next to Honest Bill.

'Was his name Tom Jordan?' she said.

Her father nodded, his eyes on the cards. Harry's spine tingled. She told herself there didn't have to be a connection. This man's death could've been a random shooting.

'Poor old TJ.' Her father caught a pair of eights and

split them into two hands. 'God knows what shady deal-ings he was involved in. There's a lot of it in the racing world, but no one deserves an end like that.' The dealer flipped him two more cards. 'He knew a good trainer when he saw one, though. Dan Kruger's one of the best there is.'

He waved a hand, standing on seventeen and eighteen. Then he shot her a look.

'Why the sudden interest in horses, Harry?'

Her eyes dropped to the pages in her hand. 'Just a case I'm working on.'

'I see.'

The dealer went bust, and Harry's father stacked his winnings into a neat blue pile. She flipped over a page. As long as she had his attention, she may as well try him with some other pieces of the jigsaw.

'What do you know about diamond dealing?'

'Ah, diamonds again.' He threw her a glance. 'Well, I'm no expert, but I know one or two people in the business.'

Harry didn't doubt it. Her father's network of contacts was partly what had made him such a successful banker. And insider trader, come to that. She tried again.

'Does the name Garvin Oliver mean anything to you? He's in the diamond trade. Or his wife, Beth Oliver?'

'Can't say I've heard of either of them.'

She ran her finger down the inventory list, looking up the names of the diamond buyers who'd purchased the large stones.

'How about Fischer? Or Gray?'

Her father shook his head, then eased out a stack of purple chips on to the betting spot.

'Five thousand.'

Harry's eyes snapped to the table. What was he doing? By her calculations the count was minus five. That meant more high cards than low cards had been dealt, leaving the hot tens and aces in short supply. He should be betting low, not raising his stake.

She tried to catch her father's eye, but he was busy counting chips. The blonde had left her seat and Harry's father had snagged her betting spot for himself. He pushed out another five thousand euros. Now he was playing two hands.

Harry felt her body tense. Had she lost track of the count? Bets of that size only made sense for a count of plus twelve or more, when the remaining deck was rich in high cards. This deep into the shoe, a count of minus five put her father at a glaring disadvantage.

Was he playing dumb, a camouflage move for the surveillance team upstairs?

The dealer slid the cards out of the shoe. Harry's eyes widened as her father drew a pair of aces on one hand and a blackjack on the other. He split the aces, catching a ten on each. A gasp went round the table as the dealer flipped over his hole card and stood on seventeen. Then he paid her father over seventeen thousand euros.

Harry blinked. The deck was sizzling with aces and faces. Had her card-counting skills crumbled along with the rest of her judgement?

By now, more players had left the table, and her father nabbed another three betting spots. He stacked up five hands at five thousand euros each, and Harry closed her eyes. By her reckoning, the count was minus seven. It just didn't make any sense.

She heard the *snick-snick* of cards being dealt. She opened her eyes to see her father doubling down on three of his hands, and splitting the other two. Two of the split cards caught another pair and he split them both again.

'My God,' someone said from behind.

By the time he drew his palm across his cards, her father was playing nine hands. The lowest stood at seventeen, the highest at nineteen and he had sixty thousand euros on the table.

Harry pressed her fingers to her mouth. The dealer flipped his bottom card, revealing a total of sixteen. The worst possible hand. House rules dictated he had to hit.

Harry's heart raced. If her negative count was right, the dealer was likely to draw a low card. A four or a five could wipe her father out. But her father was playing as though the dealer would draw a high card and bust.

The dealer slid a card out from the shoe. He flicked it over, and a gasp went up from the crowd. He'd drawn a five. Twenty-one.

Harry felt dizzy. For an instant her father froze, and his tan paled. She stared at him. Had he really read the count wrong? Or maybe she was the one losing her touch. Maybe the dealer's five was just dumb luck, the kind that rolled in from time to time no matter what the numbers said.

Her father stacked up his few remaining chips, a tiny tremor in his hands. He beamed at her, his eyes over-bright.

'The important thing about losing is to get over it quickly.' He pushed a single blue chip out on to the baize.

Harry shook her head, wondering at his ability to skip right over his losses. But then, for him, the next hand was always the one that just might change everything.

He patted her arm. 'Come to the yard sometime and see Dawn Light train. He'll be running in your name, after all.'

Her name.

She pictured it engraved into Garvin's files, the police only a few steps behind her. She stared at the pages in her hand.

Diamonds and horses.

She wasn't sure what the link between them was, but maybe Dawn Light was the place to start.

16

PRIVATE PROPERTY – KEEP OUT.

Harry stared at the notice on the wrought-iron gates. Most people would have heeded it and turned right around, but to Harry it was an invitation to snoop.

She drummed her fingers against the steering wheel and peered into the dark. Beyond the gate, her headlights picked out a long, deserted avenue. She stuck her head through her smashed-up window, her breath smoky against the cold air. It was six thirty in the morning, and the only sound was the squawk of bad-tempered crows.

She'd been up since five, unable to sleep. After her father's blackjack bender, she'd escorted him home to the Westbury Hotel and checked into a room of her own. It had felt a lot safer than her isolated cottage, but sleep still hadn't come. In the end she'd risen early and, armed with the directions her father had given her, she'd driven out of town and made her way cross-country for almost an hour. She hadn't had time to get her car window fixed, and the blast of pre-dawn air had soon turned her cheeks numb. Bit by bit, the motorways had given way to valleys and hills, until finally the land had flattened out into the desolate plains of Kildare.

Harry climbed out of the car, hugging her fleecy jacket around her. She inhaled the earthy smell of damp grass and mud as she checked over her shoulder. The lonely ribbon of road unravelled into the distance. On either side of it was flat, open country. No trees, no buildings, no hedges, no fences. No landmarks to tell one monotonous stretch of grass from another. Harry shuddered. How could anyone live with all this empty space?

Hunching against the cold, she stepped up to the gate and tried the latch. It clinked open. She hesitated, peering up at the walls. As far as she could tell, there weren't any cameras.

She pushed the gate open, climbed back into her car and drove on through. She cruised up the avenue, searching for signs of life. Her father had taken her to more betting shops than racing stables, but one thing she knew about training yards was that their day started early.

The avenue bent to the right, and her headlights swept across a large, ramshackle farmhouse. Withered-looking ivy struggled up its walls, and the window frames were cracked and peeling. Harry parked in the turning circle near the door and killed the engine. A ruckus of barking started up in the house and for the moment, she kept her headlights on.

Lights blazed in the front porch, and the door swung open.

'Who's there?' A tall man in boots and a wax jacket stepped outside. He put a hand to his eyes, shielding them from the glare of her headlights.

Harry opened the car door. Immediately, two Alsatians loped out from the house, low growls rumbling in their throats. They prowled towards her and she snapped the door shut. Her taste in dogs ran to breeds about knee-high; in her view, anything bigger could cause bodily harm, so she tended to keep her distance.

'I'm looking for Kruger Racing Stables,' she said.

The man clicked his fingers and the dogs slunk back into the house. He stepped towards the car.

'And you are?'

'Harry Martinez.'

She felt his stare, his eyes in shadow under thick dark brows. She took in the tall, lean frame and the faint barn-yard aroma of his clothes.

He inclined his head to one side. 'Dawn Light?'

'That's right. Are you Dan Kruger?'

He bent down to peer in at her, one hand on the car roof. The gesture was oddly intimidating and Harry felt herself shrink back. He looked past her down the avenue.

'This is a private entrance. You should have come in through the yard.' He pronounced it 'yawd', and Harry noted the clipped, South African vowels and softly rolling

137

'r's. Up close, she could see he had a boxer's nose, slightly crooked on the bridge as though it had once been broken.

'Sorry,' she said. 'I thought this was it.'

He frowned. 'I run a tight schedule around here, you should've called first.' Then he straightened up and clicked his fingers, gesturing for her to get out of the car. 'Now that you're here, I suppose you may as well walk round with me.'

Harry's eyes slid to the two Alsatians panting by the door. He followed her gaze.

'Don't worry about them. They won't touch you while I'm here.'

She flipped off her lights and eased out of the car. The dogs pricked their ears, but didn't move. Kruger turned and shut them in the hall, then tramped around the side of the house. Harry trotted after him. The air was thick with the mulchy smell of horse manure and hay, and she kept her breathing shallow. By now, the darkness had thinned and she could make out the shapes of wheel-barrows and pitchforks, just in time to save her shins.

A horse whinnied up ahead, high and long, like a set of squealing tyres. Hooves whacked against concrete and voices hollered over the racket. Kruger disappeared through a tall wooden gate, and after a moment's hesitation Harry followed. She stepped into a large, brightly lit courtyard, then immediately jerked to a halt.

Looming above her was a towering, coal-black horse. Steamy breath surged from his nostrils, and his bulging chest muscles quivered. Harry backed up against the wall.

The horse smacked his hooves against the ground as the young stable lad beside him struggled with the girth.

'Easy, boy.' The lad looked to be about sixteen. His pale face was pinched, his skinny frame no match for the pumped-up powerhouse in his care.

Harry shot a glance at Kruger. He'd moved further into the yard, deep in conversation with a short, grey-haired man and a statuesque woman in jeans. Harry sidled along the wall. The black horse stomped towards her, tossing his head. She froze, his bulk blocking her path. Her blood pumped a little faster round her veins. Maybe she'd apply her knee-high rule to more than just dogs.

The lad tried to shoulder the animal aside. 'Come on, Rottweiler, cut it out.'

The horse drew back his lips, baring dinosaur-sized teeth. He stretched his neck out to Harry, and she could feel the warmth of his breath on her face. The lad yanked at the reins but the horse strained against them, showing the whites of his eyes in a manic, crazed stare.

Then without warning, the horse reared up. He soared above Harry like a black dragon, his forelegs thrashing inches from her nose. She cried out and flung her arms across her face, crouching into the wall. Hooves thwacked the ground, and she braced herself for a bone-crunching blow.

There was a loud yell and a crack. Harry peeped through her arms. The pale-faced lad looked terrified. He was whipping the horse's chest, and another lad had raced over to help. The animal's squeals raised goose bumps on Harry's body, but she couldn't move.

'Hold his head!' It was Kruger. 'Bend him, Eddie, make him drop his head!'

The two lads wrenched at the left-hand rein, forcing the horse's head to one side. The animal dropped his forelegs with a crash to the ground. Then he lashed out with his hind legs, back-stepping into the centre of the yard. He clattered and snorted, his glossy coat slick with sweat, but somehow the two lads managed to hold him.

Slowly, Harry lowered her arms from her face. Her limbs trembled and her armpits felt damp. She straightened up and waited for her heart to stop thumping, glad of the chance to recover her dignity while everyone seemed preoccupied with the horse. Everyone, that is, except for the woman with Kruger. Harry caught her stare, and blinked. The woman's eyes were pinned to her like thumbtacks.

Harry dropped her gaze, covering her unease with a brisk pretence at brushing herself down. Then she made her way over to Kruger, her legs still wobbly. But before she reached him, he moved away towards his horse.

'Are you all right, miss?'

The grey-haired man turned a wizened face towards her. He was the same height as Harry, his adolescent frame at odds with his wind-battered face.

She nodded, feeling oddly to blame. 'I think so.'

She watched Kruger's retreating back as he ambled towards the frenzied animal. The horse eyed his approach, still bucking and tossing his head. Kruger's gait was casual, almost shuffling.

Harry could still feel the tall woman's stare. This time she stared back, noting the moss-green eyes and the strong brows that flared above them.

'You're obviously not used to horses.' The woman arched one of her magnificent eyebrows.

Harry felt her cheeks tingle. Being comfortable with menacing animals seemed to be a way of keeping score around here. She lifted her chin.

'I don't come up against them much in my line of work,' she said.

The grey-haired man shook his head. 'It wasn't your fault. That's Rottweiler's Lad. Bad-tempered brute at the best of times, but he's been in a sulk since Billy-boy beat him yesterday.'

Harry raised her eyebrows. 'He sulks?'

'Oh, yes. They can all throw tantrums. Rottweiler hates being shut up in the dark, Steady Peggy bites if you approach her from the wrong side. Worse than children, sometimes.' He squinted over at Kruger. 'No excuse for him behaving like a hooligan, though.'

Harry followed his gaze, not sure if he meant the trainer or the horse. By now, the stable lads had released Rottweiler, and Kruger had stopped in front of him. The trainer was standing quietly, shoulders down, head held high. The horse snorted and pawed the ground, but Kruger remained motionless, as though smelling the air.

The grey-haired man stuck out a hand. 'Vinnie Arnold,

head lad around here. You're Sal's daughter, the boss says.' He winked at her. 'Not that I'd need to be told; you can see it in them dark Spanish eyes.'

Harry smiled and shook his hand. The tall woman sniffed and wheeled away, calling over her shoulder.

'I'll be with the leg wound in box two.'

Harry watched her stride off, then glanced over at Kruger whose capacity for stillness was beginning to make her fidget.

'Maybe I should've made an appointment.'

'Don't mind him, he'll get over it.' Vinnie lowered his voice. 'We're all a bit shook here today, to be honest. One of our owners was killed yesterday.'

'Yes, I heard about that. It must be hard.'

'Terrible. Who'd do such a thing? Been with us nearly three years. A tough businessman, TJ, but he knew his horses.' He nodded at Kruger. 'The boss'll miss him.'

Harry followed his gaze. The trainer and his horse still stood in the centre of the yard. Kruger's stance was authoritative, yet gentle at the same time, and the combination was having its effect on Rottweiler's Lad. The horse had stopped thrashing and rolling his eyes, although he still held his head high, ready to bolt at the first false move. What kind of message was being transmitted between them?

Vinnie glanced at his watch. 'First lot left ten minutes ago, Rottweiler's the last of them.'

For the first time, Harry took in the rest of the court-yard. It was lined on three sides with peak-roofed stable boxes, like a terrace of small townhouses. Horses poked their heads out like nosy neighbours, while the stable lads worked around them.

'He's almost done,' Vinnie said. 'Never takes him long.'

Harry glanced back at Kruger. He was still immobile in the centre of the yard. The horse was now inching towards him, his head low, his posture docile. He whiffled softly through his nose, and finally Kruger put out a hand to pat him on the neck.

'Put him away, Eddie, he's not going out.' Kruger handed over the reins, then checked his watch. 'If Rob ever decides to turn up, he can ride something else.'

Harry saw the look of alarm on young Eddie's face, and guessed he wasn't wild at the prospect of being alone with Rottweiler. She didn't blame him, but Kruger seemed not to notice. The trainer strode back across the yard, barking out orders as he went.

'Vinnie, put Rottweiler on the list for Cassie to check out later. His off fore looks stocked up to me.'

'Yes, Boss. She's in with the leg in box two now.'

'Boxes three and eighteen haven't eaten up, and Steady Peggy has a swollen eye, so she'll need to see them as well.'

'Rightio.'

Vinnie bustled off. Kruger rounded on Harry as though it was her turn for instructions, then seemed to remember who she was. He cleared his throat and looked away across the yard.

She studied his dark profile. There was something

faintly simian about the thick, prominent brows and flattened nose. Maybe looking like a primate helped him bond with his horses. Then she remembered the extraordinary effect he'd had on Rottweiler's Lad, and decided that was a cheap shot.

'That was impressive,' she said, trying to make amends. 'The way you calmed him.'

Kruger clicked his tongue, then yelled across the yard, making Harry jump. 'Eddie, be firm with him, for God's sake, don't let him push you around!'

Eddie was tugging at Rottweiler's reins, his eyes wide in his underfed face as the horse barged into him.

Kruger cursed under his breath, then turned back to Harry. His gaze was unblinking, although with those dense eyebrows it was hard to be sure.

'Horses read our body language better than we know,' he said. 'Give them the wrong cues, and you're in trouble.'

Harry felt herself bristle. Was he blaming her for Rottweiler's antics? She managed a tight smile.

'I heard he just had a bad day at the races.'

Kruger gave her a long look. Then he closed his eyes and massaged the bridge of his nose. When he looked at her again, the shadow of his brows had lifted and for the first time she saw his eyes. They were a dark, tired-looking brown.

'Look, I'm sorry. About the horse, and for the way I've –' He shook his head and sighed. 'The fact is, Rottweiler's not the only one who had a bad day at the races.'

Harry dropped her gaze. 'Yes, I know. I heard about TJ.'

'The police have been round, asking questions. The lads, everyone, well . . . We're all a bit shell-shocked.' He shook his head, as if that would help him make sense of it. 'It's bizarre. Who'd want to kill TJ?'

Harry bit her lip. 'Weren't there any witnesses?'

'Too crowded and noisy. No one saw or heard anything.' His jaw tightened. 'Shot at close range, the police said. Like an execution.'

Harry's stomach flipped. Execution.

Garvin on his knees, a gun to his head.

A chill skittered through her. She shoved her fists deep into her fleecy pockets. Stupid to hope the two killings weren't connected. TJ's name was on Garvin's list, wasn't it? Right there next to her own. Now he was dead, along with Garvin.

Did that mean she was next?

17

'When you came to the house, I thought you were a reporter.'

Harry shot Kruger a surprised look. It was the first thing h 'd said in ten minutes. She hunched her shoulders against the cold, glancing back at the band of horses ambling across the flatlands towards them. The wind whipped up tears in her eyes, and she began to regret accepting his invitation to watch the horses train.

'What made you decide I wasn't?' she said.

His eyes moved over her face, tracing the outline of her brows, her nose and her mouth, until she felt her cheeks tingle. At least one part of her body was warm.

He turned his gaze back to the meandering troop of horses.

'It's not hard to tell you're Sal's daughter.'

She nodded, then looked back over the bleak plains,

breathing in the ripe smell of wet earth and leaves. The Curragh sprawled unfenced for thousands of acres, and it numbed Harry's brain to think of such godforsaken isolation.

The horses sashayed closer towards them, bridles chinkling and hooves squelching in the mud. By now, the darkness had lifted, leaving a grainy light that made the world look like a black-and-white movie.

'So which one is Dawn Light?' she said.

Kruger frowned. 'He's not here yet.'

'He's back in the yard?'

'He won't be in the yard till next week.' Kruger strode towards his horses, flinging her an impatient look over his shoulder. 'I thought you knew that.'

It was Harry's turn to frown. Mentally, she replayed the conversation with her father, and then remembered the racecourse marked down on Garvin's list. Was that where Dawn Light was? She scurried after Kruger.

'Is he in Kenilworth?'

'Of course he's in Kenilworth. He's been there for two months.'

Harry blinked. She had the feeling she was missing something here, but like a wet bar of soap, she couldn't catch hold of it. Kruger turned away and addressed his posse.

'Trot them down, canter back for three furlongs, then half-speed for the final four.' He craned his neck to see through the pack of twenty or so horses. 'Jimmy? Keep Billy-Boy back, he had a hard race yesterday.'

The jockeys responded with nods and 'Yes-Boss's, like well-drilled cadets.

An engine growled somewhere behind Harry. She turned to see a Mercedes pull up on the grass beside Kruger's mud-caked jeep. Vinnie, the head lad, clambered out of the passenger seat, shaking his head at Kruger and rolling his eyes. A blond-haired man in a red sweatshirt climbed out from behind the wheel.

'Am I late?' He was short and whip-slim, with a broad grin that told Harry he didn't give a shit about the time.

A scrawny figure slid out from the back seat. It was Eddie, the stable lad. His gaunt face seemed to have gained a little colour, and his eyes were devouring the sporty contours of the car.

Kruger glared at the blond-haired man. 'Rottweiler's developed a leg, he's not out.'

'So I heard.'

The man stared at Harry. He pushed up his sleeves to reveal sinewy forearms. Then he stepped towards her and held out his hand.

'Rob Devlin.'

Harry introduced herself and shook his hand, though in truth he'd stepped so close it was hard to move her arm. His breath smelled like fermenting fruit, sweet from the fumes of last night's alcohol. He stood eye to eye with her, gripping her fingers a shade firmer than was necessary.

'I hear Rottweiler gave you a taste of his temper,' he said.

148

His teeth were white and even, his eyes a clear grey, but his skin was showing signs of damage. Right now, it looked rugged and outdoorsy, reddened by the wind, but in a few more years he'd have the battered complexion of a man who'd spent his life at sea.

'It was probably my fault.' Harry eased her hand out of his grasp, sensing the muscles along his ropy arms. 'I think I startled him.'

Privately, Harry was convinced the horse was just nuts, but after all, these people were animal lovers.

Kruger clicked his fingers. 'Jimmy, let Rob up on Billy-Boy.' He fixed his eyes on Rob. 'Hold him back. It's been raining all night, I don't want to risk his knees on sloppy ground.'

Rob pushed past him as though he hadn't heard, moving towards the back of the bunch. Hooves scrunched the dirt and tails swished as the horses seemed to sense it was time to move. At a signal from Kruger, they jogged away in pairs, the jockeys hunched like monkeys on their backs. Rob Devlin took up the rear.

Harry stood beside Kruger and Vinnie, watching the horses go. Eddie hung back, joined now by the unfortunate lad who'd just lost his ride.

Vinnie clicked his teeth. 'We'd be better off letting one of the work riders handle him.'

Kruger raised a pair of binoculars to his eyes. 'We'll see.'

Harry studied the trainer's tall, rangy frame as he watched his horses in the lead-grey light. He looked like he should be out hunting big game on the savannah, not shivering in a boggy field in Kildare. She listened to him debate tendons and near-hinds with Vinnie, and had to admit that he seemed at home here too.

Hooves thudded in the distance. Kruger shifted his feet, adjusting his binoculars.

'Here's the first pair.'

Vinnie lifted his own binoculars while Harry peered across the field. Two horses scudded towards them, covering ground at a steady pace.

Kruger grunted. 'Artemis isn't balanced, look at his action.'

Harry shot him a look. Artemis. Another name from Garvin's list.

The two horses thundered past, snorting in tempo with their pounding hooves. Kruger tracked them for another few hundred yards, then lowered his binoculars. Harry chewed her lip and decided to try out a few names.

'My father talked a lot about your horses.' She studied Kruger's stern profile as she tried to remember the names on Garvin's list. 'Honest Bill and Excelsior, for instance. Are they still in your yard?'

Was it her imagination, or did his jaw just tighten up?

'Rob's riding Honest Bill now,' he said, then he snapped his binoculars back up to his face. 'Excelsior's dead.'

Kruger stepped away, focusing on the next pair sprinting up. Harry caught Vinnie's eye and made a rueful face. He matched it with a kindly one of his own, as if trying to make up for his boss's abruptness.

She edged closer to him, lowering her voice. 'Was it a fall?'

Vinnie nodded. 'His first race here after Cape Town. Nothing worse for a man than going home with an empty horsebox. A sickening journey.'

Harry felt the hairs rising up along her arms. Cape Town. There it was again, that recurring South African theme. Everything pointed to a connection between Garvin's operation and the horses in Kruger's yard. She remembered the filename for his list of horses: VW-Cargo. If the diamonds were the cargo, did that mean the horses transported them?

She eyed Kruger's rigid back. His body language screamed 'do not disturb', and she'd no doubt the signals were intended for her. She sidled up beside him, just as the next pair of horses charged by.

'Do you often race your horses in South Africa?' she said.

Kruger clicked his tongue, and shot her a glance from behind his binoculars. 'Why would I do that?'

'Oh, I don't know.' She ignored the testy set of his mouth. 'They hold a lot of big races out there, don't they?'

'It's too far for the horses to travel.' He whipped the binoculars down from his face and cursed. 'Vinnie, what happened there? I missed it. How did Merlin go?'

Vinnie gave a thumbs-up sign, binoculars still glued to his face. 'He's a front runner, no doubt about it.'

Kruger huffed out a long breath, making a big deal

151

about the interruption. Harry ignored him. That was the nice thing about dealing with someone rude: it gave you permission to be rude right back.

'So you never race them in South Africa?' she persisted.

He threw her an exasperated look. 'Of course I don't. What would be the point? We've plenty of suitable races in Ireland and the UK.'

Harry frowned. Her fragments of information began to feel a little jumbled.

'Boss, here comes Billy-Boy.'

Kruger whipped his binoculars back up to his face. 'What the hell is he doing?'

Harry followed his gaze. Two more horses pounded towards them, but unlike the others who'd paired stride for stride, these two didn't seem well matched. They were separated by a gap of eight lengths.

'He's holding him too far back.' Kruger's voice sounded strangled. 'What's he playing at?'

Harry squinted at the trailing horse. Rob's red sweatshirt was like a lodestar in the drab light.

'He's going for it, Boss.'

'I'll fucking kill him.'

Harry shot Kruger a glance. His jaw had hardened and his tan looked darker. She sensed Eddie stirring behind her, sidling up for a closer look. She snapped her eyes back to Rob. He was crouching lower over Honest Bill's neck, and he'd started to pump his arms.

'Jesus!' Kruger snatched his binoculars down, then jammed them back up to his face. Vinnie shifted beside him.

Honest Bill took off like a missile. His stride lengthened and he seemed to glide overground, closing in on
the lead horse.

Kruger flailed his arms. 'Devlin! Pull back!'

The lead horse must have sensed he was being pursued,
because he suddenly picked up pace. Honest Bill stormed
after him. The two horses stampeded across the gallops,
hooves thundering, mud clots splattering. Honest Bill's
ears lay flat against his head, his neck stretched forward.
Yard by yard, he was closing the gap between them.

'He'll bloody ruin him!'

Harry's heart thudded in her throat. The horses drew
level. Then with a final burst of acceleration, Honest Bill
sailed out in front.

Slowly, Kruger lowered his binoculars, his gaze fixed.
Harry bit her lip, and even Vinnie looked wary. The
horses slowed down, then Honest Bill turned and cantered
back towards them.

Kruger stood still, his head held high. It was the same
pose he'd used with Rottweiler's Lad, but this time there
was no gentleness in his stance.

Rob pulled up beside them and slipped down off the
horse's back. His eyes slid towards Harry and he grinned,
while Kruger bent down and ran his hands along Honest
Bill's legs. When he spoke, his voice was low.

'You did that deliberately. You engineered that gap so
you could push him into it.'

Rob shrugged, and cast an arm around Honest Bill's
neck. He leaned in against the horse's sturdy shoulder,

feet crossed at the ankles. He looked like a boy with a much-loved pony.

'He's a sprinter, Dan, he loves it.' Rob patted the horse's neck. 'Look at him, for God's sake.'

Harry had to admit, the horse looked pretty chirpy. He nudged at Kruger's shoulder, his ears pricked, his black eyes full of curiosity.

Eddie sidled up alongside him, and stroked the horse's flank. The boy's face was flushed, his sharp cheekbones jutting out like blades. His gaze was pinned to Rob in undisguised admiration.

Kruger straightened up and glared at the jockey. 'If his knees are fucked, I'll make sure you never ride for anyone again.'

Then he looked at Honest Bill and his shoulders lost some of their rigidness. He cupped the horse's velvety-looking chin in his hand and stroked the broad forehead, murmuring to him like a father with a sick child.

Harry watched the two men, their dislike for each other oddly neutralized by their affection for the brave horse between them.

She sighed. How the hell did Garvin Oliver fit into this peculiar world?

18

Kruger fired up the jeep's engine.

'There's breakfast for everyone back at the house. Care to join us?' He studied her face. 'You look like you could do with some bulking up.'

Harry raised her eyebrows. She'd never known anyone swing so wildly between rudeness and polite invitations. She shook her head and strapped herself in.

'Thanks, but I'm fine.'

Right now, she needed to get away and figure out her next move. She sank back against the seat and closed her eyes. Maybe she was wasting her time. After all, what had she learned? She was certainly no closer to finding Beth and proving her innocence to Hunter. She felt her shoulders droop. Maybe she should back off and let the police handle things.

The jeep bounced like a space-hopper across a patch

of rough terrain. Harry's eyes flared open, the jolt kick-starting her adrenaline like a splash of cold water. She straightened up, trying to throw off the lethargy. Kruger was right. She needed fuel.

'Actually, coffee and toast might be nice,' she said.

Kruger shrugged, bumping the jeep out of the fields and back on to the narrow road. They drove in silence for a while. Up ahead, a squadron of crows dive-bombed into the flatlands, then swooped back up to the skies. Apart from them, the Curragh seemed to be empty.

Brakes squealed into the silence. Harry twisted in her seat, craning her neck. Behind them, a Mercedes wheeled round a bend, then roared straight towards them. Kruger clicked his teeth in annoyance, maintaining the jeep's steady speed.

Harry dug her fingernails into the seat. Tyres screeched as the Mercedes slowed down, inches from the jeep's rear end. Harry could see Rob Devlin's grin through the wind-screen. Eddie was in the passenger seat beside him, beaming. Rob pumped his engine with challenging revs, then swerved out into the road and shot past.

Harry sneaked a glance at Kruger. With his flattened nose and grim mouth, he looked like a prize-fighter, and his expression discouraged chitchat. Harry bit her lip.

'Looks like Rob has one fan, anyway,' she said.

Kruger threw her a cynical look. 'You mean Eddie? *Ja*, Rob's his hero, all right. Trots round after him like a puppy dog. Eddie's been apprenticed to the yard for years, and all he's ever wanted is to be a champion jockey, just like Rob.'

'And will he make it?'

Kruger shook his head. 'Hasn't got the hands for it. No sense of pace, either. At best, he'll be mediocre.' He shrugged. 'I suppose one of these days, I'll have to break it to him.'

Harry felt a pang on Eddie's behalf. Sometimes, life just didn't deliver.

They continued in silence until they reached the yard, where Kruger pulled up at the back of the house. Rob's Mercedes was already there.

Harry clambered out of the jeep and followed Kruger into a scullery filled with coats and boots. The air smelled fusty, like dried-out rain. Kruger toed his heels, dislodging his feet from his wellies. Harry eyed her own trainers. They were caked with a kind of brown gloop that she seriously hoped was mud. She watched Kruger slip on a pair of shoes, and wondered what the protocol was here. Did he expect her to pad around the house in her socks?

Kruger glanced at her feet. He looked like he was itching to lift them up and check them like horses' hooves.

'Do you mind leaving those here?' he said.

Harry managed a smile and kicked off her trainers. Then she followed him in her socks out of the scullery and into a wide hall. The carpet was frayed and the walls were lined with horse portraits. The salty scent of bacon flavoured the air, and suddenly Harry was starving.

Then she froze. Two wolf-like shapes had sloped out in front of her. Kruger clicked his fingers and the dogs came to heel, tongues dangling, heads dipped below their shoulders. Harry swallowed. Why would anyone want a pair of dogs that looked like they should be guarding Hell?

Kruger indicated a room to his right. 'Grab a seat. We'll leave the kitchen to the others.'

She eased past him, trying not to make any sudden moves in case the dogs took it as a signal to pounce. She watched Kruger move off down the hall, his sidekicks skulking behind him.

'Nasty brutes, aren't they?'

Harry spun round. Rob Devlin was sitting behind a large, old-fashioned desk, his feet propped up on its surface. 'Santa's little helpers, that's what I call them.'

He still had his boots on, and Harry could see the muddy smears he'd left on the desk. Clearly the household rules didn't apply to him. She bunched up her toes, feeling at a disadvantage standing there in her socks.

Her eyes roamed the room. Like the desk, all the furniture looked dated and heavy, with too much dark wood and faded upholstery. Rob swung his legs down to the floor.

'What did you think of Billy-Boy?'

Harry shrugged. 'I don't know much about horses, but he seems pretty special.'

'He's special, all right. Dan'll put him out to stud in another season or two, but right now he's at his peak.'

Harry perched against a second, smaller desk by the wall. 'Tom Jordan owned him, didn't he?'

His eyebrows shot up. 'You knew TJ?'

'No, but I think my father did.' She paused. 'I heard what happened at the racecourse yesterday.'

Rob dropped his gaze. 'I still can't believe it. Why would anyone kill TJ? And with his kid on his shoulders. My God.'

'Did you know him well?'

'Well enough. He and Dan had been business partners for years.'

'He was a partner in the yard?'

He nodded. 'Dan's the horse expert, but TJ's the money man. Or was.'

'How does that work?'

Rob shrugged. 'Dan picks the yearlings and TJ pays for them. Lately, Dan's been speculating with his own money, too, buys horses to sell on to owners later. He breaks them in, trains them, mostly for the flat. Then he races them till they're about three, sells them on for stud and splits the profits with TJ. Nice operation. Until now.'

Harry thought of her father and Dawn Light. 'But he trains for other owners as well, doesn't he?'

'Sure, he'll buy and train for anyone with enough moolah, and he'll take a piece of the action, too. But the best yearlings always went to TJ.'

'Like Billy-Boy.'

'Exactly.' He got to his feet and moved round the desk towards her. 'Fantastic bloodlines, another one of Fort Wood's progeny. Dan was lucky to get him.'

'Fort Wood?'

'Champion Sire in '98. Most of his progeny have been strong.'

He stood right in front of her, breaching her personal space. If it wasn't for the desk, she would've backed away. She stirred uncomfortably against it.

'So Dan picked well,' she said.

'Dan always picks well.' He topped her height by just a few inches, which probably made him tall for a jockey. In spite of his wiry frame, there was something intensely male about him.

'Did he pick Rottweiler?' Harry said.

Rob grinned. 'Yep, and the old devil's a winner, no doubt about it. The South African bloodlines haven't failed Dan yet.'

Harry stared at him. 'South African?'

'Billy-Boy was bred in Kimberly, same as Fort Wood. Rottweiler came from a stud farm in Port Elizabeth.'

'Wait a minute. Are you saying Dan buys some of his horses from South Africa?'

'He buys all of his horses from South Africa. Everyone knows that. It's a sort of trademark with him.'

'Even Dawn Light?'

Rob nodded. 'Dan bought him in Cape Town a couple of months ago. He's still in Kenilworth, gets shipped in next week.'

'Why so long in Kenilworth?'

'That's where the quarantine station is. Gotta make sure he's free of all those midges and mozzies; little buggers carry disease.'

Harry nibbled her lower lip. So Dawn Light wasn't out in Kenilworth to race; he was waiting to get the all-clear before being flown home. She edged along the desk, sliding out of Rob's orbit, and wondered how it all tied in.

A long-legged woman swept into the room, stopping up short at the sight of Harry. It was the statuesque lady with the supercilious brows. She turned to Rob.

'Where's Dan?'

The jockey gave her a lazy grin. 'Gone to fetch breakfast for his new ladyfriend here.'

The woman drilled him with a look that would've made Harry squirm, then stalked back out of the room. Rob laughed softly to himself.

'Who's that?' Harry said.

'Cassie? She's the stable vet.' Rob winked at her. 'She vets every woman that comes within an inch of Kruger. Scares most of them off, too.'

'They're together?'

Rob made a face. 'She'd like to think so. Kruger's just a passenger in the whole thing, if you ask me. Doesn't care much about anything outside of his horses.'

Harry made a mental note to stay out of the woman's way. She crossed to the window overlooking the main yard. Water slopped on the ground outside as the stable lads hosed the horses down. Rob joined her. When he spoke, his voice was low.

'Things might have to change around here, now that TJ's dead.'

Harry shot him a glance. His face looked sunken in the harsh, direct light, but his jaw was firm.

'I know one thing though,' he went on. 'Wherever Billy-Boy goes, I go. Me and him, we have a big future together.'

'Billy-Boy's not going anywhere.'

Harry spun round. Kruger was standing behind them, carrying a tray. He glared at Rob, plonked the tray on a nest of tables, then planted himself behind the larger desk. Harry felt like a schoolgirl caught bad-mouthing the principal. Her instinct was to keep still in case she drew his fire. In the end, hunger won out and she reached for the toast.

Kruger shuffled through some paperwork, and for the first time Harry noticed the two laptops in the room. There was one on each desk and without thinking, she noted the connected cables, then found herself scanning the shelves. Profiling her surroundings for technical weaknesses was second nature to her by now, but normally she did it the minute she entered a room. Looked like her instincts were backsliding again.

She found what she was looking for on a shelf near the window. A small box, not much bigger than a paperback. A row of green lights flickered along one side, the tell-tale antenna poking up from one corner. A wireless access point. She glanced back at Kruger. The technology seemed out of place in this old lady's room, where everything else looked like part of a restoration project.

She sipped her coffee, and caught Rob eyeing the tray.

162

He turned abruptly, fists stuffed in his pockets, and began to pace the room. His slim build looked clenched in some kind of struggle, and Harry glanced at the plateful of toast. Who knew what kind of punishing starvation he endured to keep his weight down?

Kruger looked over at him. 'You're still riding in Cape Town on Sunday?'

'Yep. International Jockeys' Challenge. You're looking at the new champion.'

Kruger ignored the swank. 'I'll put you down for Artemis at Leopardstown when you get back. With luck, the ground will dry out before then.'

'It better. He's pig-slow on soft going.'

For the next few minutes, they ignored Harry and talked about weather and drainage. She tuned them out and wandered over to the horse portraits on the wall. Noble-looking animals stared down at her with bright, intelligent eyes. She stared back. What was the connection between Kruger's horses and Garvin's diamond operation? Was he really using them as couriers? She stopped in front of a majestic chestnut, with a forehead as broad and wise as a saint's. Was Kruger involved in whatever was going on? Or was he another victim, just like her?

She flicked him a glance over her shoulder. He caught her look and broke off his conversation, his eyes straying to the picture on the wall.

'That's Honest Bill when he first came to the yard,' he said. 'Your father wanted to buy him, but TJ held firm.' He punched a few keys on his laptop. 'Incidentally,

163

you can tell Sal I've found him another colt. A yearling from Fort Wood's line has come up for sale in Cape Town. I'll be there in a few days to check him out.'

'My father's buying another horse?' Harry thought about his losses the night before and wondered how he could afford it. 'What about Dawn Light?'

'Don't worry about him, he's in safe hands. Our travelling groom has already flown out to escort him back. Apparently, he's a nervous flier, but Eve will sort him out.'

Harry frowned. 'Eve?'

The name sparked a circuit in her brain, but it fizzled out.

'Eve Darcy. She's the best flying groom in the business.' He nodded at the photograph on the wall. 'That's her with Billy-Boy.'

Harry snapped her gaze back to the photo. A young woman stood beside Honest Bill, one hand on his neck, the other holding on to his bridle. She was slim and boyish, the peak of her jockey's helmet casting a shadow over her face. Harry peered closer. Then her tummy flipped in a jolt of recognition.

The woman was smiling out at her with Beth's tilted eyes.

19

'Mani, you are awake?'

Takata's voice croaked into the darkness. Mani hunched deeper under his blanket and kept his eyes shut. In spite of the chilled night air, he was sweating.

Tomorrow his contract was up. He would leave the mine for good, free of its choking dust and suffocating tunnels. But without the diamonds, it would all be for nothing. His fingers tightened around the stone in his fist.

'Mani?'

Jackals yowled outside the compound. Mani shivered, the sweat turning cold on his skin. Just one more day, that was all he'd needed. One more day for Volker to clear his baggage through the x-ray machines. Without Volker, how would he get the diamonds out?

Takata's bunk creaked. 'You must not think about Alfredo. There was nothing you could do.'

An image of Okker flooded Mani's brain: his bulk bending over Alfredo's corpse, his blade ready to slash. Nausea slithered in the pit of Mani's stomach. He opened his eyes. Takata was leaning across his bunk towards him.

'Tomorrow when you are home, tell Asha her old father is well.' He laughed, his chest rattling. 'Tell her I am putting on weight.'

A spasm of coughing tore at the old man's lungs. His bony shoulders jerked with each convulsion, his skeletal frame ready to snap in two. Silently, Mani held out the bottle of water he kept hidden under his bed. He watched as Takata sipped between ragged gasps, unable to meet his eyes. They both knew the old man would never be well. His lungs were caving in, shredded by sharp, silica particles and asbestos fibres thinner than hairs.

Mani listened to the crackles of the old man's chest. When Mani's father had died, Takata had helped with food and money, though he had so little himself. 'You do not owe me anything,' he would say. 'We are neighbours, that is all.'

Now Takata had two more weeks before his contract was up. Mani hoped the old man lived long enough to return home to his daughter. If he died in the mine, they would never let his body out.

Takata eased back against the wire frame of his bunk. 'Tomorrow, everything is ready?'

'There is nothing to worry about.' Mani's throat was dry. 'Go back to sleep.'

'When it is over, you will return to Cape Town?'

'Yes.'

Takata tutted in the dark. 'Fatima, my cousin, she lives in Cape Town. Everywhere there is drugs and disease. Her sons are all dead.'

'I know, you told me. But I do not live in a shanty on the Flats.'

Takata leaned towards him in the dark. 'You are sure everything is ready?'

'Yes. Now go to sleep.'

Mani squeezed his eyes shut. The endless drone of insects thrummed in his ears and suddenly he felt short of air. What would happen when he failed to bring the diamonds out? The dealers waiting on the next shipment had already killed his mother. Who would be next? He pictured Asha's almond-shaped eyes and his head swam.

He clenched his fists, the stone cold against his palm. Cockroaches scrabbled in the dark all around him. Eventually, Takata's slow, bubbling breaths told him the old man was asleep.

Mani eased back his blanket, now sodden with sweat. He scanned the room. The other men were just hunched-up shapes, hawking and moaning in the dark. He got to his feet, slipped the stone in his pocket and picked his way between the bunks. He headed for the toilet at the back of the room, the stench of human waste guiding him through the dark.

Insects scuttled across his path. Cold air and dust

whipped through the broken windows. They were all at ceiling height, all out of reach. Except for the one over the toilet.

Mani stared up at it. It was set about twelve feet high along the wall. He stepped on to the stained, ceramic bowl and sprang against the window ledge, scrabbling for purchase. He hauled himself up on to the sill, then eased through the open window and dropped on all fours to the ground.

He checked his surroundings. Ahead of him, the double electric fence choked off the advancing scrubland. The acacia trees were black against the horizon. Beyond them, to the north, lay the Kuruman Hills, where blue asbestos dust poisoned the red soil. Mani shivered. The runner for the diamond dealers awaited him there.

Owls screeched from their nests in the mine pits. Mani sifted through the nocturnal sounds, listening out for guards. Behind him, he knew the searchlights strobed the compound like two large orbs. He crouched in against the wall, a watchtower blindspot. Then he pulled up his trouser leg, untying the ladle and carving knife that he'd strapped on to his calf. One was for digging; the other was to protect him from snakes.

He slipped the diamond from his pocket, turning it over in his hand. The spoiled milk had done its job, purging his body in a spasm of cramps. He'd cleaned the stone off as best he could using water boiled on the dormitory's rusting hotplate.

The moonlight buffed up the silvery grey stone. It was

the biggest one he'd found, maybe more than two hundred carats. He could barely close his fist over it. He set the stone aside, gripped the ladle with both hands and began scooping up the dusty soil.

He'd found his first diamond at the age of ten, shortly after his family had moved from Angola. He'd been playing with Asha, and had discovered the stone near a thicket of giant bamboo. The land had belonged to the Van Wycks Corporation. He'd given the stone to his father and shortly afterwards, the area had been surrounded by barbed wire and buried under tonnes of waste. The land had never been mined.

Since then, he'd seen Van Wycks shut down many diamond-rich areas. They'd closed viable mines, scaled back production. They'd even turned valuable kimberlitic land into national parks. Gifts to the South African people, they'd said. But Mani knew better. It was no coincidence that mining was forbidden by law in national parks.

The ladle clinked against metal. Mani gouged out more dirt, then dug up the tin can that he'd buried a few nights before. He eased back the lid. Inside were the other three diamonds he'd found. One was small, the size of a berry. But the others were bigger than eggs.

Bats squealed overhead, flocking in and out of trees. Mani froze, straining for sounds that might have startled them. Nothing. He dropped the new stone into the can, then rattled it gently in his hands.

'Well, well, kaffir boy.'

Mani's head jerked up. Okker was standing by the wall, his submachine gun pointed at Mani's head.

'I knew I'd catch you sooner or later.' Okker smiled, his doughy face sinking into a pillow of jowls.

Mani's stomach heaved, but he couldn't move. Okker's eyes slid to the can of diamonds.

'Give that to me.'

Slowly, Mani straightened up, his knees trembling. His vision blurred as he stared into the black bore of Okker's gun. He held out the tin can.

Okker snatched at it, setting the stones rattling. He glanced inside, his small eyes bulging.

'Where did you get these?' he whispered.

Mani swallowed against the dryness in his throat. 'In the mine.'

Okker barged closer and shoved his gun into Mani's chest. 'Don't lie. This mine doesn't produce stones this size. Tell me where you got them.'

'Near the waste rock, I swear it.' Mani licked his lips. 'The machines, they throw them away.'

Okker's eyes narrowed. Mani's skin crawled in self-disgust as he wondered had he just betrayed his family. But without Volker, everything was already over.

Okker stepped backwards, setting the can on the ground. Then he shouldered his gun, taking aim.

'*Ja*, well now the stones are mine, kaffir boy.'

Mani held his breath. Okker flicked a glance behind him. Then suddenly, he relaxed his aim. He slung the gun over his shoulder, and grasped the club dangling

170

from his belt. He leered at Mani, slapping the weighted, bulbous truncheon into the palm of one hand. Then without warning, he swung it sideways and slammed it into Mani's gut.

Mani gasped. Air exploded from his lungs. His knees buckled and he sank to the ground. He crouched by the wall, dragging in air. Okker's bulk closed in on him. Moonlight flashed off metal, and Mani caught sight of the blade in Okker's hand. Then he understood. Gunfire would have drawn the other guards, who'd take their share of the stones. Okker intended this to be a silent kill.

Mani scrabbled around in the dirt. Okker raised his arm, ready to strike. Mani's fingers touched something long and cold. His snake knife.

'Say goodbye, kaffir boy.'

Mani grabbed his knife with both hands and thrust it upwards, sinking the metal deep into Okker's chest. The guard glared down at him, eyes wide, blade poised. A trickle of blood rolled down his chin. Something warm leaked over Mani's fingers. He yanked the knife out. Then slowly, Okker tumbled into the dirt.

Mani skittered backwards on all fours. Something clattered behind him, and he spun round. The tin can lay on its side, the stones on the ground. He waited for the yells, the shots, the running footsteps.

But there was nothing.

Just the chirping of crickets in the dark.

Mani picked up one of the diamonds, then stared at

Okker's mound of flesh. He thought of how black bodies had to be buried in the mine, so that no one could use them to smuggle diamonds out. His fingers closed over the handle of his knife. Black bodies may not have been allowed out of the compound.

But white bodies were.

20

Eve Darcy. Little Evie Oliver.

How could they be one and the same?

Harry padded down the hallway with Kruger close behind, like a bouncer escorting her outside. Her brain whirled. She pictured Beth's passport and the photo of Evie on Garvin's desk. School uniforms were timeless; there was nothing to say Evie's photo had to be current. Even so, it was hard to see how her age could overlap with her mother's.

Harry stepped into the scullery. Cool air sluiced her face with fertilizer smells from the yard. She shoved her feet into her grubby trainers, and tried to imagine herself masquerading as her own mother. Mentally, she superimposed Miriam's cool elegance on her own dark wildness, but the images wouldn't team up. Some things just couldn't be forced.

'I'll walk you to your car.'

Kruger's long-limbed frame loomed over her, rail-roading her out of the scullery and into the yard. She flicked a glance at his gorilla brows and thought about Eve's bruised eye. If Garvin was her father, then where did that leave her claim to be a victim of domestic violence? On the other hand, if Garvin hadn't hit her, who had?

Harry made her way across the yard, wondering how to frame her questions about Eve. Raindrops pricked her cheeks like pins and needles as the late morning sky primed itself for a deluge.

'Dan?'

Harry glanced round. Cassie, the vet, was striding towards them, zipping up her jacket against the cold. She ducked her head against the spittle of rain, calling out as she covered the ground between them.

'I've wrapped Rottweiler's leg and the swelling's gone down. You can keep working him.'

Cassie stopped in front of Kruger, a light smile on her lips. In the daylight, her hair was a deep auburn shade, like the coat of an Irish red setter. She and Kruger stood eye to eye, both titan-sized. Beside them Harry felt stunted.

'What about Steady Peggy?' Kruger said.

'Conjunctivitis.' Cassie's eyes flicked over Harry. 'I've given Vinnie some ointment.'

Silence fell, and the vet looked from Harry to Kruger as if waiting to be introduced. She hadn't been over-burdened with manners last time they'd met, and Harry guessed the social graces were for Kruger's benefit. She bit down on the urge to turn away and instead, held out her hand.

'Harry Martinez.'

The woman returned her handshake. 'Cassie Bergin. Are you one of Dan's owners?'

'My father is. He owns Dawn Light.' Harry seized the moment. 'Eve Oliver's in Cape Town, bringing the horse home.'

The name hung in the air between them, and Harry watched for signs of recognition. Cassie's eyes narrowed and Kruger turned to Harry with a frown.

'It's Darcy, not Oliver,' he said.

'Oh.' Harry feigned puzzlement. 'But didn't she used to be Eve Oliver?'

'Not to my knowledge.' Kruger's gaze became fixed. 'I didn't realize you knew her.'

Harry shrugged. 'Maybe I don't. She just looks like someone I used to know.'

She glanced from one to the other, but neither looked ready to add anything. As confirmation of Eve's identity, it didn't amount to much, but right now she didn't know how to push for more. She made a show of checking her watch, then turned to Kruger.

'Thanks for this morning. Next time, I'll call ahead.'

She wheeled away, aware of Cassie giving her the head-to-toe scan that women use to size each other up. Harry did a quick run-through of her own appearance: scruffy jeans, bedraggled hair, face puffy from lack of sleep. Really, the woman had nothing to worry about.

Harry made her way round to the front of the house and climbed into her car. She sped down the avenue and out the gate, anxious to put distance between herself and Kruger's yard. Raindrops swatted her through the broken window. She tore along the road that cut through the plains like a runway on a deserted airstrip. The only signs of life were a horsebox and a man on a bike.

Her fingers clenched the wheel. Had she finally found the woman posing as Beth? She pictured the photo of Honest Bill and the boyish woman beside him. The eyes were unmistakable.

She checked her mirror. Kruger's gates had retreated into the distance, casting her adrift in the wind-whipped plains. She drove on for another mile of empty road, then pulled over to the grassy kerb. It was time to call Hunter.

She dug out her phone along with Hunter's card, then hesitated. It was all very well acting like a magician and whipping Eve out of a hat, but how could she do it without disclosing her own link to the yard? The point here was to exonerate herself, not incriminate herself further.

On the other hand, someone out there was trying to kill her.

She dialled Hunter's number, but all she got was voice-mail. She left a message asking him to call, her eyes straying to the laptop on the passenger seat beside her.

Raindrops rapped on the car roof. By now the earlier pinpricks had swelled to a downpour and the windscreen was a watery blur. She flipped on her wipers, peering out at the vacant flatlands. The isolation was unnerving.

Twisting in her seat, she rummaged in the back until she found a plastic bag and did her best to patch up her broken window. Then she slid back her seat and hauled the laptop on to her knees.

She thought about the other players in Garvin's transactions. Gray and Fischer, for instance. Who were they? Maybe their names appeared elsewhere on Garvin's files. And what about that odd twelve-digit number stored along with the list of horses? Now that she knew what to look for, she could narrow her search on Garvin's crowded hard drive.

She waited for her laptop to power up, her thoughts drifting back to the laptop on Kruger's desk. People lived their lives on their computers these days; his was bound to tell her something. She shook her head, shoving the thought aside. She was in more than enough trouble already.

She turned her attention back to the screen and loaded up the duplication of Garvin's hard drive. Then she copied out the twelve-digit number from her printouts and fired off a search. She drummed her fingers against her leg, listening to the rain exploding like popcorn against the taped-up bag by her ear. 881677273934. It could be anything. A bank account, maybe? Or some kind of password? Her laptop beeped. Apart from the hidden file she'd already found, the search for the twelve digits had come back empty.

Harry frowned, then keyed in a search for the name 'Gray', but after a lengthy shakedown of Garvin's hard drive she'd turned up nothing new. Finally, she launched a search for 'Fischer', and this time she got a hit.

The screen spat out a list of seven files that contained the text 'Fischer Diamond House'. Harry pounced on them, snapping them open. They were invoices, stored in plain view alongside Garvin's legitimate data. It looked like he'd been supplying small, rough stones to Fischer on a regular basis; all bought and paid for, all above board. She scrolled through the information till she found an address: Fischer Diamond House, 9 Coen Steytler Avenue, Foreshore, Cape Town.

Something fluttered in the pit of Harry's stomach. Cape Town. It seemed that everything was converging there. Dawn Light, Eve, Kruger, Rob. And now one of the buyers for Garvin's secret, oversized stones.

Harry made a note of the phone number alongside the address in case she needed it later. Then she plugged in her wireless stick and Googled 'Fischer Diamond House'. It wasn't hard to find. It turned out to be a prestigious jewellery manufacturer, with a slick website showing slideshows of diamonds and elaborate custom designs. Harry browsed through the sparkling images, remembering the rough, unpolished pebble stowed safely in her bag. How did a humble chip of gravel get reborn into starbursts like these?

She arched her back and felt her spine crackle. Fatigue dragged at her like saddlebags of sand, and her shoulders still ached from her drop-'n-roll stunt the night before. Slowly, she packed away her laptop, resisting the urge to close her eyes and nap. It wouldn't be smart to snooze out in the open with a killer on her tail.

Her phone jangled into the silence. Her eyes snapped to the caller ID: private number. She hesitated, then took the call.

'Hello?' Her voice sounded jittery, even to her own ears.

'You can have your laptop back.'

Harry sank back against the seat. Hunter sounded tetchy, but then so did almost everyone she'd talked to today. He went on.

'If you want, you can pick it up at headquarters in Phoenix Park, the Tech Bureau guys here are finished with it.'

'Thanks.' Harry hesitated. 'Did you get my message?'

'Yes.'

She tried to gauge his tone, searching for signs that he knew about her name in Garvin's files. But his snippy monosyllable didn't give much away.

'I know who she is.' Harry's mouth felt dry. 'The woman in Garvin's house. She was his daughter, Eve.'

There was a pause. 'How do you know?'

Harry shifted in her seat. She hadn't worked out yet how to explain her sudden insight; she'd just have to bluff things out.

'It has to be her,' she said. 'Okay, maybe the ages seem a little off, but assuming the photo on the desk is old, she could be what, twenty-nine or thirty by now?'

'She's twenty-five. And she's his step-daughter.'

Harry blinked. 'You know about her?'

'We've been trying to find her to tell her about Garvin's death. We've located her employers, we're talking to them now.'

'It must have been her. The resemblance to Beth is too strong, there's no other explanation.'

Harry worked out the numbers. Eve had looked older than twenty-five, probably a side-effect of her all-weather lifestyle. If Beth were alive, she could feasibly be in her forties, and maybe in her thirties when her passport shot was taken. Whatever the age gap, it had been enough to fool Harry at the time. She bit her lip. In truth, she hadn't studied the passport all that closely. The itch to crack open that damned safe had already taken over.

'We're checking her out,' Hunter said. 'Who knows, maybe she'll confirm your story about the mysterious killer.'

Harry's stomach lurched. For an instant, she was back in Sugar House Lane, footsteps chasing her in the dark.

'He came after me last night,' she said.

Hunter paused. 'What?'

'The man with the gun. He was waiting for me outside my office.'

Harry told him about the guy in the baseball cap taking a pot-shot at her in the alleyway. She massaged the corners

180

of her eyes as she talked. Had that really only happened last night? Fatigue was dilating time, stretching it like a rubber band. She felt as though she'd been deadlocked in this nightmare for weeks.

Eventually, Hunter said, 'Any witnesses?'

'The coach driver must have seen something. I know some of the tourists in the bus saw me, but I don't know if they saw the other guy.'

'It's not much to go on.'

Harry snapped her head up. 'He fired a gun at me, for God's sake. Do you need me to produce the damn bullet?'

There was a small silence. Then Hunter said, 'We'll check it out. There may be some evidence in the alleyway.'

Jesus. What would it take for him to believe her?

Then she remembered the woman on the balcony.

'There *was* someone, a woman. She saw him smash in my car window, she saw the gun.'

'What woman?'

'I don't know her name. She lives in the tower block behind the brewery.'

'Ah. Gardenia Flats. Full of worthy citizens. No doubt she'll come rushing to co-operate with police inquiries.'

Harry flashed on the block of run-down flats, with the burnt-out balconies, the smell of cannabis and the anti-police slogans on the walls. She slumped back against the seat.

'I'll put someone on to it,' Hunter was saying. 'In the meantime, try staying in at night.'

181

Harry raised her eyebrows. 'That's it? I get shot at and all you can say is not to wander around in the dark?'

'Look, maybe I believe you, maybe I don't.' Suddenly, Hunter sounded as weary as she felt. 'Maybe this guy really did shoot Garvin. Or maybe Eve pulled the trigger, and you helped. Who's to say there ever was a man with a gun?'

'I don't believe this.'

'We'll do a door-to-door in Gardenia, just in case, but I wouldn't hold your breath. Come in for the laptop whenever you want.'

The phone beeped as Hunter disconnected. Harry felt dizzy, suffocating from the powerlessness of not being believed. When Hunter had come to her office, she thought she'd sensed a shift in his attitude. She thought he'd started to believe her. Another error of judgement.

She opened the car door and stumbled out. The rain had stopped and she inhaled the fresh, apple-sweet air until her head cleared.

She'd been a fool to think that finding Eve would be enough to exonerate her. Her standing with the police was murky at best, and the circumstantial evidence was stacking up. It was going to take more than finger-pointing at Eve to convince Hunter she was telling the truth.

And once they found her name on Garvin's files, things would only get worse.

Harry leaned against the car. Another horse box rattled past, trundling towards the yard. She gazed after it, wondering again about Kruger's laptop and the secrets it had to tell.

Her fingertips tingled. She checked her watch. In a few hours it'd be dark. The perfect cover.

It couldn't hurt to take a peek, could it?

21

Callan snapped his eyes to the wing mirror, his muscles tense. He glared at the reflection of the girl by the road until his horsebox obscured the view.

It was her, he was sure of it. What the hell was she doing this close to Kruger's yard?

He jammed on the brakes. He'd missed her once already, blinded by the headlights of that fucking bus. Why not deal with her now and get the job done?

He checked the road. No cars, no pedestrians, just a wasteland of ugly crows. He yanked the wheel hard to the right, preparing to turn the Land Rover. Something rumbled behind him. He whipped his gaze back to the mirror. A tractor lumbered out of a side entrance, its beacon flashing like an amber fez. Then it turned and chugged off in the direction of the girl.

Shit. Callan punched the steering wheel. Then he revved

up the engine and sped away. No sense involving any more witnesses. Apart from the girl, he'd left no evidence and he planned to keep it that way. Even the alley behind the brewery was clean, his cartridge and bullet safely recovered after the tourist bus had gone.

He tore along the road, picking up pace. Ahead of him, a cyclist wobbled on the verge and Callan swerved to avoid him. He slammed his horn, his palms sweaty. He flexed his shoulder, tried to relax. Nice and easy, keep it calm. For now, he was just a local out towing his horsebox. The girl could wait till later.

He drove for another mile of dreary road until he came to Kruger's yard. He slowed at the entrance, noting the jeep and the flash Mercedes parked up by the house. Then he cruised on, heading for the gallops where the barman in Newbridge had told him Kruger exercised his horses. First string out at eight, second lot at twelve. People opened up to racing journalists out here, and posing as one wasn't hard.

He reached a lay-by and pulled in. Then he buzzed open the sunroof, grabbed his binoculars and clambered on to the seat. Cold air rushed against his face as he straightened up through the opening. Leaning waist-high against the roof, he peered through the binoculars and tried to get a fix on the yard.

There it was, separated from the gallops by a low wall. Callan sharpened his focus. The binoculars were military-strength, and transported him right into the courtyard. Keyed-up horses jostled for space, flyweight jockeys on their backs. In their midst stood a tall, stern-faced man: Dan Kruger. Beside him was another man, short and gnarled like an old gnome.

A whining buzz rushed past Callan, like a swarm of invading insects. He spun round, his heart hammering, a hand on the knife he kept strapped to his belt. His eyes blurred. The fields around him shimmered like sun-baked plains. Insects, heat, guerrilla fighters. Monsters of Africa, spreading sickness and death. A sharp pain pulsed through Callan's skull. Then his vision cleared and he watched the cyclist speed away, his wheels humming.

Callan wiped his mouth, and noticed his hand was shaking. He balled it into a fist. His nerves felt jangled, on high alert. But that was what made him such a good soldier, wasn't it? Paranoia was what kept him alive.

His eyes darted to the horsebox. He pictured what was in there, and the jackhammer in his chest slowed down. He wiped his forehead and tried to ignore the echoes of his Delta commander's voice:

You're all burned out, I can't use you any more.

Callan yanked his cap low over his eyes. He knew what they said about him, the lies they told. A hundred and fifty years ago, they'd called it soldier's heart. Then it was shell shock, then battle fatigue. Vets of Korea had 'operational exhaustion'. Now they'd found another fancy name. Post-Traumatic Stress Disorder. PTSD.

Callan spat into the hedge. It was all bullshit. A few nightmares, some headaches. Who wouldn't have nightmares after the things he'd seen? But his commander had given him no choice, relieving him of unit duties indefinitely. And for what? Counselling and civvies?

Callan clenched his teeth. He'd tried civilian life once before, but as with everything else in his formative years, the experience had almost suffocated him. How could people bear the tedium? He'd broken free, leaving his native Dublin at the age of nineteen to join the British Paras. His father had sneered, predicting another failure. The old bastard had been dead for thirty years now, but not before Callan had proved him wrong.

As a Para, Callan had excelled, thriving in a world where everything was vital and adrenaline-charged. He'd blazed through tours of duty in Belfast and the Falklands, striking the enemy hard and fast, deep inside their own territory. He'd advanced through the ranks, commanding his own unit in the elite Special Forces, until his dishonourable discharge at the age of thirty-five.

Callan still burned at the injustice of it. Those fucking cowards had been running away, deserting their unit. Yes, he'd fired on his own soldiers, but you had to be brutal to be a commander. They'd hushed it up and he avoided criminal charges, but he was forced to leave the Regiment. For a while he'd drifted, homeless and unemployable, soothing his outrage with alcohol. Then he'd joined a private military company called Delta International Services.

Mercenaries had been around as long as war itself. For some, a merc was a military whore. For Callan, it was a way of feeling alive again. With Delta, he'd fought through the jungles of Angola, the Democratic Republic of the Congo and Sierra Leone. He'd endured savage, close-quarter fighting, and come out of it feeling reborn.

Then, after twenty years, his Delta commander had cut him loose.

Unstable, unreliable.

Callan whipped the binoculars back up to his face. He was trained to conquer fear, to kill without compassion. Combat was all he knew. To hell with Delta. For the last eight months, he'd been a lone soldier, an independent operative with skills for hire to the right bidder.

He adjusted his sight-line till he lit back on Kruger's yard. The client was paying more than usual this time, and Callan intended to deliver.

The horses were on the move, their smoky breath drifting around them like a low mist. Callan tracked the lead jockey. With his bright red sweatshirt, he was the easiest to tag. The rider flicked a quick look over his shoulder and Callan caught his face. Rob Devlin.

He swept the binoculars over the yard, scanning for Kruger. He found him next to the jeep, a tall, Amazonian female by his side. The woman had a hand on Kruger's arm, and Callan zeroed in on her face. Sweeping brows, strong features. He hadn't much use for redheads himself, but Kruger seemed happy to give her time. He watched them wrap up their conversation, then Kruger ducked into the jeep and pulled away. The woman gazed after him for a moment, then strode back towards the stables.

Callan lowered his binoculars. He stared across the

flatlands, gusts of wind cuffing him round the ears. His information from the runner in Kuruman was incomplete. He knew about Garvin Oliver and Kruger's yard, but he didn't know how many were involved. And now there was the Martinez girl. At first, she'd looked like a random witness, but if she had ties to the yard then her presence wasn't just a fluke.

Another good reason for eliminating her.

Callan flashed a glance at the horsebox. Then he lowered himself back inside the car and stepped out on to the road. With a quick look over his shoulder, he opened the door at the tapered end of the trailer and climbed inside.

The horsebox smelled of hay and silage, but was more spacious than it looked from the outside. It was fitted with two side-by-side stalls, separated by a padded partition. Callan ducked under the horizontal bar at the jeep-end of the trailer and headed for the mound of blankets on the floor. He hunkered down, scooping the pile aside. Underneath was a padlocked, steel trunk. He unlocked it with a key secured to his belt and slowly lifted the lid.

The hardware inside looked dull and grey in the shadows, but to Callan it gleamed like silver. One by one, he lifted the weapons out, smoothing a hand along their sleek lines.

The first was an M16A2 assault rifle, the weapon of choice for most mercs. He squeezed the grip in his right hand, then clasped the forestock in his left. The weapon was light, favouring mobility over heavy hitting. He brought the butt to his shoulder, tilted his head and fixed his sight-line down the barrel. Then he snapped the rifle out of the firing position and placed it on the floor.

Next in the trunk was the M203 grenade launcher. Callan's chest swelled at the sight of it. Combine that with the M16 and you had some serious firepower. Then came his disassembled Barrett M82A1, a monster sniper rifle for long-distance kills. The weapons clattered as he set them aside. Submachine guns, ammunition, fragmentation grenades. Finally, he lifted out his good old Browning handgun. He weighed the pistol in his hand. At ranges less than fifty metres, it'd stop a man in his tracks.

He spread the hardware out on the floor. He knew he'd never use most of it, apart from the Browning, which he'd already fired several times. This job demanded concealed, precision kills, not large-scale attacks out in the open. But getting hold of weapons was never diffi-cult, especially in Ireland. And there was something comforting about stockpiling an arsenal. It was like being back with his unit.

He checked the trunk. At the bottom lay his Commando dagger. He picked it up, turning it over in his hands. There was something spine-chilling about its leather sheath and long, pointed blade. It was designed to penetrate the neck and chest, and was the twin of the one he kept strapped under his shirt. For hand-to-hand combat, there was no better killing knife.

Callan slipped it out of its leather sheath. Daylight

flashed off the metal and suddenly Callan was sweating. His heart pummelled his chest, his whole body trembled. He felt clammy, and his bowels churned. The trailer walls receded, leaving him stranded in dark, dank heat. He backed in against the trunk. Then he hugged his knees and began to rock, moaning softly. White-hot pain exploded in his skull. A memory lit up his brain like sheet lightning. A flash of sun, another knife. Hair-raising screams, spurting blood. *Your turn next.* Callan's chest tightened. He was choking, suffocating. He felt like a dead man.

Then slowly, the pain in his head dulled and the sweat evaporated from his skin, leaving him chilled. He sank sideways on to the floor, shivering.

You're all burned out, I can't use you any more.

Callan clenched his fingers around the Commando dagger. Then he hauled himself to his feet, and staggered out the door. The wind slapped against his face, drying the tears he hadn't remembered crying.

Unstable, unreliable.

He straightened his shoulders, lifted his chin. He was a soldier, a member of the elite Special Forces. His fingers tightened around the knife. Tonight he'd infiltrate the yard, eliminating whoever got in his way.

No one was going to tell him he was finished.

22

Harry made the journey back to Dublin and spent the afternoon packing up some fresh clothes and getting her car window fixed. Then she drove north-west across the city till she reached the entrance to Phoenix Park. The sooner she got her laptop back the better.

She cruised along the tree-lined avenues. The park covered almost two thousand acres and was home to the national police headquarters, as well as the President, Dublin Zoo and a herd of fallow deer. Today, all she saw were dog-walkers in the rain.

Following the signs, she wound up outside a long, walled-off building. The place looked like a military barracks; all grey Victorian stone and parade-ground quadrangles. A barrier blocked her entry through the gates, so she parked by the kerb and made her way to the entrance on foot.

She pushed inside and stated her business to the officer at the desk. While he busied himself on the phone, she glanced around. The interior of the building looked as chilly as the outside.

'You didn't waste much time.'

Harry spun round. Hunter was standing by the desk, his thumbs hooked into his pockets. He looked like a gunslinger ready for the draw. Then he swung away, motioning for her to follow.

Dammit, she hadn't expected to run into him. Returning her laptop was a red-tape job. Why was he concerning himself with it?

She trotted after him down a long corridor, wondering if he'd found her name on Garvin's files. He'd find it eventually, but timing was everything. She'd rather he got the chance to turn up a few more suspects first.

Hunter opened the door to an office on the left and stood back to let her in. She passed through, aware of his eyes following her. He gestured for her to sit by the desk, then scooted round the other side as though anxious to put physical barriers between them. He pushed a ziplocked evidence bag towards her. Her laptop. Then he held out a receipt and a pen.

'Just sign at the end.'

So far, he'd managed to avoid her gaze but when she bent her head to sign the form she felt his eyes rake over her. Heat crept into her cheeks. Hunter cleared his throat.

'We spoke to the bus driver.'

Harry jerked her head up. 'And?'

'He remembers you. But he didn't see anyone else.'

'What about the tourists?'

'We're trying to round them up, but so far no sightings of a man in the alleyway.'

Harry slumped back in her chair. So did Hunter, and she watched him massage the corners of his eyes. His tie was crooked and his short hair stood up in peaks at the crown. Finally, he looked up and made eye contact.

'We didn't find any signs of a gun being fired, either.'

Harry flung down the pen. 'Jesus. The man was there. He's not a ghost, he must've left some kind of trace.'

'We're still looking.'

'What about the woman in Gardenia Flats?'

Hunter lifted a wry eyebrow and shook his head. 'I still have an officer knocking on doors, but I can't spare him out there much longer.' He sighed and dragged a hand across his face. He still hadn't shaved, and the stubble was picking up matching grey glints in his hair. 'Isn't there anything else you can remember that might help?'

Harry closed her eyes for a moment, casting herself back into the cobbled alleyway. Shadows in the dark. The scrape of footsteps. She shook her head.

'I've told you everything I saw.'

Hunter drummed his fingers on the desk, studying her face. 'We've located the step-daughter.'

Harry straightened up in her chair. 'Eve?'

'She's on her way to Cape Town.'

'But she still could've been in Garvin's house yesterday morning, right?'

Hunter paused. 'It's possible.'

'It's more than just possible, she was there.' Harry leaned forwards, hands clasped on the desk in front of her. 'She was the one who hired me to open the safe.'

'You don't know that.'

'It had to be her. I'm telling you the truth.' Harry fixed her eyes on his. 'And what's more, I think you know it.'

Hunter paused. 'So I should follow my instincts, right?'

'Right.'

'Wrong.' His eyes narrowed. 'Let me tell you something. Last time I listened to my instincts, it nearly cost me my job.'

Harry blinked. Hunter was still talking.

'I trusted a witness on a fraud case. Went soft on her because my instincts said she was telling the truth. Turned out I was wrong.' He leaned in closer, eyes blazing. 'You know what that makes me? Your worst nightmare.'

Harry sat back. 'I don't understand.'

'Don't you? My ass is on the line here, has been for some time. I don't need another disciplinary inquiry on my record.' His jaw muscles bunched. 'So now I play hardball. I stick with the evidence, no matter what my instincts tell me. And right now, all the evidence says you're involved.'

He glared at her, his eyes cold. Harry tried to return his stare, but for once she didn't have a snappy comeback. She got to her feet, slid her laptop off the desk and headed for the door.

Just what she needed: another copper with an axe to grind.

23

'It sounds risky to me.'

Harry rolled her eyes at Imogen's tone over the loud-speaker. 'There's nothing risky about it. I won't even be on the premises. I'll be sitting in my car, half a mile down the road.'

Harry dipped her headlights in deference to an oncoming truck. The road ahead was blacker than an oil slick, and had about as much grip. She slashed through a puddle, dousing the passenger window.

'I probably won't even find anything.' She flipped her wipers on full. 'But I'd like to be sure.'

'Why don't you just let the police handle it? They can't seriously think you're involved.'

Harry made a face and recalled her meeting with Hunter. She'd told Imogen everything, from witnessing Garvin's murder, to accessing his files and tracking down

Eve. What she hadn't told her, and probably never would, was the full story behind her exploits in the Bahamas: how she'd palmed a fortune from under the noses of the fraud squad, and how the upshot was a detective ready to put her in the frame for anything.

Harry sighed. 'Look, all I'm going to do is peek at Kruger's files and then drive off.'

Imogen paused. 'I suppose I should be glad you're willing to take a few risks again.'

Harry frowned. 'What do you mean?'

'I dunno. It just seems like . . . Well, like you've been hiding for a while.'

Harry blinked. Another car hissed past her in the rain. Had she been hiding? She recalled how she'd flown her city apartment. She'd bolted from the nightmares, groping for a fresh start, but had somehow ended up in an isolated stone cottage. And the nightmares had followed her like a stalker.

'Harry, you still there?'

Harry cleared her throat. 'Don't worry about me, I'll be fine. Anyway, you're the one with the emotional issues, remember? What about you and Shane?'

Imogen groaned. If she noticed the switch in topic, she didn't mention it. 'I called off the engagement.'

'Really? You okay about that?'

'I'm fine, we both are. In fact, I think he's quite relieved. But I'm kind of pissed off at being out of pocket for the ring.'

'You bought it yourself?'

'We split the cost. Considering the whole thing was an experiment, I thought it was only fair.'

Harry raised her eyebrows. The businesslike approach was highly commendable, but hard to reconcile with Harry's own notion of marriage. Call her old-fashioned, but where was the romance?

'Anyway, I went back to the jeweller's,' Imogen was saying. 'You know, to see if we could get some kind of refund. He offered me less than a third of what we'd paid for it. Can you believe that? I mean, the thing was hardly used.'

'Maybe you should hang on to it. For the next experiment.'

'You know what they're selling now? Right-hand rings.'

'What?'

'Yep. For single women. Diamonds you buy as a present to yourself. To assert your independence and all that. He tried to sell me one.' Imogen parodied the deep tones of a movie trailer voice-over. 'Your left hand says, "I do," your right hand says, "I can."'

'Oh, give me a break.'

'Exactly.'

'How the hell can a ring be right-handed?'

'Something to do with the different webbing between your fingers.'

Harry glanced at her hands, splaying them out on the wheel. 'Jesus.'

'Yeah.'

They were silent for a moment. Then Imogen said,

'Call me when you're done, okay? You know, just so I know nothing happened.'

Sometimes her friend fussed like a mother waiting up until her teenager got home. Harry shifted in her seat. Come to think of it, her own mother had never actually done that. She smiled into the phone.

'I'll call you tomorrow, how about that?'

Imogen fretted some more, but finally wrapped up the call. Harry disconnected and peered through the windscreen. Her headlights pooled on to the road ahead, measuring it out fifty yards at a time. Beyond that, everything was black.

She'd driven back to the Curragh after her meeting with Hunter, trying to shove the detective out of her mind. Stupid to think he might have believed her. She wondered about his past transgression, and the woman he'd trusted so rashly. He'd said it was a fraud case. Had he been working it with Lynne? If so, then no wonder Lynne gave him such a hard time. Hunter's instincts were clearly as unreliable as hers.

Harry eased her foot off the accelerator. By her calculations, she was almost there. Slowly, she cruised past Kruger's yard, noting the glow of windows and the moonlit sheen on the cars. Rob Devlin's Mercedes was still there.

She drove on for another half a mile, putting a safe distance between herself and the yard until the lights had disappeared. Then she pulled up in a lay-by under the tangled branches of a tree and switched off the ignition.

Her engine ticked into the silence. The road on either side of her was empty.

Something cold tickled Harry's spine. There was no reason to think anyone knew she was here, but she triggered the central locking just in case. Then she shook off her misgivings and twisted around to inspect the back seat of her car. The upholstery was invisible under an assortment of hardware: cables, chargers, connectors, screwdrivers. She fished through the jumble, stretching between the front seats, until finally she found what she was looking for: her omni-directional antenna.

She flopped back in her seat to examine it. It looked like a mini radio aerial, no bigger than a ballpoint pen. It was mounted on to a magnetic base, and in spite of its rough treatment in the back of her car the device seemed to be intact.

Harry opened the window and snapped the base on to the roof of the car. Then she plugged the trailing cable into her laptop and rattled her fingers over the keyboard.

The stubby antenna in Kruger's office told Harry his network was wireless. That was good news. The helpful thing about wireless networks was that they broadcast transmissions through the air. No cables, no hard-wired connectivity. And to a hacker, that meant no physical access required. The open airwaves were crackling with data, and with the right antenna you could eavesdrop from over a mile away.

Harry launched her scanner tool and waited for it to sniff out local networks. Not surprisingly, there was only one within range. With the sparse population out here, Harry figured it had to be Kruger's.

Data packets pulsed across her screen as the scanner snagged them off the air. She checked her watch. Eavesdropping was one thing, but making sense of the data was another. Kruger's packets were all encrypted, and cracking the encryption key was going to take time.

She shifted in her seat, trying to get comfortable. Maybe she could take a few shortcuts. An engine grumbled somewhere ahead and she jerked upright, squinting through the windscreen. The sound of distant cars washed to and fro like a tide, but ahead of her was just a dark void.

She turned back to her screen. The key used to encipher Kruger's data was a cryptographic mangling of two core things: the name of his network, and the secret passphrase that allowed him to plug into it. Once Harry had those two pieces of information, she could unscramble his transmissions and tiptoe through his files.

Harry picked through the control packets, searching for the plaintext network ID. Normally, it wasn't hard to find. Wireless networks were like party extroverts: every tenth of a second, they'd flounce into the air, announcing, 'Hi, my name's Netgear, anyone want to connect?' But Kruger's network was different. It was operating in cloaked mode, and the network ID was censored.

Harry frowned at the screen. The best way to nail the

information she wanted was to catch someone trying to connect. According to her scanner, one device was already online, and she was willing to bet it was Kruger's laptop. If she stuck around long enough, maybe someone else might come along.

But on the other hand, why wait?

She worked the keyboard and injected Kruger's laptop with an instruction to disconnect. Obediently, it bounced off, hoodwinked by the bogus command. Then it ricocheted back, requesting permission to rejoin. Harry siphoned off the data packets, and there in plaintext was the network name, LINKSYS.

Harry nabbed the rest of the wireless transmissions, capturing the complicated four-way handshake that played out between the network and Kruger's laptop. It was a fancy authentication dance, each challenging the other to verify its identity by encrypting random data, thereby proving they both had the same key.

But sometimes a thing can just be too complicated. The handshake gave away too many clues, and now Harry was almost there. All she needed was the passphrase.

Lights flashed somewhere to her left. Harry squinted across the field. Two beams bounced up and down, like headlights on a jeep negotiating bumpy terrain. Then suddenly they disappeared.

Goosebumps prickled Harry's skin. Was someone out there watching her? Her eyes raked the darkness, her senses on high alert. There was no sign of movement.

She tried to shake the jitters off. It was probably just

a local landowner patrolling his territory. She hesitated, then turned back to her laptop.

Flexing her fingers, she targeted the passphrase with an extended dictionary attack. Word by word, the program would step through the dictionary, hunting for a passphrase that, together with the network ID, constructed the right key. The handshake had already divulged before-and-after samples of encrypted text. If she found a key that worked on those, she was in.

Without a powerful computer to crunch through the possibilities, it could take weeks. But she was betting that Kruger's passphrase was an easily remembered word. No matter how often you warned people about weak passwords, they seldom wanted to memorize anything complicated.

An engine growled somewhere off to her side, and Harry swivelled in her seat. A tractor or a jeep revved across the field, two bright orbs flashing in the dark. Something jumped in Harry's gut. Landowner or not, it was time to move.

She shoved her laptop on to the passenger seat and gunned the car on to the road. Then she sped away from the lay-by, away from Kruger's yard, adrenaline-spiked blood roaring in her ears. She fixed her eyes to the mirror. Whoever it was, he didn't seem to be following her. She could see the red glow of rear-end lights shrinking to pinpricks as the vehicle disappeared across the field.

Harry breathed deeply, her pulse beating hard. Jesus, was she always going to be this jumpy? She scanned the verge for another lay-by. The sooner she finished and got out of here, the better.

She glanced at her laptop and frowned. The dictionary attack was still toiling away, but the wireless signal had vanished. Was she out of range? She checked her mirror, reluctant to turn back, but knew she had no choice.

She wheeled the car round, cruising back the way she'd come, waiting for the signal to kick back in. She checked the screen. Nothing. She passed the lay-by she'd left moments before. Still nothing.

Harry squinted. That wasn't right. It was as though she had no antenna.

Shit.

She slammed on the brakes, skidding to a halt. Then she buzzed down her window and groped around on the roof. Dammit. The antenna was gone. It must have snagged in the branches of the overhanging tree when she'd taken off. She hauled up the cable that trailed out the window. The magnetic base had smashed, the connector shattered. Harry groaned. Even if she found the antenna, she couldn't hook it back up.

She peered into the dark. Maybe if she just moved a little closer to the yard, she could pick up the signal without the boosting aid of an antenna. She eased the car back into gear and cruised further down the road, the banging in her chest sending vibrations down her arms. But by the time she reached the gates, she still hadn't stumbled across a signal.

She coasted to a halt, staring at the deserted stables. Her throat felt dry. With trembling hands, she picked up her laptop and eased the car door open.

She had no choice. She had to sneak inside the yard.

24

Harry hunkered down by the yard entrance and shivered. Prying on someone's network over the airwaves was one thing, but snooping around their property in the dark was another.

Rain misted down on her like wet cobwebs, and somewhere a shutter banged in the wind. She glanced back at her safe, warm car and wondered what the hell she was doing. Then she scrooched closer to the gate, hugging her laptop to her chest.

Ahead of her was Kruger's house, the buttery glow of a ground-floor window the only visible light. The jeep and Mercedes stood side by side, the nose of Rob's car jammed tight against the house as if he'd barely managed to hit the brakes in time. To the right was the main yard, and behind that a wide, barn-like structure that Harry guessed housed the stables.

She peeked at her laptop. Still no wireless signal. She lowered the lid to hide the glowing screen, then peered across the yard. Her best chance was to position herself in line with Kruger's office to maximize the signal from his antenna.

She screwed up her face, trying to recall the layout of the house. Navigational puzzles were never her strong point, but she remembered the office window overlooking the yard. She stared across the open quadrangle. Camping out there would be too exposed. The stable building was probably her best shot.

Harry slipped through the gate and skirted along by the wall, hunching into the shadows. Then she scuttled across to the jeep, taking cover behind it. She hadn't seen any security cameras, but that didn't mean there weren't any. At this stage, she'd have to take her chances.

Hooves smacked against brick in the distance, and a long whinny quivered through the dark. Harry crept past the cars and alongside the house, ducking under the brightly lit window. Then she hesitated. Really, she should sneak on by, but it couldn't hurt to take a peek. She inched her head above the windowsill.

Kruger was leaning against an oversized mantelpiece, his dark brows shielding his eyes. Cassie Bergin stood beside him, warming her hands by the fire. Both were tall and striking, and together they looked well matched. It would've been a cosy scene, if it wasn't for the argument they were having.

Harry amended that. Cassie was arguing; Kruger was

207

tuning her out. The vet leaned towards him, her face strained as she talked. He wouldn't meet her eyes. Even in pantomime, Harry could tell that Cassie wasn't getting anywhere. Then Kruger turned away, moving out of Harry's range, and Cassie seemed to run out of steam. Her shoulders sagged, and her face looked slightly crumpled. Harry raised her eyebrows. She thought of Kruger's abruptness, his edgy silences, and wondered what made Cassie care.

She ducked her head and inched past the window. Then again, what the hell did she know about relationships? The last man she'd thought about getting involved with had ended up trying to kill her. By anyone's standards, that had to amount to a staggering lack of judgement.

A snarl tore at the air behind her. Harry froze. Kruger's Alsatians. She swallowed. Her legs felt paralysed. She couldn't move, couldn't even turn her head. A low growl bubbled in the dog's throat. Harry hunched her shoulders, bracing herself. There was a scrabbling sound, something ticked against glass. Harry shot a glance at the window behind her and let out the breath she'd been holding. For now, the dogs were still inside with Kruger.

Electricity sparked into her limbs. She raced across the yard, heading for the barn-like stables. Her ears strained for frenzied barking, for footsteps and yells. She stumbled inside the barn and ducked back against the wall, clutching her laptop. She listened. Apart from the sounds of her own hammering chest, there was nothing.

Harry closed her eyes and sank to the ground. Jesus.

208

The sooner she got out of here, the better. She breathed deeply, her nostrils filling with the musty scent of manure. Then she opened her eyes and took in her surroundings.

The stables were bigger than an aircraft hangar. Dozens of stalls lined either side of a wide, concrete corridor. Skylights beamed a row of pale oblongs on to the floor, like a moonlit zebra crossing. Some of the horses were still awake, their heads poking out over their stalls. The nearest one threw her a curious look and snickered.

Harry darted a glance outside. She had a sideways view of Kruger's house and, by her calculations, one of those windows had to be his office. She eased open the lid of her laptop. The dictionary attack was still crunching away. And at the bottom of the screen was a pulsing wireless icon. The signal was back.

Harry slumped against the wall and shivered. Her clothes were damp and her limbs felt stiff, but she settled in to wait. As soon as she had the passphrase, she'd decode Kruger's data, sniff through his files, and then get the hell away.

Metal shrieked against cement outside, as though someone had collided with a wheelbarrow. Harry jerked to her feet. Footsteps scuffed in the dark. Her eyes darted left and right. There was nowhere to go. She scrambled towards the stalls, peering in over the half-doors. Muscled horseflesh lurked in the shadows. She kept going till she found an empty stall, then slid the bolt open and locked herself inside. She crouched against the wall, sweat drenching her back.

Someone whistled gently in the dark. Footsteps shuffled closer towards her, then stopped.

'Hey there, Billy-Boy.'

Harry's eyes widened. It was Rob Devlin. A bolt clanked, a stall door rattled. Shoes whispered through loose hay. Harry stiffened. He was in the neighbouring stall.

'My old pal.'

Harry hunched lower, inhaling the sawdusty smell of the ground. Next door, Billy-Boy whinnied.

'Had some good times, haven't we, old fella?'

Rob's tongue sounded thick in his mouth, and Harry wondered how much he'd had to drink.

'Champion jockey, champion racehorse.' A hand smacked against horseflesh. 'Travelled the world, haven't we, Billy-Boy? Trophies, TV interviews. Not bad for a skinny kid from Laytown.'

Billy-Boy whiffled through his nose, and Rob laughed softly.

'Yeah, I know, not skinny enough. No food again today. 'Nother five pounds to lose for tomorrow.'

Billy-Boy's shoes clicked against the concrete. When Rob spoke again, his voice was quieter.

'Alcohol's okay though, isn't it? Better than food any day. Gets us through, hey, boy?'

Rob was silent for a moment, and Harry bit her lip. She pictured the jockey's wiry frame, recalled his reckless vitality, and wondered how long he could collude with alcohol and still remain a champion.

Rob crooned at his horse some more, murmuring affectionate, who's-a-good-boy noises that she thought only dog-lovers did. Then suddenly his voice changed.

'Don't think I can take this much longer, Billy-Boy.' His words were muffled, as though he'd buried his face in the horse's neck. 'Shrinking myself down, day after day.'

Rob took a long, shuddery breath and with a shock, Harry realized he was crying.

'I'm just so bloody tired,' he whispered.

Harry dropped her gaze to the ground. She shouldn't be here, listening to this. It was a private confession between man and horse. After a few minutes, Rob cleared his throat and seemed to pull himself together. He gave Billy-Boy a hearty pat.

''Nuff of that, hey, boy? We'll be okay. We can do it.'

He patted the horse some more, then left the stables. When he was gone, Harry exhaled a long breath. She tried to reconcile Rob's broken spirit with the daredevil rider for whom speed had seemed to be everything. She failed.

She shook her head, then checked her laptop. The dictionary attack had finally finished, and a message flashed across the screen:

'Passphrase found: BILLY-BOY.'

Harry rolled her eyes. What was it about these men and their horses?

All of a sudden, her plan to tap into Kruger's network seemed overly dramatic. What did she hope to find? Secret files that would prove he was a diamond smuggler? Right now, the notion seemed unlikely. But she'd come this far; she may as well finish the job.

She checked the wireless network icon. The signal had weakened, deflected by the stable structure. She eased open the stall door, checked left and right, then crept out towards the entrance. Settling herself in line of sight with Kruger's office, she went to work on her keyboard.

Now that she had the passphrase, she could decode Kruger's transmissions and read them in the clear. Not only that, she could join the network and interfere with his data.

In a few deft strokes, she'd hopped on to the network. Easy as catching a bus. Then she packaged up her first weapon and fired it at Kruger's laptop. It was a keylogger, a covert piece of spyware that would slip into Kruger's hard drive and record every keystroke he made. What's more, it would email the information to Harry. Soon, she'd have an audit trail of every word he typed.

Footsteps scrunched somewhere behind her, and she froze. She caught her breath, turned her head. Too late. Pain torpedoed through her skull. The ground filled her vision, then slammed up into her face.

25

Harry opened her eyes. Pain pulsed through her head and churned down into her stomach. Her brain reeled, and she snapped her eyes shut again.

Straw prickled her cheeks. Her sinuses filled with the dense odour of horse, and beside her, something rustled in the straw. She squinted through half-closed eyes. She was lying face down on the ground somewhere, the darkness thicker than a blanket.

She clenched her teeth, then eased herself up on all fours. The world tilted, and for a moment she thought she'd throw up. She clambered to her feet, dizziness pitching her against a wall. She clung to it, sweating.

A black shape stomped towards her, hot breath fanning her face. The sheen of sweat cut through the blackness, outlining the horse's looming, muscular physique.

His eyes were liquid in the darkness.

Harry pressed herself closer against the wall. 'Easy, boy.'

The horse snorted and whipped away, swinging round and round the stall. There was very little room, and with every circuit his powerful haunches thundered inches from her face.

Sweat drizzled down her back. Who the hell had dumped her in here? Had Rob come back and hit her from behind? Maybe it was Kruger and his bad-tempered dogs. She shook her head, trying to clear the log-jam in her brain.

The horse lurched to a halt and pawed the ground in front of her. The air was thick with his earthy smell. He'd worked up quite a sweat, his coat hairs spiking up in damp peaks. Harry dropped her gaze, avoiding eye-to-eye contact in case it signalled aggression. That was how it worked with dogs, wasn't it? She didn't know if the same applied to horses, but it was the only circus trick she had up her sleeve.

The animal flared his nostrils at her, then swerved away, resuming his manic circling of the stall.

Harry's eyes raked her small prison cell. By now, she'd adjusted to the gloom, and could make out the door on the other side of the stall. It was shut tight, probably bolted from the outside. She scanned the walls and ceiling. Unlike other stalls that opened up to the rafters, this one was fully enclosed. The door was the only way out.

Harry held her breath and inched towards it. She kept

her movements fluid so as not to startle the horse. For now, he seemed preoccupied with his frenzied loops around the stall. She inched some more, thinking about Garvin's diamonds and how they tied in with Kruger.

Her guess was that a syndicate of illicit diamond traders was operating out of the yard. Garvin appeared to be the front man, importing the smuggled stones and arranging for their distribution. The yard's regular shipments of South African bloodstock probably acted as a cover for secreting stones out of the country.

She thought about TJ: horse owner and Dan Kruger's business partner. He'd been shot, just like Garvin. To Harry, that was sufficient proof of his involvement, although she was sketchy about his role. Then she recalled her conversation with Rob.

Dan's the horse expert, but TJ's the money man.

Maybe TJ bankrolled the syndicate's operation, and then took a cut of the profits. But why had he been killed? Or Garvin, for that matter?

As for Eve, Harry was inclined to think she was a lone operative. For starters, she'd stolen Garvin's diamonds. That was hardly the action of a trusted partner-in-crime. Or step-daughter, for that matter. But she could be wrong. Eve was in Cape Town now, preparing to ship another racehorse home. And presumably, along with it, another consignment of stones.

The question was, who else in the yard was involved?

The horse pricked his ears, sensing her movement. Harry froze. The big creature wheeled round, fishtailing towards her like a giant serpent. He tossed his head, and his rump cannoned into the wall.

What the hell was spooking this animal?

'It's okay, easy buddy.' She tried to imitate Rob's crooning tones, but under the circumstances it was hard to pull off.

Suddenly, the horse squealed. He reared up on his hind legs, soaring above her like a black spire. His forelegs slashed the air. Hooves swished near Harry's face and she gasped. His legs crashed to the ground, and he rolled his eyes, the whites gleaming in a half-crazed stare. Harry's insides turned cold. Mostly, she couldn't tell one horse from another, but this monster was unmistakable. It was Rottweiler.

He hates being shut up in the dark.

Harry remembered what Vinnie had said, and her breathing ramped up. She had to get out of here. She shot a glance to her right. The door was only a few feet away.

Rottweiler's ears lay flat against his head and his eyes still rolled in their sockets. Harry's gut clenched. She thought about calling for help, but right now, making noise seemed like a foolhardy move. She licked her lips and tried again.

'You don't like me being here, do you?' She wasn't happy with the way her voice cracked. 'That's okay, I don't like it either. I'll just—'

The horse drew back his lips and unleashed a hair-raising scream. Harry hunched her shoulders, cowering against the wall. The animal bared his teeth. His nostrils looked huge, like potholes in the dark. Harry willed herself to stay still. Then he whirled around, clenched his muscles and bucked. Legs sprang out like missiles and clipped her on the shoulder. Harry cried out, cradling her left arm. The horse lurched away and thrashed against the walls, his huge chest heaving.

Harry sank back against the wall, breathless. She tried to straighten up, but the pain in her shoulder was agonizing. She watched the big creature flailing around the stall. Foam bubbled at the corners of his mouth, and bloodspats speckled his shoulders. It occurred to Harry that he was as scared as she was, but knowing it didn't really help.

She edged the last few feet towards the door, trying not to snag the horse's attention. Then she turned and groped with her good hand in the dark, scrabbling over the wood for hinges, gaps, anything that would give her purchase. But there was nothing. The door was smooth, and bolted tight from the outside.

Rottweiler started up a shrill whinny, and Harry spun round. His back was towards her, his neck outstretched to the ceiling. She strained to listen for sounds from outside. With all this disturbance, surely somebody would come?

But all she could hear was the horse's tortured scream.

She peered through the shadows, scouring the stall for weapons, or for tools that might break down the door. Her shoulders sagged. Nothing but woodshavings and straw.

Rottweiler's rump backed in towards her, his muscles bunching. She stared at the powerful haunches, her brain racing. Maybe the horse was the only weapon she had.

Bracing herself, she held her ground by the door and fastened her eyes on Rottweiler's backside. The timing was critical. If she got it wrong, the horse would probably kill her.

She stared unblinking at his hindquarters, waiting for a sign. He backed up some more. Then he curved his body. Dipped his head. His muscles bulged.

Now!

Harry dived to the left, pitching on to the straw. In the same instant, Rottweiler whipped out his hind legs, lashing out a deadly kick into the space where she had been. His hooves smashed against the door, splintering one of the planks. Then he swung away, pounding his shoulders against the walls, looking dizzy and disoriented.

Hot pain screamed in Harry's shoulder. She winced, and shot a glance at the door. The splinter was good, but it wasn't enough. Her throat felt dry. Rottweiler blundered about the stall, his haunches still towards her. Stumbling to her feet, she limped back to the door. Then she stood in front of it like a bullfighter, and waited for the horse.

It didn't take him long. He ripped into a bucking frenzy in the middle of the stall, backing up closer to her with each lethal kick. She pinned her gaze to the slashing

218

hooves. When she was close enough to see the nails on his shoes, she dived.

She wasn't quick enough. A hoof cracked against her bad arm, slicing pain into her bone. She screamed, and slammed down on to the straw. She lay there, unable to move. If he decided it was time to trample her to death, she wouldn't have the strength to stop him.

Wood cracked, splinters shot into the air. Harry peeked at the horse. He bucked and squealed by the door, crashing his hooves into it. Another section snapped. With a final kick, the horse shattered the central plank, then wheeled in furious circles around the stall.

Harry tried to sit up. Pain shot down her arm, and she sucked in air through her teeth. She clutched her shoulder, scrambled to her feet. She dragged herself to the door and slipped her good hand through the fractured wood. She reached around and shot the bolts back.

She fell against the door, swinging it open and spinning out of Rottweiler's way. He thundered past her and clattered out of the stables. Harry leaned against the open door, her chest heaving. Then she staggered out, still clutching her shoulder, and followed the horse into the yard.

Kruger's house was in darkness, the place deserted. The jeep and the Mercedes were gone. Her heart sank at the desolate surroundings. No wonder no one had come; there was no one around to hear.

She made her way, half running, half jogging, to her

car. She clambered in, locked the doors, and rested her forehead on the wheel. As the last of the adrenaline shuddered out of her body, she gave up the struggle and wept.

26

The door crashed open and Mani flinched, his limbs rigid under the blanket. For a split-second there was silence. Then a battery of guns drilled like jackhammers into the darkness.

The room filled with screams. Mani flattened himself against his bunk. Bullets ripped into the ceiling, tore up the floorboards. Cement crumbs sputtered down on to his head.

'*Opstaan!*'

The guards barged through the room, yelling and blasting shots into the air. The noise was deafening.

'*Uit met julle! Val in!*' Outside! Line up!

Mani's heartbeat drummed. They'd found Okker.

'Mani, what is it?' Takata's voice quivered. A guard lunged at the old man and dragged him on to the floor.

'*Opstaan!*' Get up!

The guard rattled bullets into the floor, shattering the wood. Mani ducked against the splinters. When the guard rounded on the men behind him, Mani sprang off his bunk and bent over Takata. He wasn't hit. Gently, he put an arm around the old man's bony shoulders and lifted him to his feet.

'What is happening?' Takata's scrawny fingers clutched at Mani's shirt.

Mani didn't answer. All around him, wild-eyed men scrambled towards the door. He guided Takata in behind them, hunching against the bursts of submachine-gun fire. The old man stumbled, sinking to the ground. Skinny arms reached out from behind and helped to lift him up. A voice breathed in Mani's ear.

'What is it? Do you know?'

He turned to look at the gaunt miner supporting Takata's arm. Mani didn't know his name, but had heard he was a schoolteacher from the Congo. He'd left his home when the war there had destroyed everything.

Mani looked away. 'I don't know anything.'

He shoved his way outside, guiding Takata, leaving the schoolteacher behind. The pre-dawn air was cool, the sky still dark. He lined up against the wall with the other men, keeping Takata close. Facing them stood six guards, guns braced against their shoulders, eyes lowered to their viewfinders. Mani's bowels contracted. An execution squad.

The rest of the men spilled out of the dormitory, jostling in front of him. Mani shrank back against the

222

wall. The man beside him blessed himself with a trembling hand. Then the tallest of the guards stepped forward. Janvier, the Belgian mercenary and Okker's second-in-command.

'Filthy, murdering pigs!' He spat on the ground. 'You think you can get away with this?'

His face was brick red and greasy with sweat. His fingers flexed around the muzzle of his gun.

'Bastards!'

Torchlight flickered somewhere to Mani's left. Voices grunted, and something scuffed along the dirt. Tremors shook Mani's limbs. They were trying to move Okker's body. He shot a glance at Takata, who was staring at the light, eyes wide in skeletal sockets. The old man knew that was where he hid the stones.

Janvier prowled up and down the line of men, oily sweat sliding down his face.

'Somebody killed Commander Okker.' He ran his tongue over his lips. 'That means I'm in charge now.'

A murmur rolled through the group of miners. Mani felt Takata's hand on his arm, but he kept his gaze fixed straight ahead.

'I want to know who did it.' Janvier cocked his gun with a snap. 'And you will tell me.'

Mani stiffened. His calf burned from the knife and ladle still strapped to his leg. Maybe he should have left them with the body, but he'd wanted to remove any signs of digging in case it prompted a search for the stones. If they found the knife on him now, he'd be shot.

Janvier swung his weapon back and forth, eyes darting along the line of men. 'You're nothing but a bunch of lazy bastards!'

Mani dug at the strapping with his foot, loosening it till it slipped to his ankle. Sweat trickled down his back. Janvier stepped closer, taking aim at the men in the front row. The guard's breathing was harsh, as though he'd been running.

'You think you can creep up on us, one by one, and just slit our throats in the dark?'

Up close, Mani could see that Janvier's hands were shaking. The guard swivelled left and right, training his weapon along the rows of men. Mani jiggled his leg, and the ladle and knife slid to the ground. He felt Takata's eyes on him. Then the old man shifted, leaning against him, his feet scuffing the dirt. Mani lowered his gaze. Takata had dragged the knife behind him.

'Tell me who did it!'

Janvier jerked his gun downwards and pumped bullets into the dirt. The men in front leapt backwards, yelling. Eventually, the clatter of gunfire stopped. Janvier's chest heaved, his uniform drenched in sweat. Then he grabbed one of the miners by the shirt and shoved him away from the rest. The man staggered backwards, his lanky frame quivering. Mani swallowed. It was the schoolteacher.

Janvier trained his gun on him. 'Who killed him?'

Mani stopped breathing. The schoolteacher shook his

head, his hands in the air. His sunken eyes were transfixed by Janvier's gun, his head still shaking long after the question had been answered.

Janvier snapped his fingers at the guard closest to him, the pale young soldier who'd taken Mani to the x-ray unit.

'Kill him,' Janvier said, without looking round.

Blood pounded in Mani's ears. He wanted to move, but he couldn't. The schoolteacher's head kept on shaking.

The young guard opened and closed his mouth. 'Sir?'

'For Christ's sake. It's not hard. Watch.'

Janvier adjusted the grip on his gun and fired. Bullets exploded into the schoolteacher's chest, pummelling his body. He jerked twice, then slumped to the ground.

Mani's head reeled. The man beside him began to moan and the acrid smell of urine filled the air. Mani stared at the blood spilling from the schoolteacher's chest, and felt himself sway. What had he done? He should have stepped forward, tried to stop it. It should have been him, lying dead in the dirt. But then there'd be no one to save Asha.

He clenched his fists. Noble courage or self-preservation? He hated himself for not knowing which it was that kept him quiet. Then he felt Takata's hand on his arm.

'Think of my Asha,' the old man whispered. 'Nothing else matters.'

Janvier kicked at the empty cartridges by his feet. Behind him, dawn leaked into the eastern sky. Suddenly, Janvier lunged, hauling two more men out from the front row. He jabbed them backwards with his gun till they stood beside the schoolteacher's body.

'This time, two of you will die. Next time it'll be three.' Veins pulsed like livid snakes on Janvier's temples. 'We'll keep going till I get an answer to my question.'

He clicked his fingers at the pale young guard, who hesitated, then raised his gun with trembling hands. Mani jerked forward, not sure of his intentions, but Takata seized his arm.

'No, Mani!' The strength in the old man's grip was astonishing. 'You will do this for me. You will owe me now.'

The young guard wiped his forehead on his sleeve. Mani looked at Takata. The old man's eyes blazed into his. The guard cocked his gun, took aim. Mani snapped his gaze to the two cowering men, standing by the school-teacher's body.

'Wait.'

Mani jerked his head back. Something icy trickled into his stomach. Takata was pushing through the rows of men. But Janvier ignored him, nodding at the young guard.

'Do it.'

'Wait.' Takata's voice was strong, his shoulders square. It must have cost him all his strength. 'I killed him. I killed the commander.'

Janvier flung the old man a scornful glance, then threw back his head and laughed. 'You? You're already half-dead, you couldn't kill anyone.'

226

Takata dropped something with a thud at Janvier's feet. Mani stared. It was his carving knife. Okker's blood was still caked around the handle.

Janvier's eyes widened. He stared at the knife, then raised his eyes to Takata. The veins on his forehead bulged. Then he levelled his gun at the old man's chest and blasted him with gunfire. Takata's body whipped backwards into the air, then crumpled to the ground with a sickening crack. Janvier swivelled back to the other two men and rattled bullets into their heads.

Mani froze. All around him, the men yelled and scrambled against the wall. Mani's eyes were transfixed by Takata's broken form.

You will owe me now.

A hooter shrieked through the compound, calling the miners to the early morning shift.

'Round them up, get them down the mine!' Janvier hawked and spat on the ground. 'Now you know who's in charge around here.'

The guards stampeded through the men, using the butts of their guns to line them up. Sweat flashed through Mani's body. He fought the urge to run to Takata. He had to get out. He had to follow Okker's corpse, get the stones to Kuruman where the runner called Chandra was waiting for him. He shoved through the rabble of men, then came face to face with Janvier.

'Get back in line!'

Janvier's eyes bulged and his face was crimson. Behind

227

him, the young guard looked pale and ill. Mani swallowed.

'But my contract, today it is up. Today I go home.'

Janvier smiled, showing nicotine-stained teeth. 'Your contract has just been extended.'

27

Harry pulled the tall stack of cards towards her. Six decks, three hundred and twelve cards.

Lifting from the top, she split them into six individual packs and arranged them, horseshoe-shaped, on the table in front of her. Her father sat opposite, his eyes locked on the cards.

He'd called her hotel room earlier that morning. There was someone he wanted her to meet, he'd said, someone with information. But he'd refused to elaborate, and so far they'd just practised shuffle-tracking.

She grabbed two of the small packs. Her shoulder crunched with every move and she tried not to wince. She'd spent several hours in A&E the night before, where it turned out Rottweiler's kicks had dislocated her shoulder. With little fuss and no warning, the medics had manhandled it back into its socket. Harry flinched at the memory. It was one of those occasions where the cure was worse than the disease. They'd offered her a sling but Harry had declined, not wanting the immobility. She'd settled for painkillers and an assurance that the discomfort would ease in a couple of weeks.

She flexed the two packs, one in each hand, then spliced them together with a snap. She repeated the riffle, then switched the top and bottom halves of the pile and set it in the centre of the table. She reached for the next two packs. Her father never took his eyes off the cards.

He'd been shuffle-tracking for as long as she could remember, and had taught her how to do it when she was ten. The objective was to track a valuable clump of cards as it flickered through a dealer's shuffle. As a card-counting strategy, it was quite advanced and few people had the skills to pull it off.

Harry shuffled the final two packs and set them on top of the restacked pile in front of her. Then she tipped the cards over on their side and presented them to her father to cut.

Somewhere in the pack was a slug of aces. Harry had grouped them together before the shuffle, blackening their edges with a marker along one side. By now, the shuffle had diluted them with other cards, but not enough to eliminate a rich cluster still lurking somewhere in the pack.

Her father lifted the white plastic cut card and held

it over the stack. His forehead twinkled with sweat, and not for the first time Harry wondered was he losing his touch. To comfortably predict when the aces would roll into play, he had to pinpoint the slug to within two or three cards. He hadn't managed it once in the last half hour.

She watched his unblinking stare, and pretended not to notice the tremor in his hand. Then he sliced the cut card into the centre of the block.

Harry lowered her eyes. She swivelled the pack towards him so that he could see the blackened segment he'd been aiming for. He was half a deck out.

'Dammit!' He dragged a hand over his eyes and down through his beard. Then he yanked his chair closer into the table and squinted at the cards.

'Do it again.'

Sudden pain lurched across Harry's skull, and for a second she closed her eyes. Her father touched her arm.

'Are you all right, love?'

She opened her eyes, managed a nod. 'Fine. Just a headache, that's all.'

The medics had lectured her about concussion, and in the end had prescribed more painkillers and rest. But after everything that had happened, sleep was proving elusive.

'Leave those.' Her father studied her face. 'You're white as a sheet, we can do this another time.'

'I'm fine, really. Come on, Dad. Eyes on the cards.'

She smiled encouragement at him, then separated the

pile into six more decks and laid out another horseshoe shape. While her hands were busy with the cards, her brain disengaged and looped over the events of last night.

She'd been lucky, and she knew it. If she hadn't recovered consciousness when she did, she could easily have been killed. Claustrophobia would have driven Rottweiler more and more berserk, and his lethal hooves would have pulverized her. As it was, they very nearly had. She remembered the horse's squeals, and something cold clutched her stomach. Whoever had locked her in that stall knew what he was doing.

And now he had her laptop.

Her fingers tensed on the cards. The laptop hadn't been in Rottweiler's stall, unless she'd missed it in the dark. Either way, someone else had it now. With the right expertise, they'd find the data she'd stored from Garvin's hard drive. Not to mention the spyware she'd dropped on to Kruger's machine.

She shuddered and thought of the man in the baseball cap. He'd killed Garvin, had probably killed TJ, and she still had no idea why. Had he been the one who'd locked her in the stall? It seemed unlikely. Only someone close to the stables would know about Rottweiler's phobia. Which meant someone else was after her now.

Her brain clamoured, screaming overload. She drove the thought away.

Focus on the cards.

She swallowed, and presented the shuffled pack to her father. He inserted the cut card, and she rotated the pack

232

to show him the blackened edges. He was closer this time, but not by much.

'Godammit!' He thumped the table, then got up and paced the room.

'You weren't that far off,' Harry said. 'And you're getting closer all the time.'

He didn't answer. Shuffle-tracking was all about precision, and they both knew it.

She watched him prowl the luxurious suite. When they'd weaned him off the ventilator, it had taken the physiotherapists weeks to get him back on his feet. Physically, he was mostly intact, but now and then, a stranger appeared. Mood swings, fatigue, lapses in concentration. Common after-effects of brain injury, the doctors had said.

Her father came to a halt by a period chaise longue, lowering himself into it as though it was a rickety old beach chair. Harry looked away. Maybe he was just getting old.

She picked up the stack of cards. 'You said you had someone you wanted me to meet.'

He checked his watch. 'She'll be here any minute.'

She? Harry hoped her father wasn't about to introduce her to a new ladyfriend. It wasn't that she had any objections to him dating; she just didn't like getting dragged into the screening process.

He flashed her a tired, sheepish smile. 'I asked you over early so you could drill me on the cards. You don't mind, do you?'

Harry smiled back and shook her head. Then she slotted the cards into a plastic dealer's shoe and began dealing blackjack hands. The cards snapped out, crisp and clean. There was something satisfying about the freshness of a brand-new deck.

The last time she'd tracked a shuffle had been in the Bahamas. She'd been card-counting in a six-deck blackjack game and for two hours she'd watched the count climb. Plus ten, plus twelve, plus sixteen. Hand after hand, the low cards spilled out. She waited for the prized high cards to pour out of the shoe, but all she got was an ugly, low run. By the time the plastic shuffle card appeared, the count was plus nineteen and most of the high cards hadn't made it to the table.

She'd watched the dealer lift the last undealt pack out of the shoe. She'd stared at the bundle of cards, transfixed. It had to contain almost every paint and ace in the game. She locked her gaze to the precious slug as the dealer slapped it on the discards and began his shuffling routine. She tracked the riffles, eyes like lasers, drilling into the decks. When the dealer offered her the cut card, she slotted it right next to the slug. The dealer switched her cut section to the head of the pack, her rich parcel of cards now on top. Then he started to deal.

For the next twenty minutes, the shoe had been a burst of colour, paints and aces in every hand. In the end, Harry had left the table with a profit of over two hundred thousand dollars.

'I'm flying to Cape Town at the weekend.'

Harry gaped at her father. 'What?'

'With Dan Kruger. He's found me another yearling, wonderful bloodlines. I'm going with him to the sales.'

Harry's stomach tightened. For reasons she couldn't explain, she didn't want her father going to Cape Town. Not with Kruger, anyway.

'But you don't know anything about buying thoroughbreds. Why not just leave it to Kruger?'

Her father looked wounded. 'I have some feel for it.' Then a mischievous grin slid across his face. 'Besides, they hold the bloodstock sales in GrandWest Casino.' He laughed and rubbed his hands together. 'Racehorses and blackjack. What could be better?'

Harry sighed. Talking him out of the trip was going to be harder than she thought. She crossed the room and sank into an armchair opposite him. The upholstery was softer than velvet, and she fought the urge to close her eyes. Her whole body felt dislocated, not just her shoulder.

She wedged herself into an upright position. 'How much do you really know about Dan Kruger?'

Her father shrugged. 'I know he's one of the best trainers in the country.'

'Apart from that.'

'What else is there to know about a man whose entire life has been horses? He grew up with them. His father was a moderately successful trainer in South Africa, I believe. Dan started off as a jockey, but then of course he grew too tall.'

235

Harry bit her lip. 'I met him yesterday. After you told me about Dawn Light. I thought I'd look him up.'

'Oh? What did you make of him?'

She made a face. 'Communicates better with horses than people, if you ask me.'

Her father laughed. 'That's Dan, all right. They say it's because he was deaf.'

Harry frowned. 'He didn't seem deaf to me.'

'Oh, not now. But for the first five or six years of his life, apparently, he couldn't hear anything. Lived in his own little world. No friends, schooled at home. Spent all his time with the horses in his father's yard. They say that's where he learned to talk to them.'

Harry raised her eyebrows, trying to picture Kruger as a small boy, isolated in a world of silence. She could understand how the solitude might have shaped his aloofness.

A rap at the door made her jump. Her father heaved himself to his feet and crossed the room.

'Ros, my dear, come in, come in.'

A woman with short, mahogany-dark hair stepped into the room. She was probably in her fifties, with a top-heavy figure that looked imposing in a cream wool suit. The gold buttons and black trim were straight out of Parisian haute couture. Harry's father played host.

'Harry, I'd like you to meet Ros Bloomberg.'

Harry took in the woman's strong features, and the smoky shadows that ringed her brown eyes. A distant memory stirred, then melted away. Harry blinked, decided she'd imagined it. Then she smiled and shook hands, wondering where all this was going.

Her father beamed at her, as if reading her thoughts. 'Ros is a diamantaire.'

28

'So you buy and sell diamonds?'

'That's right,' Ros said.

Harry sipped the coffee her father had made them and watched the other woman's face. A whisper in her brain still told her she knew her from someplace.

Ros leaned back against the chaise longue, her strong, dark profile and Chanel suit somehow in keeping with the period décor. She looked like the matriarch of a business dynasty posing for a glossy magazine.

'I've been in the diamond business for thirty-five years,' she said.

Harry's father patted Ros's shoulder as he passed behind the sofa. 'And running her own company for most of it.'

'Thanks to you.' Ros fixed Harry with a frank gaze. 'I was twenty-five, a gemology graduate with big ideas and no money. Your father was the only one who believed in me.'

Her mild American accent was easy on the ear, the mellowness at odds with her forceful appearance. Harry noticed she wore no jewellery, its absence lending her glamour a businesslike edge.

Harry's father perched on the arm of the chaise longue. 'You would have found another investor eventually.'

'I was high-risk, and you know it.' Ros looked at Harry. 'He convinced his bank to finance me. Against a lot of opposition, I might add.'

'But they never regretted it, did they?' He beamed at Harry. 'Ros's company is one of the leading traders in rough diamonds. She's got buying operations everywhere. Russia, Australia, South Africa, you name it. Trading offices in Tel Aviv, New York, all over Europe.'

Harry raised her eyebrows. Her father was beginning to sound like a company brochure. Ros smiled.

'Your father said you needed information,' she said. 'I don't know how I can help you, but I'm always ready to do a favour for Sal.'

'That's very kind of you.' Harry could hear her own uncertainty, and hoped it didn't sound rude. But in truth, she wasn't sure how Ros could help her either.

Her father cleared his throat. 'I've explained to Ros that you're a computer forensics investigator.' He flicked Harry a doubtful glance, as if to check he'd got the terminology right. 'And that you're working on a case involving some people in the diamond trade.'

Harry shifted in her seat. 'Dad—'

He held up a finger. 'Ros knows everyone in the business, Harry. Those names you asked me about, if they're in the diamond trade, she'll know who they are.' He stood up and crossed to the other side of the room. 'Now, if you'll excuse me, I'm going to leave you girls to it. I've a few calls to make.'

Having brokered the meeting, he disappeared into the bedroom, humming. Harry set her cup on the marble table in front of her, forgetting for a moment about her aching shoulder. Her ligaments screamed a reminder, and she sucked in air, then eased back against her seat. She threw Ros an apologetic look.

'Look, I appreciate the offer, but I really don't think these names will mean anything to you.'

Ros smiled. 'Try me.'

Her tone was mild, but there was a command behind the smile that wasn't lost on Harry. She was starting to get a sense of how Ros might have become such a successful businesswoman.

She squinted at the woman's dark features. 'Have we met somewhere before?'

Ros broke eye contact. She set her cup carefully on the table, then smoothed her hands along her skirt. She flicked Harry a shy glance.

'Your father didn't think you'd remember.' She tilted her head to one side, contemplating Harry. 'You were only a little thing, just six or seven years old.'

Dimly, Harry recalled a face. Fresh, smiling, full of

fun. A younger-looking Ros. She frowned, trying to nail the flashback down. Ros shifted in her seat.

'Your parents had separated for a while. You and Amaranta spent weekends with your father from time to time.' She smoothed another invisible wrinkle from her skirt. 'He used to invite me along.'

Harry nodded. During the course of their marriage, her parents had been apart more often than they'd been together. She stared at Ros. A memory fragment was taking shape, foggy as an old photograph. A beach, maybe, or a park somewhere. Ros laughing, Harry skipping alongside her. Amaranta, stern-faced, lagging behind, determined not to enjoy herself. And suddenly Harry recalled her own feelings of guilt when later her mother had asked if she'd had a good time with her father.

She glanced at the bedroom door. 'So your relationship was more than just business, then.'

Ros hesitated. When she spoke again her voice was gentle. 'Yes.'

'I see. And now?'

'Your father and I will always be a part of each other's lives. I'm sorry, that must be difficult for you. But he and Miriam—'

'You don't have to explain. My parents haven't been together for a long time. I don't have any loyalties you need to tiptoe around.'

But even as she said it, Harry couldn't help feeling an unexpected lurch on her mother's behalf. She didn't know why. Her mother certainly wouldn't care.

She flapped a hand. 'Look, skip it. It doesn't matter.' She made herself smile. 'My father thought you could help me, so maybe I should just try you with these names.'

Ros clasped her hands together, and looked as anxious as Harry to move on to safer ground. 'Of course.'

Harry cleared her throat, tried to re-focus. 'Let's start with this one. Does the name Garvin Oliver mean anything to you?'

'Yes, it does, as a matter of fact. Is he the one you're investigating?'

'I'm afraid I can't really tell you that.'

'I'm sorry, of course you can't.' Ros looked serious. 'I heard that he was shot.'

Harry raised her eyebrows, and Ros went on.

'It's the scuttlebutt among all the dealers right now, it's really shocked everyone.'

'He was well known?'

Ros shrugged. 'Well enough. He was a diamond trader, dealt in small rough, mostly from South Africa. I have to admit, I never did business with him if I could help it.'

'Oh? Why not?'

'He was a bully. And I didn't like his professional reputation.' Ros's lips tightened. 'I've heard rumours your fraud squad were investigating him for selling bogus merchandise online.'

Harry flashed on DI Lynne. That explained his interest in the case. 'Did Garvin deal in illicit stones?'

'Well, let's just say he wasn't too fussy about where the stones came from.'

'Meaning what, exactly?'

Ros sighed. 'Look, this industry is fraught with secrecy and sharp practice. I'd be lying if I said otherwise. Diamond mining has an appalling history. Violence, human rights abuses . . .' She swallowed and looked at her hands. 'You've no idea.'

Harry watched the woman's clenched fingers. Ros lifted her chin.

'Most of us want that to change. Reputable diamantaires will make sure the stones they buy are certified as conflict-free. We don't take stones from war zones, or from mines where conditions are inhumane.' She jerked to her feet and began pacing the room. 'God knows, no one wants to fund terrorists or support slave labour. But Garvin Oliver didn't care one way or the other.'

Harry digested the information. The more she heard about Garvin Oliver, the harder it was to be sorry he was dead.

'Did you ever hear of him dealing in smuggled stones?' Harry said.

Ros shrugged. 'Not directly. But smuggled stones and legit stones aren't easy to tell apart. Rough gets smuggled on to the market all the time. Out of the mine, out of the sorting office, out of the manufacturing plant. Someone's always stealing diamonds.'

Harry flashed on Eve crouched in the safe, her duffel bag crammed with stones.

'What about Garvin's step-daughter, Eve?' she said. 'Did you ever meet her? Or his wife, Beth?'

'Not the daughter. But I met his wife once. Pretty, frail-looking woman. Like a pixie.' Ros came to a halt by the window. 'I believe she committed suicide.'

Harry shot her a look. 'I didn't know that. I heard she died in a car accident.'

'She drove off a pier. They say no other car was involved.' Ros shook her head and stared out the window. From that angle her looks were striking, the olive skin and flared nostrils giving her an exotic look. 'I met her at a dinner party in New York. Garvin bawled her out in front of everyone for not packing the right shirt. He was purple with rage. It was quite shocking.'

Harry was silent for a while, trying to imagine what Beth must have felt to make suicide seem like her only option. Her mind drew a blank, and finally she said,

'I've a couple more names for you. Have you heard of a dealer called Gray?'

Ros turned and crossed back to the sofa. 'No, I don't think so.'

'How about Fischer?'

Ros's eyes widened. 'Jacob Fischer? As in, Fischer Diamond House?'

'That's the one.'

'Jacob is a master diamond cutter, fifth-generation, one

of the most respected in the business.' She drew herself up. 'I've known him for more than twenty-five years.'

'And Fischer Diamond House?'

'A world-class diamond-polishing operation. Been around longer than I have.' Ros's tone suggested that longevity alone was enough to put Fischer above reproach. 'Jacob buys only the highest-calibre rough. He employs about twenty expert cutters, but he still insists on working with the larger stones himself.'

Harry chewed this over, not sure how any of it helped. She was running out of names to try. Then she remembered the photos in Garvin's hidden files.

'What about names of diamonds?' she said. 'Would you recognize them?'

Ros threw her a curious look. 'Yes, if they're premium stones.'

Harry scoured her memory for the names Garvin had recorded against some of the larger diamonds. 'Yellow Mist, that was one. Does it ring a bell?'

Ros shook her head.

'What about Helios, then?' Harry said. 'Or Pink Heart?'

'Sorry, never heard of them.'

Harry slumped back against the chair. 'Well, maybe they haven't come on to the market yet.'

'Or maybe they're bogus names, designed to hype up the value.'

Harry frowned. 'How does that work?'

'Every gem trader knows the value of a name. If a

stone has a romantic story attached to it, it jacks up the price.'

'So people make them up?'

Ros shrugged. 'It happens. It rarely fools the experts, though.' She narrowed her eyes. 'If these are Garvin's stones we're talking about, then a stunt like that would be just his style.'

Harry nodded and chewed her bottom lip. She could hear her father on the phone in the other room. Ros gestured towards the sound of his voice.

'I'm worried about him. He looks so tired.'

Harry dropped her gaze. 'He's doing okay.'

She didn't feel like explaining about the fatigue and the memory lapses, didn't feel like admitting he wasn't the man he'd been before the accident. But then, if Ros was as close to him as she said, she probably already knew.

Ros scanned the sumptuous suite. 'He always did have a weakness for living in luxury.'

Harry's glance flickered over the plush carpets and the oak-panelled walls. The truth was, her father didn't really live anywhere. One day, he'd stay in a five-star hotel, the next in a cheap B&B. The luck of the cards decided which.

'He likes the freedom of hotels,' Harry said, not untruthfully. 'He was so long in hospital, he was beginning to feel institutionalized.'

Ros eyed the room service tray on the table. 'Isn't this just another form of institutionalization?'

Harry looked away. She was probably right. The way he lived, her father rarely had to do anything for himself.

Ros leaned forward. 'I know what he is, you know. I know why he went to prison, what he did. But it doesn't matter. Sal will always be important to me.' She cleared her throat and sat back. 'I just wanted you to know that.'

Harry sighed. There were a lot of people who felt like that about her father. They offered him loyalty, admiration, tolerance. Love, even. The rest of the population just wanted him back behind bars. Including her own mother, probably. As for Harry, it had taken a while, but she'd finally accepted that even though he was incapable of being an everyday parent, it didn't mean he wasn't a good father.

She gave Ros a speculative look. Her elegance reminded her a little of Miriam, although that was where the similarity ended. Ros had a simmering energy about her that would never boil through Miriam's shell.

Immediately, Harry felt guilty about making the comparison, and shoved her hands in her pockets. Her fingers brushed against the small diamond that by now she took everywhere with her. She studied Ros's face.

'What can you tell from a rough stone just by looking at it?' she said.

Ros smiled. 'Plenty. Weight, colour, clarity, potential cut.'

'Can you tell where it came from?'

'Of course. An expert diamantaire can tell the country, the region, sometimes even which mine.'

Harry stared at her for a moment, and then came to a decision. She extracted the stone from her pocket. It glowed with a dull light, like a fragment of an ancient chandelier. She held it out to Ros on her upturned palm.

'What can you tell me about this?'

29

'Well-formed octahedron, good colour. Fine white. 1.25 carats, I'd say.'

Harry watched as Ros peered through her jeweller's loupe, the stone clamped in a pair of tweezers.

Ros frowned. 'There's a tiny gletz running through it.'

'A gletz?'

'A crack. Puts the whole stone at risk, I'm afraid. It could shatter on cutting, hard to tell.' Ros lowered her magnifying lens and handed the stone back to Harry. 'But you could probably cut a good round brilliant from it, maybe half a carat.'

Harry rolled the stone between her fingers. Despite all the handling, it still felt cold.

'What's it worth?' she said.

Ros shrugged. 'About two thousand dollars. Not much more.'

Harry gestured at the loupe. 'Mind if I take a look?'

Ros handed her the small lens. Harry raised it to her eye, brought the stone up close and felt a jolt of surprise. Liquid crystal filled her vision, plunging her into a world of silvery valleys and glaciers. She stared, mesmerized. The molten landscape shimmered rather than dazzled, like folds of silk. Harry lowered the loupe and blinked.

'The cut will bring out the real fire and brilliance,' Ros said.

'I like it this way.' Harry handed back the loupe. 'Can you tell where it's from?'

'Northern Cape, South Africa. Possibly the De Beers Finsch mine, but more likely Van Wycks.'

Something stirred in Harry's brain. VW-Stock. VW-Cargo.

VW for Van Wycks?

'Is Van Wycks a mining company?' she said.

'One of the most powerful, after De Beers. They own mines all over the world. Canada, Australia, Angola, as well as South Africa.' Ros reached for her coffee. 'I'm a Van Wycks sightholder, I buy from them regularly in Cape Town.'

She must have noticed Harry's confusion, for she went on to explain.

'It's based on the system De Beers invented with their London sights. Van Wycks pick their favourite hundred or so diamond merchants and invite them to their head-quarters once a month to pick up a box of rough stones.' She cocked a wry eyebrow at Harry over the rim of her

250

cup. 'You pay for your box before you open it, and if you complain about the contents, you're never invited back.'

Harry made a face. 'A bit high-handed, isn't it? Couldn't you just buy the stones somewhere else?'

Ros shook her head, swallowing a mouthful of coffee. 'The sight is the only supply channel they open up. If you try to buy elsewhere, you'll find junk in your sightbox, lose a fortune and get expelled from the major supply line.'

Harry blinked. It sounded a lot like bullying to her, and she couldn't imagine Ros going along with it.

'It's not exactly a free market, is it?' she said.

Ros snorted. 'The diamond industry has never been about freedom, believe me. More about the control of supply and demand.'

'You mean, price-fixing?'

'Big time. The larger mining companies had so many diamonds, they could dominate the market.' Ros topped up her coffee from the silver pot on the table. 'They've been stockpiling rough for decades, grabbing mines all over the world, hoarding rough until they had more than anyone else. All so they could set up a cartel.'

Harry glanced at the pebble in her hand. 'Was Van Wycks in the cartel?'

'Absolutely. If a diamond producer refused to join, the big boys made sure they regretted it.'

'How?'

'By flooding the market with stones just like theirs

until the price collapsed. The bigger companies could weather the storm, but no one else could.'

Harry raised her eyebrows. 'Bully-boy tactics, in other words.'

Ros sipped her coffee and shrugged. 'Some people wanted out, but Van Wycks wasn't complaining. The cartel made them huge profits. If the price of diamonds weakened, they just suppressed production and cut the flow. When the price recovered, they turned on the tap again.'

'You make it sound like the supply of diamonds is limitless.'

Ros hesitated. 'Well, let's put it this way. If every diamond the cartel has hoarded was allowed out on to the market, the price would collapse. But they're too smart for that. They stockpile the stones in a vault and dripfeed them out.'

Harry frowned. 'How big is the stockpile?'

'A few billion dollars' worth. And that's just Van Wycks. Most of the big companies have stockpiles of their own, as do the Russians and the major Australian mines.'

Harry blinked. 'Jesus. I thought diamonds were meant to be scarce. I thought that was the whole point.'

Ros gave her an odd look and didn't answer. Harry shook her head. It seemed like such a scam. How could a diamond be paraded as valuable if it wasn't even rare?

She stirred uncomfortably. 'You make the whole industry sound like one big hoax.'

Ros sighed. 'I'm afraid it was, for as long as the cartel operated. Even the advertising had a sort of brainwashing aspect to it. Most people don't realize, but hardly anyone bought diamond engagement rings before the 1930s. It used to be opals or rubies.'

'The cartel changed all that, I presume?'

Ros nodded. 'They decided to cook up a link between diamonds and romance. They launched an aggressive ad campaign, even got Hollywood to insert special diamond scenes in their movies. Talk about subliminal advertising. Anyway, they rewrote tradition and the rest is history.'

Harry rolled her eyes. 'Diamonds are forever.'

'Exactly. Even that little slogan has its own subliminal message: "Once you've bought it, never sell it." That way, you see, there's no real secondhand trading, and the cartel has a larger market for new stones.'

Harry nodded, remembering Imogen's efforts to sell her 'used' ring. Then she sank back against her chair. The whole thing was clever, no doubt about it. Diamonds and love. One, a commodity that people didn't need, and the other a life force they couldn't do without. Fabricate a connection between the two, and a hard-headed businessman just couldn't go wrong.

Harry hugged her arms to her chest, the stone buried in her fist. She felt oddly manipulated, as though someone had been making a fool of her all her life. She glared at Ros. The whole industry was built on illusion, and this woman was a major player. Ros's frankness was

253

disarming, but Harry couldn't help wondering what was behind it.

She squeezed her fingers around the stone. 'You're doing a good job of talking down your livelihood here.'

Ros lifted her chin. 'On the contrary. I believe the industry is strong and can survive without all the skulduggery. I've been campaigning for transparency and regulation in the diamond business for years.'

Harry's eyes flickered over Ros's bare fingers and neckline. 'I notice you don't wear any diamonds yourself.'

'I wear them for pleasure, not business.' Ros dropped her gaze. 'Well, that's what I tell my clients, anyway.'

Then she sighed and got to her feet. She drifted around the room, idly picking things up and setting them down again. She came to a halt by the window, then turned to face Harry.

'If you want to know the truth, I haven't worn diamonds in over seventeen years.'

Harry frowned. 'May I ask why?'

Ros hesitated. 'A journalist approached me once and said things about the diamond industry I didn't want to believe. In the end, I agreed to go to Africa with her and see for myself.'

She resumed her ramble around the room. When she spoke again her voice was low. 'I'd thought it was all lies and exaggeration. But it wasn't.'

Harry shifted in her seat, wondering what was coming next. Ros went on.

'We visited some of the mines in the Northern Cape.

The conditions were barbaric. The miners were forced to live like animals, imprisoned in compounds no better than concentration camps.' Ros plucked at her fingers. 'I saw bodies of men tortured to death with electric shocks. We were told they'd stolen food.'

She exhaled a long breath, then continued. 'For those who survived the torture, there was always the dust. Kimberlite rock contains a lot of serpentine.' She flicked a glance at Harry. 'That's asbestos, to you and me. It's a horrible, lingering death. The mine owners could easily have suppressed the dust but they didn't.'

Harry swallowed. She tried to think of a response, but failed. Ros crossed the room and sat back down on the sofa.

'Then the journalist took me to Sierra Leone.' Ros clutched her fingers together. Her throat was working hard, her eyes on her hands. 'By then, the RUF rebels were in control of the diamond fields. Their signature tactic was to amputate people's limbs.' She looked at Harry. Her eyes were dark marbles of pain. 'If you gave money to beggars in Sierra Leone, you had to put it directly into their pockets. Most of them didn't have hands.'

Harry drew in a sharp breath. Instinctively, her brain shut down, refusing to picture the images Ros was conjuring up.

Ros glanced at her and nodded. 'And here's where we come in. The international diamond industry bought a hundred million dollars' worth of diamonds from the

RUF every year. We funded that war.' She looked back down at her hands. 'It was hard to see the beauty in diamonds after that.'

Harry felt the blood drain from her face. Her mind reeled, partly from horror and partly from a kind of collective guilt that she felt powerless to do anything about. She stared at Ros and felt the need to blame her, a reaction she didn't care to analyse.

'But you stayed in the business.' Harry heard the accusation in her own voice and wasn't proud of it.

'Of course I didn't stay in the damn business, what do you take me for?'

'But—'

'I wanted nothing more to do with it. I didn't want to fund wars, or fuel atrocities like that. I left, and planned on never coming back.'

Harry hesitated. 'So what changed your mind?'

Ros rested her elbows on her knees and massaged her temples. 'I realized that running away wasn't going to change anything. People would still be tortured and killed, just as before. But I was well known in the industry, I had influence. I could do more good by going back.' She straightened her shoulders. 'Since then, we've established a certification system for conflict-free stones. It's not foolproof, but it's a start. The conditions in some of the mines have improved, but not in all of them.' She sighed. 'Africa's a beautiful, brutal place and it's very hard to change it.'

Harry chewed her lip, and found she couldn't meet Ros's eyes. She fiddled with the stone in her hand.

'What about the cartel?' she managed eventually. 'Is it still in operation?'

Ros shrugged. 'The monopoly is supposedly waning. The cartel's market share has dropped, and allegedly they've shed a lot of their stockpiles. But, if you ask me, the big mining companies always find a way to work the system.' She pointed a finger at the stone in Harry's hand. 'And that includes Van Wycks. Their market share in small rough has fallen, but I've heard rumours they're trying to establish another monopoly, this time in larger stones.'

Larger stones. Harry's mind flew back to Garvin.

'You said Garvin Oliver dealt in small rough,' she said. 'How small?'

'Anything up to two carats, nothing more.'

'What would you say if I told you he'd been trading in Van Wycks stones of two hundred carats or more?'

Ros shook her head. 'That's impossible. Stones that size rarely get traded around, and the Van Wycks mines haven't produced them in years.'

'I've seen them. Or photographs of them, at any rate.'

Ros stared at her. 'How many?'

'It looks like Garvin imported a few hundred in the last year.'

'A few hundred? That's impossible. If that was a regular supply, it'd flood the market. You're sure they're Van Wycks stones?'

Harry thought of the filename, VW-Stock, and nodded.

Ros gaped at her. 'The old rules of supply and demand

still hold, particularly for large stones. I can't believe Van Wycks would allow it.'

'Maybe they don't know about it.'

Ros looked seriously alarmed. 'Then Garvin was getting involved in something extremely dangerous.' A fold of worry pleated between her brows. 'And maybe you are too.'

An icy fist squeezed Harry's chest. Ros was right. Gunmen, diamond cartels, torture and death. Her head swam with the enormity of it all, and suddenly she wasn't sure she could handle it.

She rolled the diamond around in her hand, its interior world of shimmering light hidden. She bit her lip. Maybe it was time to ask for help. Maybe it was time to go back to Hunter.

30

Harry rubbed her eyes and squinted at the screen.

FRANCIS (down) (down) **I** (space) **REFUSE** (space)
TO (space) **ENTR** (space) (left) (left) **E** (right) (right)
STEADY (space) **PGGY** (backspace) (backspace)
(backspace) (backspace) **PEGGY** (space) **UNTIL**
(space) **SHE** (space) **IS** (space) **FIT.**

Harry's eyelids drooped, and it took a couple of panto-sized blinks to keep them open. She skimmed through the next section of the keylogger file, piecing the text together.

It was the first espionage report from the spyware program she'd airdropped on to Kruger's machine. Page after page, it revealed every key he'd hit over the last twelve hours. By now she'd plodded through most of it, and so far all she'd found were innocent emails, along with evidence of Kruger's clumsy typing style.

She arched her back against the plush leather chair, listening to her spine crunch. The painkillers were finally kicking in, dulling the aches in her head and shoulder. She was still in her father's suite, making use of its free workstation and internet access while he escorted Ros downstairs.

Harry pecked at the page-down key, browsing through the file she'd downloaded from her web mail account. Her brain felt sluggish, like a wet sponge, as she struggled to absorb what Ros had said. If Harry's guess was right, Garvin's supply of large stones was fouling up the Van Wycks operation. According to Ros, Van Wycks worked hard to keep two key things alive: the exorbitant price of large diamonds, and the myth that they were scarce. Garvin's pipeline posed a serious threat to both.

Was that why he'd been killed?

Something rippled along Harry's spine. Tangling with crooked diamond traders was bad enough, but going up against the tyranny of a global cartel was more than she could handle. As soon as Ros had left, she'd phoned Hunter, gripped by an alien need to ask the detective for help. But Hunter had been unavailable. In the end, she'd left an urgent message asking him to call.

Harry scanned through the rest of the file, noting that Kruger had gone online to check his flights to Cape Town. Then he'd written another terse email to one of his owners, and finished up with a Google search. She stared at the search query he'd entered:

HARRY (space) MARTINEZ

Her stomach dipped. Kruger was checking her out. She chewed her nail, her eyes on the screen. Was he just curious? Or was there something more behind it? She shook her head and shut down the file. She knew what his search would have netted him: references to her company, Blackjack Security; résumés of her professional expertise; and newspaper articles linking her to her father's insider trading.

'Harry, I need your help.'

She turned to see her father stepping back into the room, his eyes shining. He rubbed his hands together in the way he always did whenever he was up to something.

'I've been talking to Dan Kruger,' he said. 'It seems TJ's widow may want to sell Honest Bill. I'm going to see Dan to discuss it.'

Harry frowned, aware of a nagging sensation in her gut at the idea of her father in Kruger's yard.

'Just how many racehorses do you plan on buying?' she said.

Her father shrugged. 'Who knows? It's like a hand of poker, Harry. The next one just might be the big winner.' He beamed at her. 'Could you run me out there?'

Harry hesitated. Returning to Kruger's yard hadn't

261

been in her game plan. How could she go out there when someone on the premises wanted her dead? A tight band squeezed her chest. She flashed on Rottweiler's thrashing hooves, his high-pitched squeals. Then she pictured her father out there by himself.

'Sure, I'll drive you,' she said, then checked her watch and thought of Hunter. Why hadn't he returned her call? 'We should go straight away. I may need to get back later to meet someone.'

She waited while her father fussed with his coat, then together they made their way to her car. For the next twenty minutes, they stop-started in city snarls and by the time they reached the Naas road, her father was asleep.

Harry opened her window a chink. The cold air was bracing, the sunlight so sharp the air almost sparkled. Relieved of the need to chitchat, she settled into the drive and in another half an hour had reached Kildare. Her eyes widened. In the wet, the Curragh had looked like an ancient bogland, but now the landscape was brighter, as though the sun had buffed it up with Brasso. Under other circumstances, it might have lifted her mood.

She followed the stretch of road until she spotted Kruger's yard. She eased her foot off the accelerator, her heart double-thudding and her fingers tense on the wheel.

'Dad, we're here.'

She made a left in through the gates, every particle of her body willing her to turn around. She pulled up at the rear of the house, then forced herself out of the car. Her father followed. The *thunk-thunk* of their slamming doors drew looks from some of the lads in the yard. A short, grizzled man broke away from them and hurried over. It was Vinnie Arnold.

He and her father shook hands like old pals, pumping each other's arms and exchanging hearty shoulder-slaps. Then Vinnie gestured towards the stables.

'Billy-Boy's in his stall. I'll take you over, the boss'll catch up with us later.' He edged away. 'Sorry to rush you, but we've had a bit of a mishap with Rottweiler. Young Eddie who minds him hasn't turned up yet, so we're short-handed.'

Harry's father smiled. 'Don't worry, that's fine. Coming, Harry?'

She shook her head. She'd sooner stick herself with pins than set foot inside the confines of another stall. 'You go ahead, I'll wait here.'

She watched them walk away, her eyes doing a quick scan of the yard. Horses clippety-clopped around the quadrangle, stable lads fussing over them like nursemaids. A tingly sensation danced along Harry's spine. In spite of the bustle, she felt an overwhelming urge to back up against a wall. She could have sworn someone was watching her.

Shaking the feeling off, she turned away from the yard and ambled over to a fenced-in paddock on the other side of the house. She followed the fence line until she reached a gate, then she froze. Ahead of her in the paddock was Kruger.

He was jogging across the field, his dark hair flapping

263

in the breeze. A copper-coloured horse cantered freely alongside him, his muzzle almost touching Kruger's shoulder. Neither of them had noticed her. Suddenly Kruger jerked to a halt, his body tilted back. The horse skidded and turned, his eyes on Kruger. Then the trainer wheeled round and sprinted in the other direction. The horse romped after him, his tail and mane fanning out like swatches of gold in the sun.

Harry leaned her elbows on the wooden fence, mesmerized. The pair looked like playmates in a game of follow-the-leader.

She watched as Kruger halted again. Then he backed up in an s-shaped course across the field. The horse whirled round and snaked after him, bending his body like a large fish, changing tack at the slightest twitch of Kruger's hips and shoulders. The horse's hooves swished through the long grass. His carriage was proud, a mirror of his trainer's erect posture. Without warning, Kruger turned and ran again, this time heading towards Harry. The horse bounded after him like a big friendly dog.

Harry saw Kruger noticing her. He slowed to a jog, then to a walk. The horse matched his pace as they both approached the fence. Harry stirred, feeling a need to explain her presence.

'I'm here to drop my father off,' she said.

'So I see.'

He stopped by the fence, hitching one foot on to the bottom pole. He was wearing soft leather chaps over his jeans, and together with the dark workshirt they made him look like a rangy cowboy. She tried to picture him shutting her into Rottweiler's stall, but for some reason the image wouldn't come.

The horse poked his head over Kruger's shoulder, and Harry could feel the warmth of the animal's breath on her cheeks.

'That looked like fun,' she said. 'You two must have known each other a long time.'

'He got here yesterday, I just started breaking him in.'

Harry blinked. 'I'm impressed.'

Kruger cradled the horse's downy muzzle in his hand. 'Communication and trust, that's what it all boils down to.'

'You say that like it's easy.'

'With horses, it is. They're honest, they don't lie. Not like people do.'

Harry shifted her gaze, acutely aware that she'd just finished snooping through his emails. Then she remembered his Google search and figured he'd done some snooping of his own.

'So how do you do it?' she said.

'Communicate with horses?' He shrugged. 'You need to become the dominant horse.'

She frowned. 'You mean, there's a pack hierarchy, like with wolves?'

Kruger nodded. 'Every herd of horses has its leader, its protector. He struts along, proud and confident, and the others respect him.'

'And he fights his way to the top?'

Kruger shook his head. 'He hardly ever uses physical force. Often he's not even the biggest in the herd.'

Harry frowned. 'How does he get to be leader, then?'

'He has a special quality. A powerful presence and dignity that the other horses just don't question.'

She raised a cynical eyebrow. 'You mean, like charisma?'

He shrugged. 'If you like. He uses it to lead the herd with his body language. He's got special signals for stop, change direction, circle against a predator, that kind of thing. The herd trusts him.' He patted the horse beside him. 'Once you can project the dignity and signals of the dominant horse, then you win their trust.'

'So it's all down to body language?'

'Everything in your body is information to a horse. He reads your posture the same way a deaf person reads lips.'

For the second time that day, Harry had a vision of Kruger as a small boy living without sound. She stared at his dark, serious face and wondered if she could trust him as much as his horse did. Six months ago, she'd been inclined to put people on pedestals, but now she viewed the world through a filter of suspicion. There had to be a happy medium in there someplace, but so far she hadn't hit on it.

Kruger studied her for a moment, then said, 'Why don't you try?'

Harry gaped. 'What? Talk to the horse? You must be kidding.'

'Come on. Just stand straight and tall, full of confidence, and he'll stand with you.' He opened the gate, and ushered Harry through. 'Remember, every movement is a word, so just keep still. Listen to the horse and let him listen to you.'

Harry edged into the paddock, shaking her head. 'I'm really not sure about this.'

Kruger relaxed against the fence. 'Just stand still.'

Harry eyed the horse in front of her. His ears twitched, and he held his head high as if sampling the air. Kruger's slumped posture seemed to neutralize his influence, and the horse turned all his attention to Harry.

The big animal fidgeted and tossed his head. Harry squared her shoulders and stood her ground. She could smell the warm, grassy scent of his coat, and took in the bulging muscles of his chest and hindquarters. For an instant, she flashed on Rottweiler's pumping legs, and her insides flooded with memories of her own misery and fear. The horse in front of her squirmed, his head drooped. His muscles quivered and his head bent even lower. Then his ears flattened sideways and he edged away, his whole demeanour wretched.

Harry blinked. What kind of anxieties had she projected on to the unfortunate animal?

Kruger pushed himself off the fence and stood between Harry and the horse. She could feel his body heat. He faced the horse, tall and square, and immediately the animal responded. The horse lifted his head and pricked his ears, and a soft whinny chugged in his throat. Kruger turned back to Harry, his gaze dark and intent, his body close enough to touch.

'A horse can pick up self-doubt a mile away,' he said. 'You might be able to hide it from humans, but you can't fool a horse.'

His dark eyes held hers and for a moment she thought he might step even closer, whether to touch her or yell at her, she wasn't sure. Then she saw his gaze shift behind her.

'Dan, Vinnie's looking for you.' Cassie's voice was sharp.

Harry turned to find her watching them both, her eyes boring into Harry's like white-hot drills. Harry recalled her sensation of being watched, and wondered just how long Cassie had been spying on her.

31

Callan squinted through his viewfinder and zoomed in on the Martinez girl. Even at this distance, he could tell it was her: neat figure, thick, dark curls; a way of holding herself ready for anything.

He leaned forward, angling for a clearer shot. Sunlight skewered through his skull, intensifying the pain in his head. He winced, his eyes watering. Then the redhead drifted across his line of vision, obscuring his view of the girl.

Shit.

Callan flexed his fingers and panned across the yard, his sightline coming to rest on the white-haired man with the neatly trimmed beard.

It had to be her father. Same dark eyes and brows, same olive skin. The likeness was unmistakable. Callan anchored himself deeper against the Land Rover's open roof, then squeezed the shutter and snapped off a few shots. He swept the lens back across the yard and captured a clear photo of Harry talking with the redhead.

That would do for now.

He ducked back into the jeep, clambered out on to the road, then let himself into the horsebox. He closed the door behind him, shutting out the light. The trailer was cool and dark, like a cave sheltered from the sun. His head didn't throb so much in here. He inhaled the familiar smell of horsehair and hay, this time overlaid with something different: the sweetish stink of blood.

He glanced at the body on the floor beside him. He'd get rid of it soon, dump it in a ditch along a lonely stretch of road. His eyes fell on the butchered face, the sticky mess of blood. He'd abducted the youth from the yard the previous night. His name was Eddie and he was twenty-five, though he only looked sixteen. But apart from that, he'd given Callan fuck-all information. He'd died too bloody soon.

Callan spat into the hay. Fucking midget jockeys. No stamina. Weak as birds, the lot of them. He'd lost interrogation targets before. They often died before revealing information, not because they were heroes but because their bodies just couldn't hold out.

That was why he needed the photographs. He always took them, just to show his clients, although often they didn't want to see. But now they had another purpose.

He browsed through the shots he'd just taken. The Martinez girl looked puny beside the strapping redhead.

He flicked a glance at Eddie. That was the problem. Too much physical force could kill a weak prisoner before you'd persuaded him to talk. But dangle the threat of torturing a loved one, and co-operation was usually instant. His eyes dropped to the photo of the girl's father. The man looked relaxed, his smile slightly phony. Callan lifted the camera and aimed it at Eddie, snapping off a few close-ups of his face. He checked the results and nodded. That should be persuasive enough.

He tucked the camera into his pocket, then shrugged a shoulder against his face. His skin still felt oily from the 'Black is Beautiful' camouflage cream he'd applied the night before. All the white mercs used it to blacken their faces at night. In Africa, Callan had worn it on a daily basis for years. Sometimes it still oozed from his pores.

Another bolt of pain lanced Callan's skull, and he squeezed his eyes shut. For a moment, the trailer see-sawed, pitching like a boat in a storm. He groped for the wall, tried to steady himself. His gut lurched and he slumped to the floor, waiting for the dizziness to pass.

Lack of sleep, that was all it was. He'd been up all night with that bonehead Eddie. He'd ditch the body, then grab some kip in the trailer.

He took a deep breath, trying to settle the queasiness, then leaned his head back against the wall. It'd be easier just to kill the whole bloody lot of them, instead of trying to find out who else was involved. Who the fuck cared about a little collateral damage? Certainly not his employers.

When Van Wycks had hired him, they'd been very clear. Eliminate everyone. No loose ends. What better way to satisfy his client than by annihilating the whole yard?

It wasn't the first time he'd been hired by a mining company. Usually his clients were governments, or splinter groups angling for power, but his Delta unit had been assigned more than once to the diamond fields of Angola. His orders had been to seed all the roads with landmines to kill off would-be smugglers. No doubt about it, big corporations liked hiring mercenaries just as much as governments did. Mercs were unofficial. And therefore highly deniable.

Callan shifted on the floor, testing the dizziness. The trailer had stopped swaying. Something hard dug into his hip, and he shoved it away. The laptop. The kid had been carrying it when Callan jumped him in the yard. He'd tried powering it up, but all it did was ask for a bloody password. The glare of the screen had triggered the damn headache.

He kneaded his forehead, rocking slightly. He knew what the headaches and panic attacks were, he didn't need a fucking therapist to tell him. They were memories. Bad ones, from African sinkholes of death. *A flashing knife, tearing flesh*. Callan punched his forehead, trying to pound the recurring image away. Sierra Leone. Ambushed. Drug-crazed rebels lining them up, taking aim with their diamond-purchased guns. Their leader going from prisoner to prisoner, slicing open their throats.

Callan had been at the end of the line, waiting his turn. It hadn't come. Delta reinforcements had lifted them out. But the rotten stench of fear still seeped from his pores, just like the camouflage cream.

He hunched his shoulders and kept on rocking, his eyes shut tight. The episodes were happening more and more often. They were lasting longer, too, becoming more intense, paradropping him back into vivid memories so real he could feel the pain.

Callan shivered. What if his commander was right? What if he was all burned out, and no one ever hired him again?

He stopped rocking and opened his eyes. A cool calmness stole over him. Maybe it was time he took out a little insurance.

He slipped the camera out of his pocket and, with trembling fingers, scrolled back through the photos. These people were smuggling diamonds. Big diamonds, according to the runner in Kuruman. And they were getting ready to make another shipment. He stared at the photo of the Martinez girl.

Supposing he took the shipment for himself?

He huddled back against the wall, his eyes sliding left and right. Van Wycks wouldn't like it, but who said they needed to know? He'd still fulfil his contract, he'd still eliminate the smuggling network. The stones would just be a bonus.

Adrenaline buzzed through him as a strategy crystallized in his head. He needed more information. When would the shipment be delivered? Where and by whom?

His eyes flickered over Eddie's carved-up face, then back to the photo of the girl. It was a pity. She was attractive. But it was her turn next.

32

'What exactly are you doing here?'

Harry glanced up at Cassie, then turned back to secure the latch on the paddock gate, taking her time about answering. Finally, she said, 'Waiting for my father.'

When she looked up, Cassie was still glaring at her. Her eyes were a curious shade of khaki, her gaze as unblinking as a cat's. Harry noticed she'd waited till Kruger was out of range before making her blunt inquiry.

Cassie folded her arms across her chest. 'So do you plan on taking an interest in your father's horses?'

Harry raised her eyebrows. The truth was, the less she had to do with horses the better, but the woman's manner made her feel contrary.

'I might,' she said.

The green eyes flicked down to Harry's shoes and back

up again to her face. Harry fought the urge to ask how her faded blue jeans had measured up. Then Cassie turned on her heel and struck out across the yard.

For a moment, Harry watched her go, the vet's long stride covering ground as though she was on wheels. Then Harry took off after her.

'Cassie? Can I ask you something?'

The vet didn't look round. 'I've a wounded horse to see to.'

'It'll only take a minute.' Harry trotted to catch up. 'It's about Eve.'

Cassie shot her a look. 'What about her?'

'How long has she worked here?'

'Two, three years. Why?'

'Does her step-father ever come to the yard?'

Cassie stopped at the entrance to the stables, her face blank. 'Her step-father?'

'His name's Garvin Oliver. Have you ever met him?'

'No. Is he connected to the yard?'

Harry shrugged, trying to read Cassie's face. 'I heard he was a business partner of Kruger's.'

Cassie looked away. 'Dan Kruger doesn't take on partners, believe me. Business or otherwise.' She snatched up a black case that had been left near the door and marched into the stables. 'Now, if you don't mind, I've got some wounds to dress in here.'

Harry frowned, and scooted after her. 'But what about TJ? He was a business partner, wasn't he?'

'For a while. But Dan was getting ready to buy him

276

out.' Cassie spun round to face her, her mouth tight. 'One thing you should know: Dan's a loner. He always will be.'

Harry blinked. Cassie turned and veered into a nearby stall. Something rustled behind its half-door, a large mass shifting in the straw. Hairs bristled on the back of Harry's neck. She edged closer to the stall and peeped in over the door.

A large, black horse stood diagonally across the box. His head was low, his shoulders twitching, and a criss-cross of wounds glistened across his legs and backside. It was Rottweiler.

Harry nibbled at her lip. She had to admit, she'd given little or no thought to what had happened to the horse after he'd bolted from the yard.

'Stay where you are.' Cassie flung her an accusing look, then bent down to squirt liquid into the gashes on Rottweiler's legs. 'You'll upset him. He doesn't like you.'

Harry took a step back. Absurd to feel offended by a horse's opinion. 'Is he okay?'

'Just about. We found him wandering on the roads this morning.' Cassie ran a gentle hand over the horse's leg, then grasped his ankle and clicked her tongue. Obediently, Rottweiler lifted his hoof. 'He'd broken out of his box.'

Harry glanced around the stall. It had a fresh, woody smell, and opened up to the rafters, the partitions offering a view into the neighbouring boxes. Fixed to one wall was a long mirror, about five or six feet up from the ground. Cassie caught her look and shook her head.

'Not this box. Some idiot put him into the enclosed stall at the end.' She eased Rottweiler's foot back on to the straw, then took some damp-looking gauze from her bag. 'Everyone knows he hates being shut in. He's lucky he didn't kill himself.'

Or someone else, Harry thought.

Cassie went on: 'He kicked the stable door in. Must've made quite a racket. Eddie was the only lad on duty, the others were out celebrating Billy-Boy's win. Dan'll kill him when he shows up.'

Harry frowned, picturing Eddie's pinched face. Was he the one who'd locked her in Rottweiler's stall? He seemed so young.

Cassie wrapped Rottweiler's leg, fixing the bandage in place with sticky green tape. The animal's muscles quivered, but he allowed himself to be handled, stoic as a seaside donkey.

'What's the mirror for?' Harry said.

'Dan put it up. Rottweiler gets lonely if he's on his own, so now when he looks to his left, he always sees another pair of ears.'

Harry squinted at the horse. He turned his head and for a moment they traded looks. Hard to reconcile this forlorn-looking animal with last night's satanic gladiator.

Cassie murmured encouraging noises to the horse, the tape making sucking sounds as she wrapped it round his

278

leg. Harry marvelled at how relaxed the woman was around those hooves. Last night they'd been like blades in the dark.

'I don't know how you do what you do,' Harry said.

Cassie frowned at her. 'What do you mean?'

'This life, the horses, all of it.' Harry spread her arms out to indicate the stables, then fixed Cassie with a direct look. 'I couldn't do it. Wouldn't want to take it on.'

Cassie paused, blinking. 'Really?'

'I'm a city gal, I guess.'

Cassie sat back on her heels and contemplated Harry. The tight set of her mouth seemed to soften for a moment. Then she nodded and busied herself with another bandage, her cheeks slightly flushed. She cleared her throat.

'Look, about earlier—'

'Doesn't matter.'

Cassie opened her mouth to speak, but seemed to change her mind. The sound of ripping tape broke the silence, then Cassie said, 'Was there anything else you wanted to ask me about Eve?'

Harry noted the shift in tone. With the territorial hackles about Kruger smoothed out, maybe now she'd get some information. She leaned her elbows on the half-door.

'I was wondering where the name Darcy came from. Is she married?'

'Not that I ever heard. If she is, the husband's long gone; she's been seeing Rob for over two years.'

'Rob Devlin?'

'Mm-hm.' Cassie dabbed some ointment on the horse's leg. 'Against my advice, I might add.'

'Oh?'

'Getting involved with a jockey is not for the faint-hearted, believe me.' Cassie got to her feet, brushing wisps of straw from her trousers. 'At best, the life is terrifying, at worst it's destructive.'

'You talk like you have personal experience.'

Cassie threw her a jaded look. 'I do. My husband was a jockey.'

Harry gaped. She took in the vet's imposing physique and tried putting the picture together. Cassie smiled and shrugged.

'I know. Bizarre, isn't it? Lou was actually quite tall for a jockey, just like Rob, but even so, we still made an odd pair.'

'You're divorced?'

Cassie's smile faded. She bent down by Rottweiler's foreleg, testing the tightness of his bandage with her fingers. When she spoke again, her voice was muffled.

'I thought it was normal at first. All the dieting, the saunas. Just part of the life. Lou was a very successful jockey, just like Rob.' She sighed, then began packing up her bag. 'But the fact is, lighter jockeys get the rides, and Lou did everything to lose more weight. Laxatives, self-induced vomiting, stimulant drugs. He exercised in plastic suits and went without food for days, sometimes losing six or seven pounds in a morning.'

'Wow.'

'Yeah. Half the time he was so cramped-up and de-hydrated he could hardly function. I don't know how he had the strength to ride.'

Harry recalled Rob's misery in the stables the night before. 'Do they all do that?'

'It's pretty common. With Lou, it wound up in alcohol-ism and depression.' She shook her head. 'He was battling with a weight problem he just couldn't beat, you see. He was too tall. Just like Rob.'

'What happened to him?'

Cassie joined her outside the stall. 'The police found him wandering around town one morning, half-starved, barely able to stand. They sat him down in an interview room, then left him to call me.' She shot the bolt home on the stall door, her eyes on Harry's. 'While they were gone, he hanged himself.'

Harry caught her breath. 'Oh my God.'

'Sorry, I hate bringing it up like that. I'm fine with it now; it was almost three years ago. But I know it makes other people uncomfortable.'

Uncomfortable didn't cover it. Harry was silent for a moment. Then she said, 'Are you saying the same thing's happening to Rob?'

'I don't know. But if you ask me, there are signs he's headed that way.'

Rottweiler rustled across the straw towards them and poked his head out over the half-door. Cassie stroked his downy-looking muzzle.

'I've tried talking to Eve,' she said. 'But she's pretty head-strong. Never listens to anyone.'

She rummaged in her pocket, then fed the horse half a Polo mint. The noise he made, you'd think it was a gobstopper. Cassie went on.

'Maybe the relationship will just burn itself out. It's turbulent, to say the least. Lots of rows and yelling, then someone storms off. Usually, it's Eve.'

Cassie shrugged, then headed out of the stables, talking over her shoulder. 'Hey, look, what do I know? Maybe they're made for each other.'

Harry scurried after her, blinking as they emerged into the sunlight.

'Like you and Kruger?'

Cassie flicked her a look, but didn't answer. Harry struggled to keep pace with the vet's long strides, and tried another question.

'So how long have you and Kruger known each other?'

'Four or five years. Lou used to ride for him sometimes.'

Harry found herself speculating whether Cassie had been seeing Kruger before her husband died. The vet must have sensed it, for she said,

'In case you're wondering, Kruger and I didn't get together till last year.'

Harry felt herself colour. 'I wasn't—'

'Yes, you were.' Then Cassie flapped a hand. 'It doesn't matter. Most people jump to the same conclusion. Juicy rumour is more fun than the truth, I suppose.'

Harry pictured Kruger's enigmatic face and could see

how people might gossip. She recalled the one-sided argument between him and Cassie that she'd witnessed through the window.

'He looks the sort of man it'd be tough having a relationship with,' Harry said. 'Kind of hard to read, if you know what I mean.'

'Like I said, Dan's a loner. Sometimes I'm not sure he wants to be with anyone. But I stick around.' Cassie gave a wry smile. 'Stupid, right?'

'Not necessarily.' Privately, Harry thought it sounded a little needy, but now was not the time to say so.

Tyres swished in the distance. She glanced up to see a car rolling into the yard. Cassie cleared her throat.

'I'm going with him to Cape Town this weekend.'

Harry shot her a look. 'For the sales?'

'For a holiday. Together. He works too hard.' Cassie smiled, then drifted away towards the house. 'I finally talked him into it.'

Harry stared after her. It seemed as if the whole world was drawn to Cape Town.

Car doors slammed, and her gaze shifted to the two men striding towards them. Her eyes settled on the leaner of the two. Spiky schoolboy hair, lean, hard build. Her gut tightened. It was Hunter.

He halted in front of her, his face stony. Harry swallowed.

'You got my message?' she said.

'Yes.' He spat the word out like a bullet.

'I wanted to talk to you. Clear up a few things.'

283

His eyes narrowed. 'Is that a fact? Well, there are a lot of things you need to clear up, Ms Martinez, and now's your chance to do it.' He gestured at the car. 'I'm taking you in.'

33

'I can't believe this. Am I under arrest?'

Harry shifted on the hard wooden chair and stared up at Hunter. He was standing on the other side of the table, arms folded, one shoulder up against the wall.

'Not yet,' he said.

He looked pale, the schoolboy image jaded. He'd refused to answer her questions during the drive to the station, and had left her waiting in the interview room for the past half an hour. Harry clasped her hands together and did her best to look earnest.

'I was coming in to talk to you,' she said. 'You didn't have to come after me like I was some kind of fugitive.'

'Didn't I?'

Harry blinked, and tried again. 'What exactly am I supposed to have done?'

Hunter pushed himself away from the wall and placed

his hands flat on the table, leaning in till his face was level with hers.

'We found your name on Garvin Oliver's files.'

A charge travelled down Harry's spine. She'd known they'd find her name eventually, but that didn't make it any easier to deal with. She raced through her options. If she admitted she knew about Garvin's files, then Hunter would know she'd tampered with his evidence. If she played dumb, there was a chance her chicanery with the laptop just wouldn't come up.

'I don't understand,' she said.

Hunter smacked the table, and she jumped.

'Don't give me that.' His eyes narrowed. 'According to forensics, someone accessed Garvin's hard drive not long before you handed it over.' His gaze was flinty. 'You know exactly what's on those files.'

Harry's gut contracted. Dammit. For once, she should've played it straight. She sighed and held up her hands.

'Okay, I took a copy. I shouldn't have done it and I'm sorry.'

'You're *sorry*?'

'Look, in my defence, it was your mistake the laptop got left behind, not mine.'

Hunter's jaw clenched and she decided not to pursue that line of attack. Instead, she made another 'I surrender' gesture.

'Okay, that didn't give me the right to make a copy. But I only did it to protect my back. It seemed to me that until I found out who this Beth woman was, you weren't going to believe a word I said.'

'You couldn't just trust us to get to the bottom of it?'

'Frankly, no.' She saw his mouth tighten, and felt her own temper climb. 'Hey, you started jumping to conclusions the minute you found me in Garvin's house. Throw in some insinuations from DI Lynne – who'd give anything to see me behind bars, by the way – and I really didn't rate my chances.'

'We found you beside a dead body and an empty safe – of course we drew fucking conclusions.' The look he gave her was cold. 'None of that gives you the right to tamper with evidence.'

'I had to do something. Whoever killed Garvin is probably gunning for me. You weren't going to protect me.' Harry flung her arms in the air. 'What was I supposed to do, sit around and wait for him to find me?'

Hunter glared at her for a moment, then yanked out a chair and sat down.

'There's more against you than just a bad history with Lynne.'

Harry lifted her chin. 'Such as?'

'Tell me about Dan Kruger. You've been spending a lot of time with him lately.'

'No I haven't. I met him for the first time yesterday.'

'What for?'

'I wanted to know why my name was on Garvin's files.' She ignored his sceptical eyebrow-lift. 'Dawn Light was the only lead I had, and I tracked him to Kruger's yard.'

Harry noticed she was reluctant to bring her father's name into things, and hoped Hunter wouldn't pick up on it.

'What about Tom Jordan?' Hunter said. 'How did you meet him?'

'I didn't. I never knew him.'

His eyes drilled into hers. 'But you know he's dead?'

She shrugged. 'So? It's been all over the news.'

He tilted his chair back, arms folded across his chest. 'This morning you and your father met with a woman called Ros Bloomberg. In the Westbury Hotel.'

Harry gaped at him. 'Have you been following me?'

'She's well known in diamond circles, or so I'm told. Now, why would you meet up with someone like her?'

'She's an old friend, she was trying to help.' Harry's palms felt clammy. 'I'd figured Garvin was dealing in smuggled diamonds, and I thought Ros could fill in some of the gaps.'

'Who told you Garvin was smuggling diamonds?'

Harry frowned, confused. 'You did. You told me his operation wasn't legit that day you came to my office.'

Hunter rocked his chair on its hind legs and acted as though he hadn't heard. 'Maybe you knew about it because you were involved. Maybe you took a copy of his files because you needed them to keep the operation going.'

Harry shook her head. Her brain felt as though someone had gone over it with an eraser. 'That's crazy, you can't believe that.'

Hunter let his chair drop with a crack to the floor. 'Maybe you and this step-daughter of his are working together.'

'No! I told you, I was trying to find out who she was.'

'We know more than you think, Ms Martinez. We know that Garvin sourced illicit diamonds through Cape Town, and we know he used Kruger's horses to get them out. Eve handles that part, though God knows how.' He curled his lip. 'Maybe she makes them swallow the things, or shoves them up their backsides. It's been done before with drugs.'

Harry's heartbeat ratcheted up. 'Look, I don't know Eve Oliver or Darcy or whatever her name is. The first time I met her was when she hired me to crack open that safe.'

He cocked a cynical brow. 'Really? Bit of a coincidence, isn't it? She hires you to open Garvin's safe while your horse is lined up for the next shipment?'

Harry opened her mouth but found she had nothing to say. After all, he was right. It *was* a bit of a coincidence. Hunter drummed his fingers on the table.

'Only it's not your horse, is it?' He studied her face. 'It belongs to your father.'

Harry shifted in her seat. 'Well, yes, but—'

'And your father's the one with the connections to this so-called diamond expert, Ros Bloomberg.'

'They did business together years ago, but so what? He did business with a lot of people.'

'Oh, we know all about your father's business deals.'

Hunter's eyes bored into hers. 'Did you know that he's travelling to Cape Town with Kruger in the next few days?'

A pulse beat hard in Harry's throat. For the first time, it occurred to her that her father's position was almost as rocky as hers.

'Just what are you getting at?' she said.

Hunter shrugged. 'Let's face it, as an ex-con, your father's credentials are even worse than your own.'

'You're trying to hang this on him because of his credentials?'

'He's got a lot of unexplained income.'

'He gambles, that's how he makes his money these days.'

A quiet voice cut across her. 'Like you did in the Bahamas?'

Harry snapped her gaze to the man by the door. She took in the dark hair, the slightly shabby suit and tie. Detective Inspector Lynne.

Hunter frowned and got to his feet. 'What are you doing here?'

'I heard you'd brought her in.' Lynne stepped into the room, easing the door shut. 'Just thought I'd drop by.'

Harry watched the two men square up. Hunter gripped the back of his chair, his posture tight. Lynne stood by the door, quiet and watchful. Like a fox with a banty rooster.

'You're wanted outside,' Lynne said to him.

Hunter hesitated, glancing at Harry. Lynne smiled.

'Don't worry about her. I'll keep her company till you get back.'

Hunter glared at his colleague, then marched out of the room. Lynne turned his gaze to Harry.

'So he hasn't arrested you yet. If it was me, I'd have taken you in days ago.'

Harry clamped her hands together. 'He's got nothing to arrest me for. It's all a mistake.' Even to her own ears, her denials sounded weak.

Lynne drifted over to the empty chair and sat down. All his movements were smooth and soundless, as though he'd been well oiled.

'He's been holding off,' he said. 'Some part of him wonders if you're telling the truth.'

Harry almost snorted. 'That's not how he comes across, believe me.'

'He's being careful.' Lynne was watching her closely. 'It wouldn't be the first time he misjudged a suspect.'

'I know, he told me.'

Lynne tilted his head. 'Did he, now?'

'Said he trusted a witness when he shouldn't have, went too easy on her.' Harry folded her arms. 'Well, you can take my word for it, he's not going easy on me.'

'That's what he said? He went easy on her?' Lynne gave a humourless laugh. 'That's an interesting way of putting it.'

Harry frowned, shifted in her seat. He leaned in closer.

'Hunter jumped into her bed, that's what he did. Every chance he got. Couldn't keep his horny hands off her.'

Harry stiffened. Lynne nodded, his lip curling.

'That's right, he was screwing a prime suspect. Who just turned out to be the perp, by the way.' A muscle jerked near his right eye. 'Claims he didn't know, but he fucked up big time. And on my case. Came close to dismissal, and nearly dragged me down with him.'

Lynne's fists had clenched on the table between them. He seemed to notice and leaned back in his chair, letting his eyes roam up and down Harry's body. She hugged her arms tighter across her chest, and his lip curled into another sneer.

'Hunter knows how to pick 'em, I'll say that. The last one was a good-looking woman too.' He gave Harry a penetrating look. 'Or maybe he just has a weakness for women who tell lies.'

Harry willed herself to hold his gaze. 'I'm telling the truth.'

'You're an accomplished bluffer, Ms Martinez, we all know that. How else would you have made so much money playing poker?'

'It wasn't all from poker.' She allowed herself to blink, suddenly tired of the staring contest. 'Sometimes it was blackjack.'

Lynne peered at her as though she was a crystal ball that had gone unexpectedly cloudy. 'I hope we don't find any other unexplained wealth in your possession.'

Harry dropped her gaze, the diamond in her pocket burning like a hot coal. She was saved the trouble of answering by the sound of a commotion outside. Then the door swept open and Hunter stood on the threshold. His lean frame filled the doorway, every muscle taut. For an instant, Harry pictured him in someone's bed, and heat prickled her skin like a rash. She shoved the image away.

'They've found a body,' Hunter said.

Lynne got to his feet. 'Whose?'

Hunter ignored him and glared at Harry. Deep lines bracketed his mouth, and his nostrils flared slightly.

'His name's Eddie Conway, a stable lad at Kruger's yard.'

Harry heard a hitch in her own breathing. Young Eddie, the skinny lad who looked after Rottweiler. Hunter drilled her with a look, his eyes blazing.

'Your laptop was found right beside him.'

34

Mani lugged the jackleg drill closer to the tunnel wall. The weight wrenched at the wound on his arm, and pain scorched through him. He felt himself sway, his vision cloudy. Around him, the dust churned like black smog.

The wound on his arm was changing. The skin had turned hot and discoloured, the gash wet from a stinking discharge. Mani flashed on Ezra's gangrene, stagnant and toxic, and without thinking he looked round for Takata. The realization slammed into him like a tank.

Takata was dead.

Mani's head swam. Takata had taken a bullet to save Mani's life, so that he in turn could protect Asha. But how could he save her when he was trapped down here in the mine?

Mani slumped back against the wall, cradling his bad arm. He swallowed against the lump in his throat, trying not to picture Takata's kindly face. The old man had trusted him, had believed he would not fail. But Mani knew he already had.

Metal *tink-tinked* into rock as the other miners worked on the tunnel. Mani heaved himself upright and reached for the drill, balancing it on its supporting leg. The last time he'd drilled a hole, Okker had bludgeoned him with his club. Now the guard was dead, his fat body laid out somewhere overground, along with Mani's diamonds.

Mani tensed and fired up the motor. The drill bit hammered into the rock. Vibrations shuddered through him, inflaming his wound.

What if the other guards had already discovered the stones?

A feverish heat swept over him. He released the trigger, his arms limp. What did any of it matter? By now, Okker's body had probably left the compound, the stones far out of reach.

'Dos Santos!'

Mani turned and squinted through the shifting dust. A guard stood at the mouth of the tunnel, summoning him with the barrel of his gun. Mani glanced at the other men, then stumbled across the loose boulders and out into the main shaft. His miner's lamp hosed away the shadows from the guard's face. It was the pale young soldier who'd balked at killing the schoolteacher.

The young guard jabbed the air with his gun. 'Get into the lift.'

Slowly, Mani turned and trudged towards the metal

cage. His hands began to shake. Had they found out he'd killed Okker? Were they going to shoot him, just like they'd shot Takata? Mani shuffled into the lift, the guard close behind. The cage clanked upwards, drilling through a column of thickening heat. Then it groaned to a halt, and Mani stepped out into the sunlight.

The guard kicked at a bag on the ground. 'Here's your stuff.' Then he thrust a sheaf of papers at Mani. 'Your contract is up. Go through x-ray, then leave by the main gate.'

Mani dragged his mask down under his chin, staring at the papers that authorized his release. Then he peered at the guard. For a moment, the young soldier held his gaze, then he signalled with his gun.

'Move!'

Mani stuffed the papers into his overalls and picked up his bag. He followed the barbed-wire corridor to the x-ray unit. To his right, beyond the wire, was the main exit area, and he stared at the huge, fortress-like gates. A pickup truck rumbled beside them, waiting to leave. In the distance, heading from the white workers' quarters, two men were making their way towards the truck. Between them, they shouldered something large and wide, stumbling under its weight.

A body bag.

Mani's heart pummelled inside his chest. Was Okker's body still in the compound? Mani tore his gaze away and raced into the x-ray theatre, identifying himself to the operator behind the screened-off booth. True to his

296

word, Volker had gone. His replacement was younger, new to the job, his movements slower than a toad. Mani clenched his fists, shifting from foot to foot. If he could just get to the truck before it moved out, maybe he'd still have a chance.

The operator finally looked up and nodded. Mani dumped his bag on the x-ray conveyor belt and stepped inside the cubicle. The door slid shut, the C-arm juddered, then began its slow crawl along the walls.

Sweat ran down Mani's face. Twenty-five seconds to scan him head to toe. Surely the truck would still be there? He thought about the Belgian guard, Janvier, ditching the body without involving the police. The guards never called the authorities into the mine. Too many of the killings were down to them.

The C-arm finally clunked to a halt. The Perspex door slid open and Mani jumped out of the capsule, waiting for the operator to unlock the main exit door. Bolts clunked, a buzzer sounded. Mani pushed through a waist-high metal gate and collected his bag from the end of the conveyor belt. Then he shouldered his way through the large steel door, lurching out into the sun.

The truck was still there.

Mani dragged himself towards it, fighting the feverish aches in his limbs. The truck's engine revved, the exit gates creaked.

'Wait!' Mani scrambled to the cab door. 'Can I travel with you?'

The driver scratched his beaded hair and shrugged.

He glanced at the man in the passenger seat and they consulted in isiZulu for a moment. Then the driver turned back to Mani and smiled, showing gaps in his crooked teeth.

'You can come. But the big man in the back, he take up a lot of room.'

The two men flung back their heads and cackled. Mani thanked them and moved to the rear of the truck, flinging his bag into the open wagon. Then he heaved himself up, settling in against the side. The driver was right. Okker's body and canvas holdall took up most of the space.

The steel gates creaked and the truck eased into gear. Mani relaxed against the throbbing wagon, taking in the wide-open skies and the expanse of scrubland ahead. He inhaled the strong perfume of the sweet acacia trees. Soon he'd be out, away from the mine. Soon he could look for the diamonds.

A clatter of shots fractured the air. The truck jerked to a halt. Mani snapped his head around. Janvier stood a few feet away, his gun trained on Mani's head.

Slowly, Mani raised his hands in the air. The guard's eyes were small in his shovel-shaped face. He glared at Mani, then dropped his gaze to Okker's body bag.

His eyes shot back to Mani. 'Who said you could leave?'

Mani swallowed, groped for his release papers. 'Everything is in order, my contract is up.'

Janvier ignored him, his eyes flicking back to Okker.

A muscle bulged in his brick-shaped jaw. Then he stepped to one side and yelled at the driver.

'Back up! I want him x-rayed.'

Mani swallowed. 'But I have already been cleared.'

'Not you.' Janvier spat on the ground. 'The body.'

The truck whined into reverse, backing up to the x-ray unit. Mani gripped the wagon sides, his gut twisting. The truck screeched to a halt, and Janvier yelled at the two men in the front.

'Get that body into x-ray.' Janvier narrowed his eyes at Mani. 'You! Take his bag.'

The two men lugged Okker's body out of the wagon and dragged it into the x-ray unit, scuffing it along the ground. Mani lifted Okker's holdall and clambered down from the truck. Then for the second time that day, he stepped into the x-ray theatre.

'Put the bag on the conveyor belt.'

Mani did as he was told, while the driver and his friend wrestled the zipped-up body into the scanner capsule. They left it slumped against the sides, then stepped outside.

Janvier grabbed Mani's shirt and slammed him up against the wall behind the screened-off booth. He jammed his gun barrel into Mani's throat, so hard it made him gag.

'What do you think?' Janvier shoved his big face into Mani's. Behind him, the scanning motors hummed. 'Will they find anything?'

Mani choked, then dragged in a harsh breath. His lungs

299

heaved, fighting the suffocation. Janvier bared his teeth and rammed the gun in deeper. Mani's throat closed over, his tongue bulged. He squeezed his eyes shut and waited for them to find the stones.

The humming stopped. Mani's eyes flared open. Janvier shot a glance at the x-ray operator.

'Well?'

The operator shrugged. 'All clear.'

Janvier jerked his head around. 'What are you talking about?'

'There's nothing there.' The operator gestured at the screens. 'See for yourself.'

Janvier stared at the monitors. Mani twisted his head. The crooked silhouette of Okker's body was like a ghost on the screen. Beside it was the grainy image of his holdall.

Janvier roared and lunged back at Mani, hurling him to the floor. 'Bastards, all of you!' He spat in Mani's face, then wheeled away, barging out the door. 'Load it back up!'

Mani scrabbled to his feet, trembling. The two men from the truck scuttled back inside and bundled Okker's body out. Mani followed with the holdall, hurling it on to the wagon next to the body. Then he climbed up beside it and crouched into a corner.

The driver revved the engine, and the truck lumbered back towards the exit. The steel gates groaned, parting slowly. Mani braced himself, waiting for someone to stop them. Then the truck sailed out through the gates, bumping on to the dirt road.

Mani hugged his knees, his pulse racing. His eyes locked on to the steel gates, the razor-wire fences. No guards charged out, no armoured jeeps. The truck jiggled along on the open road. The prison compound dissolved into the distance, merging with the shimmering dust and scrubland. Finally, Mani closed his eyes and rested his forehead on his knees. He stayed like that for two or three miles. Then he lifted his head and eyed up Okker's body bag.

He shifted in closer, stealing a glance at the driver and his passenger in the cab. They were arguing, paying no attention to their stowaway. Mani reached for Okker's holdall and unzipped it. He rummaged through it, burrowing through shirts, pants, socks and shoes. Mani flung the contents out, scrabbling around the bottom of the bag.

Where was it?

Then his fingers closed over something cold. He lifted it out, the metal glinting in the sun. Okker's knife.

Mani flexed his fingers around the handle, his eyes flicking back to the body bag. Then he gritted his teeth, grabbed the zipper tab and ripped the bag open. A baked stench rushed out into Mani's face. He turned away, his belly heaving. Then he covered his nose and mouth and peeled back the bag. Flies buzzed into the air. The sickly stink of rotting meat filled Mani's nostrils. He forced himself to look at Okker. The body was bloated, the skin turning greenish-blue. Fluid leaked out of the staring eyes that had sunk back into the skull.

Mani clamped his mouth shut and tried not to breathe. He tightened his grip on the knife. With his other hand, he groped at Okker's belt, feeling around the sides. He frowned, then wedged his hands under Okker's back and heaved the body up. The underside was damp and sodden. Beneath the body, still clipped to the belt, was Okker's wooden club.

Mani detached it and lifted it away from the body, letting Okker slump back. He stared at the club. The bulbous head was weighted with a rounded sheath of lead screwed into the wood. Mani fumbled with the knife, untwisting the screws. The lead cap slipped off, revealing the shortened club stem that Mani had whittled away with his knife.

He backhanded the sweat from his face, then lifted the lead cup. It rattled in his hands. Inside it were four misty-white stones, nestling like eggs in a basket.

35

Leave no trace.

The first rule of forensics and Harry had blown it. Dammit. She thumped the steering wheel with her fist.

When she'd copied Garvin's hard drive, she'd set up her equipment to block any writes to his disk. Or so she'd thought. In her rattled state, she must have got it wrong and left tell-tale prints all over his files.

Not that it mattered. She flipped on her headlights and edged into the traffic. Tampering with evidence was a misdemeanour compared to the trouble she was in now.

Her first instinct had been to deny the laptop was hers, but the Blackjack tag was hard to argue with. In the end, she'd told Hunter about her ordeal in Rottweiler's stall, but she could tell from the stony look on his face he was having trouble believing her. She'd told him to check her records in A&E, even shown him some of her bruises. He'd quickly turned away, said he'd look into it.

Harry sighed. Sometimes she was better at telling lies than she was at telling the truth.

Hunter's face drifted into her head. The tired hazel eyes; the boyish haircut at odds with the caveman stubble. She shook her head. Lynne's revelations had shocked her, she had to admit. He'd given her an insight into Hunter that she wasn't sure she wanted.

She swung past Trinity College, duelling with a bus for space on the inside lane. Traffic was heavy for this time of night. She flashed on Eddie's body, abandoned in the dark. The police said he'd lain in a ditch overnight. She swallowed hard. Eddie could have locked her in Rottweiler's stall, but he seemed too young to have acted on his own initiative. On whose orders, then?

She thought about Kruger, recalling her hypnotic encounter with him in the paddock; how he'd stood so close and sensed her self-doubt as if she was one of his horses. Heat suffused her face. The man was easier to deal with when he was distant and rude.

Maybe Rob was the one who'd told Eddie what to do. The jockey had been there that night, after all. And he was involved with Eve. He'd probably given her the black eye.

Harry pictured the jockey's blond good looks, his wiry strength. Then she remembered his pain in Billy-Boy's stall. Was Cassie right? Was he dicing with alcoholism and eating disorders, the endgame being self-destruction? A career like that couldn't last for long.

Maybe the diamonds were his retirement plan.

And then there was Cassie. She'd been at the yard that night too. She was close to Kruger. Or as close as you could get to a man like that. If he was involved, there was a good chance she was too.

Or maybe she was operating independently of Kruger. Cassie had struck her as a strong woman. Was she really the type to pursue a losing relationship? Maybe it was all a front, and her involvement with Kruger was just a way of staying close to the yard.

Close to the diamonds.

Harry frowned. Maybe, maybe. The whole bloody yard could be involved for all she knew. Her intuitive antennae weren't exactly humming with signals. She ground the gears, swerving too fast at the next turn.

What the hell did any of it matter now? Hunter was already connecting the dots; he didn't need her help. He knew Kruger's yard was the link to everything: to Garvin, to TJ and now to Eddie. And since he'd found her name on Garvin's files, she'd nothing left to hide. No more snooping, no more interfering. From now on, she just needed to lie low.

And so did her father.

She checked her watch. She'd call his room when she got to the hotel. Hunter's colleague had driven him back to Dublin in her car, dropping the Mini at the police station while she'd made her way there with Hunter. She'd told her father she was working a case, but she wasn't sure he believed her. She had to persuade him to

305

cancel his trip to Cape Town. Any ties with Kruger now just put them both in the frame.

Harry geared down, making another turn. Her shoulder ache was back, the pain bone-deep. Hunter had interrogated her for over three hours before he'd finally let her go. All she wanted now was to sleep.

By the time she arrived at the Westbury Hotel, it was almost ten o'clock. She bumped down into the underground car park and pulled into the first vacant slot. Then she scurried across the cavernous space, every muscle tensed for flight. But no one molested her, and two minutes later she'd reached the hotel lobby. It was brightly lit and filled with people, and immediately she felt more secure. An illusion, she knew, but it lifted her spirits.

Her room was on the first floor, next to the lifts. The corridor was quiet, a discarded tray the only sign of life. Fumbling for her keycard, she slotted it into the lock, wincing at the twinge in her shoulder.

Painkillers and sleep, in that order.

She pushed the door open. The room was dark and she groped along the wall. Where the hell was the light switch?

Something rustled in the corridor behind her, and she half-turned. A shape flew at her. She caught her breath. Got ready to scream. Strong arms hurled her into the room and slammed her to the ground.

Her head smacked against the floor. She tried to scream. A fist punched her chest, blasting air out of her lungs. She gasped. Couldn't breathe. Lungs wouldn't inflate.

The door banged shut, blocking out the light. Hands thrust her on to her stomach and wrenched her wrists behind her back. Muscles ripped along her shoulder, and she cried out. Metal clinked, felt cold against her skin. Her attacker snapped the handcuffs tight, then yanked her round to face him.

She stared up at his blocky shape, her heartbeat drumming. His eyes glowed white in the dark. And jutting over his forehead was the peak of a baseball cap.

A charge shot through Harry's chest. She started to scream, but he lashed out with his foot, crunching it into her ribs.

Harry doubled over, pain stabbing her side. Jesus. He was going to kill her. He loomed over her.

'Let me explain how this works.' His voice was harsh and low. 'I ask you questions, you give me answers.'

Harry huddled into a foetal position, hating the whimper that mewled out of her throat. The man in the baseball cap continued.

'If I don't like your answers, we have a problem. If you scream, we have a problem.'

He slipped something out of his pocket and held it out to her. Harry froze. It was a tapered, deadly looking blade.

He smiled. 'Like it?'

He took a step towards her. Harry moaned, scrambling into a sitting position. Her heart slammed against her chest.

'It's a Commando dagger, very thin.' He jabbed the

307

knife towards her and she flinched. 'Thin enough to slip between a person's ribs. Or skewer them right in the eye.'

Harry let out a choked sob. She dug her heels into the floor, heaving herself backwards. The wall stopped her up short. He hunkered down beside her. A sudden chink of moonlight lit his face. His skin was scored like the hide of a tortoise.

'See that?' He held the blade close to her face. 'It's double-edged, unusually sharp.'

Harry shrank back against the wall. 'What do you want?'

He pointed the needle-sharp tip at her eyeball. 'I want names. Information.'

'But I don't know anything!'

'Wrong answer.'

He inched the dagger closer to her eye. Harry moaned, twisting her face away. He grabbed her chin, immobilizing her.

'Who ships the diamonds?'

Harry swallowed. 'I'm not part of that, I swear. I got involved by accident, I don't know anything.'

He twirled the blade like a screwdriver, drilling it closer to her eyeball. 'Try again.'

'I swear, I'm not—'

The back of his hand whacked her across the face, whipping her head away from the blade. Then he grabbed her chin and yanked it back. The knife was still poised, ready to thrust. Tremors racked through her body.

His fingers squeezed her chin. 'Bad fuckin' start. Maybe this'll jog your memory.'

He jerked her chin aside and stood up. Harry closed her eyes, hot tears squeezing through her lashes. Damn Eve Darcy to hell for dragging her into all of this.

'Look at me!'

Harry snapped her eyes open. The man in the baseball cap towered over her, an envelope clasped against his barrel-shaped chest.

'Take a look.'

He extracted a photograph and held it in front of her face. It showed a heavy-set, dark-skinned man, standing next to some kind of aircraft. His black, wavy hair and full features spoke of Indian ancestry.

'I don't know him,' she whispered.

'That's the "Before" picture.' He pulled out another photo. 'I prefer the "After" shot.'

He shoved it into her face. It showed the same man, this time lying on the ground. Gashes ripped his face, and where his eyes should have been there were raw, bloody potholes.

Harry gagged, and twisted away. Dear Jesus.

'Look at it!'

She dragged her gaze back. He'd switched to another photograph. Eddie's thin face stared out at her, a black horse in the background. Another shot replaced it. The stable lad's face was spattered with blood, and his right eye was missing.

Harry's stomach heaved. 'Please—'

'Try this one.'

He held out another shot. Her heart went into freefall.

It was a photograph of her father, standing in Kruger's yard.

Her brain reeled. Dear God, no.

She shook her head, kept on shaking it. The police had seen him home, he had to be all right. Small moans escaped her throat.

The man in the baseball cap crouched down beside her and shoved his face into hers.

'Your father doesn't have any "After" shots yet.' He whipped his blade up close to her eyes. 'But he will if I don't get some answers.'

Harry stared at the dagger, her whole body quivering. He was probably going to kill her, no matter what she said. But maybe she could protect her father.

'Okay, okay!' Her teeth were chattering. 'I'm part of the syndicate, I can tell you what you want to know. You don't need to hurt him.'

He narrowed his eyes. 'Don't I? Maybe you're lying, just telling me what I want to hear.' He grabbed her by the chin, crushing her jaw. 'Are you playing me?'

'No!' She flashed on Hunter, and the hours she'd spent trying to convince him she wasn't involved. Now she had to make this killer believe that she was.

'I was working with Garvin Oliver.' Her body wouldn't stop shaking. 'We were a team. You saw me in his safe, I couldn't have opened it without his say-so, could I?'

He pressed the blade flat against her cheek, the tip nestling near the corner of her right eye.

'What else?' he said.

Harry's brain raced. 'In my pocket. There's a diamond. It belongs to the syndicate, you can have it.'

He released her chin, holding the knife in place. She felt his fingers grope inside her jeans until he found the small stone. He brought it up to his face.

'What the fuck is this?' His fist clenched over it. 'Oh, you'll give me diamonds, all right, but not fuckin' pebbles like this. Tell me about the stones!'

Harry scrambled round in her head. 'The horses. We bring the diamonds in through the horses.'

'Stupid bitch, I already know that.' He pressed against the blade. 'Who else is involved?'

Harry took a deep breath, stalling. 'What'll happen to them if I tell you?'

'Not your concern. Let's just say I've got my orders and I intend to carry them out.'

'Orders from who? Van Wycks?'

She saw the flare of recognition in his eyes and knew she'd got it right. He shoved harder against the blade.

'Enough fucking questions. Tell me who's involved!'

Harry flashed on Eve. If she told him her name, this man would surely kill her. She swallowed, her eyes on the dagger.

'Eddie Conway.' No one could hurt Eddie now. 'He was just a kid, a gofer.'

The man in the baseball cap angled the dagger, digging his knuckles under her eye socket. 'You're wasting my time.'

'No, wait! Eve! Eve Darcy.'

Something small shrivelled inside her, but she had no

311

choice. Eve would have to take her chances. The man with the baseball cap twirled the blade between his fingers. One slip and it would slice into her cornea.

'Go on,' he said.

'She's Garvin's step-daughter. She's been in on it from the start.'

'What about the yard? Who's calling the shots?'

Harry clenched her teeth. If she knew who to name, she'd do it. But picking someone out would be like handing down a random death sentence.

'I don't know,' she whispered.

'If that's all you've got, then you're no use to me.' The blade brushed against her eyelashes. 'And neither is your father.'

He clamped her cheeks with his free hand and anchored his knee on to her chest. Then he pointed the dagger at the pupil of her eye.

Harry caught her breath. The blade filled her vision, like a snake ready to strike. Moonlight flashed on metal. The man in the baseball cap winced, and for a second, he seemed to hesitate. His eyes glazed over, as though he wasn't seeing her. Sweat oozed from his skin, and she could feel his muscles trembling. The knife still quivered over her eye.

Harry's brain looped in circles. Say something, anything! There had to be something else she could use.

'The diamonds!' She forced the words out through his iron grasp on her cheeks. 'The next shipment, I can get it to you.'

He blinked. Re-focused. Loosened his grip.

The dagger tip still hovered over her eye.

He stared at her. 'Go on.'

'Cape Town. It comes in through Cape Town in a few days.'

'Where in Cape Town? Who transports it out?'

'I do.' Harry panted, playing for time. If she told him about Kenilworth and Dawn Light, she'd have nothing left to trade. 'Eve contacts me with the exact time and place. I meet one of our couriers out there, then arrange to ship the stones home.'

She held her breath, her gaze transfixed by the dagger. He studied her for a moment.

'Here's what we'll do,' he said eventually. 'We'll wait here for your friend Eve to call. Then I'll go and collect the diamonds myself.'

'And kill me?' Harry licked her lips. 'Won't work. Our couriers don't know you. You think they're just going to hand the stones over to a stranger? If they don't see me around, they'll call the shipment off.'

He spat into the dark. 'You think I'm just going to let you go?'

'You have to.' Harry clenched her teeth, hoping it would hide the terror in her voice. 'Without me, you'll never get access to the diamonds.'

His eyes narrowed. He leaned back, lowering the knife to his side. Without warning, he punched her hard in the stomach. Harry gasped, trying to double over, but his weight pinned her in place. Then he grabbed her by the hair and yanked her head off the floor.

'Now, why would I trust you to deliver the stones back to me?'

Harry sobbed against the pain. 'Because you have no choice.'

'I can think of a better reason.' He arched her head back, and thrust his blade against her jugular. Something warm trickled down her neck.

'You'll deliver the stones to me because if you don't, your father is a dead man.'

36

Mani trudged along the deserted road. His bones jarred with every step. He'd been walking for almost four hours, and had trained himself not to look up. The infinite blackness was too hard to take, with Kuruman nowhere in sight.

A hyena yip-yipped somewhere in the distance. The heat of the day had long gone, the darkness tumbling like an ink spill. Mani had travelled with the truck as far as the main road, then the driver had let him out.

'This is as far as we go,' the driver had said. 'Kuruman, it is twenty miles to the north, just follow the tarred road.'

Mani had nodded and watched the truck veer off the highway, bumping out across the scrubland. There were no towns that way, no other roads. Just arid wasteland. Perfect for burying a body.

Mani adjusted the bag on his shoulder, and thought of the diamonds inside it. At the last minute, he'd decided not to hide them in Okker's body. White corpses were rarely x-rayed, but what if this time they'd changed the rules? So Mani had hollowed out the end of Okker's club, gambling that the x-rays wouldn't penetrate the lead sheath.

He plodded along the edge of the road, his feet scuffing against the sand that blew in from the Kalahari Desert. His arm throbbed, the toxic wound leaking infection into the rest of his body. The poison was already making him lightheaded. How long before delirium distorted his brain?

Mani took a deep breath. It was almost over. Soon he would find the runner called Chandra and give him the stones. Then Mani's job would be done. Ezra had told him what would happen next.

'Chandra, he will take the stones to Cape Town. His contact will phone him with the time and place.' Ezra had raised his head off his filthy bunk, his eyes pleading. 'Once Cape Town have the stones, it is over. You can leave. They will call off their people and we will be safe.' Then his gaze had clouded. 'Until the next time.'

Mani clenched his teeth, his eyes fixed on the road. There would be no next time. He would go back to Ezra's stinking shack and force his brother and Asha to return with him to Cape Town. Mani rubbed the grit out of his eyes. He remembered the first time he'd asked Asha to come away with him. She had refused. Her father was old and sick, she'd said. She would not leave him. So she'd stayed behind and married Ezra instead.

But now Takata was dead.

A wet cough racked Mani's chest. He doubled over, his lungs feeling as though they were filled with crushed glass. After a moment, the spasm passed. He straightened up and continued along the tarred road.

Dust had been layering his insides for the past thirteen years, ever since his first trip down the mines as a child. Mani tried not to wonder what kind of sickness was brewing in his lungs.

He dragged on, the semi-desert stretching out around him. After two more miles, he lifted his gaze. A cluster of pinpricks glowed in the distance.

Kuruman.

Adrenaline streamed into Mani's legs. He shifted the bag on his shoulder and quickened his pace. He walked for another four miles before he reached the town. Then he followed Ezra's directions, circling west around the outskirts of Kuruman, passing briefly through its traffic and bright lights before heading back out into the thornveld.

The man called Chandra operated from an airstrip six miles outside the town. Mani tramped on past the shadows of sand dunes and the mounds of asbestos from abandoned local mines. Dust caked his lips. A solitary light burned in the distance, and he fixed his eyes on it. Soon he could make out a small, single-storey building and next to it, a narrow runway.

He willed himself to walk the last few steps. As he approached the building, the silhouette of a man moved into the open doorway.

'What do you want?'

Mani licked the salty crust off his lips. 'I'm here to see Raj Chandra.'

The man walked towards him. 'I am his brother, Sanjeet, you can deal with me.'

Mani squinted at the dark, fleshy face. 'I think I must speak with Raj.'

The man called Sanjeet stared at him for a moment. His eyes were round, his hair thick and oily-looking. Then without a word, he turned on his heel and went back inside the building.

Mani stood shivering in the dark. It would take him three more days to walk back to Ezra's shantytown. He wondered if Asha would hate him when he told her about her father.

Sanjeet returned alone. He stood in front of Mani and held out a tumbler of water. Mani hesitated, then snatched at it, gulping it down. He wiped his mouth with an unsteady hand.

'Thank you.'

Sanjeet nodded, then dropped his gaze, fiddling with a gold watch on his wrist. The strap seemed too big for him, despite his chubby arms. He glanced back at Mani.

'My brother is dead.'

Mani froze, the water in his stomach settling like a stone. 'Dead?'

'Last week. I found him on the runway.' Sanjeet looked out across the semi-desert, his expression puzzled. 'Someone had cut out his eyes.'

Mani's head reeled. He felt as though he'd travelled to the edge of the world only to find there was nothing there. He swallowed against the spiralling panic.

'But I have something to deliver,' he said. 'Something for Cape Town.'

Sanjeet shrugged. 'If you have money, I can take you anywhere you want.'

'But your brother, he has a contact in Cape Town, someone who—'

'My brother had many contacts, but he never shared them with me.' Sanjeet jerked his chin in the direction Mani had come. 'He also had a big house in Kuruman and a fancy car, and he didn't share those with me either.' Sanjeet fiddled with the oversized watchstrap. When he spoke again, his voice was low. 'But now everything he owned belongs to me.'

Sweat beaded on Mani's scalp. Asha and Ezra wouldn't be safe till the stones were delivered to Cape Town. But who would take them there?

Sanjeet gestured over his shoulder. 'I can have it ready in ten minutes.'

Mani peered into the dark. The dim shape of a light aircraft straddled the end of the runway.

'My brother never let me fly it.' A smile flickered across Sanjeet's face. 'But now I am in charge.'

Mani's breathing turned shallow. Maybe he should

return to the shantytown now, take Asha and Ezra away. They could run, take the diamonds for themselves. Then he felt his gut shrivel. The way Ezra spoke of the people involved, he knew they would come after them. And they would find them. The stones were too important.

He peered at Sanjeet. The man did not know anything. If the stones were to be delivered to Cape Town, Mani must take them there himself. He eased his bag off his shoulder and fished around inside, extracting the smallest of his stones. He held it out to Sanjeet, the smooth facets pearly in the moonlight.

'Can you take me to Cape Town?' Mani said.

Sanjeet stared at the diamond, his eyes growing rounder. He took the stone between his fingers, held it up to his face. Then his glance slid to Mani's bag.

Mani tensed. Sanjeet probably guessed there was more than one stone. If he decided to take the rest of them, there was nothing Mani could do to stop him. He was too weak to defend himself now.

Sanjeet glanced over at the aircraft, then nodded and slipped the stone in his pocket. He gestured towards the airstrip building.

'Come inside. You can rest while I get things ready.' He rubbed his hands together and looked up at the sky. 'It's a clear night, we should be there in two hours. We leave in ten minutes.'

Sanjeet was true to his word. In less than fifteen minutes, Mani was buckled into the cramped, two-seater plane. Sanjeet sat in front, flipping switches. Mani's heart pumped. What was he going to do once he got to Cape Town?

The engine buzzed to life. Vibrations rippled over Mani's frame. He clutched his bag closer to his body and thought about Cape Town, the city that had been his home for the last two years. He pictured the university and wondered if he'd ever return there.

The light aircraft joggled along the runway, circling into position. For a moment, it stopped and rumbled in place. Then it bounded straight ahead, bobbing on the uneven surface. The engine whined higher and higher, building speed. Mani gripped the armrests, bracing his stomach. With a heave, the aircraft veered upwards and climbed into the sky.

Something clunked against Mani's foot. He glanced down. A mobile phone had slid out from under the pilot's seat, its descent on the tilted floor checked by the cable attached to it. Mani blinked.

His contact will phone him with the time and place.

Mani bent to retrieve the phone. It was bulkier than the usual mobile, with a chunky antenna poking out of one end. The bars on the screen told him the battery was charging, presumably from the aircraft's engine.

Was this Raj Chandra's phone?

Mani glanced at Sanjeet. The mobile could be his, but after all, it was Raj who used to fly the plane. Mani slid the phone into his bag, for the moment leaving it connected to the charger. The plane bumped through a pocket of turbulence and Mani clutched the armrests, trying to recall what Ezra had said about Cape Town. He pictured his brother's broken-toothed grin.

'Chandra, he does not say much about his contact.' Ezra's eyes had half-closed in the smoke-filled shack. 'Just that it is a woman called Eve.'

37

Harry hugged her knees, huddling in closer to the wall. Her body felt heavy, as though terror had somehow weighted it with lead.

The man in the baseball cap was long gone, but for the last half hour she'd been unable to move. Still crouched on the floor of her hotel room, she kept listening for sounds, wondering if he'd come back.

A dry sob juddered through her. He wouldn't come back, he didn't need to. He knew she'd do whatever he said.

Harry shivered in the dark, and thought of the pact she'd made. Her father's life for the diamonds. A fair exchange. Except that she had nothing to trade.

What the hell had she been thinking?

She rested her head against the wall. The truth was, she'd had no choice. Her lies were the only thing keeping her alive.

She rubbed her cheeks, her skin tight from dried tears. She thought about standing up, but the effort seemed overwhelming. In any case, where would she go? Right now, she was everyone's target. Hunter thought she was working with Eve, and so did the killer from Van Wycks. To the syndicate, she was probably just a snooper, but they still wanted her out of the way. In the end, somebody was bound to get her. Bullseye.

Harry shook her head, wondering if delayed shock was making her delirious. Slowly, she clambered to her feet, steadying herself against the wall. Her wrists felt bruised, and the tenderness in her abdomen reminded her of the punches she'd taken.

She staggered into the bathroom and switched on the light, wincing at herself in the mirror. She looked like some kind of nocturnal demon. Her hair was a wild tangle, her dark eyes huge in a ghostly face. A thread of dried blood zig-zagged against her throat, giving her a vampirish look.

She ran the tap and sponged at her neck with a towel. Pinkish water swirled down the plughole, and an image of Eddie's empty eye socket exploded inside her head. Dizziness sideswiped her and she moaned, clutching at the sink with both hands.

Breathe!

She thrust Eddie's grisly image away. Blood drizzled back into her head and slowly she raised her eyes to her reflection in the mirror. She looked drained, her posture slumped and cowering. Just like the wretched horse in

Kruger's paddock after she'd infected him with her own self-doubt.

She gripped the cold enamel sink. Godammit, enough hiding. She splashed her face with water and swallowed another dose of painkillers. Then she dug out her spare laptop, hooked it into the hotel broadband and began a search for flights.

A cold finger brushed against her spine at the notion of travelling to Cape Town. Hunter hadn't exactly said not to leave town, but flying to another hemisphere was probably pushing her luck. And her plan when she got there was open-ended, to say the least.

But she had to go. According to her story, she was the syndicate's point man for the next Cape Town shipment. The Van Wycks killer would expect her to fly out there.

She booked herself on a flight leaving the following day, and made a hotel reservation. She'd pick up her passport from the cottage before she left for the airport. Then she checked her email, downloading another report from the keylogger on Kruger's machine. She trawled through the data till her eyes began to cross, but she didn't find anything of interest. Now that the police had a reason to examine her laptop, they'd probably crack her email and download the reports for themselves. Maybe Hunter would find something he could use.

Harry eased back in her chair, every breath dragging fiery pain along her ribs. How the hell had she got caught up in any of this? A few hours ago her plan had been to lie low, and now she was more involved than ever.

She closed her eyes, aching for sleep, but she still had one thing left to do. She dug out her phone and called her father's room.

'Yes?'

Harry blinked. 'Miriam?'

'Ah.' Her mother paused. 'Harry. You're looking for your father, I presume?'

Inwardly, Harry sighed. Girls were supposed to be close to their mothers, comfortable chitchat always on tap. Somehow it had never worked out that way for her.

'Is he there?' Harry said. 'I need to talk to him.'

'Where are you? Your father said you'd been taken in by the police.' Her mother's voice rose to a hiss on the last word.

'I wasn't "taken in". I explained to Dad already, they just had questions about a case I'm working on.'

Another voice carped at her in the background. 'Tell her she should have phoned.'

Her sister, Amaranta.

Harry closed her eyes and felt the spurt of annoyance climbing over her like an itch. She pictured her sister: ash-blonde, like Miriam, and just as elegant. They'd probably been on a shopping trip together in town.

Amaranta was still issuing instructions. 'Tell her to call over sometime, she doesn't visit you enough.'

Harry didn't feel like explaining that she was only down the hall. She pressed on before things got awkward.

'Look, can I talk to Dad?' she said.

'Your father can't come to the phone.' Miriam's voice

was firm, as though she was already two rounds into an argument on the subject. 'He's asleep and I'm not going to disturb him.'

Harry squinted at the phone. Since when had Miriam been her father's protector?

'Is he okay?'

'He's worn out. Doing too much. No telling him that, of course.'

She could hear Miriam sucking in on a cigarette, and pictured her long, manicured nails flicking away the ash.

Her mother exhaled into the phone. 'I suppose you've heard of his absurd plan to fly to Cape Town.'

'That's one of the things I want to talk to him about. He can't go.'

'I've told him that, but you know how he is.' Harry heard her dragging in another nicotine hit. 'It only spurs him on all the more.'

'But it's dangerous, there's too much going on here.'

'He won't listen, even to you, Harry. God knows, he's never been particularly focused on the future, but since he got out of hospital he's been worse than ever. The here and now is all that counts with him.'

Harry chewed her bottom lip. Her mother was right, in more ways than she knew. Harry had considered telling her father everything, but far from agreeing to cancel his trip, he'd probably insist on getting involved. And in truth, he was probably safer out in Cape Town with her. At least then she could keep an eye on him.

'Do you know when he's flying out?' she said.

'The day after tomorrow.'

'Can you ask him to call me? Tell him I'll meet him out in Cape Town.'

Miriam missed a beat. 'What?'

'It's this case I'm working on, I need to go out there.' Harry rushed on, forestalling more questions. 'There's something else I need from him, but I need it now. It's a number for one of his business contacts, her name's Ros Bloomberg.'

Harry tensed, waiting for her mother's reaction. Did she know about Ros? Most wives would, but then Miriam had made a practice of surviving her husband's transgressions by simply blanking them out.

'Harry, I'm not waking him. It can wait till tomorrow.'

'It can't. I need—'

'Hold on a minute.'

The phone clattered in Harry's ear. She clenched her teeth, her mother's abrasiveness setting them on edge. She didn't expect gushing affection, but a softening of attitude would be nice once in a while. But then, Miriam had always been remote. Even as a child, Harry couldn't recall her mother ever cuddling her. For a long time, Harry had blamed herself. She knew her resemblance to her father grated on Miriam, a constant reminder of the husband who'd let her down. But recently Harry had learned there was more to it than that.

Miriam had had an affair before Harry was born. She'd been ready to leave the marriage, when unexpectedly she'd become pregnant with Harry. Sal was Harry's father, there was no doubt of that, but Miriam still wanted to leave him. Her lover, however, had backed out. Taking on another man's child was more than he'd bargained for, and he'd ended the affair. Miriam had lost her bid for freedom, and in her eyes Harry was to blame. A shaky start for any mother and daughter.

'Roslyn Bloomberg, is that the one?'

Harry jumped. 'Yes, that's her.'

'Her card was on the dressing table.'

Miriam called out the number and Harry jotted it down, feeling complicit in some kind of deception against her mother. Blast her father and his complicated affairs.

'Harry, is everything all right?'

It was the unexpectedness of the question as much as the insight behind it that made the tears sting the back of Harry's eyes. She blinked them away.

'Yes, everything's fine.' She swallowed, then risked a question of her own. 'You and Dad, are you two—'

'Don't be ridiculous.' Miriam paused. 'I'm just keeping an eye on him.'

'Oh. I see.'

An uneasy silence hung between them, then they both rushed to fill it with polite farewell sounds. Harry disconnected and stared at the phone, wondering if either of them would ever have the courage to break through the other's shell.

Then she sighed and shook her head. Maybe some things were best left alone.

She checked the number she'd scribbled down and

called Ros Bloomberg. When she answered, Harry identified herself, apologizing for the late-night call.

'No problem,' Ros said. 'How can I help?'

'Remember we talked about Jacob Fischer, the diamond cutter in Cape Town? You said you'd known him a long time.'

'I have, he's a good friend.'

'Do you think you could persuade him to meet with me? I'm leaving for Cape Town tomorrow, and I'm hoping he can answer some of my questions.'

'You're going to Cape Town? I'll be heading out myself in a couple of days for the Van Wycks Sight. Why don't you wait and we can meet him together?'

'I'm working to a deadline on this, I'm afraid. I really need to see him as soon as I can.'

'Well, I'll try.' Ros sounded doubtful. 'But I warn you, Jacob's a busy man. Even his wealthiest clients need to book appointments weeks in advance. Leave it with me, I'll see what I can do.'

Harry thanked her and ended the call. Then she shuffled back to her room, cradling her bruised midriff. She eased herself on to the bed, and stared up at the ceiling. At this point, she wasn't sure how Fischer could help, but his name had been on Garvin's hidden files, along with information about the diamond shipments.

Something nudged at the base of her brain when she thought of Garvin's files. She frowned, chasing it, but the more she worried at it, the fainter it got.

She closed her eyes and let it go. It probably didn't

matter. Fischer was just a long shot, anyway. She had one priority when she got to Cape Town, and that was to find the diamonds.

And to do that, she'd have to find Eve.

38

Harry wasn't sure what she'd expected of Cape Town, but this definitely wasn't it.

She edged her airport rental car along the N2 freeway, nose to tail with early morning traffic. Swollen clouds hugged the skyline, like a bloated tarp draped over the city. Jackhammers clattered at regular intervals, roadworks pockmarking the route. In the overcast light, everything looked run-down and grey.

Hard to believe she was right at the bottom of Africa.

Her eyelids drooped. It was eight in the morning and she'd been travelling for sixteen hours straight. She rolled down the window, her gaze drifting over the parched wasteland bordering both sides of the freeway. Baked air bussed her cheeks. According to the dashboard, the temperature outside was already twenty-eight degrees.

Harry checked the map on the passenger seat beside

her. She'd scrutinized it on the plane, memorizing the route as though cramming for an exam. Take the N2 from the airport, follow the Waterfront signs to Eastern Boulevard, then cross over Coen Steytler. She recited the directions under her breath, her muscles tense as she turned her gaze back to the traffic. Navigational challenges always made her head bleed.

Before she left Dublin, Harry had tried calling Kruger. She'd hoped to find out where Eve was staying, but all she'd got was his voicemail. She'd try him again when she got to the hotel. She hadn't quite worked out a pretext for her inquiry, but she'd worry about that later.

Harry chugged along the freeway in a stop-and-go wave, glad of the slow pace since it gave her time to read all the signs. She craned her neck, trying to get her bearings. The barren landscape to her left was changing, suddenly cluttered with rows of rickety metal shacks. They looked like ramshackle garden sheds, their construction a patchwork of cardboard and corrugated iron. Washing lines looped through the narrow spaces between them, garments flapping in the bluish haze generated by outdoor fires.

The shantytowns of the Cape Flats.

Harry stared at two small boys playing with a rusty shopping trolley. Her knowledge of the area was sketchy, but her guidebook had filled in some of the gaps.

The Flats had served as a dumping ground for apartheid. African workers had been forbidden to live in the city. But since the white people in Cape Town still needed their labour, the Africans had been corralled into outlying townships, which soon sprawled into squatter camps. Cape Town forced thousands of its residents into the Flats, after the government bulldozed their homes and designated the areas as whites-only.

Harry watched as the two boys clambered into the trolley. Behind them was a blue, free-standing cubicle, like a telephone box without a door. An elderly man was urinating into it.

A horn blared, and Harry jumped. She waved an apology to the driver behind, closing the gap that had opened up in front of her. She squinted through the wind-screen. The clouds had shifted, revealing a hard, blue sky. A column of heat climbed up her spine. Somewhere in this unfamiliar city, Eve was getting ready to take another shipment of stones. And somehow, Harry had to intercept the delivery.

Her eyes darted to her rear-view mirror. She'd seen no sign of the Van Wycks killer in the airport or on the plane, but she could easily have missed him in the crowds. Her stomach tightened. It wasn't likely that he'd cut her loose and not keep tabs on her.

She rounded a bend, checked her map. Up above her the last of the clouds were parting. A hulking, grey mass eased into view. It was vast and rugged, and loomed up from the earth like King Kong, taking charge of the city. The almighty Table Mountain.

Harry's eyes widened. She was close enough to make out its stony terrain, and the trees that grew in a permanent tilt from the wind. She drove on, the mountain glowering at her like a giant chaperone.

The congested freeway finally loosened up and soon the docks appeared on her right-hand side. She exhaled a long breath, relieved to tag a landmark on her route. She plunged into the city with the rest of the traffic. The main streets were wide, the architecture mixed. Austere Victorian, ornate Dutch gables, modern high-rises. Harry clung to her directions like a drowning woman to a raft, squinting at the bilingual signs in English and Afrikaans. Ten minutes later she'd pulled up in the car park of the Southern Sun Hotel.

She lugged her bags over to the entrance, trying not to strain her sore shoulder and ribs. The sun-cooked wind blew like a hairdrier on her face, but inside, the foyer was blessedly cool. Chandeliers sparkled overhead, and underfoot the huge marble slabs were polished to a mirror finish.

Harry crossed to the desk and checked in, then made her way to her room on the twelfth floor. It was small, but otherwise lived up to its four stars. She flung her suitcase on the bed, along with the laptop and forensic field kit she'd picked up from her office before leaving.

Her jeans were clinging to her like molten tar, so she peeled everything off and stepped into the shower. The bathroom was tiled with more polished slabs, and suddenly Harry thought of the old man with his open-air urinal. The sea of dilapidated shacks floated across her vision. She huddled under the water, not liking the jab of guilt that bit at her like indigestion.

Apartheid had clearly left a legacy of extremes. She'd only been here an hour, and already her awareness of it was knotting her insides.

She lifted her face to the jet of water, trying to hose away the image of the crumbling shanties. Then she dried herself off, slipped into a white cotton sundress and sat on the bed to consult her map. If she was reading the scale right, the Victoria and Alfred Waterfront was only a short walk away. She grabbed her bag and headed for the door. Breakfast would perk up her metabolism.

Outside the hotel, a white-hot sun grilled her bare arms. She tacked her way across the grid of streets, jostling with the tourists and fighting off the crawling sensation down her spine that told her she was being watched.

The air grew dense with the salty tang of fish. Masts and cranes giraffed above the rooftops at the working end of the harbour. At the other end, jazz and marimba bands whipped up a carnival atmosphere amid the restaurants and bars lining the promenade.

Harry crossed the footbridge over the quays and pulled up a seat outside the nearest café. Seagulls shrieked overhead, blitzing the tugboats docked at the water's edge. A waiter appeared and took her order for coffee and an omelette. Then a low voice behind her said,

'Mind if I join you?'

39

Harry spun round. Rob Devlin was standing behind her, watching. Adrenaline spiked through her veins.

Had he been following her?

She managed a smile. 'How did you know I was here?'

He cocked a wry eyebrow. 'It couldn't just be a co-incidence? Everyone ends up at the waterfront sooner or later, and it's not exactly huge.'

Harry darted a glance around the harbour. Tourists were surging along the promenade, pouring in and out of the restaurants and African craft shops. It'd be some coincidence to bump into an acquaintance here.

She fixed her smile in place as he took the seat oppos-ite hers. He was dressed for the sun, his T-shirt and Bermuda shorts showing off his hard, wiry limbs. He ordered an orange juice from a passing waiter, then leaned his elbows on the table and stared at her.

'We seem to be seeing a lot of you lately.' His eyes flicked up and down the length of her body. 'Not that I'm complaining.'

Harry folded her arms across her chest. There was something aggressive about the way he flirted. A kind of hostile masculinity that had nothing to do with liking women.

'You here to buy another horse?' he said.

'My father is. He gets in tomorrow. I'm just along for the ride.'

'Come and see me race on Saturday. International Jockeys' Challenge.' He leaned back and spread his arms out wide. 'Take a good look. Champion jockey two years in a row, about to make it three.'

'Congratulations.'

It came out a little drier than she'd intended, but oddly he didn't seem to mind. He grinned at her.

'Yeah, I know, I'm a cocky little shit. But I'm also one of the best jockeys around.'

Harry found herself envying him his brash self-confidence.

A small cruise ship drifted through the harbour, parping its horn like a tuba. Rob turned to look, and she took the opportunity to study him. His cheeks were sunburned, his blond hair tousled from the wind. Women paid hairdressers a small fortune to achieve the same effect.

His orange juice arrived. When the waiter left, Rob slipped a flask from his pocket and emptied half its contents into his drink. He saluted her with the glass, his look challenging, then took a deep slug.

338

Harry watched him. His grey eyes were clear, but maybe the flushed cheeks had more to do with thread veins than over-exposure to the sun. He set down the glass and squinted at her.

'You ever ridden a horse fast?'

'I've never ridden a horse, period.'

He threw her a scornful look, as if she'd just confessed she'd never driven a car.

'There's nothing like it.' His eyes glazed. 'You're flying over that track, it's like you're joined together. Just you and the horse. You can read each other's mind.'

'Like Kruger does?'

'Maybe.'

'How?'

He shrugged. 'Little things. The bob of his head, the way he bunches his hindquarters. His pull on the reins. I can always tell how much he's got left in the tank. And when it's the right moment to ask for it.'

'Sounds exhilarating.'

He stabbed a finger at her. 'That's exactly what it is. Exhilarating.'

The waiter arrived with Harry's omelette, the savoury aroma triggering her digestive juices. Rob glared at her plate, then gulped down his drink and rattled his ice at the waiter.

'Same again,' he said.

Harry hesitated. Tucking into breakfast in the face of his starvation seemed a little crass, but in the end her own hunger won out. She forked up a mouthful of egg.

Then it occurred to her he'd probably know where Eve was staying.

'Which hotel are you in?' she said, between bites.

'Western Lodge. The better places were booked out – some kind of diamond convention in town.'

Harry thought of Ros and the Van Wycks Sight. The diamantaires were gathering. She kept her tone light.

'Is Eve staying there, too?'

'No.' He averted his eyes from her plate. 'Not sure where she is.'

'Hasn't she been in touch?'

He frowned, and was saved from answering by the arrival of his drink. He doctored it with his flask, then took a deep draught and leaned back in his chair. Harry was about to repeat the question, when he said,

'No one's heard from Eve since she left.'

Harry's fork stopped halfway to her mouth. 'What about Kruger? He must have been in contact with her.'

'I already called him.' Rob's teeth sounded clenched. 'He doesn't know where she is either.'

Harry's insides sank. 'You mean, she's missing?'

''Course she's not missing. Probably just playing the tourist for a few days, not answering her phone, that's all.'

'Is that usual?'

He shifted in his chair. 'Not really.'

Harry set her fork down with a clatter, her appetite gone. She needed Eve, and it wasn't a good sign that no one knew where she was. Rob narrowed his eyes at her.

'Why all the questions about Eve?'

340

'No reason.'

He leaned forward, his eyes blazing. 'Do you know something I don't?'

'No, I—'

'Because if you do, and I find out, then it won't be just Eve who's in trouble.'

Harry blinked. The alcohol seemed to have stoked up some internal rage inside him, and she wasn't sure quite how to deal with it. Silence seemed the best idea.

A pulse jumped at the corner of his eye. Then his face seemed to register that somehow he'd crossed a line. He leaned back, spread his palms upward.

'Hey, I apologize. I don't know where that came from. Worried about Eve, maybe.' He gave her a rueful look. 'We had a fight, if you must know. She went off in a huff.'

He watched for her reaction, inviting sympathy, but Harry couldn't care less about his domestic disputes.

'You expect her back, though, don't you?' she said.

'Sure. We fight all the time, but she always comes back.' He lowered his gaze, stared at his drink. 'It's not my fault, you know. Sometimes I overreact, but she's so stubborn, it just drives me mad.'

Harry frowned. People often told her that she was stubborn. Usually, what they meant was she wouldn't do things their way. She watched Rob's fist curl around his glass, the sinews on his arms standing out like tree roots. She remembered the bruises around Eve's neck, and shuddered.

Her phone chirped from the bottom of her bag. She dug it out. Private number. Maybe it was Ros calling with news on Fischer.

'Hello?'

'Look over at the bridge.'

Harry caught her breath. The harsh voice made her insides shrivel.

'I said, look!'

She snapped her gaze to the footbridge behind Rob. Her gut jolted. Standing by the walkway was a thickset man, his grey T-shirt taut over hard-looking biceps. He raised his baseball cap and waved.

'Enjoy your flight?'

The voice grated in her ear. The Van Wycks killer. Under his cap, a grey buzz-cut glinted in the sun. Her head swam. She watched him hook the cap back over his head.

'What do you want?' she whispered.

'Is blondie there involved?'

Harry shot Rob a glance. His attention was fixed on his glass. 'No.'

'You're lying.'

Harry glared over at the footbridge. The man in the baseball cap was leaning against the railings, one arm folded across his barrel-shaped chest. When he spoke again, his teeth sounded clenched.

'I want the diamonds.'

'I don't have them yet.'

'When?'

Harry's heartbeat drummed. 'These things take time.'

'You don't have time. Neither does your father.'

Harry tried to swallow, but her mouth was parched. 'I'll know tomorrow. She'll contact me, she'll tell me where and when.'

Rob's head jerked up, his gaze razor sharp. The voice in her ear grew harsher.

'You know what'll happen if you mess me around.'

'I won't, I swear.'

He didn't answer. Sweat flushed over her body in waves. Finally, he said,

'You've got two days.'

The line went dead.

40

Harry blundered through the crowds on the promenade, the blood roaring in her ears.

Two days.

Sweat flashed over her. Two days to find Eve in this alien city. She spun round, disoriented. Nearby street performers rapped out drum tattoos, chanting in complex rhythms. Acrobats whooped, tourists clapped. Harry's brain whirled, rudderless and off-course.

She scanned the surge of tourists for Rob's wheaten hair, but he'd disappeared. She'd scrambled out of the café with a mumbled excuse as soon as the Van Wycks killer had gone. Now she wished she'd stayed where she was. At least Rob knew his way around.

A sob hitched in her chest. Then she scrabbled in her bag for her phone. Her father. It wasn't too late to call him, warn him to stay away. What had made her think she could protect him out here, when she couldn't even protect herself? Her hands shook as she called her father's hotel room.

No answer.

Shit. Her head swam, and the dock seemed to tilt beneath her feet. She stumbled over to the railings at the edge of the promenade. Water lapped at the wall below her, and in the distance a yacht honked. She inhaled the briny harbour scent, trying to clear her head. Then her phone buzzed against the palm of her hand.

Harry stiffened. She checked the display. Private number. She swallowed and took the call.

'Yes?'

There was a pause. 'Harry, is that you?'

Harry sank back against the railings. 'Ros. Oh, thank God.'

'Are you okay? You sound odd.'

'I'm fine.' Harry almost laughed, giddy with relief at a familiar voice. 'Just glad to hear from you.'

'Where are you?'

Harry scoured the area, groping for a landmark, then gave it up. 'Somewhere by the waterfront.'

'In Cape Town? Good. I've talked to Jacob Fischer, he can meet you now if you're free. He's got an appointment, but he'll push it back half an hour for you.' Ros sounded puzzled. 'You're lucky, he doesn't usually change his schedule for anyone.'

'That's great.' At this stage, Harry didn't know how Fischer could help, but right now she was all out of options. 'Have you got his address? I don't have it on me.'

'He's on Coen Steytler Avenue, opposite the Convention Centre. Big marble-fronted showroom, you can't miss it.'

'I'm on my way now.'

Ros paused. 'Jacob knew Garvin Oliver for years, you know. I think that's why he wants to talk to you.'

Harry felt the skin pucker along her arms. Jacob Fischer's name had appeared only once on Garvin's hidden files, as the buyer of a 270-carat stone. It was hard to tell how involved he might be, but at the moment she didn't trust anyone.

She thanked Ros, disconnected the call, then dug her map out of her bag. From memory, Coen Steytler Avenue wasn't far from her hotel. She stepped away from the docks on to the busy main thoroughfares. The mid-morning sun cooked her skin. Traffic blared through the shimmering streets, and towering above them was Table Mountain, slate-grey and craggy. Harry shuddered. It looked like a place where giants and trolls might live.

By the time she found Fischer Diamond House, her back was drenched in sweat. Ros was right, the jewellery showroom was hard to miss. Grey and white marble fronted the building, with silvery diamond logos embedded in the stone. The glass entrance door was locked, but Harry found a bell and announced herself to a crackling intercom. The door buzzed open and she stepped inside. Instantly, the temperature dropped fifteen degrees, and Harry gasped with relief.

The woman who'd buzzed her in approached with a tray bearing orange juice and flutes of champagne.

'Mr Fischer will be with you shortly. Would you like some refreshment?'

Harry thanked her and snagged an orange juice, gulping it down while her eyes swept the room. A curved showcase took centre stage, display lights blazing on to rows of jewels. More showcases lined the walls, the whole setup under surveillance from discreetly mounted cameras.

A door opened at the other end of the room and a bearded man shambled over towards her. He was as round as a beachball, and had to be a hundred pounds overweight. His thighs pushed together with every step, pulling his knees inwards in a pigeon-toed gait. The steel-grey hair and goatee put him in his late fifties, though with all the padding it was hard to tell. He held out his hand.

'Jacob Fischer, pleased to meet you. Ros said you'd come by.' He sounded breathless from his short haul across the room. Without waiting for her reply, he heaved himself around like a ship on a turning manoeuvre and began retracing his steps. 'I hope you don't mind, but we'll have to talk while I work.'

'That's fine.' Harry trotted after him, noting the limp ponytail hanging halfway down his back and the small gold hoop in his ear. 'I appreciate your seeing me at all.'

She followed him back through the unmarked door and down a narrow passageway. His trouser legs swished as he walked. Harry winced. Chafing had to be a problem for him. He slid her a glance over his shoulder.

'Ros said you had questions about Garvin Oliver.'

347

His accent was stronger than Kruger's, the vowels more compressed, the 'r's harder.

'That's right,' Harry said. 'I'm hoping you can clear up some details for me.'

'Are you with the police?'

'Not exactly.' Harry crossed her fingers. 'I'm a forensics investigator, Garvin's come up in another case I'm working on.'

He paused beside a metal door and contemplated her for a moment. He teased at his beard, his chest wheezing. She hoped he wouldn't ask to see any kind of ID, but he seemed preoccupied with some knotty problem of his own. Then he ran a tongue over his lips.

'Can you tell me more about how he died?'

'He was shot in his home. They're not sure who did it yet.'

Jacob nodded, his forehead spangled with sweat. He punched the keys on a combination lock by the door, and Harry noticed that his fingers were trembling.

'Did you know Garvin well?' she said.

Jacob shrugged. 'We studied gemology together thirty years ago. We stayed in touch.'

He lumbered ahead of her into a long, narrow workshop where half a dozen men sat hunched over wooden benches. Harry trailed behind him. The room smelled like a toolbox, full of oil and dust.

'Did you ever buy any rough diamonds from Garvin?' She had to raise her voice over the whirring of motors and grinding tools.

'Sometimes,' Jacob said. 'Small rough, mostly good quality. Not everyone would deal with him, but I threw him a lifeline now and then.'

'Why?'

'Because I could.' He rolled to a halt beside one of the workers. 'Garvin was one of the unluckiest men I ever knew.'

'Really? That's a view of him I haven't heard before.'

Jacob didn't answer. He bent over the desk to inspect a small envelope the size of a sugar sachet. He poured out the contents, a tiny pile of crystals, the whole heap no bigger than a pinch of salt. He pushed his finger into it and the crystals clung to his flesh. Then he screwed a loupe against his eye and peered at them. Harry noticed he was holding his breath, probably afraid his wheezing would puff the flecks away.

He grunted, then sprinkled the crystals back in place. He plodded on to the next bench, talking over his shoulder. 'Everything Garvin did turned to shit.'

'The impression I got, that was mostly his own fault.'

'*Ja*, it was. But sometimes things went wrong that were outside of his control. Look, he's been shot, hasn't he?'

'Are you saying you're not surprised he's dead?'

Jacob shrugged. 'Like I said, the man was unlucky.'

He paused by the next bench. The workman was holding a complicated-looking steel clamp up to the loupe in his eye. On the bench in front of him was a spinning turntable, coated in fine, black dust. The workman lowered the clamp tip against the wheel, let it grind there for a moment, then brought it back to his loupe. He repeated the sequence every few seconds.

Jacob caught her eye. 'He's cutting facets into the diamond. Fifty-eight in all.'

Harry's eyes widened. Fifty-eight angled surfaces on a stone so small she couldn't even see it. She gaped at the workman, then turned her attention back to Jacob.

'You don't just deal in small stones, though, do you? You bought at least one large rough from Garvin. What was it, 270 carats?'

Jacob shot a glance at the nearby workers, then narrowed his eyes at Harry. He breathed heavily through his nose for a moment. Then he turned and tramped into an office off the workshop, signalling for Harry to follow. He shut the door, then collapsed into a chair behind the desk. Dark moons of sweat ringed his armpits.

'Where did you hear that? It's bullshit,' he said.

'There's a record of the transaction on Garvin's files. Large white rough, 270 carats.' Harry pulled up a seat. 'You bought it about a year ago.'

'I don't care what his records say, it's still bullshit.' His gaze skittered away from hers, his mouth a thin line.

Damn. She needed him chatty, not scared and tight-lipped. She shrugged and aimed for a careless tone.

'Look, the police have his files, they know who he dealt with. Tell you the truth, we couldn't care less where you get your stones.' If he noticed the casual 'we', he didn't give any sign. 'All we want is information about Garvin.'

Jacob fished a handkerchief out of his shirt pocket and

dabbed at his forehead with it. 'It was a lapse in judgement. I should never have bought it.'

'Oh?'

'He swore it was legit, said he'd been shipping others just like it into Antwerp for months.' He mopped his face some more. 'Of course, Antwerp never asks too many questions.'

'Did you know he'd acquired the stone illegally?'

He wouldn't meet her eyes. 'I knew it was a Van Wycks stone. And I knew it was impossible to buy one of such size out on the open market. Van Wycks have throttled back large rough production, suppressed it altogether in some of their pits.'

'So it had to have been smuggled directly out of the mines?'

Jacob nodded. 'The only other place you'd find a stone like that is in the Van Wycks stockpile itself.'

'It was that unusual?'

For a moment, he didn't answer. Then he looked up, his dark eyes shining.

'Would you like to see it?'

41

Harry stared at the suede drawstring pouch that Jacob had set on the desk. He cradled it with his palm, stroking the soft-looking fabric as if it was a kitten.

'When Garvin first showed me the stone, it took my breath away,' he said.

'I'm surprised you still have it. I thought you'd have sold it on by now.'

He looked shocked at the notion. 'A stone like that, it can't be rushed. It takes time to cut it. And nerve.' He gave her a sheepish smile. 'If you want to know the truth, I was afraid of it. Large diamonds can be treacherous. They're hard, but they're brittle. Hit a structural flaw, and they can burst into powder.'

Harry recalled the photo in Garvin's file; the large, cloudy crystal as big as an egg. Jacob fingered the pouch.

'I studied it for weeks, not daring to cut it,' he went on.

'There was a small gletz, I couldn't be sure how deep it went. Then finally, I cut a window on to it, a small facet to view inside. The gletz wasn't deep, and the interior was clear. Plenty of light.'

Jacob ran his tongue over his lips, guarding the pouch jealously with his hand. Harry wondered had he changed his mind about showing her what was inside. She let him talk on, wondering where all this was going.

'I made some plastic models, experimented on them until I was ready,' he said. 'It took me almost a year to cut this stone. I did it myself, by hand. One hundred and ninety-seven facets.'

Harry raised her eyebrows, not sure what to say. His fingers looked too pudgy to hold a knife and fork, let alone carve tiny angles on a stone. Jacob loosened the neck of the drawstring pouch.

'People think the diamond trade is about selling stones, but they're wrong.'

'They are?'

He held up a finger. 'The diamond trade sells light. Brilliant light, liberated from the rough. It bounces inside the cut stone, reflecting off the facets. The better the cut, the more reflected light there is.' He clenched his fist. 'That's what gives a stone its fire.'

Harry blinked. She wondered at the generations of skill and artistry that had evolved into this unlikely-looking master cutter. Jacob dropped his hand back to the pouch and slipped his fingers inside.

'A cutter must think like a beam of light, he must

imagine himself inside the stone.' He extracted something from the pouch, closing his fist over it. 'A cutter must turn it from a stone into a jewel.'

He gave Harry a direct look, then held up the stone between his thumb and forefinger. Harry gasped. She couldn't help it. The diamond was a plump pyramid of light, as big as a golf ball. Jacob twirled it in his thick fingers. Its shimmering surface was a mound of facets, thrashing out shards of dazzling light.

Harry felt a tug in her chest. 'It's beautiful.'

She stared at the sparkling jewel and thought of the atrocities that stained the diamond trail. Something squirmed inside her. She thought of the massive corporate stockpiling; of the clever marketing and the elaborate hoax that conned the world into thinking that diamonds were rare. The stone flashed slivers of light. Was there anything instinctive in her reaction to its beauty? Or was it all just conditioning?

She looked away, not liking the notion that she'd been played all her life like one of Pavlov's dogs. She cleared her throat.

'How much is it worth?'

The question sounded crude in the face of such craftsmanship, but she felt on firmer ground with it.

Jacob shrugged. 'I had to cut away a lot of the weight, but it's still almost a hundred and eighty carats.'

'So, how much?'

He sighed. 'Fourteen, fifteen million.'

Harry's eyes widened. 'Rand?'

'US dollars.'

Harry gaped at him and worked out the sums. He'd bought it from Garvin for five million euros; say, seven million dollars. On the roughest of exchange rates, that still doubled his money.

'Not a bad profit for a year's work,' she said.

Jacob shook his head and slipped the stone back in its pouch. 'It's cost me more than that already. I paid dearly for this stone, much more than I ever gave to Garvin.'

Harry frowned. 'How come?'

'Van Wycks. They found out I'd bought it.' He shrugged, palms turned outward. 'They weren't happy.'

'But what could they do?'

'I'm a sightholder, they control my supply of Van Wycks stones. They made sure I paid for my mistake.'

'I don't understand.'

Jacob sighed, then twisted in his seat, grunting as he returned the pouch to the small safe behind him. He straightened up, panting from the effort, then slumped back against his chair.

'They hauled me in, threatened me with expulsion from the Cape Town Sight. They didn't do it, but for months afterwards, my sightboxes were filled with rubbish. Small stones, poor colours. Worthless leftovers. Two or three million dollars down the drain each time.'

'They made you pay millions for worthless stones?'

'The price of your sightbox is fixed, there's no haggling. Take it or leave it.'

'So why didn't you just leave it?'

Jacob snorted. 'And lose my only supply channel? Complain or refuse to buy and you're out for good, expelled from the sight.'

'Aren't there other suppliers?'

'Not for Van Wycks rough. It's very high grade, outstanding quality. And the large stones are so rare, the retail profits are astronomical. The Cape Town Sight is the only place to get them.'

Harry shook her head, marvelling at the power games. 'So who decides which diamantaire gets what?'

'Head of Buying, Montgomery Newman. He was the one who threatened to expel me. I've an appointment with him shortly, as a matter of fact.' Jacob snorted. 'Some last-minute ass-licking to make sure I'm still in his good books.'

'You've redeemed yourself with him, then? How?'

He shifted in his seat. 'Let's just say I've had to prove my loyalty.'

Harry studied his face. A tiny muscle pulsed beneath his eye, and she wondered just what Van Wycks had asked him to do. She saw him sneak a look at his watch, and her mind groped for the questions she needed to ask.

'Just a couple more things,' she said. 'Did you ever hear of a buyer called Gray?'

Jacob frowned. 'I don't think so. Who is he?'

'That's what I'm trying to find out. It looks as though he had an exclusive arrangement with Garvin. Apart from the stone he sold to you, Garvin sold all of his large rough to Gray.'

Jacob's brow cleared, and he shook his head. 'There was no buyer called Gray, you can depend on it. It was Van Wycks, operating incognito. When they hauled me over the coals, they told me they would mop up his stones.'

Harry screwed up her face. 'What?'

'Mopping up – it's common practice in mining corporations, has been for decades. Van Wycks was buying back its own smuggled stones.'

'But why?'

'Same reason they do just about everything. To control the price. If they didn't buy them back, the stones would flood the market and the price would drop. Mopping up happens all the time. The big mining companies used to spend fifteen million dollars a week mopping up diamonds in Angola.'

'Do you think Garvin knew?'

'I doubt it. Van Wycks probably operated through an entity in Antwerp so Garvin wouldn't make the connection. Anyway, even if he guessed, so what? They probably paid him a fair price, so what did he care?'

Something crawled along the base of Harry's spine. Van Wycks had such power, such total control. They dominated the world's most prestigious diamantaires, bullying them as though they were fat kids in a playground. Van Wycks made all the rules, meted out all the punishments. The tyranny of the cartel was absolute.

She chewed her lip, and wondered what had pushed them to eliminate Garvin. Sure, he'd become a thorn in their side, but they'd had him under control for the past year, if what Jacob said was true. They'd successfully diverted his stolen diamonds back into their own stock-pile. So what had changed that made it necessary to kill him?

Jacob checked his watch, then heaved himself to his feet. 'If you don't mind, I'll walk you to the door. I need to keep that appointment.'

He led the way back through the dusty workshop, his large girth quivering with every step. When they reached the corridor, Harry said,

'Did you ever deal with Garvin's step-daughter, Eve?'

'I never met his family, it wasn't that kind of friend-ship.'

Harry trudged after him into the showroom. The question had been a long shot, but there had to be some way of snagging a breadcrumb on her trail. She hitched her bag higher on her shoulder, preparing to shake his hand as he waited by the glass door. Then a thought struck her.

'Did Garvin ever approach you again?'

His gaze slid sideways. 'I never bought any more large stones from him.'

'But did he offer them to you?'

He sucked in air and looked at his shoes, though he probably couldn't see them over his stomach. Then he said, 'He came back once. Two months ago. But I told him I wasn't interested.'

'Why did he come back? Was he getting tired of selling to Gray?'

Jacob wiped his palms along his trousers, then punched a release button and tugged open the glass door. 'Maybe.'

He stepped aside, gesturing for her to leave. Harry didn't move.

'So he wanted to branch out. Van Wycks can't have been happy with that.'

His gaze shifted past her down the street. 'Maybe they didn't know.'

She stared at his face. It was slick with sweat. Van Wycks did know, Harry was sure of it. They knew he was preparing to sell his stones elsewhere. And once they realized they could no longer control him, they'd decided to take Garvin out.

Jacob still wouldn't meet her eyes. She was willing to bet that he'd told Van Wycks about Garvin's change of plan. He'd sold Garvin out to prove his allegiance to the cartel.

Jacob was right. His fabulous stone had cost him.

She thanked him for his time and headed outside. The baked air swaddled her, squeezing perspiration from her pores. Mentally, she replayed everything she'd learned, but knew she was no closer to finding Eve.

Harry hiked along the broiling streets, heading back to her hotel. Maybe sleep and food would fire up her brain. Then her phone rang from the bottom of her bag, and she jumped. She ducked into the shade of a high-rise office block to check the caller ID. Her limbs relaxed, and she took the call.

'Imogen? I meant to contact you.'

'I bet you did. I haven't heard from you in two days, where've you been?'

Harry winced. 'Cape Town.'

'*Cape* Town? What on earth are you doing there?'

'It's a bit involved to explain over the phone.'

Imogen paused. 'You're still trying to find that Oliver woman, aren't you?'

'Yes.' Harry bit her lip, guilt pricking her like a needle jab. She hadn't been much of a friend to Imogen lately, cutting her out of the loop and going off for days on end. But things were too dangerous to involve Imogen now. 'I'll need to stay here a few more days. Can you cope in the office?'

'Is that why you needed the satphone?'

'What?'

'The satellite phone. The number's doodled here on your pad . . .'

Dimly, Harry recalled copying something out when she was trawling through Garvin's hard drive. The odd twelve-digit number he'd stored in his hidden file.

'. . . 881677273934,' Imogen recited. 'It's a satphone number, isn't it?'

Harry blinked. 'How do you know?'

'Me and Shane talked about an African Safari honeymoon. Mobile coverage is pretty limited in remote areas, so we looked into satphones.' Imogen snorted. 'Won't be needing one now, will I? Anyway, 881 is the country code set aside for satellite phones. Yours looks like an Iridium network number to me.'

'It's not mine, so don't call it.' It came out sharper than Harry'd intended. 'Sorry. Can you call it out again?'

She fished in her bag for a pen and paper. Imogen repeated the number in a tight voice, then said,

'What's going on? Are you okay?'

Harry closed her eyes, and swallowed against the lump that had bobbed up in her throat. She'd give anything to confide in Imogen; to let someone tell her what to do, reassure her she wasn't alone. Images floated across her brain: Eddie's grisly, empty sockets, her father's smiling face. Her eyes flared open. She couldn't take the risk.

'Sorry, Imogen, I know I'm being a pain in the ass, but I'll make it up to you, I promise. Gotta go, I'll call you later.'

Harry disconnected, heaving out a long breath. Then she frowned at the digits she'd scribbled down. Why would Garvin store a satellite phone number alongside the list of horses that transported his stones? Was this how he communicated with his couriers on the ground? Was this how he checked in with Eve?

She stared at the number and wondered who would answer if she dialled it.

42

Mani opened his eyes. The shack was dark and quiet.

He shifted on the hard bunk, his bones aching. Light threaded between the corrugated walls, and slowly his vision adjusted to the clutter around him: cooking pots, clothes, dishes and water drums. Leaning against one wall was the rusted side panel of a car.

He heaved himself up and sat on the edge of the bunk. Sweat rolled down his back, and the smell of rotting fruit seeped out from the wound in his arm.

His bag lay flattened where he'd been sleeping on it. He groped inside, checking for the diamonds and the clunky mobile phone he'd taken from Sanjeet's plane. They were still there.

Sanjeet had dropped him at a makeshift airstrip a few miles from the Cape Flats. Mani had swayed in the wind-swept plains, wondering where to go. Impossible to return to his student lodgings. He didn't belong there now. In the end, he'd made his way to the shantytowns near the N2 motorway. Takata had cousins there, family that might help.

The sound of women's voices drifted into the shack from outside. Mani slung the bag over his shoulder and got to his feet, picking his way across the uneven floor. He stepped out into the sunlight, eyes squinting.

A stout woman stood by the door, rinsing plates in a plastic bowl. Wisps of grey hair poked out from under her blue bandana. She turned to him with wide eyes.

'What you doing out here?' She flapped her cloth at him. 'Look at you, why you not lie down like I say?'

Mani tried to smile. Her name was Fatima. She was Takata's cousin, though she looked much older than him, probably in her seventies. He blinked up at the sun.

'I think I need some air. I will walk a little.'

She plonked her fists on her hips. 'How you can walk? You need to rest.'

'I won't go far.'

He turned down the dusty track that ran between the shanties. Behind him, Fatima muttered, sloshing water in her bowl. He wished he had something to give her. She had lived in the shantytown for over forty years. Before that, she'd grown up in District Six, a neighbourhood not far from the Cape Town docks. She'd been evicted to the Flats when her home had been rezoned for whites and demolished by the government.

Now she shared an eight-by-ten-foot space with nine other members of her family.

Mani stumbled on the rough dirt track. Dizziness whirled inside his head. Maybe Fatima was right, maybe he was not fit to walk. He clutched his bag, fingering the shape of the phone inside. The battery was running low. He'd switched it off at night, trying to make it last. Something squeezed his chest. Maybe he'd already missed a call.

He trudged past the converted cargo container that the community used as a school. The air was thick with the charred smell of fires, and the sourness of open latrines. The shantytown was much like the one near the mine, where he had lived since he was ten. Mani watched a group of enterprising women selling sheeps' heads at the next corner. Buzzing flies stuck to the meat in clumps. His stomach churned, and he lowered his eyes, feeling like a traitor. These people had courage. Hope, even. But he knew he could not bear to live in a place like this again.

Suddenly, his bag vibrated against his arm. The phone chirped inside, and Mani snatched it out. He stared at the display. The number started with 021, the Cape Town area prefix.

He swallowed and took the call. Without saying anything, he put the phone to his ear. Emptiness echoed over the line. No one spoke.

His heart pounded his chest. The caller was expecting Chandra. Perhaps there was a code, something he was meant to say. How could he know? He had to explain himself before they hung up.

'Hello?' He licked his lips. 'Am I speaking to Eve?'

The line hissed in his ear. He rushed on.

'Raj Chandra, he is dead, but I am here in his place.'

No answer.

'My name is Mani dos Santos, I am Ezra's brother. I've brought the stones.'

He heard a small stirring on the line. Then a woman spoke.

'You have the diamonds?'

Her voice was soft. Cautious. Mani tightened his grip on the phone.

'Yes. Three of them, over two hundred carats each.'

The woman paused. 'What happened to Raj?'

Her accent was gentle, soft around the edges. Mani swallowed.

'Someone killed him, cut out his eyes. I don't know who.'

He heard her catch her breath. When she did not respond, he said,

'I am here to keep Ezra's side of the bargain. Please, just tell me where to deliver the stones.'

Harry sat down on the bed, the hotel phone clutched to her ear. Her brain whirled. This man thought she was Eve.

She'd paced her hotel room for several hours before she'd worked up the nerve to make the call. In the end, she'd decided to just dial the number and listen.

'Please,' he said again. 'Tell me what to do.'

He sounded unsure, as though he didn't know the rules. That made two of them. Her pulse hammered in her throat. She played for time.

'How do I know you're not lying to me?'

'I am telling the truth, I swear it to you! I work in the Van Wycks mine, just like Ezra. I have brought the stones out for you. Please, I swear it.'

Harry swallowed. He sounded young. So he was a miner, he smuggled the stones out. But something in his voice was not what she expected. It resonated with her, but she couldn't get a fix on it.

The miner coughed at the other end of the phone, a wet, slashing sound that seemed to grip him in spasm. He sounded in pain.

Asbestos, to you and me. It's a horrible, lingering death.

Harry squeezed her eyes shut and hugged her arm around her waist. The ragged coughing ripped across the phone line. She dug her bare feet into the soft carpet, her toes clenched. Had she made a mistake? Or was this her route to the diamonds? Maybe she no longer needed Eve. This person called Mani would give her the stones, then she'd pass them on to the Van Wycks killer. Circle closed, game over.

Harry shuddered. Something told her it wouldn't be that simple.

The bout of coughing passed, and Mani croaked into the phone. 'Please, are you still there?'

She hunched her shoulders and began rocking on the bed. 'I'm still here.'

'Tell me what to do.'

Harry kneaded her forehead. 'Where are you now?'

'The Cape Flats. I can meet wherever you say.'

Harry pictured the corrugated metal shanties by the freeway. Her brain scrambled, hunting for pointers to her next move. This man might know more than she thought. If she was going to meet him, it might be wise to stick to a place that Eve may conceivably have used. She thought of Dawn Light, the next courier in the chain.

'Kenilworth Quarantine Station,' she said. 'Do you know it?'

'I can find it.'

Harry checked her watch. It was almost seven in the evening. The racecourse was probably closed, and it would soon be dark. Too dark to meet up with strangers.

'Tomorrow morning, eleven o'clock.'

'I will be there.' Mani's voice was hoarse. 'Please, I beg you, please don't hurt my family.'

Harry stopped rocking, her breath caught. Mani continued:

'I'll keep Ezra's part of the deal, I'll deliver the stones. You have already killed my mother, you know I will do as you say. Please don't hurt the rest of my family.'

Harry clamped a hand over her mouth.

You have already killed my mother.

Her brain whirled, and she flashed on her father's face.

Something wrenched at her insides. She knew now what she'd recognized in Mani's voice. She knew, because she was consumed with it herself.

It was fear.

43

Harry's fingers clenched on the wheel.

Please don't hurt my family.

She could still hear his voice, weak and afraid. Mani
was a victim, just like her. If he failed to deliver the stones
to Eve, would his family take the punishment? A low
murmur of dread hummed along her spine. She thought
of what she was about to do to him, but her brain skittered away, searching for somewhere safer to land.

The map. Focus on the map.

She squinted at the road, trying to concentrate on her
route. Kenilworth Racecourse was tucked away in the
southern suburbs of Cape Town. The streets were laid
out in a simple grid so it should have been easy to find,
but Harry's nerves were jangled and she'd already made
a few false starts.

Peering through the windscreen, she searched for road

signs. The suburb was flanked by winelands and gardens, which probably made it expensive. The houses looked large and handsome, all of them guarded by electronic gates and signs that read: 'Warning! Premises protected by ARU'. It took Harry a few passes to decipher the small print. ARU stood for 'Armed Response Unit'.

Harry shuddered, wondering at the tensions that splintered this city. What use was a graceful mansion if it made you live in fear?

She criss-crossed over on to Rosmead Avenue and finally spotted the racecourse entrance to her right. She turned in, edging her way into the car park. It was almost full. She snagged a vacant spot and climbed out of the car. The morning sun blazed like a furnace, and already she could feel the sweat trickling from under her arms. Car doors slammed nearby, and a bevy of women tottered past, their party frocks fluttering in the breeze. Behind them, three men lugged a picnic hamper bigger than a tea chest.

Harry frowned. Damn. It hadn't occurred to her it might be race day.

She followed the picnickers into the grounds. There was quite a crowd and she dodged off the tarmac path to avoid them, detouring across the grass. It was spongy underfoot, the air lightly scented from occasional tubs of flowers. Party-goers had set up camp along rows of blue and white benches, the champagne and cooler boxes already open though it was still only ten in the morning.

Harry scanned the area for signs of the quarantine

station. All she knew was that it was located somewhere in the racecourse. She threaded through the crowds. The women were like butterflies in their bright summer dresses. The men looked more casual, though designer labels seemed to be the norm. Everyone was laughing a little too hard, just to show what a great time they were having.

Harry passed by the empty parade ring, an immaculate oval of green, and stopped at the edge of the racetrack. Her gaze raked her surroundings. To her left was the grandstand, a huge mosaic of blue and yellow seats. Behind and to her right, was Table Mountain, rising up like a movie backdrop. She didn't know what a quarantine station looked like, but nothing here seemed to fit.

'Harry?'

She spun round. Dan Kruger was staring at her from the other side of the parade ring. She felt herself tense as he crossed towards her, and she worked hard not to back away.

'What are you doing here?' he said.

The last time she'd seen him he'd been dressed like a cowboy, in jeans and leather chaps. Today he'd swapped the rancher look for cool, cricket whites. Harry had to admit, they sat well on his long-limbed frame. She squinted up at him.

'I could say the same of you. Your flight only came in a couple of hours ago, didn't it?'

He shrugged. 'Sal's resting up back in the hotel, but I'm okay.'

Harry's stomach tightened at the mention of her father. 'Which hotel is he in?'

'The Commodore. By the looks of him, he'll sleep most of the day.'

Harry gnawed at her lip. Her father's hotel was probably as safe as anywhere for him right now. Her gaze shifted past Kruger to the tall woman striding purposefully towards them. Cassie.

The vet's summer dress fluttered around her long legs, and her bare arms looked well toned. Her russet hair was coiled up in a bun, adding to her height. The overall effect was of a graceful, well-proportioned athlete.

Cassie moved next to Kruger, linking her arm through his. She greeted Harry, inquired about her flight. Then she said,

'Seems a long way to come when you don't really like horses.'

Harry frowned. The vet's smile took the edge off her words, but even so Harry noticed the shift in tone. She wondered what had changed since they'd last met.

'I'm just here to keep my father company.' Harry looked from one to the other. 'Have either of you heard from Eve?'

Kruger hesitated, glanced at Cassie. Then he said, 'No, why?'

'I met Rob yesterday. He said no one knew where she was.'

Cassie flapped a hand and edged away. 'She'll turn up. They've had another blow-out, that's all. Not the first, and won't be the last.'

The vet seemed tense, anxious to be gone. Maybe it was Harry's jangled state of mind, but she found herself speculating about the real reason Cassie was in Cape Town. Was it just to be with Kruger? Or was there more to it than that?

Cassie was the stable vet, after all. She probably examined the new arrivals in the yard, and had more opportunity than most to recover any hidden stones. If she was part of the syndicate, then Eve's radar silence might have unnerved her. Maybe Cassie was here to track her down.

A tannoy system crackled into the silence, announcing the runners for the next race. Kruger turned to Cassie.

'Why don't you go ahead and place those bets?' He patted her arm to dispel the look of resistance she gave him. 'I'll meet you up in the stands.'

He eased his arm out of hers and she edged away, her expression cagey. When she'd disappeared through the crowds, Kruger said,

'She wanted to make a holiday out of it, do some sightseeing.' The concept seemed to puzzle him. He glanced around the racecourse, and his expression relaxed. 'I'd rather be here. Besides, there's a three-year-old running that I want to see. And Rob's riding in the Jockeys' race in an hour. Are you going to watch it?'

'I may not have time. I've an appointment with someone.'

He threw her a curious look. 'Are you here to see the bloodstock sales?'

She could tell from his tone that he didn't think it likely.

'Not really.' She scrambled for something else to say,

before he could quiz her further. 'How many horses do you plan to buy?'

'Two. Maybe four. I never buy in odd numbers.'

Harry raised her eyebrows. He hadn't struck her as the superstitious type. He smiled and shook his head.

'That's more scientific than it sounds. I always increase the herd in two's. For all their pack hierarchy, horses tend to form friendships. They usually have one special companion, another horse in the herd they can trust.' He gave her a direct look. 'A bit like humans, in a way.'

Harry looked away, not knowing how to respond. Whatever she might have told Cassie, she couldn't deny there was something mesmerizing about this man. She folded her arms across her chest.

'Aren't you worried at all about Eve?'

'She can look after herself. Eve's one of the toughest women I know, never seen her afraid of anything. She should have been a jockey.' Kruger's gaze roamed the crowds. 'She'll be in touch. She's not due to travel back with Dawn Light till Sunday.'

'Dawn Light's in the quarantine station, isn't he? Somewhere here in the racecourse?'

He nodded and pointed across the track. 'Over there, right at the other side of the course.'

Harry squinted across the fenced-off racetrack. About a mile away, she could make out a set of low buildings, tinged a greenish grey as though in camouflage with the landscape. She scoured the track perimeter, looking for a way across.

'How do you get over there?'

'You drive round. There's a back entrance to the racecourse on Wetton Road, then you follow the dirt track. But you won't see Dawn Light. They won't let you in. It's strictly supervised.'

Harry nodded, and checked her watch: ten fifteen. She needed to get going.

The tannoy echoed over the crowd as the commentary got underway. Kruger shot her a look.

'Have you ever watched a race?'

Harry thought of her trips to Leopardstown as a child, where she'd trailed after her father. She dimly recalled peering between the legs of grown-ups, or cheering on horses in Madigan's Bar.

'Years ago, yes.'

'But up close. Have you ever seen one up close?'

She shrugged, shook her head. He was staring at her, his gaze intense. Then he seemed to make up his mind about something and grabbed her by the hand.

'Come on.'

'What—'

His grip was warm and firm. He dragged her along the railings without a backward glance. She stumbled after him, bumping through the crowds, holding on to her bag. He hauled her on, until he'd fetched up next to the winning post. He pulled her in beside him, then leaned his elbows on the rails. She felt his closeness, and a charge jolted through her.

'Watch,' he said.

The crowd pressed against her, hemming her in. She gripped on to the rails, had no choice but to wait it out. The commentator drilled through a run-down of horses, his rising pitch sending murmurs of excitement through the crowd. The man beside Harry bellowed in her ear.

'Come on, Bluebird!'

She could feel the first tremors in the ground. She tightened her fingers on the rail, felt it buzz. A rolling thunder was gathering to her left.

'*Come* on, Bluebird! *Come* on!'

The crowd surged forward, squeezing Harry up against the rails. Voices roared, urgent and male.

'Come *on*, Bluebird! Come *on*, Bluebird!'

The ground vibrated and rumbled beneath her feet. The storm to her left grew louder, the crashing sound of hooves drumming at top speed. The crowd was frantic, the commentator drowned out. Suddenly, a dozen horses exploded past her in a torrent of hammering power and speed. The noise of pounding hooves blasted through her, filling her up. The jockeys were colourful blurs, streamlined for speed: bellies flat to their horses' shoulders, faces pressed into their manes. An involuntary surge of adrenaline tore through Harry's body, her fingers tingling with the rush.

And then, just as quickly, it was over. The horses charged away down the track, the deafening noise receding. The crowd thinned, releasing Harry from the rails, and the commentator had come down off his high.

She turned to Kruger. His eyes were shining, his face

flushed. She wondered if hers was the same. He looked at her as if to say, 'You see?'

She smiled and nodded. In truth, she wasn't quite sure what she'd seen. But maybe she'd caught a glimpse of what made Rob and Kruger tick.

She gestured vaguely with her arm. 'I should go. I'm meeting someone.'

He nodded, his eyes still fiery. She checked her watch. Something twisted in her gut as she thought about her next move. She turned away, cutting across the thick grass. When she reached the parade ring, she flashed him a backward glance. He was checking his form book, marking it with a pen. Beyond him, the dim outlines of the quarantine station shimmered in the heat. It looked gloomy and isolated, like an outpost in a swamp.

She took a deep breath, then turned and headed for her car.

44

QUARANTINE AREA – NO UNAUTHORIZED
ENTRY.

Harry's pulse thudded high in her throat. She remembered the KEEP OUT sign on Kruger's gate. Maybe if she'd heeded that one, she wouldn't be in such trouble now.

She stared out at the black-on-yellow sign and kept the engine going. As long as she stayed in the car, she could still cut and run, couldn't she?

She flexed her fingers on the wheel and peered out at the steel-mesh fence. Beyond it was a row of five or six buildings, like small, brick warehouses. Opposite them was some kind of giant carousel: a revolving platform corralled by another fence, with a lone horse plodding around inside it. He didn't look thrilled about his morning workout.

Apart from the horse, there was no other sign of life.

Harry nosed the car next to a nearby clump of trees, angling it into the shade. Then she switched off the engine. She was half an hour early, but somehow she'd felt sure he'd be here before her. She eased open the door and climbed out, her gaze sweeping the area. The steel fence curved away from her, enclosing the quarantine station. Far to her left, the grandstand was barely visible, the commentator's voice a mosquito's whine.

She stepped up to the gate, which seemed to be controlled by an intercom with a red buzzer. She stared through the bars. Hooves clump-clumped on the circling treadmill, and the grassy scent of horse hung in the air. Something moved to her right. A door opened in one of the low buildings, and Harry tensed. A young black man came out, dressed in green overalls and protective gloves and boots. He glanced at her, then looked away, bending to fill a bucket from a nearby tap. Then he punched in a code on a keypad by the door and went back inside the building.

Harry checked her watch, then edged along the fence perimeter. A tremor started up in her knees, and she tried to recall Mani's voice. He was probably more afraid of her than she was of him. Like spiders. She took a deep breath. Fear was unsettling her brain.

'Eve?'

Harry gasped, spun round. A man was leaning into the fence, his fingers hooked through the wire mesh for support. He was young, in his twenties. Just a boy, really.

His skin was nutmeg-brown and his face was drenched in sweat.

Harry hesitated. 'Mani? Are you Mani?'

He closed his eyes and nodded. Then his arms began to tremble, and his fingers lost their grip on the wire. He slid to the ground, sat slumped in the dirt.

Harry gasped, took a step towards him, then stopped. He looked ill. His face was screwed up in pain. But how did she know he wasn't going to hurt her?

His hand fluttered towards the bag on his shoulder. '*Os diamantes.*'

His voice was faint. She edged forward. He turned heavy-lidded eyes towards her. They looked feverish, too glazed even to see her.

'*Os diamantes,*' he whispered.

Harry squinted at him. Her muscles were rigid, ready for flight. Mani ran a tongue over cracked lips.

'*Meu irmão Ezra me enviou.*'

Harry frowned. It was Spanish, yet not Spanish. Intuitively, she glimpsed some meaning in his words. *My brother Ezra sent me.*

'*Pegue isso,*' Mani said.

She chewed her lip, shook her head. Then she gave an elaborate shrug to show she couldn't understand. '*Lo siento, no le entiendo.*'

His eyes flickered in her direction, and he seemed to look at her with interest for a moment. Then his head fell back against the fence, rolling from side to side.

'Meu irmão Ezra me enviou.'

His voice sounded pleading. Was he delirious? His consonants had a faint Russian sound that swallowed his vowels up. Then suddenly Harry understood. He wasn't speaking Spanish; he was speaking Portuguese.

'Please.' She clasped her hands together, kneading her knuckles. 'Can we speak English?'

He looked at her, confused. 'I . . . Yes. I am sorry.'

He hunched his shoulders and began to cough. His lungs crackled like firewood, and Harry winced. She noticed his left arm was bandaged near the shoulder, the dressing badly stained. Even as he coughed, a brownish fluid seeped into it.

The hacking subsided. Mani fumbled for his bag, groping inside it with his right hand. His left arm seemed to be useless.

'The diamonds,' he said. 'I have them, they are here.'

He fished out a parcel of grubby fabric held together with string. He tossed it on the ground towards Harry, his eyes pleading.

'Take it.'

Harry stared at the small package. She couldn't move.

Mani groped in his bag again and dragged out a bottle of water. He tried to unscrew the top with his teeth, his left arm limp by his side, but the bottle slipped from his grasp on to the dirt. Harry jerked forward.

'Here, let me.'

She unscrewed the top, then knelt down to hold the bottle to his lips while he drank. Up close, she could see that his bandaged arm was badly discoloured, the swollen flesh oozing a smell of decaying bananas.

Mani nodded and widened his eyes to show he'd finished. She handed him the bottle, then sat back on her heels.

'You're ill,' she said. 'You need a doctor.'

He squinted up at her. His eyes looked wary. 'I have friends here, they will help. Please, just take the stones.'

Harry eyed the small package beside her, her insides churning. His diamonds were for Eve, to protect his family. How could she take them and leave him here like this?

She clenched her fists, then darted a glance around. The area was deserted, the only sounds the thumping hooves and Mani's wet breathing. She set the parcel on her lap. With shaking fingers, she untied the string, unfolded the fabric. Inside were three pearly-grey stones. She picked one up. It had the cold, oily feel she remembered from Eve's small diamond, the same octahedral shape. But it was bigger. Much bigger. So big she could hardly close her fist over it.

She flicked a look at Mani. 'These are from Van Wycks?'

His eyes widened. 'Yes, I swear. Just like all the others. Ezra told me where to look.'

'Where do you find them?'

'The dumps, the waste dumps near the pit.'

He stared at her, his eyes wide with panic, answering her questions as though she was setting him a test.

382

She looked at her lap. She hated to frighten him, but there were things she wanted to know.

'Are there more?'

'So many more.' A furrow appeared between his brows. 'Van Wycks, they must know, but they do not mine them.'

'What happens to the stones?'

'They bury them. Under tonnes of waste.' His voice was growing weaker. 'As if . . . as if they do not want people to know.'

Harry stared at the colossal diamond in her hand. It should have been unique, a breathtaking wonder. Yet Van Wycks had so many like it, they didn't even bother to mine them.

'Were you the first to find them?' she said.

'No, no, it was Ezra. Ezra is always looking.' Mani made a choking sound, half-laugh, half-cough. 'For my brother, there is always another stone.'

Always another stone. The phrase resonated inside Harry's head. She flashed on her father's jaunty smile. Always another hand. Always another horse.

'The gambler's creed,' she said, almost to herself. She looked up to find Mani staring at her, puzzled.

'You are not what I expected,' he whispered eventually.

Harry dropped her gaze, a grinding sensation starting up in her gut as she wrapped the diamonds back in their cloth. She had never hated herself so much.

Mani grasped her wrist. 'My family, please, you will keep your promise? Nothing will happen to them?'

Harry couldn't meet his eyes. She had nothing to say.

'Please!' His fingers tightened. 'I have done what you asked!'

Harry fixed on her father's face. She clamped her teeth together, pulled away. She didn't think she'd ever make peace with herself afterwards, but right now she had no choice.

Mani reached out towards her. 'Tell me you will not hurt them, please!'

His voice cracked. Harry backed away. She wanted to hunch her shoulders, cover her ears. Anything to block it out. Inside, her head was screaming.

'I'm sorry,' she whispered.

Mani gaped at her. Then he crumpled back against the fence. The rattle from his lungs ripped through the silence between them. After a moment, he said,

'You are not Eve, are you?'

Harry clapped a hand to her mouth, edged away. She couldn't speak. Then a quiet voice behind her said,

'No, she's not Eve.' Metal *snip-snapped*. 'I am.'

45

The sweat on Harry's skin turned cold. Eve was standing a few feet away, her gun trained on Harry's face.

'Nice to see you again, Harry.'

Her build was slighter than Harry remembered, the chest and hips thin and straight as an arrow. The T-shirt and shorts could have been made for a child, and the gun looked too big for her hands.

Harry heaved out a long breath. There was something oddly inevitable about meeting Eve again. The woman had been the start of everything, after all; somehow Harry had always known she'd run into her one more time.

'Hello, Eve.' Her limbs felt heavy, as if she'd reached the end of a long road. 'I've been looking for you for days.'

'I bet you have.'

Eve narrowed her eyes, heightening their oriental

slant. By now, her bruises had paled to citrus shades. Her short, choppy hair was spikey at the crown, and reminded Harry irrelevantly of Hunter. She found herself wondering would he finally believe her when he found her body riddled with bullets.

'How did you know I was here?' Harry said.

'Let's just say a friend told me.'

A friend. Rob? Kruger? Or maybe even Cassie. It could have been any one of them. Harry felt her brain drag. She'd been asking herself the same questions over and over, ever since the wheels had come off her life. But at this point, what did it matter?

Eve gestured towards Mani with a flick of her gun. 'Who's this?'

Harry flashed a glance at his face, feeling oddly protective. His eyes were almost closed, his breathing laboured. She aimed for a casual shrug. If Eve didn't know his name, she wasn't about to give it away.

'You should know, he's one of your couriers.'

Eve smirked. 'Oh really? You think you know everything, don't you? I've never seen him before.'

'Oh, that's right, I forgot. You deal with Raj Chandra, don't you?'

The smirk disappeared, as though wiped by an eraser. Eve flexed her two-handed grip on the gun. She stood with her feet apart, arms braced and outstretched. Going purely on size, she could have been a child with a grown-up's weapon. But her stance said she knew what she was doing.

Eve's jaw was tight. 'You don't know anything.'

'You'd be surprised at what I know.' Harry inched to her left. 'For instance, I know that Garvin was smuggling large stones from the Van Wycks mines. And I know that Kruger's horses provide the transportation cover. Which is where you come in, of course.'

Eve adjusted her stance, and didn't reply. Harry inched a little more to her left. The gate with the red buzzer was just a few feet away. She kept on talking.

'I even know some of the other people involved. Tom Jordan, Eddie Conway.' She watched Eve's face. 'I've been talking to Rob and Kruger, too.'

Eve's eyes flickered. 'It doesn't matter what you know, you're too late.'

'I've talked to the police, they're all over this.' The buzzer was close. If she could just back up a little, maybe she could lean her shoulder into it. 'They're probably already looking for you.'

Eve quick-stepped towards her. 'Don't move!'

Harry's heart flipped. Eve's arms were taut, the gun steady. The bore was on a level with Harry's eyes and she stared into the hypnotic black tunnel. Ice trickled over her insides.

Eve jerked her head. 'Move away from the buzzer. Do it now!'

Harry shuffled forward, transfixed by the gun. When the fence was out of reach, Eve said,

'Now, put the package on the ground, then get over there beside your friend.'

Harry hesitated. Out of the corner of her eye, she was aware of Mani stirring. She stole a glance at his face. His eyelids fluttered, getting ready to close, and his lips were moving. No sound emerged, but Harry knew what he wanted. He wanted her to give the diamonds to Eve. As if she had a choice.

Her eyes slid back to the gun. Then slowly, she set the parcel at her feet. Her hands were shaking. The bundle looked small and grubby in the dirt. She wanted to snatch it back, make a run for it to her car. Instead, she stumbled over to Mani.

Eve bent to retrieve the parcel, her eyes and her gun still trained on Harry's face. She kneaded the cloth between her fingers. The stones clacked inside. Her uptilted eyes grew slightly feverish.

'Seems like this is my lucky day.'

Harry didn't answer. She couldn't. Beside her, Mani had slipped into unconsciousness, his chest rattling like hail against a window. Eve straightened up, still talking.

'With Garvin dead and Raj not answering his phone, I thought the shipment was off.' She weighed the parcel in her hand and laughed. 'I knew you were worth keeping an eye on.'

She seemed giddy, almost high, as though handling the diamonds had triggered an endorphin rush. Hooves clumpety-clumped somewhere behind Harry as the horse picked up pace on his workout. For all she knew, it was Dawn Light. She squinted at Eve.

'Mind if I ask how all that stuff with the horse works?'

388

Eve shrugged. 'Different ways. Rectal suppositories. Vaginal insertions for the mares. Sometimes I just bury it in their feed. Who's going to check? The horses are a perfect cover for moving in and out of the country.'

'So you're going to ship these ones out with Dawn Light?'

Eve laughed. 'Oh, these aren't for shipping. Not through the usual channels, anyway.' She cradled the parcel against her chest. 'These ones are for me.'

Harry blinked. 'You're double-crossing the syndicate?'

'The syndicate?' Eve snorted. 'Is that what you call them? It makes them sound so respectable.'

'Them? Aren't you a part of it?'

Eve's smile turned bitter. 'I've been trying to get out for a long time. Now I finally have the chance.'

'Because Garvin's dead?'

Eve's gaze shifted. 'He's not the only one calling the shots.'

'Who else is involved?' Harry stared at Eve's lemon-and-lime bruise. 'The same person who gave you the black eye?'

Eve shifted her feet. 'Like I said last time we met, leaving is more dangerous than staying sometimes. They catch you at it, and you're dead. You've got to plan it right. You need money to disappear, lots of it.'

'Is that why you broke into Garvin's safe?'

'*You* broke into Garvin's safe, Harry, let's not forget that. Your fingerprints are all over that little escapade, remember? I even left your business card lying around.'

Harry closed her eyes and nodded. So she'd been right. Eve had deliberately set her up.

'So I was your fall guy?' Harry couldn't keep the jaded tone out of her voice.

'More like a smokescreen, I'd say.' Eve shook her head and laughed. 'For once, luck was on my side. I met your father when he first came to see Kruger. Nice old guy, isn't he? Said he'd be running Dawn Light in your name.'

'He has his reasons.'

'I know, I checked up on him. Quite a shady past, I was surprised. He talked about you a lot. How you're such a whiz with computers, how you even run your own security company.' She flicked Harry a curious look. 'Must be nice to have a father who's so proud of you.'

Harry swallowed and didn't answer. Eve went on:

'Anyway, it got me thinking, so I checked you out. And there you were, MD of Blackjack Security, and now an owner of Dawn Light. You even had a shady past of your own, if half of what I read about you is true. You were perfect.'

'Thanks.'

If Eve picked up on her tone, she didn't show it. 'The police were already getting close, investigating some of the owners. TJ, for one. He's getting real edgy about it.'

Harry frowned at the present tense. Didn't she know he was dead? Eve was still talking.

'I badly needed to get into that safe, but I had to cover my tracks too. So I put you in the frame. The police'd be so busy looking into you that by the time anyone thought of me, I'd be long gone.'

390

Harry nodded. As a way of muddying the waters, that'd just about do it. Eve smiled.

'As it happens, that all worked out even better than I thought. All except for one thing.'

'What's that?'

'Garvin's safe was full of junk. Nothing but a bunch of marbles.' Her mouth turned sour. 'It wasn't enough. I needed big stones, stones like these.'

'So you stuck around for one last haul?'

'Exactly.'

Sweat trickled down Harry's back. The sun scorched through her dress, and by now it was clinging to her like a wet sheet. She studied Eve. She looked cool in her T-shirt, but her hairline sparkled with sweat. Harry nodded towards the gun.

'That must be getting heavy, now you only have one hand.'

Eve tightened her grip on it, her knuckles pale. 'Don't worry about me, I'm just leaving. Throw me your car keys.'

'What?'

'Your car keys, give them to me!'

Harry blinked. 'I left them in the ignition.'

Eve sidestepped over to the car, her eyes riveted to Harry's face. A chill settled over Harry's shoulders, in spite of the sizzling heat. What was Eve going to do, kill her then drive off?

'One thing I don't understand.' Harry kept her tone conversational. Just two old pals, having a chin-wag.

The way she saw it, the longer she talked, the longer she stayed alive. 'How could you go into business with a man like Garvin? He abused your mother, didn't he?'

'My mother had a habit of marrying abusive men.' Eve peeped in the driver's window, then snapped her eyes back to Harry. 'My father used to beat her up. Beat me up too, sometimes. He died when I was ten, thank Christ.'

'Was his name Darcy?'

Eve nodded. She set the parcel of stones on the car roof, and opened the door. 'After him, along came Garvin. He moved in, took all her money, beat the shit out of her as well.' She leaned in and yanked the keys out of the ignition. Her eyes never left Harry's face. 'Only this time, I didn't know. My mother sent me away to boarding school. Wanted to protect me, I guess.'

Harry frowned. 'But you found out eventually, didn't you?'

'A few months ago. I found her lying on the floor in the kitchen. Her ribs were broken.' Eve swallowed hard, her throat working. 'He'd smashed them with a kitchen chair.'

Her hand clenched over the car keys, and she raised her fist. Her thin chest heaved. Then she hurled the keys high over the steel-mesh fence. They chinkled to the ground, somewhere out of sight. Then she slammed the car door shut and snatched up her parcel of stones.

'She told me everything then. Said she'd finally had enough, that she was leaving. Then she died.' Eve shook the parcel at Harry like a fist. 'She didn't prepare, you see, she hadn't got a plan. She thought if she just took off he'd let her go.'

'Are you saying he killed her?'

'Wouldn't surprise me. Some people called it suicide, but I don't buy that. She died trying to escape him, that's all I know. In my book, that makes him a murderer.' She gave Harry a direct look. 'You asked me a few days ago if I was glad he was dead. The answer is, hell, yes.'

Harry stared at Eve. Her elfin frame was quivering, the mix of rage and fear coming off her like a vapour.

'Who gave you all the bruises, Eve? Was it Rob? Or were you involved with someone else? Kruger, maybe?'

Eve touched the skin around her eye. 'Like mother, like daughter, isn't that what they say?'

'Bullshit. I thought you were smarter than that.'

'I am.' Eve jutted up her chin. 'I'm getting out, remember?'

She flashed a glance over her shoulder, then backed up towards a green jeep parked further along the track. Her gun was still zeroed in on Harry's face. Eve flung the parcel in through the jeep's passenger window. Harry jerked forwards, as though yanked by a connecting string.

'Wait!' The diamonds. She couldn't let them go. 'Don't you want to know who killed Garvin?'

Eve double-fisted the gun and stepped over to the driver's side. 'He made a lot of enemies, it could be anyone.'

'TJ's dead too, did you know that?'

Eve froze, her hand on the door. 'I don't believe you.'

'It happened the day you cleared out Garvin's safe. He was shot at Leopardstown. You'd probably already left.'

Eve narrowed her eyes and didn't answer. Harry rushed on:

'Then Eddie Conway was murdered, the very next day. Someone gouged his eyes out.'

Eve gasped. 'That's a lie! Eddie was only a kid, he was barely involved.'

'He was involved enough to be killed.'

'But he didn't know anything! He helped me recover the stones, sometimes, that's all. I needed someone to hold the horse's head.'

'Then he knew about the diamonds.'

'I doubt he recognized what they were. He just had orders to help me when no one else was around, and to keep his mouth shut.'

'Orders from who? Who else would've been around to help?'

Eve clamped her free hand back on the gun. 'I still think you're lying. Why should I believe you?'

'Anyone at the yard'll tell you. And what about Raj? Why do you think he's not answering his phone? Why isn't he here to deliver the stones? Because he's dead too, that's why. They all are. Van Wycks has hired someone to eliminate the syndicate. He's killing them one by one, Eve. And now he's coming after you.'

Eve didn't answer. The gun trembled in her hand. Harry edged towards her, her heart drubbing against her ribs.

'Give me some of the diamonds, Eve. Just one would

do, you don't need them all.' She inched forward. Baby steps to keep herself alive. 'The Van Wycks killer, he thinks I'm one of you. I can buy him off. I've already done the deal. If I give him the stones, he'll back away.'

Eve shook her head. She was breathing hard. 'You're lying. These stones are mine, I've earned them.'

Then she yanked open the door to the jeep.

'Wait!' Harry gestured towards Mani. 'What about him? What about his family?'

'What?'

'It's part of the deal, isn't it? He delivers the stones and his family stays safe?'

Eve shrugged. 'That's not my call. All I do is ship the stones home.'

'Then whose call is it? Tell me who else is involved!'

Eve ducked into the jeep and fired up the engine. She wheeled into a U-turn, tyres scuffing in the dirt. Harry raced to the open passenger window, grabbed at the door-frame. The jeep yanked her arms and she lurched after it, screaming in through the open window.

'The syndicate, they'll know what you've done, won't they? Whoever you're running from, they'll come after you for the stones.'

The jeep skidded to a halt. Eve peered across at her, the engine revving and the parcel of stones on her lap.

'Not if I say you have them.' Her eyes locked on Harry's. 'Then they'll come after you, won't they?'

46

Harry blundered out through the revolving doors of the Cape Town Medicare Clinic.

Baked air coddled her skin, thawing the chill left behind by her plunging adrenaline levels. An ambulance shrieked past in a whirl of lights and she thought of Mani as she'd left him, strapped to a trolley with an oxygen mask over his face. His chest had been rattling hard enough to break.

She fingered the car keys in her pocket. The young man in the quarantine station had found them for her. He'd also called the emergency services, after she'd leaned on the gate buzzer and screamed till her throat had burned.

The ambulance driver had tutted when he'd seen Mani. 'Doesn't look like he'd have medical insurance, does he?'

Harry glanced at him in alarm. 'But you can get him into a hospital, can't you?'

'Somerset will probably take him.'

'Will they look after him there?'

The driver had dipped his head to peer at her over his glasses. 'They'll do their best.' His tone was doubtful. 'But it's a public Emergency Service. Over-crowded, under-funded.'

So Harry had ordered him to take Mani to the nearest private clinic. She'd followed in her car and spent the last half hour filling out forms. All she knew about Mani was his name, but it turned out no one cared as long as they had her credit card number.

She unlocked her car and lowered herself into it. The interior was stifling, and smelled of hot plastic. She thought of Eve, and wondered where she was headed. Not that it mattered. Nothing did, now that the diamonds were gone.

She closed her eyes and sank back against the head-rest. Turning on the ignition seemed like such an effort. And where would she go? Back to a hotel full of strangers? Or down to the waterfront to wait for the Van Wycks killer?

She snapped her eyes open, groping for her phone. She put in a call to directory inquiries, who connected her to the Commodore Hotel. A few seconds later, her father's voice came on the line.

'Hello?' He sounded groggy.

'Dad, it's me.'

'Harry, love.' There was a creaking noise, as if he was winching himself into position. 'Are you in Cape Town?'

'Yes.' She felt her throat close over. 'You okay?'

'I've been asleep.' He sounded mildly surprised.

'Stay in bed, you need the rest.'

'I can't believe you're here, I thought your mother was making it up.'

'Got in yesterday.' She noticed she'd adopted a certain economy with words. Less chance her voice would let her down.

'Harry, is everything all right with the police? Your mother said—'

'Yes, everything's fine. Look, Dad, you need to stay in the hotel. Don't wander around.'

'Nonsense, Cape Town's perfectly safe. But I'll stay in the Commodore for a while. Cassie Bergin's meeting me here for lunch. The vet lady, did you meet her?'

Harry blinked. 'Yes.'

'She's at the races with Dan, but between you and me, I think he's left her in the lurch, so she's coming back. Why don't you join us?'

'Can't, I'm afraid.'

Harry clamped her teeth over her lower lip to stop it from trembling. Before the coma, she might have told her father everything. But now he seemed too frail.

There was a pause. 'Harry, are you sure you're all right?'

'Yes.' Her voice felt strangled. 'Just in a bit of a bind, that's all.'

'Ah. A bind. I know all about them.'

Harry squeezed her eyes shut, tried to laugh. 'I bet you do.'

'What would you do if you weren't afraid? That's what you've got to ask yourself. I do it all the time. If I wasn't afraid, would I raise the stakes? Play another hand? Would I double down?'

'This isn't cards, Dad.'

He paused. 'Did I ever tell you that when I came out of that coma, I was scared to death?'

Harry's eyes popped open. 'No. No, you didn't.'

'Brain injuries change you, you know. Some people get depressed, violent even. Others go home and need prompt cards to help them shop. I was afraid to leave the hospital.'

'You never said.'

'Crowds were the hardest. Couldn't handle them. And some of my oldest friends were like strangers. I felt disconnected, like I'd landed on the moon. Still do, truth be told.'

'I . . . I had no idea.'

'So I force myself to keep doing normal things, and my confidence grows, bit by bit. We've got to take fear right out of the equation, Harry. Otherwise, we'll never do anything.'

Harry nodded, though she knew he couldn't see her. Then she cleared her throat, shovelling away any telltale tremors.

'You're right, Dad. I know.'

'Good.' She heard the smile in his voice. 'Come to lunch?'

'I can't, I'm sorry. Stay safe. I'll call you later.'

They said their goodbyes and Harry disconnected. Something squeezed her chest at the thought of her father being afraid. How could she add to his problems now?

She leaned forward and switched on the engine, then eased the car out towards the main road. Her body felt numb. She navigated the route back to her hotel with her brain only half-engaged. Her system was on a go-slow, refusing to deal with anything except the basics of moving around.

By the time she reached her hotel, it was almost two o'clock. She let herself into her room and flopped down on to the bed, and when her phone rang, she answered it almost absentmindedly.

'Hello?'

'Time's nearly up.'

Her stomach jolted, and she jerked upright on the bed. 'Who's this?'

'You know who it is.'

A lazy trickle of sweat crept down her back. She pictured the solid biceps, the baseball cap. Her insides gave a sickening lurch.

'What do you want?' she whispered.

'Have you got the stones?'

Harry licked her lips. They were drier than dust. 'I need more time.'

'I said two days. Then your time runs out.'

'But—'

'Tomorrow evening, seven o'clock. Table Mountain. Take the cableway up to the top. I'll find you.'

The line went dead. Harry's phone burned against her ear, and her head filled with the roar of her own thrashing blood. She clamped a hand to her mouth.

Jesus!

The room swirled. She dropped the phone and hugged her arms round her waist. What the hell was she going to do now?

What would you do if you weren't afraid?

Harry closed her eyes and pictured her father. The jaunty smile, the snowy beard, the hands that weren't quite steady any more.

She felt her fists curl. There had to be some way out of this. She snapped open her eyes and sprang to her feet, then started to pace the room.

Think!

Everybody was after her now. The Van Wycks killer. The diamond syndicate. Everybody wanted Mani's stones.

Harry jerked to a halt by the window. Table Mountain hogged the view, and she glared out at it. It loomed up, vast and prehistoric, its top flattened as though sliced by a cleaver. A frothy brim of cloud boiled up over it, like smoke from a volcano.

Harry shuddered. Tomorrow, she'd go up there. But first, she had to replace Mani's diamonds. She wheeled away from the window, snatched up her phone and dialled Ros's number.

'Ros? It's Harry. Sorry, but I need more information.'

'Are you okay? You sound wired.'

'I'm fine.' Harry paced up and down beside the bed, her limbs jittery. 'Well, maybe I am a little wired. Look, I need to get hold of some diamonds.'

'I'm your gal.'

'Van Wycks diamonds, big ones. Three or four of them, uncut.'

'How big?'

'I don't know.' Harry pictured the clacking stones in Mani's parcel. 'Big enough that you'd have trouble closing your fist over one. What's that, two hundred carats?'

There was a pause. 'Harry, are you out of your mind? Didn't you listen to anything I told you? Van Wycks hardly ever produce stones that size. And even if you could get hold of one, do you have any idea how much it would cost?'

Harry clenched her fist, recalling what Jacob had paid for his. 'A lot, right?'

'Six, seven million dollars at least.'

Shit. Harry's nest-egg from the Bahamas was a tidy sum, but it wasn't going to stretch that far. She kept pacing, the blood flaring through her veins.

'You said Van Wycks hardly ever produce them. What happens when they do?'

'They award them to selected diamantaires in the Cape Town Sights.'

'Like you?'

Ros laughed. 'You really weren't listening, were you?

402

I told you, I'm a pariah in Cape Town these days. My sightboxes are filled with baubles.'

'Who gets them, then?'

'Jacob used to, but not lately. Bram Bierkens is a bit of a golden boy, so's Jan De Rooy. They're both in Antwerp. But it doesn't matter who has them, Harry. Even if you had the money, no diamantaire would sell you an uncut Van Wycks stone.'

'Godammit, why not?'

'It's a strict rule of the Sight. No one's allowed to resell the contents of their boxes in their uncut form.'

'I don't get it.'

'It's to make sure Van Wycks keep control of the supply. If they let people resell their boxes, then an outsider could start hoarding the rough and the Van Wycks monopoly would be at risk.'

Harry stopped pacing and sank down on the bed. 'Jesus. They really have everyone in a stranglehold, don't they?'

'You better believe it.'

'So you're saying I can only buy polished stones? Could I get hold of any that size?'

'There's not that many around, but in any case you're looking at double the price.'

Harry squeezed her eyes shut, and felt something cold settle in her chest. Buying the stones just wasn't an option. Ros spoke into the silence.

'Are you in some kind of trouble, Harry? Do you want to meet up?'

Harry opened her eyes. 'You're in Cape Town?'

'I got in this morning. I told you, I'm here for the Sight.'

'When is it, today?'

'It started yesterday. Takes three days. With a hundred and fifty diamantaires, they need to spread it out. My appointment's tomorrow.'

Slowly, Harry got to her feet and moved over to the window. She stared out at the stark mountain. 'Where's this Sight held?'

'The Van Wycks building in Goodwood, just outside the city.'

Harry's extremities tingled. She recalled what Jacob Fischer had said. *The only other place you'd find a stone like that is in the Van Wycks stockpile itself.*

She could almost feel her brain shift.

'Is that where Van Wycks keep all their stones?' she said.

'Yes. In an underground vault.'

'Security must be pretty tight in there.'

'Place is like a fortress. Armed guards, swipe cards, surveillance cameras, alarms. It's elaborate stuff. And that's just for the office floors. I've never been inside the vault, but you can bet it's state of the art.'

Harry's eyes narrowed. 'What kind of swipe cards?'

'What?'

'The swipe cards. Do you really swipe them, or do you hold them up to some kind of reader?'

'I don't know, they don't give me one. They're for employees. I only get a visitor's pass.'

'But you must have seen people use them. Think, Ros, please, it's important.'

Ros sighed, and went silent for a moment. Harry could picture her screwing up her face. Eventually Ros said,

'They hold them up. There's some kind of panel on the wall.'

Hairs rose on the back of Harry's neck. 'I need a favour, Ros.'

'Another one?'

'I need a tour of that building.' Harry crossed her fingers. 'Can you get me inside?'

'What?'

'Make an appointment to see that guy in charge of the stones. Montgomery somebody.'

'Monty? How do you know about him?'

'Ask to see him today. Tell him you want to discuss the state of your sightbox. Tell him anything. Just bring me in with you.'

'I don't like the sound of this. What are you planning to do, Harry?'

'Please, Ros.'

There was a pause. 'This is more than just a case, isn't it? What's going on, Harry?'

Harry closed her eyes. 'I'm up against the cartel here, that's all I can say. Can you just trust me? Please. I need your help.'

'Does Sal know anything about this?'

Harry's eyes flew open. 'No, and you can't tell him,

either. He's got enough to cope with. Promise me you won't tell him?'

Ros was silent for a long moment. Harry could almost hear her weighing things up. Then Ros said,

'Let me see what I can do.'

47

'We'll call you my assistant,' Ros said. 'Just try not to say anything.'

Harry nodded. Her stomach was clenched like a fist. They were in Ros's car, travelling east out of the city towards Goodwood. Against her better judgement, Ros had wangled an appointment with Montgomery Newman for three fifteen that afternoon.

Harry fiddled with the strap of her bag. 'Maybe we shouldn't use my real name.' She'd no idea if Van Wycks knew of her existence, but it seemed prudent to cover her tracks. 'Let's say I'm Catalina Diego, okay?'

Ros shot her a surprised glance, and Harry looked at her hands.

'It's a name I use now and then.'

'Yes, I know.' Ros was smiling fondly at her. 'I remember she used to come to the park with us sometimes.'

Harry felt her mouth open. She hadn't thought anyone else remembered Catalina.

Catalina Diego had been her imaginary friend when Harry was five years old. She was blonde and angelic, and took the blame for most of Harry's misdeeds. She'd grown up with Harry, evolving from childhood playmate into an alias for her hacking scams.

Harry shifted in her seat. She'd bet that even Miriam wouldn't remember Catalina. She glanced at Ros, the memories of her becoming more solid. A tea party on the grass; Ros pouring milk for Catalina with the utmost seriousness.

Harry cleared her throat. 'So, tell me more about this Monty guy.'

She wasn't sure what she wanted to know, but right now she needed the distraction. Ros checked her rear-view mirror and swerved into the outside lane.

'He's a director of Van Wycks, been with them over forty years. Most people are afraid of him, though they probably wouldn't admit it.'

She switched gears, handling the powerful Mercedes with ease. She wore a navy linen dress with no accessories of any kind. The combination gave her an air of ladylike formality.

Harry twisted the strap of her bag round her fingers. 'He decides who gets what in their sightboxes, doesn't he?'

'That's right. In line with global markets, of course. If there's an excess of yellow diamonds in the market, for instance, then he won't include any in the Sight.'

'In case it depresses the price?'

Ros smiled. 'Attagirl, you're learning. Supply and demand.'

Harry rolled her eyes. 'And then what? He awards the best stones to his usual favourites?'

'Actually, the chosen few can change at any time. You never quite know where you are with Monty. He alters his list right up to the day before the Sight, sometimes. But no one dares to complain, not even the favourites. Quibble about your box, and you're expelled.'

Ros eased the car into a bend. A crumbling shanty-town rolled into view, hugging the edge of the freeway. The sprawl of derelict shacks looked ready for demolition. Bricks and tyres anchored the roofs in place, and someone had spray-painted 'Welcom to Hel' on one of the corrugated walls.

Harry twisted in her seat. For once, she couldn't see the damn mountain.

'We're here,' Ros said.

Harry whipped her head round. Soaring out of the wasteland up ahead was a single modern skyscraper. Sunlight sparkled off every surface. Harry counted eighteen floors, and they all seemed to be made of glass.

She swallowed, dragging her eyes away. Her palms felt damp. Ros took the next off-ramp and headed down a long avenue, finally pulling up in a car park outside the tower block. Harry climbed out, squinting upwards. There were no signs anywhere, no corporate logos; nothing to say what went on inside. The polished windows mirrored the blue sky, as though deliberately trying to blend into the background.

A truck rumbled to her left. She glanced over and caught her breath. A hundred yards away, in a fenced-off compound, was a vast, concrete bunker. It was bigger than a football stadium and surrounded by armed guards. Military-style armoured trucks rumbled in and out, halting at checkpoints to the snap of weapons being primed.

Harry's insides flipped. So this was the command post of the Van Wycks cartel. She stared at the guards with their bulky submachine guns and heavy artillery belts. Suddenly she wondered what the hell she was doing.

She slipped a shaking hand inside her bag. Her fingers closed over the small black device she'd snagged from her field kit in the hotel. It was about the size and shape of a deck of cards, and she felt along the edge for the power switch. She snicked it on, then followed Ros in through the tower block entrance.

The reception area was decked out like a five-star hotel, if you didn't count the armed guards. Glossy floors, gilt-edged fittings, enough artwork to start up a gallery. The receptionist made them sign in, then handed them plastic name badges. Harry clipped hers to the pocket of her shirt, and followed Ros over to a group of sofas by the window.

She perched on the arm of a chair, too jittery to sit. Her eyes darted left and right, taking in her surroundings. To the right of the reception desk was a heavy-looking metal door. It was manned by an armed guard and, apart from the main entrance, was the only other door in sight.

Harry shifted on her chair, and noticed other visitors returning their badges to reception as they left. She'd already decided she was holding on to hers.

Suddenly, the metal door swung inward and a man in his late thirties stepped through into reception. He was narrow-chested, with thinning red hair and a complexion that spoke of anaemia. At school, probably no one had wanted him on their team during gym class.

He strode towards Ros, his hand outstretched and a faint smirk on his face.

'Ros. Mr Newman's expecting you upstairs.'

Ros got to her feet and shook his hand. 'Wesley. Still running errands for Monty, I see.'

His mouth tightened, and he didn't answer. He turned a pair of chilly eyes Harry's way, and Ros performed minimal introductions. He nodded, then turned on his heel and headed back towards the metal door.

'Follow me, please.'

His accent was more English than South African. Harry watched as he unclipped a swipe card from his belt and held it up to a reader on the wall. The panel light flipped from red to green and the door clicked open.

Something you have, something you know, something you are.

The security rule-of-thumb drifted into Harry's head as she followed Wesley through the door into a small lift lobby. He scanned his badge again, this time to summon up a ride. Harry stole a glance at his card.

Something you have.

411

She touched her bag, and felt the outline of the black device inside. It was a radio-frequency scanner. The last time she'd used it had been in a Dublin bank. The CEO had hired her to test the building security, and like a lot of organizations, they'd used proximity access cards. The cards transmitted their IDs as radio signals, which the wall readers then picked up. Just like Wesley's.

But radio signals were fair game, and anyone with a scanner could read them. All you had to do was get close enough.

The lift door opened and Wesley stepped inside, punching the button for the fifth floor, the highest on the panel. Harry followed, squeezing up close to his badge side. He smelled of soap and spray-on starch, and Harry pictured a devoted mother somewhere busy doing his laundry.

He shot her a look. The lift wasn't that cramped, and no doubt he was wondering why she was gate-crashing his space. She smiled up at him, listening for the tell-tale beep from her scanner.

Nothing.

Wesley edged away, turning his attention to Ros. 'You're wasting your time with Mr Newman, you know.'

Ros raised an eyebrow. 'You think so?'

'Of course.' The smirk was back. 'Maybe if you stopped colluding with all those bleeding-heart campaigners, he might be willing to listen.'

Ros smiled. Harry eased her bag off her shoulder, holding it lower down.

'You know me, Wesley,' Ros said. 'If I see an injustice, I'll speak up about it.'

He sighed. 'Oh, I know you, all right.'

Harry inched towards him, her bag in line with his belt.

Beep.

Wesley frowned. Harry stepped back.

'Sorry,' she said. 'Phone's out of charge.'

The back of Harry's neck tingled. Her scanner had just copied the signal from Wesley's card. Now she could clone it anytime she wanted. She wasn't sure she needed to, but it never hurt to be prepared.

The lift glided to a halt, and they stepped into a long, bare hall lined with open doors. The clatter of printers and hum of voices told Harry they were probably offices. Wesley headed for a closed door opposite the lifts. A small keypad was mounted on the wall beside it. Harry's fingertips tingled.

Something you know.

Wesley stepped up close to the keypad, and Harry moved in behind him, squinting over his shoulder. She trained her eyes, held her breath. His index finger hovered over the centre of the pad. Belatedly, he cupped his other hand around it, then jabbed at four of the keys. His hands obscured the numbers, but Harry had nailed the pattern. Four points of a diamond.

Shoulder-surfing PINs was an old circus trick, a cinch for any novice hacker. And Harry's visual acuity was better honed than most. If she could track a plug of cards through a six-deck shuffle, she could trace a four-digit pattern without a hitch.

She visualized the pad, duplicating the diamond-shaped pattern in her head. 2684, or 2604 at a pinch. She followed Wesley through the door and into another lift, with Ros bringing up the rear. Harry leaned back against the handrail.

'Quite a complex security set-up you've got here.'

Wesley punched the button for the tenth floor, which was as far as the lift went, then flicked her a smug look.

'This is nothing. This is just to segregate internal personnel. The floors we've just left are all admin staff, and who needs them wandering around the building? Next is Sales, we keep them corralled in the middle five floors.' He glanced skywards. 'Up top is Corporate Strategy. Where I work with Mr Newman.'

He slid her a glance, checking her reaction. Harry widened her eyes, trying to look impressed at his elevated slot in the food chain. He nodded, and went on:

'But like I said, this is nothing. Our real security is concentrated in the underground vaults.'

'That's the concrete fortress I saw outside?'

'That's right. It's impenetrable, take my word for it. Best protection money can buy. Seismic sensors, radar, heat detectors, magnetic fields, CCTV. Not to mention twenty-four-seven armed guards.'

Ros cleared her throat, as though reprimanding his indiscretion. He ignored her and continued itemizing:

'Concrete walls, three-ton steel doors, locks with over

414

a hundred million combinations. Even the strongboxes inside the vault need their own keys and access codes.' He threw Harry a sly glance. 'Plus lots of other stuff I can't even tell you about.'

Harry held on to her wide-eyed look. She bet he didn't really know any other stuff, and it probably bugged him that his security clearance didn't cover it. The lift doors opened and she followed him out, aware that her insides had drooped. He was right about one thing. That damn vault sounded impenetrable. But then, what the hell had she expected?

They'd exited on to another floor of offices, a duplicate of the one downstairs. The same drab carpet, the same bare walls. Wesley crossed over to yet another door, this one presumably leading through to Corporate Strategy. It was protected by a familiar, brick-sized entry device with a recessed sensor pad. Harry's muscles tensed. A biometric scanner.

Something you are.

She peered at the logo: a silver star, enclosing the word 'Axis5'. Her heart sank. Axis were specialists in live finger detection. Their sensors checked for pulse, heat and perspiration patterns that only a live finger could generate. It was meant to deter crooks from chopping people's fingers off.

She watched Wesley place his thumb on the pad. The light flashed green, the door clicked. He lifted his finger, and a small automatic flap wiped over the latent print he'd left behind.

Inwardly, Harry sighed. This one wasn't going to be hacked with a Gummi bear. Not that it mattered. What use would it be to break in here, when all the diamonds were locked in the vault?

Wesley led the way down a wide hall. Harry's eyes grew round. Corporate Strategy had quite a furnishing budget. The carpets were thick and spongy underfoot, and the walls were hung with oversized paintings so gloomy they had to be priceless. Mini-chandeliers made up for the lack of windows, sprinkling everything with a golden glow.

She passed an open door marked 'Millennium Suite', and glimpsed a large conference room with half a dozen men snacking on lobster and champagne. Some of them wore visitors' badges, just like hers. She raised her eyebrows. She bet the guys in Admin would like a piece of this.

Wesley hesitated outside a door at the end of the hallway. He wiped his palms on his trousers, then tapped with one knuckle. He eased the door open, peeped inside, then turned back to Ros and Harry with a flourish.

'Mr Newman must have stepped out. We'll wait in here.'

The office was bigger than Harry's cottage in Killiney, and scored higher on luxury, too. Everything was upholstered in cream and gold. The floor was a dark, polished wood, scattered with Oriental rugs. Wesley motioned for them to sit down.

'I'm surprised Monty's made time to see you today,

quite frankly.' His use of the name sounded a little self-conscious, as if he was trying it on for size. 'He's flying to Tel Aviv this evening, so his schedule's pretty tight.'

Behind him on the wall was a large, flat-screen TV. Harry stared up at it. It showed a long, white bench littered with mounds of tiny stones. A woman was bending over it, examining one of the piles.

Wesley followed her gaze. 'That's the security feed from the Sorting Room. Monty likes to keep an eye on things.'

Harry watched as the woman tweezed up a stone and popped it into a plastic envelope. She ziplocked it shut, then placed it into what looked like a yellow plastic lunchbox.

'That's a sightbox,' Ros said. 'They're preparing them for this evening's appointments.'

'A bit last-minute, isn't it?'

'It's always that way. Monty likes to make late changes. They'll put tomorrow's batch together in the morning.'

Something quickened in Harry's brain. She fixed her gaze to the screen. The woman was moving along the table, consulting a sheet of paper in her hand. Then she bent over another pile of stones.

Wesley pointed a remote control at the screen. 'That's Andrea, our Head Sorter.'

'Is she in the vault?' Harry said.

Wesley nodded. 'Ground level of the bunker.' He zoomed the camera out, revealing several more benches and sorters in the room. 'It's the only place that gets any natural light. Through bullet-proof windows, of course.'

'Of course.' Harry was only half-listening, her eyes transfixed by the mounds of gleaming pebbles.

The door clicked open behind her. She turned to see a tall, white-haired man standing on the threshold. He was staring right at her.

'Wesley, order the car.' His South African accent made it sound like 'caw'.

'Yes, Mr Newman.' Wesley rushed to the desk and snatched up a phone.

Montgomery Newman advanced into the room, his eyes fixed on Harry. An involuntary shiver scampered over her. She judged him to be in his mid-sixties, about her father's age. But there the similarity ended. This man was heavy and darkly tanned, with a broad face that drooped in folds like a bulldog's.

He turned to Ros. 'My apologies, but I need to cancel our meeting. I'm due at the airport.'

He smiled slightly, though the effect was mostly lost in the pleats of his skin. Harry got the feeling he'd known all along he wouldn't have time to talk to them.

Ros smiled. 'Another time, then, Monty.'

He shook his head. 'We both know there's nothing to discuss. The price of your box has been set. Six hundred thousand, same as usual.'

'For contents worth less than half that.'

Monty shrugged. 'You know what you need to do, my dear.'

He turned his attention back to Harry. His eyes were small, crowding in close against the bridge of his nose.

Harry held his gaze, trying not to blink, and felt her skin creep.

She thought of all she'd learned about the Van Wycks operation: of the market manipulation, the secretive stockpiling, the insidious marketing; of the suppression of stones, the mopping up, and the stranglehold on diamantaires. Not to mention the execution of illicit diamond traders. Harry suppressed a shudder.

Was this the face of the Van Wycks cartel?

Suddenly, he turned his back on them and headed for the door, clicking his fingers at Wesley. 'Tell Andrea tomorrow's list is ready. And see these people out.'

Harry stared after him, her heart drumming. She traded looks with Ros, then followed Wesley as he led them back through the rigmarole of protected lifts and doors. They crossed through reception and blundered back out into the sunlight. Neither of them spoke until they reached the car. Then Harry turned to Ros and said,

'I need another favour. I need you to sell me your sightbox.'

48

'Harry, are you crazy?'

Ros gaped at her across the roof of the car. Harry shook her head, darting quick glances around. Boots crunched in the nearby compound, and armoured trucks grumbled in and out. Harry eyed the surveillance cameras, then ducked into the Mercedes, motioning for Ros to do the same. When they were both inside, she said,

'I'll pay you the full six hundred thousand dollars, you won't be out of pocket.'

Ros twisted to face her, her dark eyes solemn. 'I'm sorry, but I can't help you this time.'

'Why not?'

'It's against the rules of the Sight, I told you that.'

'Come off it, Ros, you don't play by the rules any more than I do.'

Ros narrowed her eyes and studied her for a moment.

'Why do you even want it? My sightbox will be full of low-grade gems.'

'Maybe.' Harry clasped her hands together. 'But I need you to promise you'll give it to me no matter what it contains.'

Ros tapped her fingers on the wheel. Harry sensed a shift in her resolve and decided to push the point home.

'Come on, it's a good deal for you,' she said. 'Instead of making a loss, you break even. I can pay you more, if you want. Just tell me how much.'

Ros's mouth tensed. 'This isn't about money. I've been helping you because I care about your father. Because I care about you.' She turned away and fired up the ignition. 'I thought you understood that.'

Ros shot the car into reverse and swung out of the parking space.

Harry looked at her hands. 'Look, I'm sorry. I didn't mean to offend you. I made the offer in good faith, and I appreciate everything you've done, I really do.' She dug her nails into her palms. 'But I've got to have that sightbox.'

Ros flashed her a look. 'This is more than just a case, isn't it? Something else is going on here.'

Harry chewed her lip and debated telling Ros the truth. At this point there was no reason not to, and God knows, she could do with the unloading. She glanced at Ros's dark profile.

'The Van Wycks cartel killed Garvin Oliver.'

The Mercedes swerved. 'What?'

421

'You were right when you said Garvin was getting involved in something dangerous. His supply of large rough was interfering with Van Wycks.'

Ros shot her a wide-eyed look. 'And they *killed* him?'

Harry nodded. A horn blared from behind, as Ros's driving became more erratic.

'Do the police know about this?' she said.

'They're getting there.' Harry thought of Hunter, and her muscles tensed. 'But I can't afford to wait.'

'What do you mean?'

Harry hesitated. 'The killer hired by Van Wycks believes I'm involved in Garvin's operation.'

'What?'

'It's complicated.' Harry was astonished at how normal her voice sounded. 'But the bottom line is, if I don't deliver him a shipment of large stones tomorrow, I'm next on his list.' She lowered her eyes. 'So's my father.'

Ros caught her breath. She jammed her foot on the brakes, earning harsh blasts from behind, and veered into the slow lane. She shot Harry a glance, her eyes wide with alarm.

'But, Harry, you've got to go to the police!'

'There isn't time, don't you see?' Harry clenched her fists. 'Please, Ros. I need your sightbox. I don't care how much it costs.'

Ros waved that aside. 'But how will that help? All you'll get is shrapnel, tiny stones.'

'Let me worry about that. Just take me with you to the Sight tomorrow.' Harry's eyes raked Ros's face.

'I'm going up against the cartel here, I thought you'd be on my side.'

Ros clenched and unclenched her fingers on the wheel. 'The cartel is very powerful. You don't know what you're getting into.'

'Are you going to help me or not?'

For a long moment, Ros didn't answer. Harry held her breath, waited her out. Then Ros shook her head.

'You were always headstrong, even as a child. I don't like this, Harry, I don't like it at all.' Her eyes were dark with anxiety. 'But I'll do what I can for you.'

Harry sank back against the seat. 'Thank you.'

She stared through the window, avoiding Ros's gaze. She'd got what she wanted, but her conscience was chafing at her like sandpaper. She was asking a lot of Ros; much more than the older woman knew. Harry's plan could put her in serious danger if she didn't get it right.

They drove in silence for the next twenty minutes. Tension hummed through Harry's limbs. She closed her eyes and tried to relax, letting the murmuring engine tug her into a drowsy stupor. By the time Ros pulled up outside the Southern Sun Hotel, Harry was almost asleep. She roused herself, reaching for the door, then felt Ros's hand on her arm. Harry turned to look at her.

The lines around the older woman's eyes had deepened, and her forehead was puckered with worry. Harry had forgotten how close in age she was to her father.

'Be careful,' Ros said.

Tears prickled at the back of Harry's eyes, catching

her off-guard. Her sinuses filled with heat, and she could feel the beginnings of a lump in her throat. Unexpected mothering always had that effect on her, like a surge of grief welling up out of left field. Briefly, she wondered what it would be like to have a mother like Ros. Then guilt crawled over her like a long-legged spider and chased the thought away.

Harry blinked and nodded, tried to smile. Somehow, she'd work out a way to keep Ros safe.

She climbed out of the car and dragged herself over to the entrance of the hotel. Her gaze dropped to the name badge still clipped to her shirt. She tugged it off and shoved it into her bag, her fingers brushing against her radio-frequency scanner. She recalled the signal she'd cloned and shook her head.

Wesley was right. There was no way anyone could break into that vault, and she didn't intend to try. Van Wycks had spent millions protecting the assets in that bunker. But if Harry was right, they had something else of value that wasn't lying in the vault.

She crossed the lobby and headed for the lifts, the blast of air-conditioning dousing her like a cold shower. Her mind flicked back to the woman in the Van Wycks sorting room, and the sheet of paper she consulted as she filled up the yellow sightbox with stones.

Somewhere, Montgomery Newman kept a list of who got what, and Harry intended to find it.

49

'Good afternoon, Van Wycks Corporation, how may I help you?'

Harry sat up straight on the bed. Somehow, her lies sounded more plausible when her posture was good. 'Hi, this is Catalina Diego from Smartcard Systems. Could I talk to whoever's in charge of your building access security please?'

'Just a moment.' There was a pause while the receptionist presumably checked through her departmental listings. 'That'd be Theodore De Jager in IT Security. Would you like me to put you through?'

'Yes, please.'

Harry wedged the phone against her shoulder and scribbled the name down. Then she tapped at the keyboard on her lap while she waited to be transferred.

'Theodore De Jager.' The words shot out, all swallowed

together. My, this guy was important. Too busy even for vowels.

Harry waited a beat. 'Oh, I'm sorry, I must have the wrong extension. I was looking for Human Resources?'

He clicked his tongue and huffed out a breath. She bet he was rolling his eyes, too. 'Four-one-nine-eight.'

He hung up before Harry had time to thank him. She made a note, then dialled the direct line he'd given her into Human Resources. The call was picked up on the first ring.

'Hello, Heather Barrett speaking.'

Harry marvelled at how recklessly people identified themselves to total strangers. From a security standpoint, good manners were a real liability, but they certainly made the scammer's job easier. Harry jotted the name down, then went to work on her keyboard.

'Hi, Heather, this is Catalina, I'm working with Theodore De Jager in IT Security on those faulty RFID cards.'

'RFID?'

'Radio-frequency ID. You know, the swipe cards?'

'Oh, *ja*, right.' The last word came out as 'raat'. 'Are they giving us problems?'

'Turns out the last batch of cards was defective, so we need to recall them.'

'Oh, what a pain, hey?' Heather's voice was light and musical. She sounded young, maybe in her twenties.

Harry adjusted the phone against her shoulder, her hands still busy on her laptop. 'Well, it's only the new ones issued in the last few weeks, but they need to be wiped and reactivated.'

'Oh, well, mine's old, I've had it for over a year.'

'Oh no, yours is fine. I just called to get the names of last month's new hires so I can ask them to drop their cards back to Theodore.'

Heather paused. 'Can't you get the names from your own records?'

'Well, I would, but the system's just gone down, and all hell's broken loose. I'm offsite at the moment, but Theodore wants everyone contacted before the weekend.'

'I'm not sure.' Heather sounded doubtful. 'I should really check with Mrs Andrews and she's off today.'

'Oh, I see.' Harry feigned a crestfallen tone. 'I'd just feel really bad if any of these people gave up their weekend to put in extra hours, then couldn't even get into the building.'

'Oh.' Heather paused, presumably visualizing a queue of disgruntled employees locked outside their offices. 'Well, maybe I can dig up something. Hold on a minute.'

The phone clattered in Harry's ear as Heather laid it down somewhere. Harry held her breath, her pen at the ready. She tap-tap-tapped it on her pad. What if there were no new hires?

Acoustics rustled at the other end of the phone as Heather came back on the line. 'October was a quiet month on the hiring front.'

Harry tensed. 'Oh?'

'*Ja*, only three new recruits, so that should make your task a lot easier.'

427

Harry let out the breath she'd been holding. 'Great, I can probably catch them all before they head home. Can you call them out?'

'There's one in Accounts, that's Jonathan Botha, then Lynette Kemp in Sales, and Daniel Mosako in IT.'

Harry added the names to her list. She was collecting quite a roll-call.

'That's great, Heather. Can you give me their extension numbers and emails as well? I don't have the company phone list here, and I really should contact them straight away.'

Heather recited the information and Harry scribbled it down. Then she thanked her and disconnected the call.

Her fingers flew over her keyboard. By now, she'd set up bogus Yahoo email accounts for every employee name she'd acquired, including Montgomery Newman and Wesley. She finished setting up addresses for the three new hires, then considered them one by one.

Daniel Mosako was a no-go. Anyone in IT was likely to be wise to Harry's particular brand of flim-flam. But the other two had possibilities.

She dialled the number for Jonathan Botha, letting it ring out for ten seconds. No answer. Next she tried Lynette Kemp, and a woman picked up the call straight away. Harry replaced the receiver without a word and underlined Lynette's name.

She tapped her pen against her teeth, sorting through the sequence of chess moves she'd lined up in her head. Then she sent Lynette a blank email entitled 'Company

Announcement', using the Yahoo account she'd created for Montgomery Newman.

Harry checked her watch. Then she set aside her laptop and hopped off the bed. If she called Lynette too soon after her hang-up, the woman might get suspicious.

Harry wandered over to the balcony and flung open the doors. Toasty air huffed at her cheeks, and below her a tide of traffic washed to and fro. Table Mountain stood guard in the distance, and by now, the mists had rolled away from its plateau, revealing sheer and brutal-looking cliffs.

Harry shuddered. She dragged her gaze away and stepped back inside, then reached for the phone and put in a call to the Cape Town Medicare Clinic. The switchboard played pass-the-parcel with her for a while, but she finally got hold of a nurse on Mani's ward. Harry had expected more stonewalling, but the woman was kind and sympathetic. They were still running tests, she said, but for now Mani was stable. She spoke about septicaemia and silicosis, but admitted that the doctors hadn't committed to a prognosis at this stage. Harry thanked her and hung up. She stood by the bed, waiting to feel some reaction. But all she felt was a numbing chill.

She sank down on the bed and peeked at her watch. She'd give Lynette two more minutes.

Selecting a target was the most important part of any scam. Pick someone with the wrong attitude, and the game was over before it started. Customer Service staff were usually a good bet. After all, they were trained to help you out. But new recruits had potential, too. They were anxious to impress, still finding their feet. Plus they weren't fully acquainted with company protocols or personnel.

Harry checked her watch again, then dialled Lynette's number.

'Hello?' Lynette's voice was young, and a little hesitant.

'Hi, Lynette? This is Catalina over in IT Security. I'm calling about that virus warning we sent out earlier.'

'Virus warning?'

Harry paused. 'The email virus. Didn't you get the note from Theodore De Jager about it?'

'No. No, I didn't.'

Harry stretched the pause out a little. 'Uh-oh.'

'Is there a problem?'

'You could say that. Look, did you get an email from Montgomery Newman today?'

'Yes, a few minutes ago.'

'Shit.'

'I just opened it but it's blank. Is there something wrong?'

'You *opened* it?'

It was Lynette's turn to pause. When she spoke again, her voice was small. 'Yes. I'm sorry, shouldn't I have?'

'Jesus. Hold on a minute.' Harry held the phone at arm's length, cupping her hand over the mouthpiece. She counted to ten, then brought the phone back to her ear. 'This is worse than I thought. What the hell were you thinking?'

'I don't understand.'

430

'That email's not from Mr Newman. Look at it. Why would he use a Yahoo account? It's a worm. A virus. Haven't you been told about clicking on suspicious attachments?'

'But there weren't any attachments, it was just a blank email. I didn't click on anything, I swear.'

'That worm's propagating thousands of emails around the network as we speak, ever since you opened it. The whole company will be on its knees in ten minutes. Mr Newman's going to be on the warpath with this one, I can tell you.'

'Oh my God.' Lynette's voice had dropped to a whisper.

Harry sighed, allowing herself a note of exasperation. 'You're new here, aren't you? Hasn't Theodore given you your security induction course yet?'

'Well, he issued me with my swipe card, but apart from that . . .'

'I'll talk to Heather in HR about it. In the meantime, this is just a mess. I hate to say it, but it looks like you were the trigger here.'

'Oh my God. I had no idea.'

Harry pictured Lynette with her head in her hands, and experienced a stab of guilt. She felt like a brute, and in truth she should have continued to push a little further, but she didn't have the heart. Instead, she worked her keyboard and began to reel her in.

'Look, it's not really your fault.' Harry's tone was relenting. 'Who knows, maybe I won't even have to tell them it was you.'

'Really?' Lynnette sounded hopeful.

'It's my job to trace it, but maybe I don't need to be specific.' Then Harry clicked her tongue. 'Trouble is, where there's one of these worms there's usually more, and things'll only get worse. I'm surprised you haven't seen more emails coming through.'

'Well, let me check.' Lynette drew in her breath. 'Oh no, there's dozens of them coming in. More from Mr Newman, and someone called Wesley Peters. Loads from Theodore De Jager, Jonathan Botha. And Daniel someone. I don't even know half of these people.'

'For God's sake, don't open them.'

'Don't worry, I won't.' Lynette's tone suggested she never wanted to open another email again.

'This is bad,' Harry said. 'We need to upgrade your anti-virus software, install another filter to block out the worm. If we clean this up now, maybe we can keep your name out of it.'

'How do I do it?'

'You'll need to download a filter from the web. Do you still have internet access, or has your machine already died?'

'Oh, God. Hang on.' Harry could hear frantic clacking of keys, then Lynette came back on the line. 'It's okay, I'm still connected.'

'Thank God for that. Okay, there's a website you need to go to, and a link you need to click on to download the update.'

'Just tell me what to do.'

Music to a scammer's ears. Harry directed Lynette to an anti-virus website, trying to keep the smile out of her voice. Naturally, the site wasn't legitimate. It belonged to Blackjack, and Harry kept it primed with an assortment of hacker tools, all of them masquerading as trusted software packages. With gentle coaching, Lynette unwittingly downloaded a backdoor tool and launched it into the Van Wycks network.

Harry punched a fist in the air, then hit a key on her laptop. 'Those emails should have stopped by now.'

'Hang on.' There was a pause. 'You're right, they're not coming in any more. Oh, thank God.'

'Great. Right, let's keep this between ourselves and we might just get away with it. And be careful what you click on in future, okay?'

Harry wound up the call, leaving Lynette sounding weak with relief. Then she turned back to her laptop, her fingertips buzzing. Now she had a way inside.

Van Wycks probably spent millions on perimeter security. Elaborate firewalls, intrusion detection systems, anti-virus software. But a firewall was like a nightclub bouncer, and had the same limitations. It manned the network doors with reasonable efficiency, passing traffic through as long as it didn't look hostile. And sure enough, at the first sign of trouble, a gatecrasher would be out on its ear. Problem was, the bouncer only guarded the doors that were open. After all, why waste time watching ones that were already locked from the inside?

But by now, Harry's rogue software had tip-toed up

to one of those doors and silently unlocked it. It had left the key under the mat, beckoning Harry inside. With a few deft keystrokes, she tunnelled through the firewall and hopped into the Van Wycks network.

She roamed at will, burrowing through its files. Her priority was to find Monty's list of sightholders, and she keyed in all the names she knew: Ros Bloomberg, Jacob Fischer, Bram Bierkens, Jan De Rooy, although she wasn't sure about the spelling of the last two. She searched for any files containing those names, but came up empty-handed.

Harry felt herself droop. She tried different spellings, but that didn't seem to help.

Dammit, he had to keep a list of them somewhere. She racked her brain for other keywords to try. She fired off another search, this time adding Monty's name to the list, and Wesley's too for good measure.

She got a hit. A database. Her pulse rate quickened. She plunged into it, scouring the data. Then she shook her head and frowned. None of the sightholders' names were here. It was just some kind of Van Wycks employee database, nothing more.

Her insides crumpled. She dawdled through the list of names, her eyes glazing over. If it turned out to be a payroll database, she'd hike up Lynette's salary. At least that might salve her conscience.

Harry huffed out a long breath, and recalled what Wesley had said about segregating their personnel. More than likely they segregated their networks too.

Corporate Strategy's was probably sealed off, isolated on a separate, shielded infrastructure. Along with all of Monty's files.

Suddenly, her gaze sharpened. Some of the data headings listed against the employees seemed familiar. Ridge ending, valley, bifurcation. The words tapped like a woodpecker at the base of her brain. Then her heart did a quick flip. They were fingerprint characteristics. She was looking at a biometric database.

She flashed down the list of names. Monty's was there, so was Wesley's, along with a few dozen others. Against each entry was a set of biometrics used to confirm identity.

Jesus. Had she stumbled into the system that controlled access to the Corporate Strategy offices?

Her brain suddenly felt amped. Supposing she somehow inserted her own fingerprint into the system? She could sneak right into Monty's office and access his file from there.

She inspected the data in front of her, trying to recall what she knew about biometric systems. One thing was for sure, there was no use trying to slot in a scan of her own thumb, even if she had the wherewithal to do it. That wasn't how the fingerprints were stored.

Instead, the system recorded a list of distinctive features, such as irregularities in the ridges and valleys. When a finger was presented at the access device, the system looked for a match with the features stored on file.

Harry chewed her lip. Of course, there was no such thing as an exact match. If it happened, it was a sure sign of fraud. In reality, people presented their fingers at different positions and angles; the skin got stretched, distinctive features got shifted a few pixels every time. So the system had to settle for a less than perfect match. Exactly how fussy it got depended on a pre-defined threshold. For a threshold of ninety per cent, for instance, a finger that ticked the boxes by ninety per cent or more was a match. Less than that, and the finger was rejected.

Harry felt her brain click into gear. She hunched over the keyboard, ransacking the database till she found the entry she was looking for.

'Match Threshold'.

It was currently set to ninety-five per cent.

Her fingertips tingled. Supposing she set it to zero? Any finger presented would immediately score a match, whether its features were on file or not. Correlation override.

She took a deep breath and began to type.

50

Harry stared up at the Van Wycks tower block, a cold weight settling into her chest.

Clouds drifted across the looking-glass windows, the whole building draped in mirrored sky as if its very existence was an illusion. She swallowed and flicked a glance to her left. Behind the wire fence, armed guards patrolled the concrete bunker, their two-way radios squawking across the compound. They held their weapons braced against their chests, ready to challenge intruders.

Harry's gut tightened. She hitched the strap of her laptop case higher on her shoulder, then reached into her pocket for her newly minted swipe card. Cloning it had been easy. She'd plugged the RFID scanner into her laptop, copied Wesley's data across, then dumped it on to a blank card. It was like running it through a photocopier.

She palmed the card in one hand. Wesley's had his

photo burned on one side, but that shouldn't be a problem as long as no one asked to see it. The trick now was to look as though she belonged.

She dug her phone out of her bag, put it to her ear and marched through the automatic doors.

'I hear what you're saying, Wesley, but I'm late as it is.' She frowned into the phone, tilting her face away from reception as though straining to hear the voice on the other end. 'What? That's impossible. You should have thought of all this earlier.'

She huffed out a breath, her eyes down, and strode with purpose towards the heavy steel door. The guard's legs and feet slid into her peripheral vision.

'No, I can't just *drop* everything.' She did her best to sound outraged. In her experience, no one liked to interrupt a row. 'I'm on my way up to the office, Monty wants this done before he gets to Tel Aviv.'

She held the card up to the reader on the wall, keeping it palmed like a magician doing tricks. Sweat trickled from under her arms. The light blipped green. The door clicked open. She pushed against it. *Keep talking*.

'I'm going to call Monty right now, straighten this out.'

Something whirred overhead. She looked up just in time to see a surveillance camera twitch her way. Its motor hummed, and she pictured its lens zooming in on her face. The skin between her shoulder blades tingled. She hurried through the door and out into the small lift lobby.

The door closed behind her, and she took a deep breath. For the benefit of any hidden cameras, she wound up her fictitious call, then swiped her card against the reader by the lifts. The doors to the first car slid open and she stepped inside, punching the button for the fifth floor.

So far so good.

She slipped a hand inside her pocket and took out her visitor's name badge, clipping it to her shirt. A visitor with her own swipe card would've raised suspicion downstairs, but now that she was inside, the badge might give her cover to roam around.

The lift opened and she stepped out into the familiar drab hall. Chairs scraped in a nearby room, voices rumbling towards the door. Harry scooted over to the keypad mounted on the wall. She punched in the numbers, 2684.

Nothing. The light stayed red.

Shit. Harry's pulse raced. Behind her a door opened, and a burst of male laughter exploded into the hall. Harry's fingers shook as she punched in her second shot. 2604.

The light blinked green.

Harry shoved through the door and into the second set of lifts, jabbing at the button for the tenth floor. Then she sank back against the wall, her heart thumping hard against her chest. Two down, one to go.

The lift doors parted, and she peeped out. Phones trilled down the hall, and the air smelled of scorched coffee. According to Wesley, this was where Sales hung out. Harry wondered if Lynette was here, sweating over her culpability with the worm.

She crept over to the door that led into Corporate Strategy, and stared at the biometric scanner on the wall. She wiped her palms along her trouser legs.

There were no guarantees that her threshold tinkering would work. It could have been the wrong database. A backup, maybe, or a test system on standby. Harry held her breath and placed her finger on the pad.

She imagined it tracking the features on her finger, comparing them with the set of characteristics on file. It wouldn't find a match. Zero correlation. But would it let her through?

It took less than two seconds to flip back an answer. Green light.

Harry eased open the door. It was quieter here than on the other floors. No clatter of printers, no shrill phones. The champagne glow from the chandeliers made everything look lush and tranquil.

She crept along by the wall, the thick carpet muffling her steps. It was getting late, and most people had probably gone home. A few yards ahead of her, the door to the Millennium Suite stood ajar. As far as she could tell, it was empty. At the other end of the hallway was Monty's office. The double doors were closed, but she could hear the indistinct murmur of voices drifting through them.

Harry edged further down the hall. The doorknob to Monty's office squeaked and turned. She stiffened. Then she scrambled across the hall and ducked into the Millennium Suite.

'Mr Newman will be pleased. I'll contact him next week.'

It sounded like Wesley. Shit. Harry flattened herself against the wall behind the door. Anyone else and she could probably have bluffed her way out, but Wesley would know she was a gatecrasher.

She kept her breathing shallow, aware of a faint smell of fish in the room. Probably from the lobster lunch earlier. Wesley was still talking outside in the hall, but his voice was growing fainter. Finally, a door snapped shut somewhere, deadening the sound of him behind it.

Harry relaxed away from the wall, then did a quick scan of her surroundings. A glossy boardroom table took centre stage, a dozen or so chairs lined up on either side. At one end was a whiteboard scribbled over with red marker. It showed two intersecting circles, one labelled Van Wycks, the other GM Marketing, with the overlap tagged as 'synergy'. Underlined twice. Harry rolled her eyes. Bullshit corporate soundbites were the same the world over.

She cocked her head, straining for noises from the hall. Then she dropped to her knees and crawled under the boardroom table. Her nostrils were filled with chemical, new-carpet fumes. Towards the centre, the floor was fitted with a console of electrical outlets: plug sockets, phone connections, an array of network jacks.

Harry wriggled into a more comfortable position, then took out her laptop and powered it up, darting glances

441

at the door. She felt like a small animal hiding in a cave. Fishing a cable out of her bag, she plugged one end into the laptop and the other into the nearest network jack. She watched the green light flicker around the connection point on her laptop and gave herself a mental thumbs-up. The network jack was live.

She disconnected the cable, then reached into her bag and extracted a small box. It was the size of a video cassette, and had two antennae poking out of opposite corners. She plugged its power pack into an electrical socket, then snipped its other cable into the live network jack. The row of lights along its side flashed like bulbs on a Christmas tree.

It was a wireless access point, a close match for the one in Kruger's office, except Harry's had high-gain directional antennae that should help to boost its signal.

She'd decided before she left the hotel that dallying on Corporate Strategy premises wasn't such a hot idea. The job she had to do could take time, and the chances of accomplishing it undisturbed were slim. A quick in-and-out approach was called for.

She reached into her bag again, this time pulling out a roll of sticky labels. She unpeeled one and smoothed it over the box, using a red pen to print out the words, 'Do Not Remove. Property of IT Security.' Then she packed up her laptop, and surveyed her handiwork.

Her rogue access point was plugged straight into the Corporate Strategy network. Already it was broadcasting connection invitations to anyone who cared to listen.

All you needed was the passphrase, and since the access point was Harry's, naturally she knew what it was. As long as the signal reached far enough, she could finish the job from the safety of the car park.

She scooted out from under the table, then straightened up and listened at the door. Nothing. She stepped outside and headed for the exit.

'Excuse me.'

Harry stopped in her tracks, spun round. A willowy woman in a suit was staring at her from the other end of the hallway. She was model-slim and heavily made-up. She narrowed her black-rimmed eyes.

'Can I help you?'

Harry smiled and shook her head, edging towards the door. 'I'm fine, thanks, just on my way out.'

The woman frowned, and advanced down the hall towards her. Up close, her face looked dusty with powder, as though she'd dipped it in a bag of flour. She peered at Harry's visitor's badge. Her own identity swipe card was clipped to her lapel.

'Who are you meeting here?' she said.

Harry's brain scrambled. 'I'm with GM Marketing. One of the guys left his laptop behind, so they sent me up to get it.' She held up her case and tried a conspiratorial smile. 'I think the lobster at lunchtime got to him.'

The woman nodded, but didn't return the smile. Maybe she was afraid it would cause subsidence in the layers on her face. Harry sidled towards the door, her blood drumming in her ears. Then the woman said,

'Just a minute.'

Harry swallowed, and slid her a backward glance. The woman had snatched a phone out of her pocket, and was drilling Harry with a look. Then suddenly, she held the phone out to her.

'As long as you're here, you can pass this on too.' Her face powder cracked with a small smile. 'Apparently, one of them left it in the men's room.'

Harry took the phone, her heartbeat scampering with relief. 'Thanks, I'll see he gets it back.'

She pressed the door-release switch and pushed through to the lift lobby, her whole body bathed in sweat. In less than two minutes, she'd reached the ground floor and was striding across reception to the car park. She found her car and ducked into the driver's seat, settling her laptop on her knees.

Her breath was coming in quick gasps. She stole a glance around. By now, most of the other cars had gone and she was acutely aware of the surveillance cameras sweeping the area. If she stayed much longer, she'd start to look conspicuous.

Harry flicked a few keys. Her rogue access point was busy soliciting connections, and her laptop had already picked it up. It prompted her for the passphrase, and she typed it in, diving through the wormhole she'd created in the Corporate Strategy network.

Bingo. She was behind the firewall.

Her fingers clacked across the keys as she launched a sniffer program to eavesdrop on the network traffic.

Sensitive data passed across the wire all the time. Logins, confidential emails, reports, files. It was only a matter of time before she sniffed out a login she could use.

She didn't have long to wait. Ten minutes later, Wesley's credentials zipped over the wire. She captured his username and password, then logged in under his name. Now she had the keys to the kingdom.

She prowled around the network, exploring the landscape. She remembered what Monty had said. *Tell Andrea tomorrow's list is ready*. It had to be someplace where the Head Sorter could pick it up. Maybe he emailed it to her, but it didn't sound like it.

Harry fired off her search for the sightholder names: Ros Bloomberg, Jacob Fischer, Bram Bierkens, Jan De Rooy. This time, she scored. Invoices, memos, account statements, billing details. Her toes curled. She was close, she could feel it.

She leapfrogged across the network, sniffing into corners, blazing a trail of searches as she went. One of them turned up a folder labelled 'Sights 2009'. For an instant, Harry's fingers froze. Then she plunged inside and found eleven more folders, each labelled for a month of the year from January to November. She swooped into the November folder. Inside were three separate files, labelled by date: one each for yesterday, today and tomorrow.

She opened tomorrow's file, and scrolled through it. Adrenaline flooded her body. She was looking at an index of sightholders. Ros's name was there. So were Jacob's and Jan De Rooy's. Against each sightholder was an amount in US dollars, along with a detailed list of stones. She scanned some of the entries for Jan De Rooy:

Yellow closed octahedron, 15 carats

Milky white dodecahedron, 10 carats, spotted

Bluish white closed octahedron, 210 carats

Frosted white rhombododecahedron, 205 carats

Her eyes widened, and she checked the amount lodged against his name. $1,250,000. She gave a low whistle. If that was all he had to pay, then he was doing well. From what she'd learned, the 210-carat diamond alone was worth six or seven million.

Harry skimmed through the rest of the list, taking note of Jacob's allotment. Most of his stones were small, but he'd netted himself a large octahedron weighing in at 200 carats. Probably his reward for snitching on Garvin, a gesture from the cartel to signal he was back in the fold. Apart from Jacob and Jan De Rooy, only two other sightholders had earned large stones: Bram Bierkens, and a diamantaire called Saul Rubinek. Like De Rooy, they'd each copped two monster whites.

Ros's name was at the bottom of the list. Her stones were mostly under three carats, with a large batch grouped together and labelled 'common goods'. Harry raised her eyebrows. Ros hadn't been kidding when she said she was the black sheep.

Harry's fingers hovered over the keys. She checked the file to see when it was last updated. 2:55pm that afternoon, right before she'd met Monty in his office.

Tell Andrea tomorrow's list is ready.

This had to be the right file. Harry chewed her bottom lip. Then her fingers sped over the keys, switching some of the entries around. She swapped out one apiece from De Rooy, Bierkens, Rubinek and Jacob. In less than a minute, four large stones, each weighing more than two hundred carats, were assigned to Ros's name.

Harry saved the file, snapped it shut, then powered down her laptop. She fired up the ignition with shaking hands and pulled out of the car park, resisting the urge to rev up and speed away.

If her plan worked, Ros's sightbox was now worth almost thirty million dollars.

51

Three armed guards escorted Harry deep into the bunker. Their boots clattered in sync against the concrete floor, firearms rattling with every stride. A droplet of sweat meandered down Harry's back.

Ros was behind her, shepherded by three more guards. Harry threw her a worried look, but she seemed unconcerned. Today Ros was dressed in a pale green suit, another French couture number. She could have been a First Lady strolling around on a state visit.

Harry squared her shoulders and followed the guards down the winding tunnel. It was narrow and dimly lit, a windowless fortress. She thought of the diamantaires that flew here from all over the world: New York, Tel Aviv, Bombay, Antwerp, Hong Kong. At the very least, she'd expected the Sight to take place in an office, not deep inside a secret bunker.

Secrecy was the key to the diamond trade, of course. Concealment of bumper diamond reserves; clandestine choking of rough gem supplies. All of it designed to strengthen the illusion of scarcity.

They reached a huge steel door, drilled with rivets the size of table coasters. Four more guards flanked it either side. They *click-snapped* their weapons into the firing position at the first sight of Harry and her escorts.

Harry swallowed. She took in the army fatigues, the heavy guns, the thousand-yard stares. Her heart thudded. These were no ordinary security guards. These were trained soldiers, mercenaries probably. She thought of the man in the baseball cap. Jesus. Van Wycks had its own private army.

Something cold wedged in her chest. The cartel members were powerful, their tyranny above the law. What the hell had made her think she could outwit them?

Her eyes darted left and right while the squad of guards conferred. Security cameras rubbernecked her progress from every angle. Small, rectangular devices dotted the stone walls, probably heat or radar sensors.

The steel door groaned open, like the entrance to an ancient dungeon. It looked thick enough to withstand a month of continuous drilling. Harry followed the guards through, their footsteps scattering echoes off the impenetrable stone walls. A chill settled around her. The glass tower block outside was strictly window-dressing. This was where the real security was.

She stepped into a bare lobby, the stone floor and

449

walls sustaining the grim sense of incarceration. In front of her was a long glassed-in desk, with attendants installed like bank tellers behind it. One of the guards slipped a sheet of paper under the glass. The attendant frowned at Harry over his glasses, then spoke in low tones with the guard.

'Don't worry.' Ros had moved up beside her. 'I've vouched for you ahead of time.'

Harry threw her a glance. She looked cool and unruffled, and Harry felt a jab of guilt at how she'd exploited the older woman's trust. But Ros would be safe. Harry would make sure of that.

Another troop of guards marched into the vestibule, escorting a tall, middle-aged man over to the desk. His forehead was high, his remaining circlet of hair resting like a skullcap on his crown. He glanced at Ros, inclining his head in salute. There was something faintly aristocratic about the disdainful way he peered down at her.

'Ros,' he murmured as he passed.

'Jan.' She gave him a gracious smile. 'Good to see you.'

Harry's eyebrows shot up at the name. She flashed a look at his retreating back, watching as the guards ushered him through another door.

'Who's that?' she whispered.

'Jan De Rooy. One of Monty's favourites.'

Harry's eyes widened. She thought of the jumbo stone she'd plundered out of Jan De Rooy's box, and wondered how he'd react. Not that it mattered. De Rooy's windfall might have shrunk, but he'd still scored one large diamond, as had both Bierkens and Rubinek. Jacob was the only one left with scant pickings, but he was hardly in a position to bitch about it. Besides, no one was going to complain, not even the golden boys. Expulsion was too high a price.

The guard marched back towards her, his stare cold and blank. Harry felt herself tense. What if she was wrong? What if they'd already discovered the stunt she'd pulled? Maybe they'd brought her here to warn her off, not hand her a box of stones. The guard gestured with his lethal-looking firearm.

'Follow me.'

Harry and Ros obeyed, scurrying after him as he led them to an unmarked door. He opened it and motioned them inside.

'Wait here.'

Harry stepped into the room, her back tingling. Ros followed, the guard closing the door behind her. The room was small and drab, its grey carpet no cheerier than the cold stone outside. But at least this room had a window. It beamed an oblong of light on to a small, round table. Sheets of white paper covered the surface, along with an electronic weighing scale, a lamp, a jeweller's loupe and a telephone.

Harry looked at Ros. 'What happens now?'

'We wait. They'll bring in the box, then leave us to examine it in private, consult over the phone with associates if we want to.' Ros made a wry face. 'It's all a charade. No one ever says no.'

Harry clasped her hands together and began to pace the room. There were no guarantees that any of this would work. She could have accessed the wrong list. Or maybe Monty had emailed it to Andrea before he left. For all Harry knew, he could've printed the damn thing out and left it on her desk.

Mentally, she fast-forwarded to her rendezvous on Table Mountain. In another few hours, she had to deliver the stones. But even if she did, what were the chances that the Van Wycks killer would let her go? Her brain stalled, its synapses backfiring. She couldn't think of that, not now.

'This is my last sight.'

Harry stopped pacing. 'What?'

'It's Garvin. I can't get past it.' Ros hugged her chest. 'A corrupt cartel is one thing, but doing business with a bunch of killers . . . Well, I just can't be a part of it.'

Harry felt a faint trickle of relief. The more distance between Ros and Van Wycks, the better.

Ros gave her a direct look. 'But I've given you my word about today and I'll keep it. You can have my sightbox, though I still don't know what good it'll do you.'

Harry held her gaze for a moment, then nodded. She'd already made arrangements to transfer $600,000 into Ros's account, despite the older woman's protests. But she trusted her to keep her word, even without the money.

Anxiety dug lines in Ros's brow. 'Won't you reconsider? Won't you go to the police for help?'

Harry shook her head. 'It's too late. Even if I could get them to believe me, they couldn't help me now.'

'But, Harry—'

The door swung open, cutting off Ros's reply. A grey-haired man in a sombre suit glided into the room, bearing a small yellow case like an altar offering in front of him. It was a twin of the box Harry had seen Andrea fill. He set it on the table, positioning it carefully in the centre, then flipped open the locks with his thumbs. He wore white gloves and handled everything with enormous care, like a snooker ref re-spotting the black. Then without a word or a glance at either of them, he sidled back out of the room.

Harry stared at the sightbox. A flash of sweat doused her body. She moved over to the table with Ros and slowly lifted the lid.

A sheet of paper lay across the top. Harry picked it up. Ros's name was printed on it in large letters, along with the price tag of her box: $600,000.

Harry set the sheet of paper aside and forced herself to inspect the rest of the contents. The box was filled with a stack of ziplocked bags, each one full of stones. She lifted the top one up and fingered the diamonds through the plastic. They were dull and grey, like chips of driveway gravel. Harry read the label on the bag: 16 pale-grey dodecahedrals, total 17.8 carats.

The next bag contained a dozen or so brownish stones, triangular, like tiny arrowheads. According to the label they were pale-brown macles, totalling 14 carats.

453

Ros lifted out the next few bags and set them on the table. They held dozens of stones, each smaller than an orange pip. Ros's hand hovered over the next bag, and Harry heard her gasp. She watched Ros lift it out.

It contained just a single stone. A silvery-white geometric shape, with facets that gleamed as though dipped in a translucent film. Slowly, Ros unzipped the pouch and took the diamond in her hand. It was as big as a billiard ball.

Harry swallowed. Her eyes darted back to the box. She scrabbled at the other pouches: one contained a scattering of seed-sized stones; another a handful of what looked like lead shot. Then she reached the last three packets lining the bottom of the box. They didn't lie flat like the other bags. The single stones inside them were too large.

Harry glanced at Ros. The diamantaire had set her stone on the white paper and was peering at it through a loupe. Harry extracted one of the remaining bags and stared at the stone inside. It looked like a chunky nugget of broken glass. She read the label: Bluish white closed octahedron, 210 carats.

Jan De Rooy's diamond.

'What have you done, Harry?'

Harry jerked her head up. Ros was glaring at her, the expression on her face stony.

Harry blinked. 'I told you, I need large diamonds, I need to—'

'I know what you told me. Now I'm just wondering if any of it was true.'

Harry gasped. 'Of course it was true.'

'I don't know how you did this.' Ros gestured at the large stones. 'Maybe you've just been using me to steal diamonds. Is that it?'

Harry felt the words like a punch in the gut. Her head reeled. For a moment, she couldn't speak. Then she said, 'Everything I said is true. I need these stones, Ros, otherwise the killer—'

'Yes, I know what you told me about some killer.' Ros's gaze was chilly. 'Frankly, I don't know what to believe.'

'Jesus, Ros, please—'

'Don't worry, I'll keep my promise. For your father's sake, not yours.'

'Look, I only need the larger stones. You take the rest, Ros, please.'

'You can have the whole damn box and everything that's in it.' Ros snatched up the phone. 'I'll make the payment. Just take the stones and get out.'

Harry's insides shrivelled. She listened to Ros making arrangements on the phone. The older woman's profile was strong and matriarchal, but she wouldn't meet Harry's eyes.

Harry turned away. It hurt when someone you admired had such a low opinion of you, but then again she should've been used to it. The dynamics with her mother had been like that all her life. She clenched her fists. To hell with it. It didn't matter what Ros believed. She had other things to deal with right now.

She gathered up the plastic bags, packing them into the sightbox while Ros finished up on the phone. The man with the white gloves returned to the room, concluding the formalities of the financial transaction with Ros. Ten minutes later, they were hurrying back through the echoing tunnels of the bunker, their six-guard escort in tow.

The box almost scorched Harry's hands. Her muscles felt wired, on high alert, waiting for alarm bells or sirens to go off. Ros strode on ahead, not speaking, and from the tension in her back Harry knew that further protests of innocence would be a waste of time.

They passed through the gigantic steel door and out through the maze of tunnels. The soldiers cleared them at the entrance, and again at the sentry-guarded barriers. Finally, Harry stepped out of the high-security compound. Metal gates clanged shut behind her, and a ripple of fear skittered up her spine.

She'd stolen from the almighty cartel.

52

'Wait, wait and the cards will come.'

Harry's father winked at her, and she watched as the dealer flipped him an ace to go with his king of clubs. Another blackjack.

She worked hard to return his smile. She'd been trying to persuade him for the last half-hour to leave the casino and head back to the safety of his hotel, but his feverish air said the cards had already taken hold. He would stay now till his money and his luck ran out.

Chips chinkled on the soft baize, and the rattle of sorting machines filled the room. Harry shifted from foot to foot, checked her watch. It was almost time to go. Anxiety churned her stomach. An image of Table Mountain, stark and brooding, flashed into her head. She clutched her bag, and felt the irregular outlines of the four jumbo Van Wycks stones.

Harry watched her father's face. His cheeks were flushed, his eyes lit up like candles. Her insides tugged. She wanted to stay with him, to protect him. But she couldn't.

The dealer slid more cards across the baize. Her father tapped the table, and earned another ace.

'I asked Ros to join us for dinner,' he said, a frown flickering across his brow. 'But she's changed her flight. Gone home early.'

Harry looked at her hands. Ros hadn't said a word on the drive back to the hotel. It was no surprise she didn't want dinner with someone she believed was a thief. Harry couldn't exactly blame her. She may not be a thief, at least not in her own eyes, but honesty was a virtue she tended to skirt around. And look where it had got her. If she'd only been straight with Hunter from the start, maybe none of this would have happened.

At least Ros was in the clear. Once they'd parted company, Harry had returned to the Van Wycks building. From the safety of the car park, she had tunnelled once more into Monty's list and swapped the entries back, leaving Ros with her original box of low-grade gems. The only record of the switch was Andrea's copy of the file, assuming she'd taken one. But why would anyone bother to examine that? The Van Wycks transactions remained intact: sightbox money in, diamonds out, regardless of who got what. And none of the diamantaires would dare to complain. As far as Harry was concerned, her game of smoke and mirrors should never come to light.

She closed her eyes, and felt her brain tilt. Cards whispered across the felt, and the murmur of punters thrummed around her. The sounds lulled her, like a warm blanket, and she didn't want to leave. She dragged her eyes open, peeked at her watch. Her stomach lurched. Almost time.

'Harry. We meet again.'

She spun round. Dan Kruger was studying her from under his dark brows. He'd reverted to the rancher look, the workshirt and jeans stirring up images of his hypnotic bonding with horses.

Her pulse thumped. What the hell was he doing in a casino?

She remembered Eve's parting threat. Had she told the syndicate that Harry had their stones? If she had, it was only a matter of time before they came looking for her. Was that why Kruger was here?

She swallowed, tried to smile. 'I didn't think this was your kind of place.'

'It isn't. But Cassie and some of the owners wanted to come.'

His gaze wandered, unseeing, around the room, then came back to settle on Harry. He cocked his head, assessing her as though trying to predict her performance in a race.

She bristled under his scrutiny. 'What?'

'You look so keyed up.' He smiled. 'Like a horse under starter's orders.'

Before Harry could reply, Cassie drifted over and placed

459

a hand on Kruger's arm. Her brandy-coloured hair hung loosely around her shoulders, and her khaki shirt brought out the olive shade in her eyes.

'Your owners are looking for you, Dan.' Cassie turned to Harry. Her smile was frank and disarming, but the hand on Kruger's arm was territorial nonetheless. 'Dan's not a champagne trainer, that's his problem. He's no good at schmoozing clients.'

Kruger frowned. 'Waste of time.'

'See?' Cassie rolled her eyes conspiratorially at Harry. 'You need to learn how to schmooze, Dan. Or get someone else to do it for you.'

Harry watched them as if from a long distance. Theirs was a common mating ritual; the determined woman, the reluctant male. In spite of Kruger's apparent resistance, Harry was struck again by how well matched they were. They stood arm in arm, both tall and well built, and for a moment it was as if they were united against her.

Harry's skin prickled.

Cassie nodded towards the blackjack tables. 'Your father's been keeping me company while Dan goes walk-about.'

Harry looked back at the table. Her father was maintaining a flow of charming banter, but she could tell from the fixed look in his eye that underneath it all his brain was racing. She sneaked another look at her watch. She had to go, but she didn't want to leave him.

Glass shattered somewhere behind her. She turned to

see Rob Devlin backing away from a blackjack table, brushing down his clothes. He turned his gaze their way, and his face contorted with fury. Then he whirled round and stalked off. Cassie clicked her tongue.

'He got disqualified from his race yesterday. Hauled up before the stewards for reckless riding.' Worry pleated her forehead. 'He's behaving like an idiot. The owners won't like it.'

Kruger's jaw muscles tightened. 'The trainer doesn't bloody like it either. I've already told him he's never riding Billy-Boy again.'

Harry followed Rob's hard, wiry frame as he shouldered his way to the bar. His fists were clenched, aggression seeping from him in venomous waves.

She gripped her bag, felt the sweat roll down her back. One of these people had probably ordered Eddie to lock her in Rottweiler's stall. They had all been there that night; any of them could have done it. But her instincts were jammed, all her signals colliding. How could she tell who to trust?

Cassie shepherded Kruger away to mingle with a trio of men playing roulette. Harry watched them go, then moved next to her father, postponing the moment when she'd have to say goodbye. The dealer was shuffling the decks, riffling them with a snap, and stacking them into a pile. Her father stood stock-still, his eyes boring into the cards.

Harry shot him a glance. He was tracking the shuffle. The dealer tipped the six-deck stack over on its side and offered the plastic cut card to her father. He took it between his fingers, his hands steady, his gaze unblinking. He sliced it cleanly into the centre of the block, then slid a glance at Harry. He winked at her.

'Wait, wait and the cards will come.'

A charge buzzed up Harry's frame. Her eyes darted upwards to the ceiling at the dark, bulbous eye-in-the-sky. The surveillance cameras peppered the casino, positioned to monitor individual players closely enough to see the colour of their eyes. She scanned the room, taking in the other cameras and the discrete security guards.

A small crowd had already gathered around her father's table. As soon as the count went up, or when his tracked cards emerged, her father would bet high and the crowd would be three or four deep. The surveillance cameras would zoom in, the pit bosses would converge and the security guards would be alerted to the hot action at table five. In minutes he'd be surrounded by the best security the casino had to offer.

What could be safer?

She studied her father's face. Right now he seemed calm, but the question was, could he keep it up?

Her fingers tightened around her bag. 'Dad?'

'Mmm?' His eyes were still on the cards.

'You need to own this table for the next two hours. Can you do that?'

He threw her a sharp glance, and she stepped in closer, lowering her voice.

'It's important, really important. I've got to meet

someone on Table Mountain, no one must know. But I need you here, in the spotlight.' She swallowed. 'Do you think you can do it?'

His eyes held hers for a long moment. 'Are you still in a bind, love?'

Her throat closed over, and when she spoke it came out as a whisper. 'Yes.'

'Then I can do it. I haven't lost my touch yet, you know. Trust me.'

She closed her eyes and nodded, then leaned up and kissed his whiskery cheek. 'I do trust you, Dad.'

Then before he could see her tears, she turned and headed for the door.

53

Harry knew her chances of surviving Table Mountain were slim. She had no weapons. No allies on her side. No tricks up her sleeve. All she had were the diamonds.

She gripped the steering wheel, her arms throbbing from the force of her own heartbeat. The car tugged upwards and she shifted gears, following the signposts for the cableway. She squinted into the glare. In half an hour, the sun would set; another ally gone.

She gunned the engine, digging the car into the steep climb up the foothills. Table Mountain rose in front of her like a granite wall, its flanking peaks emerging as she rounded alternate bends. To the west of the plateau was the hump of Lion's Head. To the east was Devil's Peak, its pointed summit smothered in a fleecy mist.

Harry gnawed at her bottom lip. What if the cable cars weren't running? From what she'd read, the mountain range was known for its capricious mood swings. She'd seen it herself; fog rolling in at a moment's notice, seeping over the top like dry ice. The cable service paid attention to mist and high winds, and downed tools if conditions weren't safe.

The car engine laboured around another bend, and a blocky grey building loomed into view. Harry's stomach jolted. The cable station. She found a parking space along the crowded verge, then hiked the rest of the way on foot. Wind rushed through the trees, snatching at her hair. She clutched her bag with both hands.

The queue for tickets snaked up the steps of the building. The cable cars were running, and she realized she'd been hoping the service would be down. Stupid. Did she think the killer would call the whole thing off just because she couldn't get a ride?

She got in line, noting the warning signs to tourists along the way. In the event of bad weather a hooter would sound, summoning everyone aboard the last descending car. Miss it, and you were on your own. Harry squinted skywards. So far, despite the mist on Devil's Peak, the flattened table top looked clear.

Her eyes raked the dwindling crowds around her, searching for signs of the man in the baseball cap. Her mind scrambled ahead, trying to anticipate his next move. Was he already up there waiting for her? Or was he behind her, following her trail? She tightened her grip on the bag. She'd hand him the stones, and then what? Would he really just let her leave? Yet how could he kill her in broad daylight, surrounded by a crowd of tourists?

Harry shivered, every nerve ending jangling at her to turn and run. But where would she go? What other way was there to end this?

She bought her ticket, then climbed the steps to the cable car platform. She pushed into the waiting gondola with the rest of the tourists, scrutinizing every face. She recognized no one.

The doors slid shut, and the gondola lurched upwards. Harry's stomach shifted. She clung to the handrail, her feet tingling at the notion of dangling from a single stretch of wire. The gondola veered up the stony, vertical cliffs, the cables creaking overhead as the motor ratcheted them upwards. Harry stared out at the merciless, granite face, at its twisted strata that spoke of geological turbulence as old as the Earth itself.

She switched her grip to a vertical pole. The floor had started to rotate, presumably so that everyone got a panoramic vista. Devil's Peak slid into her field of vision. Its mist had thickened, and seemed to be floating their way. All around her, the tourists marvelled at Table Bay and the aerial city views, but Harry couldn't look down. Her fingers grew icy.

She fixed her gaze skywards. The upper cable station waited like an open mouth to receive them, and the gondola soared towards it, its twin rushing past on the downward trip. She spotted movement on the distant slopes: hikers slogging up a steep gully, hardier souls who'd chosen to trek up the pathways that cut through the cliffs.

Finally, the gondola creaked into the shadows of the docking station, the pulley gears grinding as the car clanged to a halt. The doors slid open.

Slowly, Harry exited with the other passengers, stepping back out into the sunlight. Her eyes darted left and right. Stretching in front of her was an expanse of rocks, pathways and thick green shrubbery. The plateau was no more than a couple of hundred yards wide. The tourists viewed it all through their cameras, pointing and snapping. Harry edged further out on to the mountain.

It was strangely quiet, apart from the wind. Gusts whipped around her ears, and the temperature had dropped. She hugged her bag close. Her eyes scoured the mountaintop, searching for the man in the baseball cap. There was no sign of him.

She clambered over the rocks, scanning the area, heading towards the waist-high wall that bordered the plateau on her right. A thick carpet of mist swirled inwards, low to the ground. It was as though she was standing on a cloud. She peeped over the wall and caught her breath. The drop was sheer. A dizzying, vertical plunge, lined with jagged rocks.

Her head swam, and she jerked backwards. In the distance, she could make out the sprawl of Cape Town, and the waterfront piers that curved into the ocean like crab pincers. Then the wind rolled out another layer of fog, draping it across the view.

The cable cars rattled behind her, ferrying more tourists up and down. She turned away from the wall. The mist was spilling on to the mountaintop like liquid cloud. Visibility was dwindling, and people were scurrying towards the station.

Where was he?

The wind was picking up. It thrashed around her head, bumping her backwards. She hunched into it, still hugging her bag against her chest. The sun was beginning to set, scattering orange light through the thickening haze, but the tourists who'd come to see it would be disappointed. If the fog kept up, the plateau would soon be blind.

Supposing he didn't show? Maybe something had happened. Maybe Van Wycks had called him off. Adrenaline surged through her. She could take the next cable car down, head for the airport with her father, take the first flight out to anywhere.

She spun round, straining for signs of the Van Wycks killer. She could barely see two feet ahead. The view of Cape Town was now totally obscured. The fog had dropped like a portcullis.

A hooter screamed across the mountaintop. Harry's heart pounded. The cableway operators were yelling through the mist, rounding everyone up. The wind snatched at their voices, hurling them away.

Harry hesitated, shivering in the wind. The Van Wycks killer wasn't coming. The hooter shrieked again, long, insistent blasts. She had to go. She took a step towards the sound. Then something hard jabbed into her spine.

'Don't move.'

54

Harry's breath froze in her throat. She stood stock-still, listening to the mournful groan of the cables as the last gondola left the station. Dizziness churned her brain.

She was stranded with a killer on this godforsaken mountain. She could smell his sour sweat, feel the hard steel of his weapon still digging into her spine.

'Turn around!'

Slowly, she obeyed. He'd stepped away from her, plumes of mist separating the few feet between them. This time, he wasn't wearing the baseball cap.

The nap of his buzz-cut rippled in the gathering wind. His weathered skin looked pale and clammy, as though he was ill. The gun he held was the same one he'd used on Garvin Oliver.

She flashed on an image of Garvin's corpse, of his lifeless thumbs being jammed against his own vault pad.

Dead man's fingers. Harry shuddered, tried to focus. The damp mist prickled her skin like rain.

He levelled the gun at her chest, a slight tremor flickering over his arms. 'Where are the diamonds?'

Harry's fingers tightened around her bag. She edged backwards.

'What about our deal?' Her voice sounded small. She swallowed and tried again. 'I deliver the stones and you let me go, right?'

'Wrong. Take a look around. Where d'you think you'd go?'

Harry's eyes flicked left and right. The wind was building up, whipping the nearby bushes into a frenzy. Another cloud bank was swirling in, shrouding the plateau. The cliff wall was close enough to touch, but she could barely see it.

He was right. There was nowhere to go.

'So that's why you brought me here.' Her voice was as flat as she felt inside.

'Lonely, isn't it?' Droplets of sweat crept down his face. 'Always is when the last car goes. The fog just speeded things up this time.' He narrowed his eyes. 'Now give me the fuckin' stones.'

Slowly, Harry opened her bag. With fingers spread to show she'd nothing to hide, she lifted out a ziplocked pouch. It was larger than the original Van Wycks bags, and she'd managed to fit all four diamonds into it. She held it up at eye level. The stones looked dull and ugly in the twilight, but the killer's eyes gleamed.

'Put them on the ground.' He was shivering now, as though gripped by a chill. 'Then step away.'

Harry's fingers tightened on the bag. Panic spiralled up her insides. The diamonds were her talisman. They'd helped to keep her alive. If she gave them up now, it'd be like handing over her soul.

She shot her arm out over the wall, stretching so that the bag dangled right over the sheer cliffs.

He jerked towards her. 'What the hell—'

'I'll drop them!' she screamed.

He froze. His eyes were fixed to the bag. It snapped to and fro in Harry's hand, battered by the wind. She tried to lick her lips, but her mouth was parched.

'One move, and I swear, I'll drop them over the edge,' she said. 'And if you shoot me, I'll just let go.'

His face curled into a snarl. He flexed his fingers on his gun, staring at the bag. A muscle twitched in one of his eyelids, like a trapped insect. Harry raised her voice to be heard above the wind.

'Here's my idea. We wait till the cable car comes back. We walk over to it, I hand you the bag. Then I step inside with all the nice tourists and we go our separate ways.'

She clamped her mouth shut to stop her teeth from chattering. Her ears strained for sounds from the cable station. Nothing but the gusting wind.

He kept the gun trained on her chest. 'I have my orders. A good soldier always follows orders.'

Then he took a step towards her.

471

Harry stiffened, her flight instincts screaming. She edged away, scraping her hip against the wall. *Think!* There had to be another way down.

Then she remembered. The hikers.

She hitched her backside up on to the wall, still dangling the bag out over the precipice. He narrowed his eyes.

'What're you doing?'

Harry didn't answer. She clambered on to the wall on her knees, gripping it with her free hand. The wind shouldered into her, trying to topple her. She peeked over the edge, and her gut lurched. Apart from a few jagged outcrops, the drop plummeted straight to infinity.

Sweat bathed Harry's body. Maybe there was a path from here, maybe there wasn't. But she'd rather die fighting for a last way out than wait meekly for a bullet in the chest.

She eyed the edge of the wall, shifted closer. Then the Van Wycks killer charged.

Harry screamed, scrambled backwards. He rammed into her, knocking her sideways across the wall. Her upper body dangled over the edge. She looked down and her head reeled, the giddy drop tilting below her. He yanked at her outstretched arm. She clung to the wall with her free hand, her grip shaky. Then a shot exploded into the air.

She felt him jerk, then freeze. The wind crashed around her ears. She flashed him a glance. His eyes looked wild, on the edge of madness. She jerked back her arm, shoved the bag down her shirt, snatched at the wall with both hands. Then he lunged at her again, overbalancing her. Another shot burst through the mist. He whiplashed backwards. Harry screamed, her grip faltered. The wind rugby-tackled her, rammed her off-balance. The cliff face veered up towards her, and she pitched right over the edge.

Her arms flailed. Her breath caught. The drop rushed up in a tailspin towards her. Her fingernails scrabbled against the wall. Scraped. Slid. Her flesh burned. She dug in. Found purchase, fingertip-deep. Shoulder muscles wrenched in pain. Her legs swung wildly, one foot hit a crevice. She jolted, no longer falling. She pressed her face into the cold stone. Clung there trembling, eyes shut tight. Tried not to think about the lethal void below.

'Harry!'

Her eyes flared open. She breathed in the smell of damp granite. She heard someone panting above her.

'Harry! Christ.'

She couldn't look up, daren't move her head. But she knew it was Dan Kruger.

Something scuffed on the rocks. She heard him grunt. Then,

'Harry, grab my hand!'

She risked an upward peek. He was stretched over the edge, reaching out. His hand was a few feet above her.

She swallowed. 'I can't.'

'You can. Just reach up.'

His voice was strong and sure. Cold sweat rolled over her. What was he doing here? She pressed her face back

473

into the cliff. Something scratched her chin. The ziplocked bag, poking out of her shirt. She knew he could see it.

Her arms quivered, pain burning her left shoulder. She thought about grabbing his hand, but couldn't move. A soft sound escaped her throat. When she felt she could speak, she said,

'Did you follow me here?'

'No, I followed Rob. Come on, Harry, give me your hand.'

As if on cue, Rob's voice drifted down to her, borne along on the wind.

'Where is she, Kruger? Tell me where she is!'

She heard Kruger shift on the rocks above. 'Get over here, Rob! Hold my waist!'

'Jesus.'

Harry peered upwards. Rob was staring down at her, his eyes wide. Then he stretched over the wall, reaching out his hand.

'Here, grab it, I'm closer!'

'For God's sake, Rob.' Kruger's teeth sounded clenched. Harry closed her eyes, fighting the burning pain in her fingers.

Something scuffled above her. Shoes scraped on rock. Small stones sputtered down on her head. She looked up. Kruger was perched on a narrow ledge jutting out from under the clifftop. He held on to the wall, reaching out to her with one hand.

'Come on, Harry, just stretch.'

Tremors racked her arms. She squinted up at Kruger, then Rob. Her head spun. Which one?

Rob was further away. He was weaker, lighter. Maybe he wasn't even sober. Would he have the strength to lift her up? And if he did, what was to stop him snatching the stones and hurling her back down? What was to stop Kruger doing the same?

Cramp twisted down her leg. Her foothold slipped, scattering a landslide of stones. She scrabbled, found a toehold. Her heart hammered as she laid her face against the cold rock. Jesus! How much longer could she hold on? Her mother's face floated in front of her. *Mom, I'm going to die.*

'Grab hold!' Rob yelled. 'C'mon, I can pull you!'

Harry's mind whirled. Rob was involved with Eve, he could be part of the syndicate. But Kruger ran the yard. Did he run the syndicate too?

Pain ripped along her fingers and wrists, tore into her arms. Now, more than ever, she needed her damned instincts.

She rested her cheek against the rough granite. 'Eve double-crossed you, you know.' She spoke into the rockface, addressing both of them. 'She's gone. Done a runner.'

Rob swore. 'Bitch! Fuckin' knew it.'

Kruger stretched down further. 'Come on, Harry, just reach up.'

Harry's fingers were shaking. Vibrations juddered up and down her arms. She was so tired. A seductive voice inside her head told her to just let go.

Just fall back, give yourself up to it.

Harry felt her eyes close. For an instant, her limbs

relaxed. *No!* She snapped her eyes open. Her biceps trembled. She stared at the hands reaching out to her. Her foot slipped, her toehold almost gone.

Choose!

With a final surge of strength, she heaved herself upwards, shot out her arm. For an instant, she was weightless, suspended in air. The abyss waited to engulf her. Then she grabbed Rob's hand.

His fingers clasped hers. Slipped. Squeezed again. He hauled her up a few inches. Kruger clambered back over the wall, leaned across Rob, grabbed her wrist and heaved. Together they dragged her up the cliff face, and hoisted her back over the wall. She collapsed on the ground, weak and shivering, her arms still trembling. She eyed the two men standing over her, saw the shock and fury mingling in their faces.

Then Kruger turned to Rob, slipped a gun from his pocket and shot the jockey through the head.

55

Rob crumpled to the ground.

Harry screamed, scuffed backwards in the dirt. Kruger turned the gun her way, and she froze. He stepped closer.

'Now it's your turn.'

He loomed above her, two-handing the gun. His jacket flapped in the wind. Harry held her breath. The gun was inches from her face, its acrid smell filling her nostrils.

He swooped down, snatched the bag from her shirt. Then he stepped away.

'First I want some answers,' he said.

Harry's breathing kicked back in. She watched him weigh the bag in his hands, kneading the stones through the plastic. He kept the gun trained between her eyes, but the expression on his face scared her more than anything. He'd just killed a man, but he looked the same as always. Remote.

Her eyes darted to Rob's slumped body. Gauzy mist screened him off like a veil, but she could still see the dark puddle spreading out around his head. A fist of regret lodged in her chest. He'd tried to help her and now he was dead. She shook her head, feeling dazed and disconnected.

Kruger flexed his fingers on the gun. 'Who killed Garvin Oliver?'

She blinked, dragged her gaze his way. 'You don't know?'

'Just answer the question. Was it you?'

'Me? No, it was Van Wycks, they were behind it, they killed everyone.' She hated the babble of panic in her voice.

'They killed TJ? And Eddie?'

She nodded, and felt her brain shifting. There could be a lot that Kruger didn't know. Maybe if she snagged his interest, she could buy herself some time. The wind gathered itself into a roar, and she raised her voice above it.

'Raj Chandra's dead too.'

Kruger's face tightened. Every particle in Harry's body clamoured at her to run. There were pathways behind her. Some of them had to lead down the mountain. She kept talking.

'Now they'll come after you.' She inched backwards, tiny movements. 'And Eve. Cassie, too, if she's involved.'

Kruger's lip curled. 'Cassie? She's not part of this. What use would she have been?'

'Van Wycks won't let you away with it.'

His mouth grew taut. 'Is that who you work for? Is that why you've been nosing around?'

'Didn't Eve tell you? I was working for her. She hired me to break into Garvin's safe.' Harry bent her knees, eased her legs underneath her. 'I told you she was trying to double-cross you.'

Kruger glared at her, the muscles in his jaw working. 'Maybe it's you she's double-crossing. She called a few hours ago and told me you had the diamonds. Said you were planning on handing them over to Van Wycks.'

Harry felt her gut sink. So Eve had made good her threat. Harry pressed her weight against her palms, stones biting her flesh. If she could just get to her feet, she could run. He'd shoot, but the fog was thick. Surely there was a chance he'd miss?

Kruger narrowed his eyes, adjusted his sightline. Clammy sweat washed over her. Say something, anything!

'Was it you who told Eddie to lock me in with Rottweiler?'

He smiled. 'Young Eddie. He had his uses. I paid him well, but he would've done what I said, even without the money. Idiot still wanted to be champion jockey. Thought I could make it happen for him.'

He aligned the gun barrel with her eyes. Harry glanced at Rob's hunched shape, licked her lips.

'You said you followed Rob here, but you didn't, did you?'

Kruger shook his head. 'Rob followed me. Fool thought I was meeting Eve, he knew I was screwing her.'

'You were involved with Eve?'

Kruger shrugged. 'It was one way of getting her to do what she was told.'

Harry thought of the black eye and wondered what other ways he used. 'Did Rob know about the diamonds?'

Another lip curl. 'He was too weak from purging himself to know much about anything.'

'So you followed me up here?'

'I didn't need to. I knew where you were going, I saw you tell Sal.'

Harry frowned. Kruger had been fifty yards away when she'd spoken to her father. He couldn't have heard. Then her brow cleared and she saw him nod.

'That's right, I still read lips,' he said. 'Comes in handy, sometimes.'

She stared at his dark, stony expression and thought of the child cut off from sound. She shuddered. His eyes looked cold and flat. The isolation may have fostered his bond with horses, but maybe it had also numbed his empathy for human beings. She thought of Mani and his fears for his family.

'Was it your idea to threaten the miners?' she said. 'Kill their families if they didn't deliver?'

He shrugged. 'Thieving bastards tried to steal the stones for themselves. So *ja*, we made an example of one or two, just to keep them in line. Garvin took care of the details. There are plenty of violent men for hire in South Africa.'

Harry's blood chilled. She recalled Kruger's hypnotic

480

communion with his horses. She'd been fooled by his solemn, strong exterior, thinking there was something deep on the inside. The truth was, there was nothing but indifference.

Kruger jiggled the bag of stones. 'Maybe Van Wycks have done me a favour.'

'What do you mean?'

He held up the bag. 'Now that everyone's dead, I don't need to share them.'

Harry swallowed. She braced her arms. Locked her elbows. Looked for a chance. She nodded at the bag.

'That's thirty million dollars' worth of stones,' she said. 'How much can one person need?'

'You've no idea what I need.'

'I thought you had a successful yard.'

Kruger spat into the dirt. 'No one has the money for racehorses any more. They're a luxury item.' A sneer curled over his features. 'Cash-rich social climbers are thin on the ground these days. Economy dips, so does the bloodstock industry.'

His face took on a brooding look. Harry tensed her legs, her muscles primed to go. Kruger went on talking.

'Owners are walking away from their horses. Foals are being destroyed because there's no one to buy them.' He eyed the stones. 'I've a yard full of thoroughbreds, millions at stake, and now there's no one to pay.'

He stared at the bag, testing its weight. The gun faltered slightly as his attention drifted. Electricity snapped over Harry's frame. This might be her only chance.

481

She leapt to her feet, spun round and scrambled. She was aware of Kruger shifting, taking aim. She zig-zagged once. A shot cracked through the air. Hot metal ripped into her arm. She jerked, screamed. Pain burned her flesh. She blundered on a few more steps. Then she stumbled over something lying on the ground, collapsed across it. It was bulky and cold. Her glance slid to the right and locked on the staring eyes of the Van Wycks killer.

Her stomach heaved. His flesh felt clammy, his shirt wet. She lay across him, her airways full of his stale smell.

'Say goodbye, Harry.'

She turned her head. Kruger was standing over her, his gun pointing at her face. Her heart thudded. Her hand closed over cold flesh. Then she swung round, clasping the dead man's hand, aiming his gun at Kruger. She squeezed the lifeless flesh on the trigger and fired.

Dead man's fingers.

Her first shot was wide. It grazed Kruger's hand, catapulting the bag of diamonds into the air. Kruger watched, stunned, as it landed on the wall. Then he turned back to Harry. She squeezed the dead fingers and fired again. He jolted backwards, blood spurting from his chest. His gun clattered on to the rocks. Harry sobbed, squeezed again, kept squeezing till the gun clicked empty and Kruger was slumped on the ground.

A low moan escaped Harry's throat. She flung the dead man's hand away, scrambled backwards, got to her feet. She hugged her chest, her whole body shivering, her right arm on fire. The wind gusted around her, and she watched as it nudged the bag of diamonds on the wall. The plastic fluttered and twitched, then the wind scooped it up and tossed it over the side of the mountain.

Harry made no move to stop it.

She backed up and huddled against a rock, cradling her wounded arm. The cableway would never start up now, not at this late hour. So she waited, shivering, until the wind had settled and the fog had finally lifted.

Then, guided by the moonlight, she began the long trek down.

56

Mani could hear voices.

He turned his head. Felt the mask over his nose and mouth. Everything was dark.

Panic squeezed his chest.

He was back in the mine.

Then he heard Asha's voice. Calm. Drifting in and out. He felt the cool sheets. He remembered, and his chest muscles relaxed.

A machine bip-bipped beside the bed. Then Asha was saying his mother's name. And Ezra's. Mani struggled against the weight of his eyelids. Why couldn't he open them?

Another voice. Soft and light. He moved his head. He'd heard it before. The girl in Kenilworth.

What was she doing here?

She'd tried to take his diamonds. Then he'd watched

484

her give them to the woman called Eve. Blackness had soon swallowed him up, but the nurses had described the dark-haired young woman who'd brought him in to the hospital. The woman who was paying his medical bills.

What did she want?

Asha's voice came and went in waves. She was talking about the diamonds. About the men who might kill them.

Mani's eyelids fluttered. Slats of light broke through them. He dragged them open. The room was out of focus, far away.

Asha was there, shaking her head, her thin shoulders stooped. The last time he'd woken up, he'd told her about Takata. She'd cried for a while, then gone away. He hadn't expected her back.

His gaze lingered on her familiar face, and the squeezing sensation flooded back into his chest. He blinked slowly, as though underwater, and wondered if Ezra was here too.

The dark-haired girl sat on the other side of the bed. Her eyes looked huge, her face drained of colour. She was saying something to Asha, leaning forward to lay a hand on her arm. Asha clutched the other girl's fingers.

Was she crying?

Mani's left arm burned. He tried to push the mask off his face. He wanted to talk. But his muscles felt leaden.

The dark-haired girl turned towards him. For the first time, he noticed the blood on her clothes and the fresh-looking bandage on her arm. Her right arm.

Mirror image.

She'd been wounded too.

He frowned, twisted his head. His brain swivelled inside his skull.

Why wouldn't they let him speak?

'Is he awake?'

Harry watched as Asha turned to Mani. There was an Egyptian cast to the girl's high cheekbones and wide, almond-shaped eyes. Like Nefertiti.

Harry flopped back in her seat. Her head buzzed with tiredness, and occasionally the room flickered like a scratched DVD.

It had taken her almost three hours to hike down from the mountain. She'd scrambled over a sloping rockface, then zig-zagged down a path of well-worn steps. By the time she'd reached the bottom, she'd been numb from cold and exhaustion.

Asha's voice floated in and out, making soothing noises to Mani. Harry struggled to keep her eyes open. She settled them on Mani's face. His skin looked dusky, coated with sweat.

Asha had explained, in her calm, slow voice, how Mani had tried to help his brother. She'd told Harry about the men who forced them to risk their lives bringing the diamonds out. And who would kill them if they didn't deliver. They'd already murdered Mani's mother, just to show what they could do.

Harry squeezed her eyes shut, flinching from the images

Asha had stirred up. Bloody and brutal. Images of diamonds and death.

Her arm throbbed, a dull reminder of how close she'd come to dying herself. The doctor who'd tended her a few hours before had been surprised at the amount of blood on her clothes. The wound was superficial, just a graze, and she'd spun him a tale that had nothing to do with bullets. But she didn't explain that most of the blood wasn't hers. It had soaked into her shirt from the Van Wycks killer as she'd lain across his corpse.

She shifted in her chair, dislodging the memory.

Mani was growing restless. One arm was hooked up to an IV drip. His good hand plucked at the oxygen mask on his face and after a moment, Asha slipped it off.

'Just for a minute,' she said.

His breath rattled above the beeping monitors. According to the doctors, the septicaemia was under control. The toxins invading his blood were on the run, and his infected wound was healing. But the damage to his lungs was irreversible. Yet in the end, it might be his schooling that would save him. His periodic absences from the mines had limited the dust exposure. With drugs and therapy, there was a chance he could get on with his life.

Mani grasped Asha's hand. When he spoke, his voice was hoarse. 'Ezra, he is safe?'

The girl looked away. 'He has gone back to the mine.'

'But he is sick.'

Harry leaned forward. 'Asha, I told you, he doesn't need to go back. Not now.'

Slowly, the girl shook her head. 'That does not matter. Ezra will always go back to the diamonds.' She squeezed Mani's hand. 'But I will not.'

Harry glanced at Mani, aware she was finding it hard to look him in the eye. 'I've told Asha. It's over. The people who were after you are all dead.'

He squinted at her, his gaze out of focus. 'How do you know?'

'I saw them die.'

'Why should I trust you?'

Harry looked at her hands. 'I don't know. I'm sorry.' She forced her eyes back to his. 'My father's life was in danger too.'

Mani stared at her for a moment, then dropped his eyes to the bandage on her arm. She took in the matching dressing on his. Asha had told her how he'd hidden small stones under his flesh. Harry swallowed. Mani had journeyed out from the belly of the earth, while she'd followed the diamantaires. Two worlds, random parts of the whole.

Two halves of the same cruel mess.

57

Harry's gaze roamed the waterfront. The cafés were crowded, the harbour a forest of masts strung with triangular flags. The last time she'd sat here, she'd bumped into Rob Devlin.

She stirred her coffee. 'Is this another interview?'

Hunter shook his head, then mock-saluted her with his beer. 'I'm off duty. Fly back this evening.'

He took a deep swallow. A cruiser boat honked nearby, and street performers chanted harmonies along the promenade.

'You're finished here, then?' Harry said.

'My superiors think the job's done.'

He fiddled with his beer mat, giving her a chance to study him. For a change, he was clean-shaven. His face had caught a light tan in the time he'd been here, adding warmth to the hazelnut eyes.

He glanced up, caught her watching him. She busied herself with her coffee.

'What about you?' she said. 'What do you think?'

Hunter shrugged. 'Does it matter? I do what I'm told these days.'

Harry frowned, trying to gauge his tone. He'd been interviewing her on and off with the local police for weeks, ever since the bodies had been found on the mountain. This was the first time his anger wasn't directed at her. Maybe he'd lost his appetite for it.

The police had talked to everyone in Cape Town connected with Kruger or Rob: Cassie, the racehorse owners, Harry's father. And by extension, Harry herself. She'd kept her wound hidden and told them as much as she could. About her first meeting with Eve, when she'd witnessed Garvin's murder; about Garvin's illicit diamond trade and his links to Kruger's yard; and about the threats to herself and her father by the Van Wycks killer.

But she hadn't told them everything. She saw no reason to mention Mani, or the role he'd played in the mines. She'd betrayed him once already. She wasn't about to do it again.

Hunter slugged another mouthful of beer. 'The Cape Town police are satisfied. Diamond smugglers kill each other in shoot-out on Table Mountain. No loose ends on *their* files.'

Harry rinsed her face of expression. She knew what the official view was. That Kruger had shot Rob and the Van Wycks killer. That the killer had managed to fire at

Kruger before he died. Harry hadn't corrected them. It was close enough to the truth, and she was happy with any scenario that didn't include her.

Hunter should've been happy too. They'd found a match for the bullets that had killed Garvin and TJ. They could prove the Van Wycks killer was their man.

She sipped her coffee. 'What does Lynne think?'

'He thinks I should arrest you.'

Harry tensed. 'For what?'

'Tampering with evidence, obstruction of justice.'

'Will you?'

Hunter shrugged again. 'Doesn't seem much point. It'd tie up resources, create a lot of paperwork. And for what?' His eyes probed hers. 'You didn't kill anyone, did you?'

Harry blinked, shook her head.

Dead man's fingers.

Her flesh crawled. She fiddled with her cup, didn't trust herself to lift it again. Wished it was a beer instead.

Hunter leaned forward. 'Where did you go after you left the casino?'

'I told you, I went back to the hotel.'

He'd been asking her the same question for the last few weeks, and she knew he didn't believe her. But it didn't matter. Nobody could prove she'd been on the mountain. The crowds of ascending tourists had been too busy admiring the view to notice a lone traveller. And apart from the lizards, no one had witnessed her punishing climb back down.

And no one would find her fingerprints on the gun.

She raised her cup to her lips, surprised to find her hand steady. She'd been screwed by circumstantial evidence before. To be found in the presence of three dead bodies would've been a handicap, whatever way you looked at it.

Her father was in the clear, too. He'd milked his black-jack table for the rest of the night, drawing hostile attention from the casino's eye-in-the-sky. The security videos confirmed his whereabouts until long after the cable cars had stopped. There was no way he could have gone to the mountain.

'They picked up Eve's trail.'

Harry tensed. 'Where?'

'CCTV shows her boarding a flight to Nairobi the night that Kruger died. She was travelling under Beth Oliver's passport.'

'Is she in custody?'

Hunter's eyes raked her face. 'They lost her at the other end.'

Harry lowered her gaze to hide her relief. She couldn't explain about meeting Eve at Kenilworth, not without betraying Mani. Eve had wanted a fresh start, had tried to break away from the syndicate. Away from Kruger. Harry bit her lip. Eve had sold her out, but some part of Harry wanted her to make it.

She glanced at Hunter. Did he believe that Eve had been her client? Suddenly, she wasn't sure it mattered.

'Kruger was up to his ears in debt, you know,' Hunter said. 'The land in Kildare was in negative equity.

And according to the experts, all those horses are virtually unsaleable in this market. He owed the banks over eighteen million euros.' Hunter leaned back, lacing his hands behind his head. 'What I don't understand is why he was up on that bloody mountain.'

Harry shrugged, feeling on safer ground. 'The Van Wycks killer must have lured him up there, somehow. We know his mission was to eliminate the diamond syndicate. Garvin, TJ, Eddie, Raj Chandra.' She'd told him about the photos the killer had shown her. 'Maybe now it was Kruger's turn.'

'And Rob?'

'He wasn't involved, I'm sure of it.' She gave him a steady look and paraphrased what she'd learned on the mountain. 'He told me he suspected Kruger of having an affair with Eve. Sometimes he followed Kruger, trying to catch them out. Maybe he followed him to the mountain, got caught up in it all by accident.'

Hunter lifted a wry eyebrow. 'Wrong place, wrong time?'

She glared at him. 'It happens.'

He nodded slowly, never taking his eyes off her. 'Hard to believe he'd be involved with a woman and not know what she was up to.'

Harry flashed on an image of Hunter in bed with a suspect, and felt her skin tingle. 'Is it so unbelievable? According to Lynne, you claimed it happened to you.'

His mouth tightened and he lowered his elbows back to the table. Harry broke eye contact.

'Sorry,' she said. 'That's none of my business.'

'You're right, it isn't.' He dragged a hand through his hair. 'But I take your point.'

For a moment, neither of them spoke. Then Harry said,

'What kind of fraud was it?'

Hunter looked up from his beer. 'What?'

'The woman. Your suspect.'

He shook his head. 'You name it. Insurance fraud, cheque fraud, identity fraud.'

'You didn't know?'

'She told me lies and I fell for them.' He shrugged. 'Fell for her.'

He drained his glass, then got to his feet. She squinted up at him. The wind twitched the tips of his hair and tugged at his short-sleeved shirt. The white cotton was snug along his biceps, loose over his midsection. Harry felt her body chemistry shift.

She tilted her head, tried to read his face. 'Lynne says you have a weakness for women who tell lies.'

He gave her a long look, full of heat and speculation. Her cheeks grew warm. Then he backed away, his eyes still on hers.

'Maybe he's right.'

58

Harry rolled the car window down. The African sun blazed against her skin, and she basked in the heat. It was the first time in weeks she'd been able to drive without wincing at the pain in her arm.

She glanced at the yellow sightbox on the passenger seat beside her, and at the stack of newspapers beneath it. The dailies were still running with the story, churning up melodrama about the bodies found on the mountain. Rob. Kruger. The Van Wycks killer.

Harry still called him that, even though she now knew his name.

Michael Joseph Callan.

According to the papers, he was fifty-five, an ex-Paratrooper and Special Forces Commander, dishonourably discharged for unspecified offences. For the last twenty years, he'd been a mercenary soldier, executing his craft in the war-torn countries of Africa. He'd been tortured by the RUF in Sierra Leone, where his captors were mostly children and teenagers. Later, he'd been hired to train the Angolan army during their brutal civil war. They'd been short of recruits, had asked him to train children. Callan had refused.

Since then, there was no record of his clandestine missions, or at least none that the papers could dig up. No one was speculating about the identity of his latest client.

Harry flashed on Monty Newman's face: the drooping jowls, the leathery tan. She shuddered, and tried to focus on the road, following the signs for the freeway heading east out of the city.

She thought about the four large stones, abandoned on the godforsaken cliffs of the mountain. Jacob had told her that diamonds were brittle. Had the wind smashed them against the rocks, shattering them into pieces? Would some lucky hiker find them one day as he trekked up the steep trails? Or would they lie undiscovered, fusing with the ancient folds and layers of the mountain? The notion seemed fanciful, but somehow Harry felt that was where they belonged.

She peeked in her rear-view mirror. Today the mountain plateau was clear. Something twisted in her chest. She couldn't look at Table Mountain without thinking about Rob. She pictured his reckless grin, the malnourished frame. He may have already been on a path to self-destruction, but that didn't make it his time to go.

She puffed out a breath, trying to scare away the tears. She'd thought a lot about the choice she'd made on the mountain, wondering what it was that had made her take Rob's hand. Maybe it was because Kruger hadn't asked where Eve was, which meant he'd already talked to her. Or maybe it was the glimpse she'd had of Rob's pain that night when he'd confided in Billy-Boy. Who knew? But something inside her had made an intuitive leap. Maybe her instincts were finally back on track.

She thought of Cassie, and wondered how her instincts would fare. Harry had driven her to the airport earlier that day. They hadn't spoken much since the bodies had been found, and the journey in the car had been awkward. Cassie spent most of it staring out the window, arms folded, lips tight. As if somehow it was Harry's fault that she'd hitched her wagon to a sociopath.

When they'd finally arrived at the airport, Cassie had turned to her and said,

'I feel like an idiot.'

Harry's eyebrows shot up. 'What for?'

'How could I have got involved with someone like that? How could I not have known what he was like?'

Cassie hugged her arms tighter across her chest, self-doubt radiating from her in waves. Harry recalled other blind relationships: Rob and Eve; Hunter and his suspect; not to mention the fiasco in her own recent past. When it came to love, people saw what they wanted to see.

'Don't beat yourself up over it,' Harry said. 'You couldn't have known.'

Cassie wouldn't meet her eyes. Harry went on.

'If it's any consolation, you're not the first of us to unknowingly fall for a killer.'

Cassie shot her a quizzical look. Harry shrugged and smiled, saw the vet's eyes widen as she took the information in. Then Cassie said,

'Look, I owe you an apology. It was never you I didn't trust, it was him. He just seemed so interested in you. Anytime your name came up, he was all ears.' She gave Harry a direct look. 'He Googled you, you know.'

'Actually, I did know, but how did you find out?'

'I snooped.' Cassie gave a rueful shrug. 'It's what you do when your relationship's built on nothing.'

There hadn't been much more to say after that. Cassie had trudged into the airport and Harry had watched her, wondering where she'd go now that Kruger's yard was gone.

A horn blared somewhere behind her and Harry refocused on the road. She was almost there. She accelerated along the freeway, scanning the horizon for the distinctive, tall building. The off-ramp wasn't far away. She glanced again at the yellow sightbox beside her.

The South African police were still asking questions, but so far, apart from Ros, no one knew about her sleight of hand with Van Wycks. She planned on keeping it that way if she could.

Harry peered at the building that loomed up ahead, and took the next off-ramp. She thought of home and what awaited her there. The stone cottage. The barriers between herself and her mother. Hunter?

She looked up at the bowling ball of heat in the sky. Perhaps it was time to go back.

She cruised down a side road, took a left into the car park and snagged a space near the door. Then she lifted the yellow sightbox and set it on her lap. Her fingertips tingled.

She'd explained to the South African police that Van Wycks had hired Michael Callan. They'd nodded, said nothing, didn't even take notes. No one ever mentioned it again. The cartel lived on, and she had little faith it would ever be brought to book. Might is right, and maybe the cartel was just too big to beat. The powerlessness of it made her fists curl. Justice of sorts may have come to Kruger and Callan, but where was the higher judgement that would bring the tyrants down?

She shook her head. Then she opened the yellow box. Stacked inside were half a dozen ziplocked bags, the stones that Ros had dismissed as pebbles. She opened the top pouch and made a spout with it over her palm. The contents spilled out with a hiss, cold and smooth against her skin.

The six hundred thousand euros she'd given to Ros had just about cleaned Harry out. She tilted her hand, watching the light play off the cloudy facets. Maybe they weren't high-grade stones, but the rest of Ros's sightbox was still worth a few hundred thousand dollars.

She squinted at them, trying to make sense of it. Ultimately, gem diamonds were useless, weren't they? Pretty baubles, with no intrinsic value. Yet the cartel had made people need them, and then pretended they were rare.

She stared at the dull, warped fragments and wondered just what she was looking at. Stones of priceless beauty? Or one of the world's most cynical hoaxes?

She sighed and poured the diamonds back into the pouch. Then she emptied the sightbox, stuffing everything into her bag. She climbed out of the car and made her way over to the main entrance, the heat of the sun swathing her like a duvet.

Maybe she should've given the stones back to Ros, but somehow she knew that wasn't where they belonged. She pushed open the door and stepped into the Medicare Clinic.

These ones belonged to Mani.

ALSO AVAILABLE

The Insider
Ava McCarthy

'It's twelve million . . . or your life'

Until recently, the toughest part of Henrietta 'Harry' Martinez's life was hiding her troubled past. But now the former hacker turned security expert is in danger. Someone wants her dead.

Her father, Sal, taught her everything he knew about taking risks but it seems he made a bad gamble with the anonymous trader known as 'the Prophet'. Sal was jailed for fraud; now the Prophet wants Harry to pay up.

With no money and little time, Harry must track down Sal's crooked partners while trying to escape the people on her tail – journalists, police and hired killers. But Harry has secret skills, honed by her father, perfected by her, skills her enemies haven't anticipated. So now the chase is on. The stakes are high. And the bets are off.

'What a delight . . . the tang of authenticity co[...] . every page'

ISBN: 978-0-00-728589-1

ALSO AVAILABLE

The Insider
Ava McCarthy

'It's twelve million . . . or your life'

Until recently, the toughest part of Henrietta 'Harry' Martinez's life was hiding her troubled past. But now the former hacker turned security expert is in danger. Someone wants her dead.

Her father, Sal, taught her everything he knew about taking risks but it seems he made a bad gamble with the anonymous trader known as 'the Prophet'. Sal was jailed for fraud; now the Prophet wants Harry to pay up.

With no money and little time, Harry must track down Sal's crooked partners while trying to escape the people on her tail – journalists, police and hired killers. But Harry has secret skills, honed by her father, perfected by her, skills her enemies haven't anticipated. So now the chase is on. The stakes are high. And the bets are off.

'What a delight . . . the tang of authenticity comes off every page'   *Daily Mail*

ISBN: 978-0-00-728589-1

What's next?

Tell us the name of an author you love

Ava McCarthy | Go ▶

and we'll find your next great book.